ALSO BY MIKE MCALARY

Buddy Boys

COP SHOT

COP SHOT

THE MURDER OF EDWARD BYRNE

MIKE McALARY

G. P. PUTNAM'S SONS / NEW YORK

G. P. Putnam's Sons
Publishers Since 1838
200 Madison Avenue
New York, NY 10016

Library of Congress Cataloging-in-Publication Data

McAlary, Mike.
Cop shot : the murder of Edward Byrne / Mike McAlary.
p. cm.
1. Byrne, Edward, d. 1988. 2. Police—New York (N.Y.)—Biography.
3. Victims of crime—New York (N.Y.) 4. Murder—New York (N.Y.)
5. Drug traffic—New York (N.Y.) I. Title.
HV7911.B97M37   1990   89-48784 CIP
364.1′524′092—dc20   [B]
ISBN 0-399-13408-5

Printed in the United States of America
1   2   3   4   5   6   7   8   9   10

This book is printed on acid-free paper.

ACKNOWLEDGMENTS

I would like to thank my friend Detective Richard Sica on two counts. As a citizen of a city in crisis, I am grateful to Sica and his partners in the 103rd Precinct for bringing the murderers of Edward Byrne to justice. As a reporter and columnist, I am indebted to Sica for opening a window to the sometimes cloistered world of the New York City Police Department. He is a man of high principle and fairness who spoke of the sensational murder case at grave risk to his career. In the end, Sica believed the assassination of a New York City police officer too important not to talk about.

I would also like to thank the detective's wife, Joanne, for a regular place at her table in a difficult time. I am more grateful for the friendship of the Sica family than can be adequately expressed.

There are dozens of other people in the NYPD and Queens District Attorney's Office who assisted me in gathering material for this book. As they fear the wrath of their supervisors, most cannot be thanked publicly. Specifically, I would like to thank my friends in Brooklyn North and Detective Edward Granshaw, retired.

After the Defense Attorney Sal Alosco, I would like to recognize my colleagues on the crack beat. Reporters Richard Esposito of *New York Newsday* and Bob Drury of Fox Television were consistently ahead of the pack in their reporting of the city's crack wars. Four of the city's best editors—Jim Willse and Hap Hairston of the New York *Daily News,* John Cotter of the *New York Post,* and Don Forst of *New York Newsday*—have taught me more than I probably deserve to know about column writing. For good or bad, I am their creation.

Finally, I would like to thank my agent, Flip Brophy; my social conscience, Denise Housman; my mentor, Mike Lupica; Counselor Edward W. Hayes; and my editors at Putnam, past and present, Chris Schillig and Neil Nyren. This project could not have been completed without their continued support.

CONTENTS

*For my parents, Jack and Ellen. They controlled
a raucous precinct—the ten-member McAlary
household—with charity, intelligence, and humor.*

PROLOGUE

The brief appeared on page twenty-one of the August 8, 1985, edition of the *New York Post.* Cy Egan, the paper's overnight rewrite man, introduced the word to the city in the second paragraph of his two-hundred-word summary.

NARCS SEIZE SUPER COCAINE

A powerful new form of cocaine—which produces the effects of "freebasing" without its fiery risks—was discovered last night during a police raid on a Bronx narcotics den.

"This stuff is safer to handle, but just as deadly in its addictive qualities," Bronx Narcotics Unit Lt. John Creegan said of the new cocaine product called "crack."

"It can be smoked in a pipe and gives the same effect as freebasing without going through the old process of purifying it with ether and alcohol where you run the risk of setting yourself on fire."

Creegan said yesterday's raid, which resulted in confiscat-

11

ing sixty-seven vials of "crack," was part of a new campaign to curb sales of the drug.

Creegan said the "crack," which sells for about $10 a vial, was seized in an apartment at 1812 Harrison Avenue, in the High Bridge section, after police made an undercover buy and then obtained a search warrant.

Arrested and charged with possession of narcotics and weapons was Tyrone Little, twenty, of 57 W. 175th Street, the Bronx. Besides the cocaine, police said a 9mm Luger machine pistol and a loaded pump-action shotgun were found in the apartment.

1

"THAT SHIT WAS SWIFT."

The other cops called him Rookie.

New York City Police Officer Edward Byrne was scheduled to work a midnight tour, assigned to sit in a marked police car outside a witness's home on a forsaken Queens block. Rookie didn't know much about the witness. He knew even less about being a cop.

Edward Byrne was only four days past his twenty-second birthday. He had been assigned to the South Jamaica precinct in January, and, seven weeks later, he was still looking to make his first arrest. An anonymous cop in a city of 27,000 blue uniforms, Edward Byrne would sit alone tonight, engulfed in boredom and surrounded by darkness. By first light he would belong to the nation, even a neglectful President wanting to know his name.

Eddie Byrne still lived in his father's house. He slept in the same bedroom to which he had come home after his first touchdown and home run, his first kiss, girlfriend, and prom. It was a New York City cop's house, which meant, mostly, that the home was located on a suburban Long Island block. Once he had put on a football uniform in that room, knowing some glory as a Plainedge High School halfback and linebacker. Upon graduation from the Plainedge school in 1984, Edward Byrne had taken out a small advertisement in his yearbook.

"It's my life," he had written.

The kid wasn't big enough to make it on even the smallest college team, so he turned from sports to books, studying criminal justice at Nassau Community College. He stayed a year and then quit. Edward Byrne had plans. He wanted to wear the blue vestments of a police officer, his father's uniform.

His father, Matt Byrne, had been a big deal on the job once. He was a member of the Club. He knew police chiefs, prosecutors, and judges. He was known for getting his work done at the right time in front of the right boss. He could read a book and he knew a thing or two about the law. So Matt Byrne was a full stride ahead of the rank-and-file cops. Before retiring in 1976, Byrne had earned a law degree and risen to the rank of lieutenant. His last job had been directing the department's legal bureau, policing other cops. Retirement found Matt Byrne doing suburban house closings and civil work. He frowned on criminal defense work—he had never put a beat cop's concept of good and evil behind him.

Matt Byrne didn't want his son Eddie to become a cop, but there was no denying Eddie the uniform. The kid took the police exam in 1986, his name went into a talent pool, and in July the transit force grabbed him, making Eddie a tunnel rat.

In New York City there is a pecking order among the various uniformed forces. Police officers and firemen are at the top of the list. Transit patrolmen are regarded as second stringers. But it could have been worse. Edward Byrne could have been called by the Housing Police Department and dumped in a project.

He spent a year in the Brooklyn subways, then put in for a transfer. The Finest called him in July 1987.

Byrne cleared the police academy and spent six months in Manhattan with a rookie outfit called the Neighborhood Stabilization Unit. By the time the kid came up for reassignment, two of his boyhood friends were working at the 103rd Precinct in South Jamaica. Matt Byrne didn't want his kid working Black Brooklyn, or even worse, the Bronx, so the old man made a phone call. The Club owed him a favor. Eddie Byrne wound up in South Jamaica, a silver 103rd Precinct collar pin on his blue shirt.

Edward Byrne was new enough to the job to savor even the most mundane police task, putting on the uniform. On the evening of February 25, 1988, the transformation from suburban kid to city cop began as soon as Rookie emerged from the shower. He walked to his dresser and took out a pair of white jockey shorts. At 6 feet and 155 pounds, he still had a teenager's hard waist, an athletic, unscarred body. A weak brown mustache split a soft, Irish face. The cop's eyes were his most remarkable feature. They were light blue, matching his uniform shirt.

Byrne put on his underpants and then a cream-colored undershirt. He had spent the evening with his girlfriend, and they had talked about marriage again.

It was a frigid, starless night. Rookie was still big on preparedness. He tugged on a thermal white undershirt and walked to the closet, where the blue uniform hung perfectly. Cops had a nickname for their uniform. They called it "the bag." The idea was to make detective and get out of "the bag." Cops who got flopped back to patrol were put "back in the bag."

Byrne stepped into the creased navy blue trousers and buttoned up his light blue winter shirt. He sat on the bed, pulled on white crew socks, and laced up his black boots. He attached a blue clip-on tie to his collar and clipped it to his shirt at the sternum with a silver NYPD tie clasp. Finally he pulled on his blue nylon police jacket. The name plate was shiny and simple. BYRNE. He carried a tin shield, NYPD badge No. 14072, in his pocket.

Eddie walked from his bedroom into the family den. Matt was sitting in a chair under his son's football trophies, watching television. The old man had one eye on the news.

"I'm heading in," Eddie said. Then the kid mentioned something about running an errand for his father the next day. Matt was only half-listening.

"Okay, have a good tour," the father said, almost absently. "Be careful."

"Good night."

The drive in from Massapequa took thirty minutes. Rookie finished getting dressed at his locker, putting on his bulletproof vest, police shield and gun-belt. The cop's gun, a Strum Ruger .38-caliber revolver, fit snugly in a black Jay-Pee holster. He had six live rounds in the gun and twelve additional bullets in a pair of Cobra speed loaders.

In June of 1986, another rookie, Scott Gadell, had been killed during a shootout with a crack dealer. The dealer, a Jamaican immigrant who had entered the country illegally, had shot the cop in the head as he'd tried frantically to reload his gun. Three bullets in Gadell's gun had misfired. Now everyone carried speed loaders.

Rookie's holster also included a pouch for the modern cop's closest friend, his ballpoint pen. Different pouches and loops on the utility belt housed two pairs of Smith & Wesson handcuffs, a flashlight, a red Swiss army knife, nightstick, and whistle. He paused at the front desk to salute the desk sergeant on the way out of the precinct. Everyone would later remember that Edward Byrne had looked bright, trim, and clean.

Rookie arrived at the guard post at the corner of Inwood Street and 107th Avenue at 12:15 A.M.

"Anything up?" he asked Police Officer Nancy Stefan. A battered yellow car had passed Stefan earlier. She did not think it important enough to mention.

"It's dead," Officer Stefan told Rookie.

He climbed into the empty blue and white, a Chevy Impala—NYPD Radio Motor Patrol No. 1041—and placed his black, leather-bound, department-issue memo book on the dashboard. The car was a warm sanctuary against a bitter morning. Normally the block would be swarming with crack dealers, but the cold had scattered them.

The cop took off his gray leather gloves and placed them on the seat along with his flashlight, portable radio, and Kodak Instamatic camera. The patrol car was parked about ten feet behind a stop sign, facing the witness's home on the southeast corner of Inwood Street and 107th Avenue. Positioned under a high-intensity street lamp, Rookie had an unobstructed view of the three-story gray wooden home, ninety feet away.

The darkened neighborhood was filled with detached wooden homes and narrow one-way streets. The homes were almost entirely broken and ruined, the sidewalks cracked and heaving. The neighborhood smelled of burned wood.

This pocket of South Jamaica looked like it had been transplanted from the Old South. White suburban cops had a nickname for the locality: They called it Tobacco Road.

An empty, plastic, white dog cage filled the backseat of Byrne's car. A reflection of the cage filled Rookie's rear-view mirror. Not that it mattered much. No one would be stupid enough to make a move on a witness with a cop on the block. Still, he positioned his side-view mirrors just to be safe.

The witness's name was Arjune. A Guyanese immigrant, on the night of November 9, 1987, Arjune had looked out his window and seen several dealers selling crack on his corner. At 6:15 P.M., he had dialed 911 to report the ongoing drug sales, but two patrolmen, George Repetti and Angelo Carbone, arrived at the corner, found nothing, and called in the report as unfounded. Thirty minutes later, Arjune called back, saying the dealers had returned. This time, as Repetti turned onto the block, he saw a kid, Yusef Abdul Qaadir, twenty, drop a paper bag. The cop found six vials of crack in the bag.

Detectives arrived on the scene just as Qaadir, nicknamed Joe Sharp, was being arrested for criminal possession of a controlled substance. The detectives overheard the central dispatcher directing the cops to a tree. Several kids, including Joe Sharp's boss, Robert Webster, were standing around listening to the transmissions on the cop's portable radios. It was evident to everyone, the detectives later remembered, that someone inside Arjune's home had given the young crack dealers up. The cops left the block with their prisoner and his $30 worth of crack.

At around 4:25 A.M., Arjune was awakened by a barking dog. He looked out the window and saw two young men he later identified as Robert Webster, eighteen, and Claude Johnson, twenty-eight. Webster was on his lawn, holding a firebomb, and Arjune watched as Webster tossed the flaming bottle through his front window. Arjune put the fire out with his hands, burning his hands, and tossed what was left of the burning bottle back out the window. Then Arjune dialed 911 again.

The witness drove around with the cops for about twenty minutes, finally spotting Johnson, who was promptly arrested. Arjune returned home at about 6:20 A.M.

About ten minutes after the cops left, Arjune looked out his window and spotted Webster on his lawn again. The crack dealer tossed two more flaming bottles at the house, but this time both of them bounced off. Again Arjune telephoned the police.

Events were not going well for police witnesses in South Jamaica. Five months earlier, in September, a Queens grandmother named Mildred Green had witnessed a crack shooting outside her cab stand. On October 2, the District Attorney's Office had put her before a secret grand jury. Two days later, a crackhead had silenced her with a shotgun blast in the head. The police department had taken a beating over the killing, and the police commissioner, regarded by everyone as a blathering idiot, had passed new guidelines for guarding witnesses.

Fearing another Mildred Green situation, the precinct commander immediately ordered around-the-clock protection for Arjune, thus creating the fateful Inwood Post. At around 10:30 P.M.

18

on November 10, Officers Repetti and Carbone were sitting in the car, when they spotted Webster, chased him down, and then led him back to Arjune. The witness made a positive identification.

It wasn't long after this that Arjune reported a man in a red Porsche cutting him off at a stoplight. The man told Arjune, "If your family isn't out of the house in three weeks, you'll be killed." Arjune sped off. He later identified the man in the Porsche as Thomas Godbolt, a dealer known in the area as Mustafa. Webster and Johnson, police already knew, worked for Mustafa, and based on Arjune's complaint, Godbolt was arrested and jailed. There were no other witnesses to the threat.

The Guyanese immigrant overnight became an American hero. Here was a man fighting back against drug dealers. In a city desperate for champions, here stood Arjune, defiant against all odds.

"I know thay are looking for me, but I don't care," Arjune once told a television crew. "I stand for justice. I don't care. Tell them I am ready to go at any time."

The cops were worried about losing Arjune, however. On February 5, 1989, the leader of the precinct's detective squad, Lieutenant Eugene Dunbar, prepared a warning to be read to all outgoing platoons. A sergeant had read Dunbar's orders to Byrne at roll call.

"As most of you know, we have a 'fixer' at 107th Avenue and Inwood Street, the residence of a Mr. Arjune," Lieutenant Dunbar wrote. "Mr. Arjune's residence was firebombed a few months ago by local drug dealers. Since that time, Mr. Arjune has had Mustafa arrested for threatening him, and Mustafa was subsequently indicted and charged with tampering with a witness.

"Last week, Mustafa, who is on parole, was violated. On Friday there was a parole hearing and Mustafa was remanded. The important point at this time is that Mustafa now knows who the complainant is in the tampering case. He did not know this until today. We also learned today that the senior parole officer and his assistant have received veiled threats.

"The men assigned to the fixer at Mr. Arjune's residence should be alert at all times for their own safety, and the sector car and the adjoining cars should be alert for any calls for assistance at 107th Avenue and Inwood."

The Inwood Post was generally regarded as a shit detail, the most tiresome detail in the 103rd Precinct. Edward Byrne had already learned to cheat boredom. He killed the first hour of his tour thumbing through the *Daily News* and *Newsweek*. The most interesting story in the newspaper concerned a drug dealer from his precinct named Fat Cat Nichols. The dealer had just been sentenced to twenty-five years to life on a narcotics conviction. All the guys had been talking about the case at roll call.

At some point Byrne reached into his plastic bag and removed a Sony Watchman and an Emerson AM-FM radio. He hung the miniature television from the rear-view mirror and placed the radio on the seat. Technically, Rookie was in violation of police procedure. A far greater transgression was cooping, falling asleep on the job. Cooping could get a cop suspended. "Late Night with David Letterman" wouldn't cost Byrne anything more than a good scolding. He switched on the television and removed his tie, placing it in the plastic bag. It was going to be a long night, but Rookie had brought along an extra set of triple A batteries.

By 2:30 A.M. Rookie was getting hungry. He was sitting on an empty stomach. His meal hour was scheduled for 3 A.M. The hour passed with no relief in sight. Eddie's replacement, a huge cop named Danny Leonard, had been ordered to sit in on the precinct switchboard. No one thought to inform Rookie of the change.

At approximately 3:10 A.M., a car approached the Inwood Post. At first Rookie thought it was his relief, but then he recognized the car as that of the patrol sergeant, making his rounds. Rookie switched off the television and passed his memo book through the open window. The sergeant, a twenty-year veteran named Ron Norfleet, scratched his signature into the book and handed it back.

"Everything all right?" Norfleet asked.

"Yes, sir," Rookie replied.

Norfleet and his driver slipped off, continuing their spot checks.

Rookie closed his eyes, sleep tugging at him. He apparently did not notice a battered yellow Dodge rolling past his post.

"Look," said a gloved passenger in the front seat of the passing car. "He's sleeping. He's sleeping."

The Driver continued down 107th Avenue for 360 feet and made a right turn onto Pinegrove Street. He stopped halfway up the block, cutting his lights and engine. The assassins—the Shooter and a Decoy—climbed out of the two-door car. They stood for a moment, studying the street. Then they doubled back toward the sluggish policeman. The Driver, wearing a safari hat and a camouflage Army jacket, remained with the car and the radio, listening to something by the rap band Krush Groove.

The Shooter was wearing a dark blue, three-quarter-length ski parka and dark green sweatpants. Decoy wore a red, green, and yellow leather jacket over a hooded sweatshirt. He also wore stone-washed green dungarees. The word "Bebos" was stitched across the back of his leather jacket. They moved quickly, expensive Nike sneakers, so-called felony shoes, silent on the salty pavement. As they reached the corner of Pinegrove and 107th Avenue, a second patrol car pulled up to the Inwood Post. Decoy stood frozen on the corner, watching. The Shooter dove into a hedge row and lay hidden. They waited, hearts racing, watching the cops.

Decoy had killed three times before. He even liked it. But now it was someone else's turn. Crack, a mutant form of the drug cocaine, raced through his excited brain, usurping his fear. The drug made Decoy's heart pump faster and his body temperature rise. His breathing was quick. Decoy had never felt so aware. He wondered if the Shooter would have the nerve to execute their plan.

The cop cars were parked driver's window to driver's window.

It was quiet enough for Decoy to hear them talking over the idling engines.

"You okay, Eddie?" asked Darin Hamilton, the second driver. Hamilton's partner, Michael Pala, said nothing.

"Fine," Rookie said. Then Eddie said something about it being hard to stay awake.

"You want coffee?"

Rookie looked at the black Casio watch on his right wrist. It was 3:20 A.M. His relief was already twenty minutes late.

"Danny Leonard should be here any minute," he said.

"We'll see you later, then."

Hamilton stepped on the gas, his car pitching toward the intersection of 107th and Pinegrove. He made a right turn onto Pinegrove and observed a parked yellow car. The cop switched on his high beams, illuminating a light-skinned black sitting in the driver's seat. Decoy was standing across the street. He thought he, too, had been spotted. Decoy lifted up his shirt, baring his tight stomach to the chill air.

"I ain't got nothing," Decoy said.

Hamilton had been too focused on the man in the car to notice Decoy. The cop switched off the beam and continued past the yellow car. He had said nothing to his partner.

"The guy must live on the block," Hamilton thought.

The Shooter waited in the darkness, chest tense, his eyes keen on Rookie's car. After five minutes, he saw the cop's head sink, sleep stealing his guard. The Shooter nodded to Decoy.

"Now," the Shooter whispered.

They reached the back of the patrol car at the same moment. The dog cage prevented Rookie from spotting them in the rearview mirror. Suddenly Decoy was standing at the cop's passenger door. He pulled back his hood, revealing his face.

"Agghh," Decoy said. "Agghh."

Rookie stirred, reaching for the holstered gun in his lap. He did not have time to be afraid.

"I'll come around," Decoy said.

Decoy took a step to his left. The groggy-looking cop still had his hand on the holstered gun.

The Shooter had stepped to the cop's window. He had the nickel-plated revolver in his right hand, the gun glistening in the yellow street light. The gun was roughly eight inches from the officer's head. Edward Byrne started to turn to the gun just as the first shot exploded through his window.

The bullet, a copper-jacketed .38, tore into the left side of Rookie's face just above the left eyebrow. The cop had closed his eyes with the flash, and gunpowder burned his eyelids. The bullet entered through a half-inch hole and rushed out the top of Rookie's skull. Glass and blood sprayed through the car. The deformed slug landed squarely atop Rookie's memo book.

With the first shot fired, and the window gone, the Shooter swung to his left, assuming a combat position. He crouched, both hands on the gun. His sneakers were firm on the pavement. A second explosion sent a bullet tearing into the dying cop's right temple. A third shot entered just above his hairline. These slugs tore off the back of Rookie's skull, a chunk of his brain landing on the seat. One exiting bullet broke the front passenger door window. Another burst through the passenger door, narrowly missing Decoy.

Still, the Shooter pulled the trigger again and again. A fourth bullet hit Rookie in the upper neck just at the border of the head hair. The bullet traveled cleanly through the neck, exiting below the right earlobe. A fifth bullet hit the cop just behind the left ear at the base of the jaw, following the preceding shot out of the neck.

The Shooter stepped back, one live round left in the gun. He looked up and down the block, ready for a witness. He saw none. The assassin had struck with enough killing force to down an elephant. The violence caused to Rookie's head was devastating, his uniform dripping with blood. The winter air was made bitter with the acrid smell of cordite.

Decoy stepped around from behind the car to the cop's window. The windshield, dashboard, and front seat of RMP 1041 were splattered with blood and brain matter. The cop's face, cut by shards of exploding glass was a blood mask. In death, Rookie's head was tilted slightly to the right. Decoy leaned into the car and started to laugh.

"That shit was swift," he said.

Decoy had to be pulled away by the Shooter. Porch lights were starting to come on along Inwood Street. The dying cop had jerked his foot onto the brake pedal with the first shot. The red brake lights had flickered on and then off, marking his passing.

"Let's go," the Shooter said.

The assassins sprinted around the corner to the waiting yellow Dodge, laughing.

"You rocked that nigger," Decoy said.

"I seen his blue eyes," the Shooter said.

"You almost fuck me up," Decoy said. "A bullet come through the door."

"That shit was swift," the Shooter said.

And then they were gone, the battered yellow Dodge accelerating onto the Van Wyck Expressway a full minute before the first police siren announced the assassination of Police Officer Edward Byrne to a horrified city.

2

"I WANT THAT P.O. POPPED."

The migration of the black middle class to southeastern Queens began with the close of World War II. Harlem had collapsed under a crushing roar of sirens. The fortunate had clamored across the Manhattan Bridge and down Flatbush Avenue into Bedford-Stuyvesant and Crown Heights, Brooklyn. But as the brownstones and brick tenements crumbled under the weight of felony and neglect, a generation of black professionals escaped further still, out into a soft Queens underbelly of manicured lawns and detached one-family homes.

By the mid-'50s, housing in the southeastern Queens neighborhoods of St. Albans, Springfield Gardens, Hollis, and Jamaica was at a premium. Some of the well-to-do blacks had once lived atop Harlem's "Sugar Hill," the nation's first ritzy black enclave. They resurfaced in St. Albans, nicknaming the area "suburban Sugar Hill." It was a heady time in the black history of the borough. Jackie Robinson may have played second base in Brooklyn, but he lived in southeastern Queens. Count Basie and Ella Fitzgerald may have sang about Harlem nights, but they slept in the new black suburbia. The famous were joined by black doctors, lawyers, stockbrokers, and engineers. Home ownership was common. The American Dream was alive and well. For a while there, whites even seemed content to share a neighborhood.

In the beginning, there were fine city services. Just as a series of low bridges kept the poor from reaching Long Island by bus, a lack of subway service kept the undesirables out of many southeastern Queens neighborhoods. In the '60s, however, with urban flight at its apex, whites pushed further east, migrating to Nassau and Suffolk counties. As whites relinquished their half of the neighborhood, city services diminished. Streets became more cracked and dirty with each passing year. Taxi drivers balked at crossing the East River with black passengers. City officials bombed the area with a half-dozen housing projects. A second exodus occurred in the early '70s, with affluent blacks following whites out onto the Island. By the mid-'70s, Attica prison had become a catch basin for troubled men from the South Jamaica and Baisley housing projects. The South Jamaica landscape became the wretched equal of Harlem and Bed-Stuy.

At about the same time whites quit southeastern Queens for Long Island, a character named Pop Freeman moved in. Freeman was a Manhattan drug dealer. The accepted drug history of the territory, as first reported by David Krajicek of the *Daily News* and Peter Blauner of *New York* magazine, is that Mafia chieftain Vito Genovese dispatched Freeman to Queens in the early '60s. Freeman had been arrested a few years earlier and kept quiet about the Genovese operation. Pop got Black Queens as a reward for doing the right thing.

Freeman couldn't have been happier with his land grant. As the neighborhood despair deepened, the business of escapism grew. There is no audience better served by drugs, Freeman preached, than a congregation of desperate men.

When Pop reached seventy, he found he no longer had the stamina to run the drug business. In 1978, he farmed out his work to a younger, more ruthless gang of drug dealers that included

Ronald "Bumps" Bassett. By then, the powdered cocaine business was flowering throughout the nation. Within two years, drug enforcement officials were calling Ronnie Bumps the equal of Leroy "Nicky" Barnes, the Harlem heroin boss. As a way of displaying his success, Bumps bought what he termed "a rich white boy's house," in Westbury, Long Island.

Still, Bumps found, prosperity has its problems. Drug lords tended to attract police surveillance. Federal agents watched and listened as Bumps extended his maneuvers into Baltimore, Detroit, Philadelphia, and Washington, D.C. During one nine-week period, the DEA traced $1.2 million in uncut heroin—with a street value of $17 million—back to Bumps. Ronnie Bumps, the agents discovered, was the quintessential black capitalist. He bought directly from Miami and hired his own people to body-pack the stuff North. With the traditional Mafia cut out, the profits were elephantine. Bumps became to drug franchises what Ray Kroc was to golden-arched hamburger joints.

In southeastern Queens, Bumps hired out some of his work to a young drug developer named Lorenzo Nichols. Born December 28, 1958, in Alabama, Nichols grew up on 139th Street in South Ozone Park. While still in his teens he joined a youth gang called the Seven Crowns. The gang sold heroin and pot, but specialized in store robberies. Nichols worked on the side stealing car radios.

He was arrested for the first time as an adult in 1976. Charged with possession of stolen property, Nichols, nineteen, was arrested four more times the same year.

Nichols was finally sentenced to jail in 1977 for holding up a Queens bar at gunpoint. He spent two and a half years in state prison. Paroled from prison on January 9, 1980, Nicholas was placed on probation until December 27, 1994. He went to work for Ronnie Bumps almost immediately. By then, other kids had a nickname for Nichols. They called the stumplike, 5-foot-8, 230-pound man "Fat Cat." The nickname had more to do with Nichols's reputation than build. Fat Cat's sister, Viola, knew the hyperactive teenager by another name. She called him "Busy."

*

Fat Cat's stay in Fulton Correctional Facility had taught him about alliances. Cocaine had found a boom market in Queens. By then, Colombian drug dealers were pouring into Jackson Heights, killing people by the dozens. Bumps, who was buying kilos directly from the Colombians, had been arrested on a Federal indictment for drug trafficking in Baltimore. Fat Cat was next in line. He figured, what with so much profit to be made, there was no sense dying in a drug war. So Nichols called a meeting with some of the other dealers in the area, including the Corley brothers, Claude Skinner, Kenneth "Supreme" McGriff, Gerald "Prince" Miller, Tommy "Tony Montana" Mickens, and Robert "Cornbread" Gray. After a night of partying in Fat Cat's clubhouse, a grocery store called Big Mac's at the corner of 106th Avenue and 150th Street, the area was split up. The Corley brothers were given control of the Forties Houses. The Supreme Team got the Baisley Houses. Tony Montana got Lauralton and Hollis. Prince and Skinner were made enforcers. Cornbread remained hidden, handling distribution. Everyone answered to Fat Cat.

Nichols's reputation grew with his waistline. Steadily, he became a kind of Robin Hood figure. An accomplished high school point guard, Fat Cat sponsored a neighborhood basketball league, outfitting his players in matching T-shirts and sneakers. College stars like Walter Berry, Pearl Washington, and Mark Jackson played in the drug games.

"You couldn't keep what was happening out in the street from moving into the playground," explained Fly Williams, a former ABA star who was reduced to playing half-court games after losing his left lung to a bullet in a shootout.

The betting action on the games was furious. A drug tournament in Harlem, called the Kings Towers Classic, had had to be disbanded after a courtside shooting. The dealer who'd run the tournament, James Jackson, used to fly players into Washington, D.C., and Baltimore for all-star games, and tricked unwitting players, Walter Berry among them, into transporting cash for him. Jackson was eventually arrested by the Feds and turned, giving up information on a heroin ring run by Mafia Don John Gotti.

In Brooklyn, the basketball games were run by another benevolent drug dealer, Donnie Smallwood. The Smallwood gang, known as the Wild Bunch, was headquartered on Saratoga Avenue in Brownsville. The gang specialized in cocaine and softball. Two crooked cops from Brooklyn's 77th Precinct played on the team. One of the team's infielders was Pearl Washington's brother, Beaver. At about the same time Pearl Washington, a star guard at Syracuse University, was being named First Team All America, Beaver was beating a rival to death with his softball bat.

The team's most lethal player was an outfielder named Anthony Jennings. The outfielder set a record for Brooklyn homicides, having been charged with four separate murders by his nineteenth birthday. Friends of the one-man maelstrom called him Nuke. In 1985, following a shootout with police in the parking lot of a Newark disco, Nuke was arrested, along with a portly Queens woman. A fingerprint check on the 250-pound dowager revealed her to be Fat Cat's sister, Viola Nichols.

At one point, Fat Cat and his understudy, Supreme, decided to sponsor a summer basketball tournament. The players knew the tournament by its proper name: Supreme's Nite Invitational Fastbreak Festival. Cocaine dealers knew it by an acronym: SNIFF. On July 30, 1987, Gregory Vaughn, a thirty-three-year-old gym teacher at Public School 150 and the former head coach of Medgar Evers College, was asked to referee a Supreme League game in Baisley Pond Park. Word on the street was that the teams were playing for $50,000 in prize money. Vaughn, the husband of a cop, had a reputation for getting kids off the playground and into schools. He made a controversial call at the end of the game. As horrified fans watched, Vaughn was beaten to death by a dealer who jumped from the stands. The SNIFF tournament was disbanded.

The Cat could often be seen on the edge of 150th Street, outside his storefront, handing out money to kids. He also gave advice on health food and exercise. Bob Drury, a reporter for *New York Newsday,* found that the Cat had led a busload of kids to Great Adventure amusement park and footed the bill for several week-end barbecues in Baisley Park.

Nichols was, first and foremost, a gang leader. He referred to everyone in his crew as Homes, short for "homeboys," and it was not uncommon for the Cat to lead his homeboys in a jog around the neighborhood. In a community devoid of heroes, Lorenzo Nichols became a kind of perverse role model. Cat had the jewelry, Cat had the clothes, Cat had the women, Cat had the gold, and Cat had the cars. Fat Cat was somebody to emulate.

The benevolent autocrat was also a killer. Although Fat Cat kept no iron gates on his storefront, and assaults on rival drug dens were commonplace, no one ever made a move on Big Mac's Deli. Fear kept them out. Fat Cat's workers regularly doused junkies who fell asleep at his door with gasoline and set them on fire. Dealers who skimmed money and drugs from the Cat were subject to varying degrees of torture. Ten dollars would cost the miscreant a beating. One hundred dollars meant a hot comb in the buttocks. Any theft over $1,000 meant death.

"Don't dis' me," Cat was heard to say, using the street shorthand for the word "disrespect." "Dis' me and you're dead."

By the spring of 1985, Fat Cat's dealings had become more and more apparent to Brian Rooney, his thirty-four-year-old parole officer. Like Nichols, Rooney had grown up in South Ozone Park. That was about where the comparisons died. Still, the fortunes of the black drug dealer and the Irish parole officer would be forever intertwined.

Rooney had always wanted to be a cop. Unfortunately, he was a man of poor eyesight. After flunking the police department's eye test in 1978, Rooney turned to the city's probation department for work. The city probation supervisor was more cop than social worker. He'd once jumped a man who was smoking pot in his elevator and arrested him. Brian Rooney didn't believe in coddling people, either.

"Look," Rooney would tell his probationers. "If you do something wrong again, *I'm* going to put you in jail. *I'm* going to put you away."

Rooney had left the probation job in 1981 for a better-paying position with the state parole division. Now Rooney carried a pistol and conducted investigations. State laws also allowed Rooney greater latitude in the area of discipline. It wasn't police work, but it was power. Still, the gun made Susan Rooney uneasy. Cops carried guns. And New York cops were being shot at the rate of one a month in 1985.

"I'll be fine," Rooney told his wife. "It's not really that dangerous. No one ever whacks their P.O. Murder is a parole violation."

Rooney grew more benevolent with maturity. He went into his pocket to feed struggling convicts. He sometimes entertained parolees' kids with magic tricks in his office. It was the street wizardry of Fat Cat, however, that Rooney himself found most enchanting. On paper, Fat Cat was working for a home improvement company. In reality, Fat Cat was improving his position in the drug game.

"I just can't imagine anybody having that much money lying around," Rooney told his wife after visiting Nichols at his storefront in June of 1985. "Hell, he's got my yearly salary in a drawer."

Fat Cat's attempt to insulate himself from arrest failed completely in July of 1985. Queens narcotics cops had grabbed Stony Bastion, one of Cat's dealers, in a buy-and-bust operation. Stony had a sheet as long as Fat Cat's arm. As a repeat offender, he faced heavy time, or as they say on the streets, state time.

"I can give you Fat Cat," Stony promised.

Bastion was registered as an informant and set back on the

streets. A few weeks later, Stony walked to a pay phone and dialed a special number.

"Hit the Cat's place," the informant said. "The place is hot."

At 10 P.M. on July 29, 1985, twenty Queens cops hit Fat Cat's storefront with a search warrant. To their amazement the cops found Fat Cat and four of his associates sitting in the store. The Fat Cat was sitting on two loaded automatic weapons. He also had a 9mm. automatic in his desk drawer. The pistol was loaded with eighteen shots. Cat had reached for the drawer as the cops burst through the door, but then thought better of the idea.

"Motherfucker," Fat Cat was heard to say.

This encouraged the cops to continue their search. In due course the cops uncovered six ounces of high-grade heroin, two ounces of coke, ten pounds of marijuana, a scale, police radio scanner, and about $180,000 in cash, including $30,000 in the desk next to the gun. The police noticed a card pinned to the wall. It was inscribed "World's Greatest Daddy," and was signed by one of Fat Cat's three children.

Word of the bust tore through the street. Fat Cat's attorney, David Cohen, arrived on the set even before police had led his client away. Oddly enough, Fat Cat hadn't even made a phone call.

"We'd never seen anything like that before," one of the arresting officers, Sergeant Michael McGuinness, later told *Newsday* and *New York* magazine.

One of those questioned in connection with the raid was a brawny Rastafarian from Brooklyn named Howard Mason. Although Mason wasn't a known drug player just yet, he had spent a quarter of his twenty-three-year-old life in jail, including a five-year bit for attempted murder. Fat Cat had met Mason in prison, and hired him on to keep order.

"Do you have a street name?" one of the cops asked.

Mason, twenty-three, said nothing. Only later did Bastion tell the cops, "That dude you was talking to with the dreadlocks. That's Pappy. He's Fat Cat's enforcer now. He the craziest guy out here. Even the Cat is afraid of Pappy."

Fat Cat posted a $70,000 bond and was released from jail the next day. By getting arrested again, Cat had violated the terms of his probation, so when Cat showed up for a 4 P.M. meeting in Rooney's office the next day, the parole officer reached for his gun.

"You're going right back in," Brian Rooney was heard to say.

At a parole hearing, Rooney advised the court that he suspected Lorenzo Nichols of being a major drug dealer and a very dangerous fellow. Nichols was violated and sent back to jail. The nervous parole officer paced the court hallway with a friend.

"What did the crazy fuck expect me to do?" Rooney wondered. "If I don't have the balls to do my job, what good am I?"

Pappy Mason emerged as Cat's man in the streets. He pistol-whipped a prostitute who stole from the Cat and shot a rival cocaine dealer in the buttocks. When a customer started to complain about the quality of Fat Cat's cocaine, Pappy shot him dead outside a Baptist church. As an afterthought, Pappy put a round through a plastic cross hanging over the body. Pappy also threatened one of Fat Cat's favorite girlfriends, Myrtle Horsheim. The mistress, nicknamed Misha, was carrying Fat Cat's son at the time.

"I don't know what you know," Pappy warned Misha. "But Busy says you sure better forget it."

Pappy Mason began to make regular visits to the Queens House of Detention in September 1985. Sometimes Pappy brought along two underlings, Chris "Jughead" Williams and Perry Bellamy. The prospect of spending life in prison had not done much for Cat's disposition.

"Listen up, Homes," Nichols was heard to tell them. "You motherfuckers better take care of Busy's problem."

Later in September, Bellamy was arrested again, winding up in the Queens House of Detention. A lanky twenty-two-year-old who'd quit school at the age of sixteen, Bellamy was heading past a prison prayer service for Black Muslims when he spotted Fat Cat standing in the hallway with two men he knew from the streets as Wykeem and Ernie. The Cat was furious.

"Man, fuck that parole officer," Nichols said. "P.O. or no P.O., he's going to get what's coming to him."

"Don't worry about it, Cat," Wykeem said. "Homes will take care of it."

Fat Cat turned back to Bellamy, one of his most trusted homeboys.

"Do that nigger, Perry," Fat Cat said. "I want that P.O. popped."

But first there was another order of business to be completed. Word of Stony Bastion's rollover had reached the street. Pappy Mason figured, quite correctly, that Stony had traded his own freedom for Fat Cat's. On October 2, 1985, at about 12:30 A.M., Stony was walking down 150th Street when Pappy, Jughead Williams, and a third man approached him from behind.

"I wanna talk to you," Pappy said. Stony started to run for the corner. That was all the confession Pappy needed. He pulled out a 9mm. and fired. Stony soaked up three in the back.

"That's one for Cat," Pappy told his associates when they gathered later to celebrate the hit at Fat Cat's storefront.

On the evening of October 9, 1985, Jughead Williams went to Pappy Mason's girlfriend's house to catch a telephone call from Fat Cat. The imprisoned drug dealer and Jughead talked for about a half hour. Later Jughead cornered Perry Bellamy outside the A&B cab stand on Baisley Boulevard.

"Yo, man," Jughead said. "I want you to do something for me."

"What?"

"I want you to bring Cat's P.O. to the park."

"Why?"

"Don't worry about it. I'm going to call him tomorrow. You just meet me at the game room, 11:30."

In the morning, the group met near a pay phone outside a MacDonalds on Sutphin Boulevard. Jughead telephoned Rooney in his office, saying that he had information on Fat Cat. Rooney was told to meet "Perry" at 7 P.M. on Sutphin Boulevard.

"Perry will take you to us," Jughead explained. "We got good shit on the Cat."

Brian called Susan Rooney at around 6:30 P.M., telling her he'd be late.

"Nothing important," Brian had said. "I just have to stop and see a guy."

Jughead spent the afternoon with Cat's crew in a game room nicknamed the Dog House. Jughead was giving the orders, but it was Pappy who carried the gun.

"Yo, man," Jughead said, showing Bellamy a picture of Rooney. "This is the P.O. and I want you to bring him in front of the park."

"For what?"

"You heard what the fuck I said. I want you to get the P.O. and bring him in front of the park."

Bellamy sat back on the pool table. He watched Jughead herd Prince Miller into the corner. It was not difficult to overhear the conversation.

"We're going to knock that motherfucker right there," Jughead explained.

"Look, Jug," Bellamy yelled across the room, "I'm not getting involved with that bullshit. Don't put me down with that shit."

"Just do what the fuck I said, Dude. That's all you get involved."

"I heard what you said over there, Jug. You're going to knock that nigger right there."

"No," Jughead said. "We was talking about somebody else."

The assassins left, Jughead and Pappy driving off in a white Datsun 280Z. Mike and Rolley Bones, Prince, and Pappy's brother Ruff followed them out in a white Pontiac 6000 and a blood-red Jeep Comanche. Bellamy was left to wait for the parole officer.

Rooney pulled his 1976 Dodge Dart to a stop across the street from the Dog House just after 7 P.M. Rooney had his briefcase on the front passenger seat. Bellamy dove into the back, stretching out.

"Just drive a few blocks over to the park on 155th Street," Bellamy said.

"I ain't got all day," Rooney replied.

The parole officer made a right onto 116th Avenue and then a left onto 155th Street. As the car reached the intersection of 119th Avenue, Bellamy spotted Mike Bones in the park.

"Pull over here," Bellamy said. Rooney jerked to a stop and shut off the engine. Then Bellamy saw Ruff hiding in the bushes on the right side of the car.

"Yo, they coming, man," Bellamy said.

"Come on," Rooney said again. "I ain't got all day."

Ruff came up out of the bushes and fired one shot, hitting the passenger door frame. Frightened, Ruff retreated toward the Jeep.

"Jesus Christ!" Rooney screamed.

The parole officer was frantic. He had just restarted the car when Pappy Mason stepped to his window. Brian saw him, recognized the ambush, and reached for the gun in his ankle holster. When he came back up, Pappy was already firing a large black 9mm. into the car. It was the same gun that had killed Stony Bastion.

Pappy fired at least twice, hitting Rooney once in the chest and a second time in the left arm. The Dodge started to roll forward. Pappy reached to open the rear door.

"Get the fuck out of the car," Pappy screamed. Bellamy jumped out, looking bewildered. He stood in the middle of the street, his hands in his back pockets. He watched as Rooney's car crashed into a truck. Fat Cat's parole officer was dead on impact.

"Get into the fucking Z," Pappy screamed.

Bellamy jumped into the Datsun and Jughead screeched off, the assassins resurfacing at Jack's Grocery Store at the corner of 150th Street and Liberty Avenue. As Bellamy exited the car, Pappy grabbed him by the shirt.

"If I hear you even say any fucking thing about this, I will kill you," Pappy said. "If I can't get you, I will get your family. Shit, I should fucking do you right here."

Rolley Bones had to step between them.

"Perry ain't like that, Pap," Rolley said.

Pappy began laughing with his brother Ruff, congratulating him on his work as a decoy. He told Prince and Jughead, "We lose one of ours. They lose one of theirs. We got to show that Busy still got the juice."

At around 12:30 P.M. Susan Rooney heard a car in the driveway of her South Hempstead, L.I., home. She walked to the window and saw Brian's partner, Richie Pasternack, with another man in black. She looked closer and saw a white clerical collar. She rushed to the door, already knowing.

"What happened?" she asked.

"He's gone," said the priest. The parole officer's eighteen-month-old son wandered out the door. "Where's Daddy?" he asked. "Where's Daddy?" Susan Rooney began to cry. She cried for a very long time.

Too many people had seen Perry Bellamy in the car with Brian Rooney. Frightened, Bellamy rushed to the 103rd Precinct immediately after the killing, and told cops Pappy Mason had done the hit. Thinking the informant a liar, the detectives threw him out of the squad room. On Friday, October 25, 1985, however, Bellamy was arrested, and at about 11 P.M. he told a homicide detective, David Dellnegro, that he was willing to talk about the killing. Dellnegro called an assistant Queens District Attorney, Joseph Keenan. By midnight Perry Bellamy was sitting in the office of the District Attorney's Homicide Bureau making a videotaped confession. He told the story in thirty-seven minutes, implicating Pappy, Jughead, and Fat Cat in the assassination of a state parole officer.

*

The cops had never heard anything quite like it before.

Perry Bellamy: We were all there when the P.O. got kicked. We had walked down to the Dog House. But before we walked down to the Dog House, Jughead had called the P.O.

District Attorney: Were you present when Jughead called the parole officer?

PB: Yeah.

DA: Okay, what happened then?

PB: Jug called the P.O. on the phone and he was on the phone with the P.O. and he asked the P.O. to come down the Dog House, that Perry would be waiting for you. "Perry will bring you to a spot where I will meet you."

DA: Okay, had you ever met the P.O. before?

PB: Oh, yeah. Three or four times on 150th Street.

DA: Who were you with when you met him?

PB: Serussa the Cat.

DA: Okay, and do you know his real name?

PB: (Nodding his head yes.)

DA: Is that Fat Cat?

PB: (Nodding his head yes.)

DA: Is that Lorenzo Nichols?

PB: Yeah, but we call him Serussa the Cat.

DA: Okay, do you know what Serussa means?

PB: Yeah. It means the greatest, the boss.

DA: Did Serussa introduce you to the P.O.?

PB: I found out he was his P.O. You know he used to, like, come inside the spot. He would just sit and be Fat Cat's P.O.

DA: Did the P.O. come and get you on the night of Oct. 10?

PB: Yeah. I took him to the spot. I was going to 152-13 118th Ave. But then I saw Mike Bones in the park waving me over. They was all there when the P.O. got kicked. Pappy, Jughead, Mike Bones, and his brother Rolley, Prince, and Pappy's half brother Ruff.

DA: Do you know any of their real names?

PB: I don't know any of their government names. I just knows them by their street names. Nobody be using their government names in the street.

DA: Okay, all right, what happened when the P.O. pulled his car over?

PB: After he pulled over, Ruff came out of the bushes and fired one shot. The P.O. went to start the car and it turned over. The P.O. must have seen Pappy coming from the side in his rear-view mirror. He reached down for something and then came up. When he lift up, Pappy was already there and he just open fire. That's when Pappy got him.

DA: Okay, now back up. Now did you ask Jughead why you were meeting the P.O.?

PB: Yeah, I asked him. He say "Bring the motherfucker to the spot." Just like that. Word for word.

DA: Okay, but he didn't explain to you, why?

PB: He didn't go into no detail as of why or nothing.

DA: Okay, after the shot was fired, did you see what happened to the P.O.'s car?

PB: The engine was running. The car was standing still. The P.O. was moaning when I got out of the car.

DA: Did the P.O. fire back?

PB: No. He was messed up.

DA: When the P.O. looked up, there was Pappy immediately?

PB: Yeah. When I looked up Pappy was already at my window. You understand what I'm saying? But even before Pappy got at my window, Pappy was at the bumper of the P.O.'s car. The P.O. is already starting the engine. When the engine is turned over, Pappy is at my window. The P.O. must have seen him through that little mirror 'cause he bent down like he was reaching for something. When he lift up, Pappy was already there, opening up on him.

DA: Did you notice anything else?

PB: Yeah. I notice that shit was swift.

*

Three days later, on February 28, 1985, a set of Queens detectives arrested Pappy Mason. They had nothing more to link him to the murder than Bellamy's statement. As a bonus, however, the cops discovered a fully loaded .22 cal. Derringer in Mason's boot. The cops didn't find the gun, however, until Mason reached Central Booking. Jughead Williams, having witnessed Pappy's arrest from an apartment building above the street, fled the state. Pappy was not really interested in talking to police.

"I ain't no Perry Bellamy," Pappy said.

Charged with murder and weapons possession, Pappy joined Fat Cat in the Queens House of Detention. Then, one afternoon in November 1985, Fat Cat was sitting in the prison dayroom when he got a phone call from his sister, Viola.

"Hey, Busy," Viola said. "That new stuff, people is wild for it."

"What stuff is that?"

"The stuff they be calling crack. It come in a vial. And the homeboys is going crazy for it."

Twenty-seven months later, all of it—crack, Brian Rooney, Stony Bastion, Perry Bellamy, Fat Cat, and Pappy Mason— would have a direct effect on the life of Edward Byrne. And his death.

3

"THEY CALL THEMSELVES THE BEBOS."

February 25, 1988: The detective was thinking about business again, which meant murder. The South Jamaica crack wars were in full swing, young men and women dropping left and right. The homicide detective thought about this as he stepped into the shower, hot water steaming him clean.

Richie Sica had been working too many long hours on too many small murders. He rubbed his neck. It was tight with stress. The South Jamaica streets were boiling with fury and malice, the crack vial being at the epicenter of all action and reaction. At first, in the summer of 1985, everyone had wanted to believe crack another faddish drug. They'd hoped it would go the way of acid, mescaline, and angel dust. On November 29, 1985, four months after the word "crack" first appeared in the *New York Post,* the *Times* finally got around to writing about the drug. The report, filed by Jane Gross, was headlined "A New, Purified Form of Cocaine Causes Alarm as Abuse Increases" and anchored the left-hand side of page A1. The word "crack" appeared in the second paragraph. The detectives had passed the article around the 103rd squad room, the sleuths joking with each other.

"Gee, the *Times* says crack is a problem. No shit."

By the summer of 1986, the city had seemed consumed by crack. The drug had created a cottage industry of dealers. Anyone with a bag of pure cocaine, frying pan, stove, and baking soda could get into the act. The high was much more intense. Unfortunately, the high lasted twenty minutes tops. And then it was back to the glass pipe.

The profits were enormous. A kilo of cocaine that sold for $20,000 could be mixed with baking soda, boiled on a stove, dried, cut into tiny slivers, placed in half-inch vials, and resold for $70,000.

The demand for the drug was astounding. Police throughout the city were reporting the sudden appearance of cars with New Jersey and Long Island registrations on some of the city's worst blocks. A grandstanding United States Senator, Al D'Amato, had been able to put on a pair of sunglasses and buy a vial of crack off a Washington Heights block in broad daylight. But D'Amato could have just as easily bought the drug at a bar in the Hamptons.

Anyone with a bag of vials and a gun could take over a street corner. Within days of crack's first appearance in the Bronx, there seemed to be a crack house on every block. The dealers would take over an abandoned building and hire young kids on bikes to patrol the block, looking for cops. Where school kids once worked a paper route, they now worked as lookouts. These kids routinely made $300 a week.

A steerer worked the corner, leading prospective buyers down a block into a crack house. Steerers could make as much as $1,000 a week. The dealer stayed in the crack house, his stash guarded by men with automatic weapons. As a way of dissuading theft, most deals were consummated at gunpoint. Buyers suspected of being police undercovers were made to snort coke at gunpoint. At least a dozen city cops would be shot while trying to make undercover buys in the first eighteen months after Byrne's murder. Six of them would die.

The city's murder rate jumped from 1200 in 1985 to 1800 in 1988. By 1987, nearly half of the serious crimes in the city were being committed by crack users. Three-quarters of the inmates on Rikers Island admitted using the drug. Long-term drug rehabilitation centers like Phoenix House in Manhattan and Daytop Village in Far Rockaway, Queens, were reporting a six-month waiting list in 1986 and a ten-month wait for a bed in 1987. Crack had cleaved the city in two.

By 1986, the crack trade in southeastern Queens was being called a $100-million-a-year industry. Following up on his sister's information, Fat Cat had become the King of Crack. The imprisoned dealer's mother, sister, and brothers were running the business in his absence, while Pappy Mason recruited enforcers amongst the prison population. A crack dealer, prison officials determined, had prestige on both sides of the prison wall.

By 1987, Fat Cat had become a fat target. The Cat's wife of ten years, nicknamed Mouse, lived in an expensive Elmont, Long Island, home far from the crack battle zone. The bad guys could read the newspaper as well as anyone else, so everyone figured the Cat had to be worth a dollar or two. At 3 P.M. on Friday, May 22, JoAnne "Mouse" Nichols was driving from a bank to her home when two men in a car forced her off the road. The men said they were cops and produced a subpoena with her name on it. They went on to say they were investigating Mouse in connection with the murder of Parole Officer Brian Rooney. Nichols was handcuffed and placed in a blue car. It was only after she was blindfolded and placed in a van that Nichols realized that she had, in fact, been kidnapped.

During the course of the next thirty-eight hours, Mouse was kept blindfolded in a Brooklyn apartment.

"The kidnappers threatened me with pit bulls," Mouse later reported. "They said they were going to let the dogs bite my breasts off."

Mouse listened as the kidnappers telephoned her mother and made their demands: twenty-two pounds of cocaine and $50,000 in cash. The money, raised overnight by Cat's crew, was handed over in a Brooklyn parking lot. Unknown to the kidnappers, however, the abduction had been reported to the police. Four men were arrested and convicted at trial. At the trial, Mouse testified that she had received a dead mouse in the mail before taking the stand. The envelope also included three bullets. Each bullet, Mouse reported, had been inscribed with one of her children's names.

It later turned out that the same men had also abducted and killed another of Fat Cat's workers. The men did not appear very frightened of the Cat.

A few months later, Fat Cat's girlfriend, Myrtle Horsheim, was arrested for narcotics possession in New Jersey. She wrote a threatening note to Fat Cat, signing the letter Mrs. Busy. The letter included the phrase, "What goes around, comes around." Fat Cat took this to mean Myrtle Horsheim was going to give him up on the Rooney murder.

Pappy had told her to be quiet, but she hadn't listened. In December 1987, about six months after being indicted in the Rooney murder, Fat Cat silenced his talkative girlfriend. While driving through the Forties projects with a girlfriend, in a blue Monte Carlo, Myrtle noticed a black car following her. The chase car, a black Volvo with tinted windows and gold-trim wheels, cornered her at the end of a one-way street. Two men, one carrying a 9mm., the other with a .380 semi-automatic, got out of the car. They calmly walked to Myrtle's car and opened the back door. One of the men reached in and took Fat Cat's eighteen-month-old son out of the car. The man placed the baby on the sidewalk and then turned back to the car. Both men opened fire. Myrtle Horsheim was killed instantly. The pillow talk died with her.

Fat Cat's son was later found wandering the streets. Myrtle's girlfriend recovered, but never felt inclined to identify her attackers.

That month, another debt was paid as well. Pappy had never forgotten his promise to Perry Bellamy. In January 1986, Bellamy had been on trial for murder, charged with having led Rooney into a deathtrap. The jury had sat in stunned silence as Bellamy's videotaped confession was replayed. The jury had needed all of five minutes to convict.

Pappy Mason had followed Bellamy to trial, but a witness to the murder suddenly clammed up. The jury was still deadlocked at nine to three for a conviction when the judge declared a mistrial. With no witness to be found, the D.A. was in no hurry to rush Mason back to trial.

In fear for his life, Bellamy lived on Rikers Island in protective custody. Bellamy's father, Alonzo, fifty, wanted no part of the kid or his drug business. He lived with his brother Oscar in a two-story home on 195th Street. The father of six children, Alonzo Bellamy worked making change at Wilkins Quick Wash and Dry, a coin-operated laundry on Linden Boulevard.

Alonzo Bellamy was toiling away as usual on the morning of December 4, 1987, pushing a broom through the laundromat. He did not see a young man lingering in the street. The man waited until two customers left the laundry and then entered. He walked to the rear of the store and confronted Bellamy with a gun near a set of dryers. There were no words, just the gunshot—one slug hitting Alonzo squarely between the eyes. The old man lingered at Mary Immaculate Hospital until December 22. He died without ever regaining consciousness.

The hit on Mr. Bellamy was only part of the plan, detectives learned. The rest of the plot called for a grieving Perry Bellamy to be gunned down at his father's funeral. The kid was smart enough to stay in jail.

"My son didn't have nothing in this eternal world to do with drugs," Alonzo Bellamy's mother later told David Krajicek of the *News.* "These children get bad, and it's their parents who suffer."

In any event, Bellamy was in no hurry to testify against either Fat Cat or Pappy, or as he told Krajicek, "There's not a single soul who is gonna come in and testify against that boy. The Fat Cat has become more powerful in prison than he ever was out on the street. He's got the name Perry Bellamy on a contract, too, no doubt about it."

Fourteen months later, however, in the week of February 22, 1988, it looked like justice was finally making some headway against Pappy Mason and Fat Cat Nichols.

It was an eventful week in South Jamaica. The cops had won big victories over Fat Cat and Pappy in Queens courtrooms. Following his mistrial in the Rooney murder, Pappy Mason had remained in jail on the gun charge. He'd made bail, however, in early February 1988, and the Queens District Attorney, fearing a bloodbath, had gotten Mason remanded a week later and rushed the dealer to trial on weapons possession.

On Tuesday, February 23, a Queens jury convicted Pappy Mason on the gun charge. Upon hearing the jury's verdict, Pappy turned to the prosecutor, Scott Tulman, and formed an imaginary gun with his thumb and index finger. Then Pappy pulled the trigger. Only quick action by the court officers prevented a fist-fight.

The Mason conviction dealt a hard blow to the South Jamaica crack trade. A second, more killing blow was being struck even as Detective Richie Sica stood in his shower on Thursday afternoon. Following Fat Cat's January 8, 1988, conviction on charges of drug and weapons possession, a Queens judge was sentencing him to thirty-five-to-life relating to the 1985 raid on his storefront. The judge, Vincent Naro, his life threatened during the trial, had been under police guard for months. The Cat held his face in his hands as the sentence was read. The prosecutor, Warren Silverman, had also been living under a death threat. Cops applauded the verdict wildly. The Cat, having been indicted for killing

Rooney in July 1987, still faced a murder trial and a second life
sentence. One of the cops yelled, "The Cat's nine lives are over.
Nobody takes orders from a lifer." In this great moment of tri-
umph, none of the cops could imagine the sorrow that would
befall them within the next twenty-four hours.

Richie Sica didn't know about the sentencing of Fat Cat yet, but
on the afternoon of February 25, 1988, he did know he had a
half-dozen open murder cases. All of the murders had two things
in common: crack and automatic weapons. Sica knew of single
homicide detectives in East New York and Washington Heights
carrying twice as many crack-related murders. The detective
stayed in the shower a good while, the water tranquilizing him.

Richie emerged from the shower and dressed quietly, putting on
a white shirt, striped blue tie, blue pants, and gray wool sports
jacket. It was just after 3 P.M. The girls, aged nine and eleven, were
in the basement playing Nintendo. He could feel the electric blips
of the computer coming through the floor.

The cop had fine Italian features, high cheekbones, brown eyes,
and a strong nose. He looked into the mirror and smoothed out
his curly brown hair and mustache. At thirty-nine, he still had a
powerful body, his legs and waist still free of atrophy. He was
certainly strong beyond his size, 5 foot 8 and 170 pounds.

He carried the great equalizer, a .38 cal. Smith & Wesson. The
gun, in a clip-on holster, lay on the bed. Richie clipped the brown
leather holster to his pants. The sport coat covered the gun. Still,
the gun was overrated. Like most cops, Richie had never fired the
revolver outside the police range. The detective liked being able
to say that.

He was an unlikely cop. Upon his graduation from an Elmont,
Long Island, high school in June 1967, Richie had joined the
Marine Reserves and spent two months at boot camp in Parris

Island. Some of the recruits thought the experience degrading. Richie enjoyed the experience, especially the camaraderie. Richie returned to Valley Stream in March of 1968 and found work as a mechanic at a Chevrolet dealership in Lynbrook. The money was healthy, about $280 a week after taxes, and the position stable. As a hobby, Richie did the male Long Island thing, joining a volunteer fire department in Elmont. Many of the guys were taking civil-service tests, chasing jobs and pensions with the New York City police, fire, and sanitation departments. With his schooling completed, Richie saw no reason to take another test, until someone else changed his mind.

Some personal history.

"I had become good friends with a guy named Larry Stefane. He and I played ball together, we hung around together, we were in the fire department together. Some of the other guys had talked me into taking the Nassau County police exam. Nassau called me down and asked me to stand against a wall. A guy measured me and said, 'You don't meet the height requirement. You have to be 5 foot 8 and you're only 5 foot 7 and ¾.' I made an appeal, because I really thought I was 5-8. They gave me another appointment. I went to a chiropractor, who made some adjustments. I slept on a board. In the morning, I went down and stood against the wall again. This time the guy says, 'I'm sorry, we made a mistake. You're not 5'7 and ¾. You're 5'7 and ½.'

"Larry Stefane wasn't interested in Nassau. He kept saying he wanted to be a real cop, a city cop. So we went down and took the test in October of 1970. I walk in, a guy sizes me up and says, '5 foot 9.' So we take the test. Larry scores in the high 80's. I score in the high 70's. Larry was called right after that. He went into the Academy in December. Then he got assigned to the 9th Precinct in the East Village. No one called me. I went and stayed with the Chevys.

"I remember, about six months later, I was working in Rupp Chevrolet at the time, it was late in the afternoon, and I had the radio on. And I heard about a New York City cop being killed.

I didn't catch the name. And I never thought nothing of it. This was in May of 1971. And I remember going home. It was about 6 P.M. and we were getting ready for dinner. My friend Sal came to the door, looking distraught. I asked, 'What's the matter.' And he said, 'Don't you know? Some maniac killed Larry.'

"Larry and his partner had pulled up to a grocery store. The partner had gone in for coffee. Larry was sitting in the car with the window open. This was at ten to nine in the morning. All of a sudden, this guy named Singleton just leaned into the car and stabbed Larry in the chest. Leaned right into the car and got him right in the heart. It was over nothing. Larry never provoked it. It was a spring day, and he had his window open. Larry stumbled out of the car, got off two shots, and died. Larry's partner came out of the store and shot Singleton. Didn't kill him, just shot him.

"The funeral was held in Franklin Square. The fire department carried Larry's casket on a truck. It seemed like the entire police department was there. They had the muffled drums and bagpipes. It was the saddest morning in my life, much worse than the Vietnam funerals. They were easy compared to this. Larry was the totally innocent casualty of some domestic war.

"Larry's wife, Cathy, was having a very rough time. There wasn't the support for a police widow then that there is today. Joanne and I got married in November of 1971. And what with Larry gone, Cathy wanted out of her apartment. So Cathy moved out and we moved in. That was very weird, I know. But it was a way to keep Larry alive. The same guys who used to come and visit Larry in the apartment, now they came to see me. I was also very close with Larry's mother. She told me, 'Don't ever become a cop.' I never thought of it as a vendetta, but right then and there, I decided to become a cop. It was like Larry's murder had given me some purpose. It was like, 'There's a world out there, guy. Get in it.'

"The department called me in November of 1973. I didn't hesitate. Larry's mother told my mother, 'I will never talk to Richie again.' Joanne wasn't too pleased with the decision. She wanted me to stay working as a mechanic. I had to convince her that eventually I'd be making better money as a cop. But it had nothing to do with money. I would never admit to Joanne how much losing Larry had to do with the decision. So I went into the Academy and came out with a gun and shield, No. 7860.

"I was assigned to the 13th Precinct out of the Academy on the East Side near Bellevue Hospital. I walked my first foot post on East 14th Street between Second and Third avenues. I was completely lost, couldn't even twirl the nightstick. Came home every night for a month with bruises on my leg. My first arrest was major: I grabbed a guy for blowing up a park bench with an M-80 firecracker. Spent two days in Central Booking. I never went to court on the thing. The guy's probably in the P.L.O. by now.

"In June of 1974, I was working a 4-to-12 with these guys Phil Carpenito and Roy Simpson. We got a call, 'Psycho with a rifle. Meet the complainant at the corner of 21st Street and Seventh Avenue.' This is right on the border of the Tenth Precinct. So we go and we meet the guy. He says, 'A black guy is holding my girlfriend hostage. He broke into our apartment with a rifle.' So Simpson says, 'All right, jump in the car and we'll go over there.'

"We got to the apartment house and met the sergeant, John Lawlor. The guy gives us the apartment number and says, 'Hey, one more thing, it's a big rifle.' So we head up the stairs and I'm squirming past the guys to reach the door first. I'm standing in front of the door, figuring I'm going to make my first gun collar. The sergeant pulls me back and says, 'Relax, if it's a gun collar, you got the collar, kid.' So me and Roy Simpson are on one side of the door, and Phil and the sergeant are on the other side. Lawlor knocks on the door. Nothing. Now he bangs on the door and yells, 'Police, open up.' Then *ka-boooom*. The guy fires a couple of shots through the door. Fucking busted my eardrums. The shots go right through a steel-clad door and into the wall. So now the guy is playing for keeps. Everybody fucking backs up and retreats down the hallway. I am petrified, there's no place to hide. I mean, this isn't the Marine Reserves.

"Now I had the portable radio. I pushed a button and screamed, 'Ten-thirteen, shots fired.' Nothing else. Central comes back and asks, 'What's your address? What's your address?' I screamed 'Manhattan.' Roy grabbed the radio and gave our location. And luckily, with us pinned down, an old lady across the hall from the apartment suddenly opens her door. She had heard the noise. Roy pushed into the apartment and called for backup. I'll never forget talking to Phil, asking, 'What if he comes out with the girl?' Phil just looked at me and said, 'You do what you gotta do.' And then there was more shooting. I was waiting any minute for him to come out the door. So the door finally opens, the girl sticks her head out, and we motion to her, 'Come on out, come on out.' So she comes running out. I figured Mr. Rifle would be right behind her. But he never came out. Finally the Marines get there, the guys from Emergency Service. These guys have flak jackets on and everything. The girl is hysterical. 'Where is he?' they're yelling. And she can't say anything. I mean these guys are going to war.

"Then there's more gun shots. The guy is shooting out the window at cops below us. He's got them all pinned down. These two Emergency Service guys hit the door with shotguns. We follow them in. I had the kitchen. I checked everything, even the drawers, expecting this guy to jump out firing. We finally get to the living room and there the guy is, laying dead on the floor, with a bullet hole in the middle of his head. So everybody's asking, 'Who shot this guy?' Roy comes in from the old lady's apartment, looks at the sergeant, and says, 'I dunno.' Some sergeant comes up and says he's got to give a statement to the press. 'Is it apparent suicide?' Sgt. Lawlor says, 'Looks that way.' So the guy runs out and makes a big statement in front of the cameras. 'It's apparent suicide.'

"So about five minutes later, Roy leans over to Lawlor and says, 'Hey, sarge, you know I did take a shot at this guy. He was leaning out the window firing at people in the street and I took a shot at him from Granny's window.' And that's what happened. Simpson shot the guy from Granny's window. Roy Simpson is my hero. I mean this is Buffalo Bill stuff, almost an around-the-corner shot.

"The dead guy had a pack of cigarettes in his shirt. And the sarge looks over at me, because he can see that I'm absolutely wired. He says, 'You want a cigarette?' I says, 'No.' He says, 'Okay,' and leans over the guy, tapping the pack out of the guy's pocket. He takes a cigarette, puts them back, and then stands over the dead guy smoking one of his cigarettes. I'll never forget that. Now I was a cop. Now I'm one of the fucking guys.

"It turned out the dead guy was more than just a smoker. He was also a member of the Black Liberation Army. He had a .30-cal. carbine and a whole bunch of banana clips. I mean he was ready to do war. He had an army satchel with a picture of a cop in it, Detective Thomas Shea, from the 103rd Precinct. Shea had killed a thirteen-year-old black kid named Clifford out in South Jamaica. Shea said he saw a gun. The kid was unarmed. It was a terrible situation, a huge stink at the time. And this guy had posters in his satchel, 'Shea Wanted for Murder.' The guy was gunning for a cop.

"So we all go back to the Tenth Precinct. The Manhattan D.A. is there and he starts reading us our rights. I says, 'Wait a minute.' And I had to ask Sgt. Lawlor, 'Is this what they do?' And the sarge says, 'Yeah, no problem. You just tell 'em what happened.' And there was no problem. We all got medals. The strange part was calling Joanne. I told her, 'Listen, I'm okay, but one of the guys I was working with killed this other guy.' Joanne was flabbergasted. I mean, she was liberal and college-educated. She was on the other guy's side. We had done everything wrong. This happened a lot over the years. Joanne would take the perp's side a lot. It kept me honest.

"About a month after this, I got assigned to guard a prisoner at Bellevue Hospital. I came on at about midnight. The prisoner was lying on a bed in handcuffs and leg shackles, sleeping. He had come down from some upstate prison for a psychiatric evaluation. I sat there the whole night with this guy. He slept like a baby. In the morning, a cop came back to relieve me. He says, 'Any problem?' I said, 'No, nothing. The guy slept through the whole night.

No big deal.' The cop says, 'You know who he is?' I said, 'No.'
He says, 'He killed a cop down in the Ninth. Stabbed him right
in the heart.' My blood froze. I asked, 'Who did he kill?' The cop
says, 'A rookie named Larry something. This guy here is named
Singleton.' I turned and walked out of the room. I walked back
to the station house, getting madder and madder with each step.
I didn't want to think about what might have happened had I
known who the guy was.''

Richie Sica loved the job. He learned to cherish those spine-
tingling moments of excitement and to survive the hours of te-
dium. He wrote his share of parking tickets and moving violations,
but much preferred talking to crime victims and muggers. He was
much more interested in working as a sleuth than an amateur
social worker and marriage counselor. He spent much of his first
two years on the force watching and learning, never overlooking
the obvious. While other cops struggled to find bad guys in the
police computer, Sica found them in the telephone directory.

Richie had a splendid way of communicating with people on the
streets. People liked him. They felt easy with him. He was not
much for brutality or name-calling. And at a time when many
people were still referring to cops as pigs, Sica had a way of
disarming people. It was the same with the cops he worked with.

There was, for example, a bearish cop in the precinct named
Louis Savarese. The cop had an earring and long hair, so that
made him an untouchable. No one knew very much about the guy,
except that he was quiet and a terror with a car. On one of their
first nights working together, Savarese decided to respond to a
ten-thirteen. He gunned the accelerator, the car reaching a speed
of sixty miles an hour within the distance of a half block. This was
on Christmas Eve, 1974, the East Side streets filled with holiday
revelers. Seeing a steady red light at the corner of Second Avenue
and East Twenty-third Street, Sica grabbed the dashboard, fearing
the worst.

"Lou-ie," he screamed.

Savarese exploded through the intersection, narrowly missing a gas truck. The car spun out and came to a stop in the middle of the crosswalk. Sica was furious and reached for his gun. Had he not been so shook up, he might well have shot the cop.

"Are you crazy?" Sica screamed.

"No," Savarese replied evenly. "I just don't believe in a whole lot of traffic laws."

Sica did not fully comprehend the meaning of this remark until some weeks later. The cops were standing on the corner of a typically Bohemian lower East Side block when they heard a great clamor of engines. Richie looked up and saw no less than fifty Hell's Angels in full battle dress. They were riding down the sidewalk, rolling over trash cans and shrubs. Richie figured he would die right there.

"Holy Jesus," he said, and turned to Savarese. "Do something."

To Richie's amazement, there stood Police Officer Savarese on the sidewalk, saluting the bikers. To his continued astonishment, the road warriors were waving back.

"How you doing?" the cop said to several passing bikers. "Good to see you again."

One or two Angels gunned their engines for the cop.

"How you been, man?" screamed the biggest, dirtiest biker Sica had ever seen.

"Just great," Savarese screamed back. "I'll tell the missus I saw you. Anybody seen Mongo?"

"Nah. He's in Attica on that robbery thing."

Finally, the bikers rolled past, the man-made thunder on the block subsiding.

"Hey, Lou," Sica said. "What the fuck was that all about?"

Savarese answered with a great smile.

"Oh, I know all those guys. I used to ride with them."

"You're kidding me."

"Oh, no," the cop said, touching his earring. "Before I got this job, I used to ride with Hell's Angels."

Soon all the guys were friends with Savarese, everyone understanding his eccentric manner. Savarese even went on to become one of the best-known homicide detectives in South Brooklyn. Where he was once famous for his pony tail, now he is balding and known for his fedoras. But even now, more than twenty years past his days as a road hog, cops get nervous whenever they see Detective Louis Savarese behind the wheel of a department vehicle.

Like thousands of other cops, Richard Sica's police career came to a screeching halt in July 1975. The city was facing fiscal bankruptcy. The President, Gerald Ford, had refused to intercede. The *Daily News* had reported the story with one of the greatest tabloid headlines of all time: "Ford to City: Drop Dead." The city's mayor, Abe Beame, had no choice but to lay off thousands of cops.

Richie had walked into the precinct house on July 1 and been handed a teletype message by a desk sergeant. The message listed all of those police officers being laid off on July 3. Richie found his name, shield number, tax registry number, and command listed with the S's in the middle of the sheet. It was formal. Richie Sica, two years on the job, was an ex-cop. Disheartened, Richie went back to Valley Stream and found work as a mechanic in a Lincoln Mercury dealership. The money was about the same, but without a gun and shield, Richie felt ordinary.

Six months later, Richie got a phone call. The police department wanted him back. He was told to report to the 100th Precinct in Rockaway, a knifelike slip of land running under Queens and Brooklyn.

On his first tour, Sica was paired off in a squad car with a veteran named Tom Cavanaugh. The older cop eyed Richie suspiciously.

"What did you do to get down here?" Cavanaugh wanted to know.

"Nothing. I just came back. I was laid off."

"Nah, everybody down here did something wrong."

"I didn't do anything wrong. I got laid off and they reassigned me to Rockaway."

"All right, but everybody's down here for a reason." Silence saturated the car. After some minutes Cavanaugh pointed to Richie's shirt.

"See that patch on your arm?" he said.

Richie looked at his patch. He didn't see anything wrong with his NYPD police patch.

"That patch says New York City Police Department."

"So?"

"Well this ain't the New York City Police Department down here, pal. This ain't even part of the world."

Steadily Sica began to understand. The precinct was cut off from Queens and Brooklyn by water. And true to Cavanaugh's evaluation, an awful lot of the cops around Richie seemed to have been in trouble somewhere else. Nobody talked to a Rockaway cop and a Rockaway cop never talked to anyone else. Some of this had to do with the geography, sure. But mostly the precinct was one big drunken beach brawl. Not that the people in Rockaway were mean-spirited. It's just that Rockaway was where people came to sit in the sun and drink.

During the winter, the precinct was dead, but during the summer, as New Yorkers invaded Riis Park and Rockaway Beach, the place became a madhouse. Richie quickly learned that there was a different way of doing things in the 100th Precinct.

"I worked with this one guy named Richie. Big German guy. I really liked him. Richie's wife lived with the kids upstate. So Richie would work five tours, sleep in the station house, and then head upstate for the weekend. Richie was what you call temperamental. Actually, Richie was crazy. He hated blacks, he hated Puerto Ricans, he hated everybody. But for some reason he liked me. Richie knew all the rules; he just didn't obey them.

"One day, we're working together and I stop this car. Just a routine stop. I walk up to the driver's window and say, 'License and registration.' The guy says, 'What did I do?' Now I wasn't big on writing tickets. I says, 'Just let me see your license and registration.' So the guy gives it to me. The guy's papers were good. He had a good license and a good registration. So the guy says, 'What the fuck are you stopping me for?' I said, 'Relax, you're not getting a summons. Everything is all right. You're leaving.' I gave him back his paperwork.

"Now Richie is on the other side of the car. He says, 'Who the fuck you talking to like that?' So now Richie and this guy are arguing. Richie walks around the front of the car, which is the fastest way to get run over, and he sees that the guy has his high beams on. Richie says, 'Let me see your paperwork again.' The guy hands it over. Richie tells him, 'You wait right here.' We walk back to the radio car. I ask, 'Richie, what are you going to do with this guy?' Richie says, 'I'm giving him a summons.' I said, 'For what?' He says, 'Dazzling lights.' I said, 'Dazzling lights?' and Richie says, 'Sure, look it up.' I go into the book and, sure enough, there's a thing called 'Dazzling Lights.' Richie is writing out the ticket and explaining, 'When you have your high beams on for no apparent reason, it's Dazzling Lights.' I said, 'Richie, you can't give him a summons for that.' Now he's mad at me, too. He says, 'Didn't he just bust your balls? He's getting a summons.' I sat in the car watching. Richie gave the guy his summons and we started off with our windows down. And all I could hear was the guy screaming, 'Dazzling Lights? What the fuck is Dazzling Lights?'

"Richie was very selective when it came to the rule book. He used to drink all day long. He used to be in and out of grocery stores. The more stores Richie used to go in and out of, the drunker he got. So at the end of the tour we pulled up to the station house and Richie is smashed. I mean gone. So he walked into the precinct and he's got a paper bag filled with beer bottles. He reaches the front desk and the beers fall through the paper bag. They smash on the floor. So then the screaming started.

"The guys are yelling, 'What the hell's wrong with you?' There's beer all over the place. Richie says, 'Relax, don't worry, I'll clean it up.' And with that, he goes over to the complaint room where all the 61's are kept. Richie reaches into the basket and grabs a handful of typed forms. He then goes back out and wipes up the beer with them. Then he throws a wad of them on the front desk.

"The girl is standing there with the phone in her hands, shocked. Richie tells her, 'I want to use the phone.' She says, 'Richie, what's wrong with you? I just typed all these 61's.' He says, 'I don't give a fuck, I want to use the phone.' She comes back, 'When I'm done with the phone, you can use it.' Big mistake. Richie pulls out this huge buck knife he used to carry and cuts the phone cord. Now the girl is standing there with a completely disconnected phone. She goes running to the desk lieutenant. The desk lieutenant tells Richie, 'Just go up and change.' Richie goes upstairs and the lieutenant goes in to see the captain.

"Richie comes downstairs about fifteen minutes later. The captain, a real tough, hard-nosed ex-Marine screams, 'Richie, get in here.' The guy was a bastard. He looked like a bulldog. He tells Richie, 'I'm suspending you right now. I want you to hand over your gun right now.' So Richie takes out his gun and presents it to him with an open chamber. And the captain's looking at the gun. It's a 6-shot, 22 magnum. He says, 'This is unauthorized. What are you doing with this gun?' And Richie says, 'I lost my .38 a long time ago.' Richie was suspended right then and there. They sent him to health services. Psychoed him right out of the job."

Long before Richie left the precinct, he had put in for a transfer. Actually, he was putting in for a transfer once a week. He wanted to get back to real police work. Finally, he got in touch with a friend of a friend, Jim Caruana, who worked as a sergeant in the Queens Youth Gang Task Force. The select unit had been formed after the shooting of the unarmed thirteen-year-old by Detective Thomas Shea. They worked out of the 103rd Precinct. Sica was given an interview in June 1978. The man in charge of the Task Force was a black lieutenant named Gaines. Gaines and Caruana were two of the most well-liked bosses in the city. They also liked Richie. Within a month Richie was hounding gangs on midnight cruises through the parks and streets of Queens. He learned names and he learned turf. There was a chapter of the Latin Soul Brothers who owned the area around the intersection of Parsons and Hillside avenues. This group consisted of black and Latino youngsters. Some of the other gangs included the Savage Nomads and the Sex Boys. He also spent time with a gang in the Forties Houses called the Seven Crowns. It was here, just prior to being sentenced to jail, that Richie ran into a character by the name of Lorenzo Nichols.

"I first met Fat Cat when we went into the Forties Houses to break up the Seven Crowns. They didn't call him Fat Cat then. They called him Fat Boy. Any problem in the gang and they called in Nichols to crush it.

"There were only twelve of us in the whole Task Force, so you got to know the street players pretty well. The Crowns had their drugs, but it was mostly smoke and heroin. No cocaine to speak of. Certainly no crack. Only the white kids were fucking around with angel dust. The same with pills. The Crowns wouldn't screw around with pills. Fat Cat was just a kid, but he was a big kid. He had a mouth on him, too. Still, he had some magnetism. You could see that. If we wanted guys to move, we'd go to Fat Cat. Once the Cat moved, they'd all follow.

"The gangs were very territorial. The Seven Crowns weren't allowed up on Hillside and Parsons. The Latin Soul Brothers weren't allowed to go down past South Road. Shit like that. The blacks weren't allowed to go over 102nd Avenue where the Sex Boys were. Sex Boys were white guys. They were a bullshit gang.

"The big thing back then was wearing colors. Nobody really had guns yet. The fighting was mostly hand-to-hand stuff. Occasionally you'd see a knife or a homemade zip gun. All we did basically was go and harass the gangs. It was illegal then to wear your colors. So we went around cutting the colors off of guys' backs. You'd see these guys walking down the street with big holes in their coats. The message was, no recruiting in Queens.

"We were the bad guys and I didn't like that much. We rarely arrested people. Mostly we just manhandled them. I remember one time we grabbed a bunch of guys at this apartment building called Deborah Hall. We had five or six guys cuffed. This middle-aged guy comes along and says, 'Why don't you leave all them people alone? You're always fucking with them here.' Then he says, 'You guys are suckass motherfuckers.' Now a crowd has gathered, and people are getting excited. So my two partners, Matty and Izzy, cuff this guy too. We bring him into the 103, and everybody's getting locked up. But this guy, he ain't got no involvement, really. And he's telling these two cops, 'You know, you guys suck. You don't do shit out there. You always picking on the black man. You guys are suckass motherfuckers.' So they beat him up. This went on for an hour. It got boring after a while. So finally, they give the guy a summons and throw him out the front door. The guy straightens out his coat and shirt, and then reaches into his pocket for the summons. He throws it on the ground, looks the guys straight in the eye and says, 'You're still suckass motherfuckers.' I loved the guy for that. Not for badmouthing a cop. But for his pride.

"The blackout came and the gangs disappeared. We switched to undercover narcotics work for a while, doing buy-and-bust operations in the park. In 1981, they wanted two names from every precinct and one name from every specialized unit for a new detective's list. My name got put in and I got sent to the 112th Squad in November 1981. I worked alongside real detectives for about fifteen months before they gave me a gold shield. There wasn't much that impressed me. But when I got my gold shield, and when I finally looked at it, shit, was I impressed. I still remember the first time I walked into the office with the badge in my pocket. I was in extremely plain clothes, a blue Woolrich parka. The boss took one look at me and said, 'You ain't wearing

that. You gotta go out and buy either a tan or blue trench coat.'
So I had my raincoat and I had my gold shield. I was ready for
homicide."

Detective Richard Sica caught his first homicide two weeks after
being assigned to the 103rd Precinct in February of 1985. A
Jamaican kid named David Gilzon had been stabbed to death in
a drug dispute. Two witnesses had seen Gilzon fall and another
Jamaican kid running from the scene. It took Sica and his partners, Ronnie Waddell and Ronnie Singleton, three weeks to place
a name with the face. Then the detectives came up with a scheme.

Waddell, a rangy black man, knocked on the door of the man's
apartment. The killer's girlfriend answered the door. Waddell
gave the girl his toughest look, a look he hoped would be taken
for that of a hit man. He then announced, "Listen, I'm looking
for John."

"I don't know where John is," replied the girl, lying.

"Well, look," Waddell continued. "It's in your best interest if
you let me know where he is. I gotta talk to him. I got some shit
for him."

With that, the detective spun and walked away, never having
identified himself as a cop.

Later that night, Sica and Singleton paid a visit to the woman,
their gold shields displayed prominently.

"Look," Richie said. "Your boyfriend killed another drug
dealer. His boss is looking to hit him. And if the boss can't find
John, you'll do."

The cops then proceeded to describe John's boss, a description
that coincided exactly with one Detective Ronnie Waddell.

"He was here today," the girlfriend gasped. Fearing the wrath
of Waddell, the woman surrendered her boyfriend.

Richie then set about to getting John to confess to the crime.
He sat the suspect in a chair and handed him a can of soda. They
talked quietly for several minutes. Finally Richie said, "Look. We

realize that it was probably self-defense and that you were trying to protect yourself."

The kid jumped at the chance to make less of his deed.

"That's right. He was going to hit me over the head with a bottle."

"Then what happened?"

"I pulled a knife out. I didn't want to get hit with a bottle."

"I don't blame you. I wouldn't want to get hit with a bottle either."

"Yeah, and then I stabbed him. But I didn't stab him in the heart or nothing. I just stabbed him to keep him off of me."

"Okay," Richie said, "I can understand that."

The detective got up and walked out of the room. He returned five minutes later, asking the suspect to be more specific.

"What were you arguing about?"

"We was arguing about drugs. He owed me $25 for some weed and he wasn't going to pay."

"Well, I can understand that. You guys are businessmen and you're working."

"Damn right. And this motherfucker wouldn't pay. So I cut him."

The District Attorney arrived with a video crew about a half hour later. Richie reentered the room. This was the delicate part. Nothing, prosecutors had found, has a more profound effect on a jury than a videotaped confession. The VCR had changed police work like nothing since the discovery of the fingerprint. Richie was first-generation video cop.

"Look, would you want to say it in front of the D.A. on video-tape? I don't want you to tell me something that really didn't happen. You're honest and we only want you to tell the truth."

"Well," said the suspect, "I can see that. Sure. I'll make a movie."

Whereupon the suspect made a videotape confession to second-degree murder. He was convicted at trial and sentenced to twenty-five-to-life. At first Richie felt a little uneasy about having gotten a man to implicate himself. But then a veteran detective told him, "A man has been murdered. You didn't kill him. I didn't kill him. This guy killed him. He's got to go."

Until the advent of crack, Sica's murders tended to be painfully faddish. In Brooklyn, teenagers were dying for their leather bomber jackets. In Manhattan, kids were dying for their Nike sneakers. In the Bronx, a kid was killed for his designer sunglasses. With the popularity of gold jewelry came the subway phenomenon of chain-snatching. And it wasn't a month after kids started wearing false gold caps in Bedford-Stuyvesant that detectives started finding gap-toothed murder victims. To be young and in vogue in New York, Sica realized, was to be an endangered species.

In Newark, after the mayor's son was shot for his bomber jacket, the coats were banned from an entire New Jersey school system. When court officials installed a metal detector outside Brooklyn Juvenile Court, they started finding dozens of knives and saps in the courthouse bushes. Some Long Island schools banned the wearing of gold jewelry altogether. New York City education officials went one better, installing metal detectors at the entrances to some schools.

The first craze, of course, had been the boombox radio. Chris Dennis, a twenty-one-year-old on leave from the Army, had bought such a box for his girlfriend. He was standing outside his home, listening to music, when a kid named Mark Barrett approached him. Barrett demanded the box and produced a gun. Dennis held onto the box. His girlfriend screamed. Barrett shot Dennis in the head, killing him instantly.

The soldier's father, Leslie Dennis, heard the shot and came running around the corner. He saw his dead son and the boombox laying side by side in the street. Then the bereaved father did a curious thing. He picked up the box and smashed it on the sidewalk in front of all his neighbors.

"You can't have nothing nice and live," he screamed. It was as good a comment on the times as anything being written up at Harvard University.

There was only one witness to the killing, a girl named Marlene. She started to walk off the block.

"I didn't see shit," she told Richie. "I didn't see nothing."

"What did he look like?"

"He looked black."

Richie kept after the girl, following her home.

"I saw one black guy who ran away," she said finally, slamming the door.

The following night, Richie returned to Marlene's home. The girl was petrified. Richie took a seat at the girl's living room table.

"Look," she said. "I got to live here."

"I know," Richie said. "But the kid's dead. He's twenty-one years old. He was home from the service. He wasn't bothering nobody. He bought the box for his girlfriend."

Marlene sat back, thinking.

"Do you have a boyfriend?" Richie asked.

The girl shook her head. She was pretty and young. Boys would like her.

"He runs with a hop," she said, finally. "I could identify the guy. There was no reason to do what he did. For a box? That's some cold shit right there."

Marlene picked Barrett out of a photo array. Then she remembered something else. She was feeling a lot worse about a soldier dying to protect his radio.

"I saw him last June at a barbecue across from my house. His girlfriend lives there."

The girl paused.

"He also smokes some cracks."

There was that word, or at least a version of it. Sica had never heard it before.

"He smokes what?"

"Them cracks. You know, the new stuff."

But Richie did not know. He moved on, the soldier's murder more topical. Barrett's girlfriend had moved, but left a forwarding address. Sica and his partner, Pete Pistone, grabbed the suspect the same day. His left leg was shorter than his right. Marlene was right. The killer ran with a hop.

A prosecutor named Gene Kelly caught the case. A beefy man with a high-pitched voice, Kelly looked and sounded like an over-stuffed altar boy. He was the Homicide Bureau's rising star, a terror in any kind of emotional case. Barrett never had a chance. The defendant got an appendix attack an hour before the jury came back. An infuriated Queens judge, John Leahy, packed up the jury foreman, defense counsel, prosecutor, and stenographer into a bus and set off for the hospital.

The courtroom crowded around the defendant's bed.

"Have you reached a verdict?" the judge asked.

"Yes, we have," said the only juror allowed in the room.

"And what is your verdict on a charge of murder in the second degree?"

"Guilty."

"And on a charge of weapons possession?"

"Guilty."

"Thank you, Mr. Foreman. You are excused."

On the way out the door, Judge Leahy turned to pat the defendant on the head.

"Get well soon, son. Sentencing is in three weeks."

"For me, murder is the only crime that counts. For the most part, in the ghetto, people are almost immune to murder. It's just something they live with. But then you get close to a family. You feel bad at times. Most of the time, the guy's a piece of shit. So they deal drugs? So they fight and drink? Does that mean they deserve to die?

"I don't usually like the victims. Prostitutes, drug dealers, and robbers are hard to like. In my precinct, we don't get too many dead good guys. It's like this guy Ice once said. He was a middle-aged hitman in a young man's game. He killed maybe ten people. But he didn't have an arrest record. When one of my partners,

Eddie Granshaw, grabbed him for a murder, he asked, 'Ice, what's the secret of your success?' And Ice told him, 'Ice don't never fuck with the taxpayers.'

"You start out with a body. You don't know anything about the body. None of these people have ID on them. The wallets, if they carry them, are usually stolen by the time we get there. But within the first forty-eight hours, you know everything about the guy. You know who he screwed, what he did with his money, when he last ate, and where he last worked. Sometimes you have to break bad news to the family. 'Look, your son was a drug dealer.' 'Look, your son had killed somebody before this.' They hate you for it, but you have to tell them. But then they thank you when you finally lock somebody up.

"To take somebody's life, that is the ultimate, that's it. And if you solve a case, if you catch a perp, that's the most rewarding thing. To be thanked by a family. Not all cops feel this way. I feel like that. Waddell is like that. Granshaw is like that. Pistone is like that. I get close with the families, whether they're black, white, or cops. I don't care what they are. They're still somebody's family. They didn't do the crime. But they suffer. And sometimes the only person they can talk to, that they can turn to in a quiet moment, is the case detective. You turn your back on them, it's a cold thing to do.

"Crack scared the hell out of people. A whole new society developed with the drug. We'd get a witness, a mother with kids, and she'd say, 'Look around, what am I supposed to do? I gotta live here. If I tell you who killed this guy, the crack dealers will whack my kids.' And the witnesses were right. What am I going to do for a witness? I can't sit in front of their door every day, protecting these people. They know it. I know it. Even the people that do come forward, if you stop to think about it for a minute, they gotta either really care or they gotta have a set of balls. For them to talk about these crack people and then try and go home. If they're found out, they're dead.

"But a lot of innocent people are being shot by accident. The automatic weapon has taken over. Every guy we come across, it seems, is carrying a 9mm. It's an automatic, it's got a lot of shots, like fourteen. And all these guys are spray shooters. They drive by in a car and everyone on the corner falls. I think they like the nine because of the way it sounds, 'Yeah, I got a nine.' But it's got a lot of bullets. We've still got pea shooters. Now we're up against nines and Uzis. All we've got is a .38 pea shooter. If you hit a windshield head on with a .38 slug, it can bounce off. We're undermanned and outgunned. Everybody on the street knows this. So they're afraid."

On the afternoon of February 25, 1988, Detective Richard Sica was ready to leave for work. He jumped into his truck, a black Chevy Blazer, and headed the jeep-like vehicle toward the parkway, passing row upon row of delicate wooden houses with fenced-in lawns. Traffic on the Southern State Parkway had turned the westbound lane into a parking lot. The usual thirty-minute ride from Merrick into South Jamaica took an hour. It didn't help that the detective was anxious.

The week had started badly, with cops getting fired upon. A pair of plainclothes officers assigned to his precinct's undercover anti-crime patrol had pulled over a car at the intersection of 188th Street and Jamaica Avenue. Just a routine car stop. Only the inhabitants of the car had jumped out with automatic weapons blazing. Amazingly, no one had been wounded.

The cops had retreated to the precinct and filled out a report with a description of the perps and getaway car. Copies of the police Form 61—called an unusual—had been circulated through the precinct. One copy had been forwarded to Homicide Team C, winding up on Richie's desk.

Richie began his 4 P.M. to 1 A.M. tour that day with a review of a murder that had happened on November 23, 1987. A crack whore nicknamed Princess from the Forties Houses in South Jamaica had turned up dead in the grass near an exit ramp to Greenwich, Connecticut. This was about as close as Princess ever got to royalty, lying dead with two in the head at the entrance to Camelot.

The Connecticut state police, still new to crack violence, had been very excited about the murder. They'd put a name with the body, Michelle Garland, and traced Princess back to the Forties Houses. Eventually, they'd come into the 103rd Precinct squad room, looking for assistance. Sica and his partner, Pete Pistone, had helped them explore the projects.

Earlier, during a raid on a Bridgeport housing project, the Connecticut detectives had confiscated a photograph of a young man wearing a Sherlock Holmes hat and leaning against a refrigerator, holding a bottle of Moet. An informant had identified the kid in the picture as Princess's killer. Sica began showing the picture around the Forties Houses.

"That's Divine," an informant told him.

"What's his real name?"

"I only know him as Divine. I don't know his government name."

And that's about as far as they had gotten in the first round. The talk of the streets was that Princess had stolen money from a crack dealer. The feeling was that she had been abducted from her Forties apartment, whacked in the car, and dumped in Connecticut. A witness had seen a red Jeep Cherokee with a New York tag speeding from the scene. It apparently did not matter to Princess's killers that they had left New York to commit murder in Connecticut, a death-penalty state. So much for the deterrence argument, Richie thought.

The Connecticut police, persistent in their search of Divine, had returned to South Jamaica frequently after that. A week after the Myrtle Horsheim murder, they had stopped a red Jeep Cherokee that fit the description of the vehicle seen driving away from Princess's body. The driver of the car was a young man named Philip Copeland. The passenger in the car, a dealer nicknamed

Ninja, kept calling the driver Marshal. Both men were very respectful.

"I didn't do nothing," Marshal had told Richie Sica. "I didn't shoot nobody."

Richie had taken photographs of both men and showed them around the neighborhood. The informant had come into the precinct to see the pictures.

"Have you ever seen either one of these guys with Divine?" Sica asked.

The informant pointed to Copeland's photograph.

"That's Pappy's boy, Marshal. He like the sheriff out here. I seen him with Divine. They call themselves the Bebos."

"What does the Bebos mean?

"It's short for, 'Who you be, bro?' These guys are very suspicious. Pappy is going by that name now when he talks on the phone. It's 'Bebo this and Bebo that.' He got all them kids in the Forties talking Jamaican."

The cops held onto the red Jeep. Marshal disappeared again. Eventually, Pappy Mason's half brother Donnell came by to claim the Jeep. A circle was closing, Richie Sica had felt.

In late January 1988, Richie and Pete Pistone had been called to Booth Memorial Hospital to interview a severely beaten fifty-year-old man named George Dixon. The patient, nicknamed Fruit, was being held in the trauma center. He was listed as likely to die. He had been found behind Princess's apartment with a cracked skull and broken limbs. Fruit was barely able to open one eye. Sica showed him a set of pictures. Fruit kept shaking his head no. Finally Sica showed Fruit the picture of the kid holding the Moet champagne bottle. Fruit blinked.

"Is this the man that did this to you?" Fruit nodded, and then drifted off into unconsciousness.

Richie sought out another informant, who had witnessed Fruit's beating. The detective showed him the picture.

"That's Divine," the informant said.

"What's his real name?"

"Todd."

"Todd who?"

"Just Todd. Sometimes he drives a red Cherokee Jeep."

Richie got excited. The name "Todd" rang a bell. A kid named Barry Slaughter had been dealing crack at the corner of 108th Avenue and Guy Brewer Boulevard. Although Slaughter had lived on the block his whole life, it was not within his domain to sell crack on another dealer's corner. At around midnight on November 1, a red Jeep Cherokee had pulled up to the corner. A young man had gotten out of the car and fired three shots into Slaughter's back. The dealer managed to live, but never filed a complaint with police. Slaughter's young brother, Robert, had witnessed the shooting. He told detectives, "A dude named Todd did it."

Sica and Pistone went back to Robert Slaughter with the photograph of the man holding the champagne bottle.

"Do you recognize this guy?" Sica asked.

"Sure," Slaughter replied. "That's the dude Todd who shot my brother."

One case now led to two others. A crack dealer named Crystal Bynum had been shot and killed in early October. Word on the street was that the woman had stolen $20,000 from Pappy Mason. A witness to the killing had identified Bynum's killers as a man named Todd and a guy in dreadlocks. Anonymous Todd and his pal Marshal were very busy fellows indeed.

Then in the first week of February 1988, Sica got a message from an informant named Billy. Let Sica tell more about Billy.

The informant.

"I got a call from Nassau County Police Department in late 1985. They had picked up this guy for shoplifting at the Green Acres Mall in Valley Stream. Nassau says he knows about homicides, that he wants to give information on homicides in South Jamaica. So Pete Pistone and I go out there. The guy wants to

play, we go out there. We go out to the Fifth Precinct in Elmont.
A lot of guys want to make deals. But you never know how good
a guy is until you sit down. Everybody wants to give up information when they got their back to the wall. This is a bullshit shop-
lifting case. How much can he want to talk?

"We get there, introduce ourselves, and get led into a back
room. The guy is about 5-foot-10, 180 pounds. He's wearing dungarees and sneakers. Pete and I sit down. I had a bunch of homicide folders with me. It was a small office off the squad room. We
all sat down with coffee. Right off, I see the guy is very polite. He
isn't a hard-nosed guy. I liked him right from the start. He wasn't
a wise guy. In fact, he started crying. And then he says, 'I can't
do no time. I can't do no time. I'll tell you now, all I am is a thief.
But I gotta be with my wife and my kid. Pull my sheet, you'll see.
I never hurt nobody. I'm just a thief.'

"Most guys will tell you, 'I can do the time. Ain't no problem
with that.' But this guy is totally different. Here's a guy who's
really got some feeling for his family. He was pleasant. His name
was Billy. Billy Martin. It's a name people should know because
he changed the game in Queens.

"I started with some of the old homicides. I asked him about
this guy OJ, Oren Hogan. He had been killed at 160th Street and
107th Avenue back in 1984. And Billy says, 'Yeah, that was
upstairs. He got shot in the head once and went out the window.
He was with a guy named Nate. I don't know if Nate killed him
or not, but he was there.' The information was right on. So we
tried him on another old murder, Leroy Calhoun. This guy was
killed at 159–01 110th Avenue, behind Princess's apartment in the
Forties. Billy says, 'I got that one, too. He was shot in the car. This
girl, Ernestine, was in the car with him. She lives in the Forties.
Green-eyed girl. Go talk to her. She knows who did it.' I open the
folder and look. This is a 1983 case. And sure enough, I see the
name Ernestine. Only we never knew where she lived. The guy is
two-for-two. He ain't bullshitting nobody. I look at Pete and we're
both smiling. We got a player.

"After that we tried Sheila Moore. I asked him, 'Do you remember the girl in Liberty Park?' And he says, 'I don't know if it was a guy or a girl. But I saw Ice.' He's not being skeptical about it, he's just scared of Ice. No one has ever dared to talk about Ice before. Billy says, 'If Ice ever finds out that I talked, he'll kill me. You don't know Ice. He's an enforcer for all the drug gangs. But I don't know if it was a guy or a girl. But I was parked on 170th right off Liberty. I had just dropped a friend off. He was going to go cop some crack. And I seen Ice walking with this guy.'

"He's calling Sheila a guy, but that's the way she looked, short and fat with short hair. Billy says, 'I seen Ice with his left arm around this person, and then I see him coming up with his other hand. And Ice hit him right in the head. One shot. And then he dragged him a few feet into the park.' And that's the way the body was found. She had been shot in the head and her clothes were pulled up. She had scuff marks on the back of her shoes from being dragged. So now we have an eyewitness to murder against an untouchable guy.

"I didn't say nothing. And Billy just kept on talking. 'I was there when they killed Richard Rembrandt in the projects. It was Black, Baby Wise, and a third guy. These guys ran up the stairs past me and I heard shots. Baby Wise came running back down the stairs past me. I went up and found Richard lying there, shot. Black was running across the rooftops. I left.' And it goes on like this for hours. At one point, he's saying, 'I had direct conversation with the guy that killed Johnny Lowe, too. It goes down like this. They pick me up on the street . . .' And I stopped him here, asking, 'What are you doing on the street all the time?' and Billy says, 'I'm out there eighteen to twenty hours a day. I steal and I sell to everybody on the street. I know everybody. I know the Cat. I know the Corleys. I know Supreme. I know Prince and I know Skinner. I do work for them.' And what he meant was that he delivered packages for them. Billy, it turns out, was the most trustworthy guy on the street. Skinner could give him a $30,000 package and say, 'Deliver it to this address.' Skinner knew it was going to get there. Nothing would be skimmed off. If money had to be picked up, Billy would pick the money up. There was never a problem. Fat Cat and the Corleys did the same thing with him. Billy was a gold mine.

"So I go out to the squad room, and I tell the detective, 'Listen, this guy is an eyewitness to two homicides and he's got information on six others. Could you give him a break or something.' The guys says, 'The best I can do is a Desk Appearance Ticket, petty larceny. He's going to have to come back to court.' I said, 'Fine. No problem.' We took him out to get something to eat and then back to the 103. We cuffed him just to make it look good. Then we sat him down and started going through all the homicide folders. He had information on everything and everybody. Most of it was hearsay. But he had tremendous intelligence.

"He came back again the next day and started making out a chart for us. We wrote it on the back of a manila folder. He tells us about a guy named Cornbread and a guy named Hymie, guys we never even knew existed. He draws the whole crack tree out for us, giving us everybody from A to Z, including a guy nicknamed AZ. Fat Cat's whole organization right down to the steerers. He's got everybody: names, dates, locations. He was even talking about the Rooney murder. The guys in narcotics meet him and they're wild about him. Everybody knows this is the guy.

"I swung out for a couple of days. When I came back, I took Billy down to see Greg Lasak, who was running the District Attorney's Homicide Bureau. Lasak may be the best prosecutor in the city. And I'm telling Greg all about the guy. Greg says, 'This is too good to be true. We got to polygraph him.' So they put him on the machine. He comes back, he flunked the polygraph. He's all over the place on the machine. I find out later that he's on methadone, he doesn't sleep, he's up all fucking hours of the day and night. This guy, what he turned out to be, was one scared motherfucker. After dealing with all these tough guys in the fucking project and you run across this guy, he's a fucking marshmallow. We pulled his sheet and he had ten or twelve collars, all bullshit, never did no time, never hurt anybody. Just like he said. And then we used to see him every day. We used to meet him in different places. We wanted to do a whole in-depth investigation. Set up a task force, get wiretaps, everything. We wanted to do a state racketeering case with drugs, murders, the whole nine yards. And then the D.A.'s office came to the decision that they didn't like him. Lasak had to tell me that we couldn't use him because he flunked a polygraph. The D.A., John Santucci, made the decision himself. And then the police department said, 'We don't have the manpower to do this.' Collectively, those two decisions had the net effect of getting Edward Byrne killed. No doubt about it.

"I wouldn't quit on Billy. I registered him as NYPD Confidential Informant #151. The FBI was all over the place, looking to hook up with the guy. So I sat Billy down. I told him, 'Look, we can't use you, because we can't give you any money. We're nickel-and-diming you to death. With the information you've got, you gotta do it right. Do you want to go with the Feds or do you want to stay with us?' Billy said, 'I'll go with the Feds, then.' So I called the narcotics guy, Sgt. Mike McGuiness, and said, 'Make us an appointment. We'll take him down there. You sign him up.' He signed an agreement with the Feds, saying he had to be truthful and work as an undercover. He'd be put in a witness protection program when it was all over. In addition to that, he asked for a Chevy Blazer, a 4-wheel-drive jeep, just like mine. In a pinch, Billy said he'd settle for a Suzuki.

"The Feds used Billy to start building an entire RICO case. He did everything for them. He got them into everybody. This agent named Ray Byers was running the investigation. He loved Billy as a C.I. and a person. Billy did all the introductions for the FBI. They got Billy on film with Cornbread and Hymie. Billy was able to bring in undercovers and introduce them to all the guys. I stayed very close with him.

"I got a call from my boss, Lt. Eugene Dunbar, on Christmas Eve, 1987, at around four in the afternoon. My house was jammed with people. The lieutenant tells me, 'You gotta meet me at the

Nassau County Fifth Precinct.' I get down there and Billy's been locked up. He's in the same room as before, crying. He says, 'The Feds are hanging me up for money, and I was just trying to steal some for my son, Buddha.' They had grabbed him for boosting toys out of a Toys "Я" Us in the Green Acres Mall. How could you hate a guy for that? So we begged them and they gave him a Desk Appearance Ticket. I took him back to Green Acres and gave him $20. The lieutenant gave him another $20. He went in and bought his kid toys. Then I drove him home. I'll always remember that. It was Christmas morning and we were both crying.

"The first week in February 1988, Billy came to me. He had been in a car with Marshal and Todd. Billy said Todd knew we were looking for him. He was holed up in an apartment on Guy Boulevard and South Road. Todd was very bored. He tells Billy, 'You gotta get me some Nintendo tapes. I need something to do during the day. They're looking for me, and I don't have nothing to do up in the apartment.' So Billy got him the tape. That night Billy said he wound up in a green Suzuki with Todd and Marshal. Billy brings up Princess, and Todd says, 'Yeah, we bumped that bitch in Connecticut.' And Marshal is sitting in the backseat. He says, 'Shut the fuck up, Todd, you talk too much.' And that's the statement Connecticut started with. Billy ran right over to me. He says, 'Listen, I got the statement we need.' We call Connecticut down to take a written statement from Billy. We hit the apartment on South Road, but Todd was gone.

"Three days later, another informant called Pete Pistone, giving him a description of a car Todd was using. The informant described the car as a battered yellow Dodge with North Carolina plates. Pete was given a partial plate number. Pete put all the information in his drawer and, I guess, forgot about it. Nobody else in the squad was told about the car. We never went out looking for the car until it was too late."

4

"FOUR TO THE HEAD.
THAT'S ALL IT TOOK."

At around midnight, on Thursday February 25, 1988, detectives
in the neighboring 105th Precinct reported finding the blue Buick
used in Monday night's gunfight with police. The car was parked
at the corner of 209th Avenue and 111th Street. Richie Sica and
Pete Pistone joined four other detectives in a stakeout of the car.
Three unmarked cars rolled onto the block just after 1 A.M. One
of the cars was double-parked next to the suspect vehicle, blocking
it in. Four detectives took up a position in one car at the far end
of the block. Sica and Pistone parked their car at the opposite end
of the street. The idea was to grab the suspect as soon as he
approached the Buick.

The cops sat there, talking about fishing, security work, and
landscaping. Sica was looking forward to the spring and the
chance to chase bluefish through Jamaica Bay. Pistone moon-
lighted as director of security each summer at the United States
Open at Flushing Tennis Center. Sica wasn't much for tennis.
Pistone wasn't big on fish. Eventually, the talk turned to common

ground, a love of landscaping. After discussing roses and blue firs, the small talk turned to gardening.

"We got to pull this guy Todd in," Richie said. "Let's take another look for him in the Forties tomorrow night."

"Sounds good," Pistone agreed.

Richie hadn't dressed for a stakeout, leaving his winter jacket home. No amount of small talk could warm him. The car was running low on gas, so Pistone had to turn it off every ten minutes. At about 2:45 A.M., the cops decided to peel off the stakeout.

"We'll go back to the station house," Pistone said. "You get a coat and I'll gas up the car. Then we'll come back."

Sica headed into the ancient brick station house while Pistone gassed up the car in the precinct garage. Richie climbed the stairs up into the third floor squad room and pulled his nylon uniform jacket from his locker. The detective hadn't worn any part of his uniform since getting promoted to detective in 1985. Still, it was warm, and there was no shame in being seen in a patrolman's outfit.

As Sica headed out of the station, he spotted Danny Leonard on the telephone switchboard.

"Hey," Leonard yelled. "What are you, back in uniform?"

Richie was very popular with the uniformed cops on patrol. He laughed.

"No, I needed the jacket. It's cold out."

Richie knew Leonard to be a leathery, active cop. He was not the type of kid to sit anchored to a telephone switchboard in one of the borough's busiest houses.

"What are you doing in the station house?"

"Ah, I got stuck with some bullshit here," Leonard replied.

Sica could see that the kid was embarrassed. Pistone was waiting for him with the car, right outside the front door. It was 3:25 A.M. Police officer Edward Byrne was still sitting at the Inwood Post, dozing, his stomach empty, his eyes closed, waiting for relief that would never come. Within a couple of minutes, he would be dead.

*

Although dozens of citizens heard the shots, and a few walked to the window in the first moments after Byrne's assassination, only two citizens thought enough to dial 911, the police emergency number. The first call was logged in at 3:28 A.M. An anonymous male caller stated, "There is a police officer in a car, possibly shot and bleeding at the corner of Remington Street and 107th Avenue." And then the caller hung up, never to be heard from again.

The police operator notified the department's central dispatcher, who in turn sounded a system-wide alarm. The message was heard on more than 200,000 police-band radios throughout the city. Three beeps preceded the announcement. "Ten-thirteen. Cop shot. Remington and 107th Avenue."

Pete Pistone had just reached the intersection of 169th Street and Jamaica when he heard the bulletin. Sica picked up the portable radio.

"103 PDU responding."

Pistone pushed the accelerator to the floor, the Plymouth Fury roaring to life down Liberty Avenue. The detectives had just reached Liberty Avenue when they heard Sergeant Norfleet come on the precinct radio.

"Is the Inwood Post on the air?"

Nothing. And then Norfleet again, sounding more agitated.

"Is the Inwood Post on the air?"

There could be no response.

As Sica and Pistone hurtled toward Remington Street and 107th Avenue, a second call was being placed to the 911 operator.

A computer logged the call at 3:30:05.

Caller: Yeah. Hello. . . . Yeah, ah, I live, ah, at Inwood Street, Jamaica.

911 operator: Inwood Street and where?

C: Ah . . . ah . . . on 107th Avenue. There's a police car parked in front of the house here, right . . . And I heard five bullets . . . Heavy bullets went off in the . . . ah . . . Suddenly . . . I saw

a guy running . . . I . . . I didn't see the police in the car . . . I
dunno. Maybe he is in there . . . Maybe he is not here . . . Maybe
he is safe.

The 911 operator put the caller on hold and relayed the information to central dispatch. Sica and Pistone were sitting in the
intersection of 107th and Remington, two blocks down from
Byrne. Sica was just getting ready to report the shooting as unfounded.

"Do you have anything further?" he asked.

And then Central was back.

"We have further information. It's a police officer sitting in a
car that has been shot."

Norfleet, now sailing toward the scene, tried to raise the dead
again.

"Inwood Post. Are you there?"

Pistone made a left turn onto 107th Avenue. Sica could see the
radio car parked under a street light at the end of the next block.

"There, Pete, there."

Pistone looked and saw the car. A second marked police car,
Sector George from the 105th Precinct, was rushing in from the
opposite direction. The patrolman and the detectives reached the
Inwood Post simultaneously. The patrolman, Carlyle Preudhomme, looked into the RMP 1401, but saw nothing. Then he
looked closer and saw all.

"105 George," Preudhomme screamed into his portable radio.
"Ten-thirteen. Inwood and 107."

Sica was already out of the passenger door. The first thing he
noticed was the broken window. Then he saw the cop. The top of
his head was gone. The inside of the car was coated with a red
mist.

"Oh, my God," Sica said. He reached into the car, grabbing the
cop's wrist. Edward Byrne's skin was already cold to the touch.

The 911 operator was still on the phone with the second caller.

Operator: How many shots did you hear?

Caller: I heard five heavy bullets went off. The cop was sitting

in the car . . . And I didn't see him in it . . . And I see a guy running
. . . But I hope he's safe. I dunno.

O: Is the cop in uniform or out of uniform?

C: He's in uniform

Operator to Central: I got five shots on a police officer. A sector
car is on the scene at Inwood Street and 107th Avenue. 105
George at the scene.

Operator to caller: Okay. Ah, now you say you see a man
running from there?

C: I see a man running across the street, right . . .

O: Was he black, white or hispanic?

C: He's a black guy with a brown jacket.

O: Did he have a gun?

C: Hah. I . . . I . . . can't see, I'm in my house. (Pause) I
. . . I . . . think he's all right . . . I dunno . . . Shit . . . the cop's
car just came over here.

O: All right, would you like to leave your name and phone
number?

C: They . . . I'm Arjune, I live at 107th Avenue here."

O: All right. They'll be there as soon as possible.

C: Okay. Bye. Bye.

The transmission ended at 3:33:03.

Notes from a murder scene.

"I kept hearing Norfleet trying to raise the Inwood Post. But
there's nothing. Just silence. We pulled up right across from the
kid's car. We're heading in the same direction, heading east on
107th Avenue. A radio car had pulled up at the same time. We
were parked nose to nose. And I look over and see the window
shattered. I remember seeing that first. And I remember walking
over to the car. I didn't even run. I don't know why. But I
remember jumping out of the car and hearing the uniformed cop
screaming, 'Ten-thirteen.' He was yelling, 'Police officer shot.'

"The officer was sitting in an upright position with his head tilted to the right side. His face was covered with blood. A portion of his skull was missing. I turned away and heard screaming. Arjune was standing behind his fence across the street, shrieking. It was almost like everything was in slow motion for a moment. I remember opening the car door real slow, because I didn't want to hurt him. I don't know why I did that either. I knew he was dead just from looking at him. I picked up his wrist, there was no pulse. And it was almost like I didn't want to move him, for fear of hurting him in some way. But I remember when I opened the car door, the rest of the glass from the door fell in his lap. There was a big puddle of blood in his lap. The other thing that I remember noticing was that the windshield looked like a haze. It looked like somebody sprayed the inside of the windshield, and it was from what they did, the way they shot him. It looked like an even coat. It was bright in the car. The light was on and there was a street light overhead. Those bright yellow ones. The whole area was bright. And I remember the blood was so red. So vivid. It took my breath away.

"I started to run over to Arjune then. He was ranting, 'I saw it. I saw who did it.' I had the portable radio in my hand and I put over the air, 'We got a police officer shot. Get a bus here forthwith.' Not that an ambulance would have saved him, we just wanted to get him out of the car. I didn't want him on the front page of the newspaper sitting in the car like that.

"Arjune had a pajama top on and a pair of pants but no shoes. He kept screaming, 'I saw it. I saw who did it. I saw what they did. It was two guys, and they jumped in a tan car, an Olds Cutlass. The car is missing the right rear hubcap. They drove up toward Liberty Avenue.' And I said, 'Look, Mr. Arjune. Go in the house. Please go in the house and we'll come back and talk to you later.' I thought somebody was still in the area and would see Arjune screaming. I mean, it was apparent we had a witness. Maybe we had a sniper out there. I just wanted to protect Arjune and secure the area. Arjune went back in the house, but he was still ranting about what he saw.

"I remember looking around. But I was looking for a perp. I thought somebody was setting us up. There were four of us there. Even as I was running back away from Arjune, I was still looking around. I was scared at the time, I guess. But it was a lot of things at the time, in that first instant.

"I went back to the car then and looked in again. It was very business-like by now. I remember seeing a bullet sitting there on top of the cop's memo book on the dashboard, like somebody had placed it there. It was a spent round, just sitting there. He still had his gun in his holster. It was laying in his lap. There was a folded copy of the *Daily News* on the seat beside him along with an AM-FM radio, a flashlight, and a camera. A portable TV was hanging from the strap on the rear-view mirror. It was turned off. On the dashboard he had his memo book, a note pad, batteries, a copy of *Newsweek,* and a small bag with a tie inside. The street light had a way of making everything look curiously in focus. Sort of like looking inside an Easter egg.

"Everyone took up a position. We knew the kid was dead and we knew we couldn't do anything to save him. I couldn't even tell who it was. His hair was hanging down in front and there was blood all over his face. All I saw on the nameplate were the letters B, R, and N. I thought, 'Oh fuck. It's Dennis Burn. Hell, I skied with this kid at the precinct outing.'

"Now there are cops all around the place. Darin Hamilton is there and he's white as a ghost. He's saying, 'I was just talking to him.' Hamilton's father is a Queens detective. He's there, too, looking back and forth from his own kid, to the guy in the car. You know what he's thinking. We're all thinking the same thing. This is a stone-cold assassination. There are too many holes in the kid's face for it to be anything else.

"At some point, I became aware that Danny Leonard was standing beside me. And Leonard isn't saying a thing. I didn't realize until later that he was supposed to have relieved Byrne at 3 A.M., that it might have been Danny dead in the car. Sergeant Norfleet had taken command of the situation, securing the area for a block in each direction. Two cars pulled up at the same time. Tony McManaman, this huge uniformed cop, jumped out of the car and started banging on the hood of the kid's car. Tony's a big guy. And when Tony gets in a rage, you gotta stay away from him. He'll kill you. So he started banging on the hood of the car. I had to tell him, 'Get off the car. Don't touch it. Leave it alone.' And then after I said that, I remember thinking to myself, 'Holy shit. I better not talk to Tony that way. He'll rip me apart.' But all the guys were stunned. No cop had ever seen anything like this before.

"The ambulance came and Norfleet helped load the kid onto the stretcher. Pete and Danny Leonard went with the body to the hospital.

"I started to do a canvass of the houses that were closest to the car. And everybody was saying the same thing. They heard shots about 3:30 A.M. They heard a car speed away but they didn't see anything. Which is typical. These people are used to gunshots. They don't even come to the window anymore. Hell, we had a cop living on the block and he didn't even come out of his house. Later he tells us, 'I live here. My family lives here. I don't get involved with the neighborhood.' What kind of bullshit is that? Another cop is shot and you don't come out of your house? I wanted to kill the guy.

"I mean I was fucked up. You know what it was . . . It was hate and remorse at the same time. I felt bad about this kid. But the other thing, I was enraged that somebody would just fucking kill a cop this way. If the cop was chasing somebody, and the perp turned and fired and the kid got hit and died, that's one thing. But to sit there totally unprovoked and be shot that many times, that was another thing. That was complete, outright assassination. But I was even more outraged that someone would even think of doing this. I always felt on the street, when I was in uniform, that you didn't have to respect me personally. But you gotta respect the uniform.

"It took about forty minutes for things to calm down. That's when Norfleet told me that the guy's name was Ed Byrne. I couldn't put a name with the face. Norfleet says, 'He was a new kid in the precinct. He just got here. Shit, saw him about fifteen minutes before this went down. I gave the kid a scratch and drove away.' I think Byrne may have come into the squad room once. I know I never spoke to him. I just couldn't picture his face. No matter how I tried to see the kid's face, all I could see was the way he had looked in the car. All I saw was the bloody uniform. And I guess that's the way they wanted us to see him."

No one said a word in the ambulance. Dr. James Dorsey was waiting at the entrance to the emergency room at Mary Immaculate when the ambulance pulled up. All the other bodies had come through this door. First Stoney Bastion, then Brian Rooney, Myrtle Horsheim, Crystal Bynum, and Alonzo Bellamy. A nurse had already filled out the emergency-room record identifying the police officer by name and address. She wrote: Unknown Burn, One Police Plaza.

Dorsey was averaging one gunshot wound a night. Most of the shootings, he knew, involved crack. He was catching most of the work from South Jamaica. The level of savagery unnerved him. He looked at the body and wrote on an admitting chart in a fast hand.

"20ish w/m shot in the head. Presently full arrest. Multiple gunshot wounds in head. Open exposed brain. Pronounced dead on arrival. Dorsey."

At the bottom of the chart were the notes of a second physician, Dr. Michael Kiendrak.

"This 22-year-old w/m police officer brought by EMS with detectives. Shot in the head. Came in full arrest. Surgical code was called. Was pronounced D.O.A. 3:45 A.M. M.E. notified case No. 1339. Accepted. M. Kiendrak."

A nurse assisting the surgical team filled out another record. Not that all the paper in the world was going to save Edward Byrne.

"Brought in by ambulance with multiple gunshot wounds to

head. Whitish matter oozing from scalp. Unresponsive. No visual vital signs noted. Pupils fixed and dilated. Multiple wounds noted on scalp. IV in right arm. Surgical team on standby. Pronounced dead on arrival by Dr. Dorsey. Waiting for family to arrive."

At 4 A.M. the body was rolled under an X-ray machine. The doctor handling the machine, Khaleda L. Billah, took just one photograph. She developed the X ray and then slapped it on a screen. Then she started writing. There was nothing else to do.

"Skull:

"2/26/88

"Demonstrates comminuted fractures of the skull bones. Separation of pieces of bones noted. This involves the entire skull including facial bones. Metallic fragments, most likely bullet fragments, noted in the right side of neck and also scattered throughout the skull. Accompanying soft tissue component noted overlying the vertex area. Study was limited. Only a single AP projection was obtained due to patient's grave condition.

"IMPRESSION: COMMINUTED TYPE OF FRACTURE OF THE SKULL SECONDARY TO GUNSHOT INJURY. SCATTERED METALLIC FRAGMENTS MOST LIKELY BULLET FRAGMENTS NOTED IN ENTIRE SKULL. K. BILLAH, M.D."

At 4:30 A.M., Dorsey removed four bullet fragments from the police officer's head. Two of the fragments appeared brassy-colored. The other two were lead. The rounded end of a copper-jacketed bullet was still preserved. The bullets were bagged and handed over to Pistone. Although no ballistics expert, Pistone could guess what Byrne had been shot with.

"Copper-jacketed," Pistone radioed back to his command. "Probably a .38 caliber."

By now, Mayor Edward I. Koch and his bumbling police commissioner, Benjamin Ward, had arrived. Koch didn't need a medical report or X ray to tell him what had happened on the Inwood Post. Someone had blown the cop's brains out.

"An attack on a cop is an attack on our society," opined the shaken mayor. "Whoever did this has to be hunted down like an animal."

Pistone kept his distance, waiting down the hallway with another group of cops as a nurse filled out a clothes and valuables list for the "unconscious" patient. He signed a voucher listing the items and was handed two plastic bags, including Byrne's bloody uniform, watch, house keys, tie clasp, and bullet-proof vest. The detective was then left alone in the hallway, unsteady with his burden.

Pistone walked out the door and hitched a ride back to the station house, Byrne's empty uniform on the seat beside him. There is no more ghostly experience in this world, Pistone would later tell his friends, than the experience of carrying a dead cop's empty uniform back into his station house.

The police department's chaplain, the Reverend John Kowsky, had been awakened by a phone call at 3:45 A.M. The police did not yet know the victim's full name, only that there was a cop dead and notifications to be made. Kowsky dressed quickly, putting on his collar. The phone rang again. The chaplain heard the name for the first time.

"How old?" he asked. He heard the age.

"Where are the parents?"

"His father was a lieutenant on the job."

Within minutes, Kowsky was knocking on Matt Byrne's door, standing in the den where Edward Byrne had stood five hours before talking about tomorrow with his father. The kid's bedroom still smelled of his shampoo and cologne.

"How bad?" Matt Byrne had asked the priest. He was a cop. He could take it.

"The worst," Kowsky replied.

No cop was that strong. Both parents broke down. Matt insisted on going to the hospital to see for himself. Neither the priest nor the cop's mother, Ann, thought that was a good idea. There was no reason the father had to see his son that way. Matt Byrne would never see his son's face again.

"It's bad enough that they killed him," Matt Byrne would later say. "But they didn't even give me the chance to have an open casket."

Eventually the priest found a phone, asking Matt Byrne for the numbers of his son's survivors. The priest dialed the telephone numbers and handed the phone to the ex-cop.

"Eddie's been killed," Matt Byrne told one relative after the other. The priest stood off to the side, praying very hard.

For one night at least, he did not like his job very much.

"I got back to the station house around 4:30 A.M. Lt. Eugene Dunbar, the squad commander, wanted us all back there. He took the whole squad, Team C Homicide, into a room and closed the door. Pete was there with Eddie's clothes in a plastic bag. All the bosses were just starting to arrive. And Dunbar took us into a room. One of the guys, Mike O'Brien, made coffee. I remember, just before we went into the room, the lieutenant came up to me. He says, 'You know you got this.' I said, 'All right.' And I remember when he said it, I was scared to death. I was afraid I wasn't going to solve it, or that we'd never know who did it. We went in and Dunbar says, 'Listen, I want everybody to settle down and regroup. We're going to start from scratch. The crime scene unit is out there now. The kid is dead, we can't do nothing for him. We're going to focus on the local guys first. Arjune was going to testify against the guys in Mustafa's crew. Let's start there first.' The meeting broke up at about 5:30 A.M. Most of the guys were all right after this. But I was still fucked up, back at the car window. I couldn't get the scene out of my mind. I still can't.

"The union rep, Ronnie Devita, came upstairs. He wanted to know if we were okay. He said, 'The shrink is downstairs if you want to talk to him.' I said, 'What the fuck do I want to talk to him for?' My whole life was death and murder. I couldn't go see a shrink. I went back out to the scene. It was getting light out. The neighborhood looked bigger in the light. That scared me. How was I going to find these guys?"

Decoy was back in his uncle's apartment. The Driver had dropped off the Shooter at his home, and then driven to Decoy's uncle's building. Decoy had rushed into the building and up four flights of steps. He saw two girls at the top of the landing.

"Boop. Boop. Boop. Boop," Decoy screamed. "Four to the head. That's all it took."

The girls gasped. Decoy pushed past them into his uncle's apartment. A couple of the crackheads were dozing on the velour couch.

"I'm the baddest motherfucker out there," Decoy screamed. "There's no stopping me now."

Decoy's uncle was paralyzed with fear. His nephew was bug-eyed and sweating.

"You're crazy," the uncle said.

"Yeah, that's right, we did it," the Decoy said. "Boop. Boop. Boop. We killed the cop. Just like that. Boop. Boop. Boop." One of the crackheads stirred. The Decoy slapped his leg and yelled. "It's done. There won't be no testifying now."

The uncle was feeling brave. He had been drinking all day.

"You a fool, nigger," he told his nephew. Decoy slapped his uncle in the face, knocking him to the floor. He stepped over the man and headed to his bedroom in the back of the apartment. The Decoy's girlfriend, Shareema, was in the bed sleeping. He took off his clothes and got into the bed. The half-dressed girl stirred.

"Is that you, Todd?" she asked, reaching for him.

"Sure is, baby," the Decoy whispered. "Now wake up and take a man."

The Driver could not sleep. He lay in a bedroom of his mother's home, staring at the ceiling. He had not bothered to remove his clothes. The Driver's chest was on fire. He kept hearing the gun-shots and then seeing Todd's face.

"The cop's brains were on the seat," Todd had said.

The Driver got up, put on his camouflage coat and started walking through the projects. He needed a beer. It was 4:30 A.M. The Driver got back into the yellow Dodge and started driving. He pulled over next to a One Stop Grocery after spotting a kid nicknamed Sphinx, Derrick Smith. Sphinx, eighteen, had worked with the Driver until he had joined up with Todd's crew.

"Yo, Sphinx," the Driver said, coming around the car onto the sidewalk. "What you talking about me, saying I was a traitor, going for the money with Todd?"

Sphinx wasn't afraid of the Driver.

"That's he-say, she-say talk," Sphinx replied. He started to walk away.

The Driver stepped in front of Sphinx and threw a punch, hitting the kid squarely on the jaw. Sphinx stumbled, but then regained his balance. He began to bob and weave. The Driver was slower and heavier. Sphinx hit the Driver with several jabs and then an overhand right to the cheek. The Driver retreated to the yellow Dodge, holding his face.

Sphinx walked into a hero shop, John and Rudy's, ordering a steak and cheese sandwich. He had just emerged with his hero in hand, turning the corner at 107th Avenue when the Driver jumped out of the bushes, putting a revolver to Sphinx's head. Steak and cheese spilled to the sidewalk.

"I could kill you," the Driver said. He poked the gun hard into Sphinx's right ear. The dealer closed his eyes, waiting for the explosion. Just as suddenly, the Driver let him go. He could not shoot a man.

"I like you Sphinx," the Driver said. "I couldn't kill you."

"I wasn't disrespecting you," Sphinx said. "I was just, you know, playing."

The Driver was hyped and bug-eyed, Sphinx would later recall. He had seen the Driver put the gun in his waistband.

"Look," the Driver said. "You are gonna hear about a cop being killed on 107. Listen to the news."

Then the Driver ran back to his car. He rushed into his mother's apartment and began knocking on her bedroom door. She awakened to the sight of her son standing in the doorway, a gun in his waistband, a welt on his face. It was funny, she would recall, but in that first moment she was not so afraid for herself as she had been for her son. She followed out into the kitchen and found him sitting by the window, drinking a beer.

"What's wrong?"

The Driver began to stutter. "Some-one did some-thing. I was thh-eere."

"Who?"

"Somee-one got shot in the head tonight," the Driver said. He paused, catching his words. "It was a cop."

"Did you shoot a cop?"

"No. I was there when it happened. I was in the car with Todd and another guy. They made me stay in the car."

The Driver pushed past his mother and walked down the hall, getting into his own bed. The mother turned on the radio. It took a minute or two before the announcer repeated the news bulletin. A Queens cop had been shot. A few minutes later there was an update. The cop had died of a gunshot wound to the head in Mary Immaculate Hospital. They were calling it assassination.

"Oh, my God," the Driver's mother said. "They really did it."

There was a knock at the bedroom door. Todd stirred, only half-conscious. The knock grew louder and he stumbled to his feet. Todd's head was mushy and hot. He could not remember dreaming. It took him a second or two to recall what they had done to the sitting policeman. Had they really shot him? Todd looked to his girlfriend, Shareema. She was still in a deep sleep. At this moment, the violence seemed of another lifetime. Todd rubbed his eyes and went to the door.

The dealer known as Marshal was standing there, sneering. He had spent the night with a girl in a hotel at Kennedy Airport. The alibi was named Audette Wills, and was attractive as excuses go. Todd gave Marshal a handshake and asked, "Sup?" street slang for "What's up?"

The crackheads were stirring in the back bedroom. Marshal looked nervous, his black eyes darting left and right through the apartment. The room was full of ears.

"You know what happened?" Marshal asked.

Todd grinned. Marshal was so slick.

"I heard," Todd said. He wanted to brag about it right then, to tell Marshal how swift death had come to the cop, how the officer's blue eyes had looked. But Marshal had held up a finger to his lips.

"You know there is gonna be a lot of P.O.s around here."

"Yeah, so what?"

"You got to stay out of trouble, Todd. You hot already."

"So?"

"So let's get out of the projects."

Marshal had the green Samurai Jeep parked out front. The car was registered to Pappy's girlfriend, Paris Williams. Todd put on a black leather suit and walked downstairs, rejoining Marshal. They picked up the Driver at his mother's apartment and then drove over to Carmichael's Diner on Foch Boulevard.

"I don't want no fucking talk about this," Marshal had said. Todd nodded. Todd did not tell Marshal about how he had come back to the apartment, boasting of the killing to Debbie and Muka. Todd knew the bragging had been a mistake. But he had been so proud. The Driver said nothing, thinking of Sphinx and then his mother. Talking about the killing had made it seem less real. Too many people already knew too much.

The Shooter was waiting for them in the diner's back booth along with a kid nicknamed Homes, James McCaskill.

"You should have seen the cop's blue eyes," The Shooter was saying. "The cop was younger than me."

Marshal threw the Shooter a frigid stare. What was the guy thinking? The waitress was less than ten feet away. Marshal knew already that the Shooter's mouth was going to be a problem.

"I don't want to hear no more talk about the cop getting hit," Marshal said. "You guys are crazy talking like this."

The killers paid their check, leaving a three-dollar tip. The waitress would remember them. The cops would think the tip odd, wondering what set of rules it was that these men lived by, allowing them to kill a cop and tip a waitress.

They drove into Brooklyn, stopping to buy sneakers in an East New York shoestore. The Shooter recognized a kid in the store, who told him, "You motherfuckers in Queens are bad, killing cops." The Shooter had thrown a playful punch at his Brooklyn friend.

"Boop. Boop. Boop," the Shooter said. "Blue-eyed cops shouldn't be messing with no Bebos. Bebos is the shit in Queens."

5

"I WAS THERE. I DID IT."

Edward Granshaw was feeling quite proud. This was to be the homicide detective's promotion day. An electronic alarm had awakened the homicide cop at approximately 5:30 A.M. on February 26, 1988. He was not one of those people who rise to the sound of music or news. Music was something you listened to in traffic on the Long Island Expressway. And news, well, there was enough bad news at work. Granshaw nudged his wife and rolled out of bed, headed for the shower.

"Come on," the detective said. "If we're going to make this thing, we better get moving."

The detective lived in a white colonial home off a rural road in Coram, Long Island. Granshaw worked in one world and slept in another. He could point his car in any direction, ride for three minutes, and hit a Suffolk County potato field. He was ten miles from the nearest store—fifteen minutes from the closest shopping mall. The Queens border was one area code, two counties, and fifty miles away. But it might as well have been on the other side of the world. There had never been a drug murder in Eddie Granshaw's town. His two oldest kids, a teenaged boy and girl, attended a predominately white public high school and worshipped Debbie Gibson over the rap god Tone Loc.

The detective was tall, with wavy brown hair and a cool disposition, something of a loner. At forty, Granshaw was a dead ringer for James Caan. He even talked out of the side of his mouth. He had grown up a poolroom rat in Red Hook, Brooklyn. For all his rural living, Eddie Granshaw had the street in his blood.

Many of the detective's boyhood friends had wound up in jail. One or two had been murdered, another handful dying of heroin overdoses. Granshaw had been headed for trouble, too. He had come home drunk one morning to be met at the door by his mother. Mrs. Granshaw was holding a copy of *The Chief*—the Bible of civil servants—in her right hand.

"They're giving the police exam this morning," Mrs. Granshaw had told her son. "Don't come home until you take it."

Eddie had been too inebriated to argue. He'd taken the newspaper clipping and reported for the exam, missing twenty-eight of the first fifty questions. Granshaw had sobered up halfway through the test, scoring well enough to be called for duty in 1969. He'd worked in narcotics and anti-crime before earning a detective's shield in 1981. Ultimately, he had been assigned to the 103rd Precinct, welcoming Richard Sica and Pete Pistone to Homicide Team C.

Granshaw was generally regarded as the squad's smoothest talker. The older guys had never seen anyone quite like him. Granshaw would walk the street like a foot patrolman, stopping to chat with drug addicts, welfare cheats, and prostitutes. The older detectives thought him eccentric. The kid from Red Hook seemed to actually like street people. He even had a saying, "These people may be skells, but they're my skells."

Granshaw wore no vest and carried no handcuffs. Instead he possessed a gift. The detective could talk even the most stone killer into the squad room.

"Look, we're in the same business," Granshaw would say. "You did what you had to do. Now I'm doing what I have to do. Let's be professional about this."

Once Granshaw had talked an axe-wielding Haitian psychopath out of his weapon. The Haitian psychopath had responded to a previous arrest by beating the shit out of six cops. Now Granshaw had a complainant who said the Haitian had chopped his car in half.

"We got this asshole down at the station who says you dented his car," Granshaw was heard to say. "You know he's lying and I know he's lying. But I got this fucking complaint here. The guy is busting our balls. Let's go in and straighten this asshole out."

The Haitian psychopath dropped his axe.

"Gee," Granshaw continued. "Can I be honest with you? I'm up for this here promotion. Everybody thinks you hate cops. I know better. Wouldn't it be great to show these cops up?"

"I do hate cops," said the Haitian psychopath.

"Really? Well let's teach these bastards a lesson. You put on these handcuffs I borrowed here and we'll just waltz into the precinct. We'll show the bastards up and I'll get a promotion. You can even come to my party. Don't you want to come to my party?"

"Parties are fun," replied the psychopath, putting on the handcuffs himself. "I'm not going to let those fucking cops screw up your promotion."

And that's the way Granshaw worked. He bought his prisoners sandwiches and sodas. He told them jokes. And then, more often than not, he delivered their confessions. It was Granshaw, who in the winter of 1987, finally put together a case against William Frawley, the hit man named Ice. Frawley had taken a contract to hit a dealer named Jones. He walked up to the man and shot him in the chest at point-blank range. Then Ice dropped the man to the sidewalk and started walking away. The dead man's brother, having witnessed the killing, chased Ice down the block. Ice had turned and pointed his gun at the witness. The witness had shuddered. But Ice had not fired. He had simply put the gun in his waistband, turned, and walked away.

Later Granshaw asked Ice why he hadn't chilled the witness, too.

"Ice don't kill nobody for free," Frawley had replied.

Everyone on the street, it seemed, wanted to be arrested by Eddie Granshaw. Once the astonished detectives had even seen a murder suspect shaking Granshaw's hand after making a confession.

"No hard feelings?" Granshaw said.

"Of course not," the killer said. "I'd like to thank you for arresting me."

"No problem at all," Granshaw said with an embarrassed shrug. "Hell, you could almost say it was my pleasure."

On the morning of Edward Byrne's assassination, Granshaw was to be honored at a 9 A.M. ceremony at One Police Plaza. The mayor and police commissioner would be on hand to see him promoted to the rank of second-grade detective. Granshaw had gotten dressed and put on his blue uniform for the first time in years. Then he had herded his wife and kids into the car and headed out for the city. The detective had just reached the Long Island Expressway when he heard a radio news flash. A cop in Granshaw's precinct had been murdered.

Granshaw had looked at his wife and then turned the car around. He had sped home, past the frozen potato fields, his mind racing through suspects. He had dropped his family off on the driveway and screeched off toward the city and murder.

He reached his precinct ninety minutes later and headed straight for the locker room. Granshaw was still changing from his uniform into his detective's clothes—sports jacket, starched white shirt, and tie—when an inspector approached his locker. The inspector was a book cop, too far removed from the street to be of any value to the city anymore. He was more politician than cop, one of those guys who spends his whole career looking for the right buttocks to kiss.

"What are you doing here?" the inspector demanded. "You're supposed to be at your promotion ceremony."

"I got a dead cop here," Granshaw said. "You don't kill a cop like that in my precinct."

To the inspector, there was nothing so important in this world as a promotion ceremony. His own police career had consisted of five promotion parties and about six arrests. "Detective," the inspector had said, "you are ordered to go to your promotion."

Granshaw was seething. The frantic drive into work had sobered him to a single clear decision. There was too much mindless violence in the street now. Crack had changed the game like nothing else. The detective had not come this far, up from Red Hook and out onto Long Island, to lose everything in one wanton pistol flash. Eddie Granshaw was getting out. The case of Edward Byrne, 103 PDU, Case No. 435, was to be his last stand.

"Fuck my ceremony," Granshaw said. "Fuck this department. The promotion ain't worth shit now. We got a cop killer here. And I ain't going to stand around with a bunch of bosses all day, drinking coffee and eating cake, pretending it didn't happen." The inspector had backed away from Granshaw's locker, holding up his hands, mistaking conviction for insubordination.

"Did anyone ever tell you," the inspector said, "that you have a real attitude problem?"

Granshaw watched him go and then slammed his locker. He was walking the streets by 8 A.M., his mind sharp to the hunt.

A legion of television trucks, their satellite dishes pointed toward the city, had descended on Edward Byrne's block in Massapequa, Long Island. Television reporters swarmed through the area, pushing microphones into people's faces, demanding tender remembrances of a lost neighbor. One neighbor, Jean Maher, described Rookie in glowing terms, talking about how helpful he had been during Hurricane Gloria. A high school friend named Gerry produced his yearbook, pointing to a page Edward Byrne had signed. The entry read: "Gerry, we made it. Now the fun starts. Eddie Byrne."

By 10 A.M., the network news types were in a feeding frenzy. Bulky engineers pushed and shoved at each other for camera position. Reporters screamed questions at the dead cop's friends and relatives as they entered the house. Gradually, it was learned that Byrne had an older brother, Larry, twenty-nine, working as an assistant prosecutor in the office of crime-fighter Rudolph Giuliani. Another son, Steve, twenty-six, they learned, was a second lieutenant in the Marines. The Byrnes' youngest son, Kenny, was a nineteen-year-old college student. The youngest Byrne took it upon himself to speak for the family. He had been closest with Rookie.

"Eddie was excited to be a cop," Kenny Byrne said. "And he was a good cop. He died courageously and I don't want anyone to forget that. He didn't die for nothing."

Everyone, it seemed, was tugging for a piece of Edward Byrne's uniform. The city's Nero-like mayor, Edward I. Koch, was reacting in his usual shameless manner, screeching about the death penalty. Then he went into a long-winded spiel about the responsibility of the Federal government, pinning the blame for Byrne's death on Ronald Reagan. The mayor suggested that the city declare war on South America, but said nothing about his own failures. He was facing an election in 1989 and hoping voters would forget he had lost control of the city to the drug dealers.

The police union's response was equally disgraceful. Phil Caruso, the union boss, saw the killing as a contract issue. "Edward Byrne should have had more protection," Caruso said. "He was placed in a life-threatening situation. We have to hire more cops." Most citizens were struck by two things in the first hours: the brazenness of Byrne's killers and the smallness of their leaders.

ſ   *

Meanwhile, the witness Arjune was screwing everyone up. He insisted during the first interviews that the killers had rushed from the scene in a beige four-door 1976 Oldsmobile Cutlass.

"The car is missing a right rear hubcap," Arjune insisted. But another set of detectives, who interviewed Arjune's wife, were being told that no car had been spotted. Still, Arjune was adamant. The police department, desperate for any lead, got sucked in. It would take them days to recover.

At about 7:30 A.M., a detective assigned to the Queens Nightwatch, Virginia Morrison, entered the squad room saying she had found a beige 1976 Oldsmobile Cutlass with a missing right hubcap. The car was parked on South Road near Guy Brewer Boulevard, about twelve blocks from the murder scene. Richard Sica thought immediately of Todd. Billy had told him Todd was hiding out in an apartment on the same street, playing Nintendo games.

The car was immediately staked out and shown to Arjune. The witness had then positively identified the car as the same one he had seen tearing away from the murder scene. The car's registration came back to a William Benjamin, fifty-eight, of 162-19 South Road. A check of criminal records revealed Benjamin to have shot his wife on April 26, 1987. Mrs. Benjamin had been shot three times with a small caliber gun, once in the back and twice in the stomach. After a week in the hospital, Mrs. Benjamin had dropped the charges. She'd subsequently recovered, obtaining a divorce. William Benjamin had remarried eight months ago. He was lying drunk in bed with his new wife, when the cops hit his door.

Mr. Benjamin claimed he had been out drinking until 3:30 A.M. and then returned home, drunk. He also said that he sometimes loaned the car to a crackhead named Kenneth Trappier, who worked in his garage. He had last loaned the car to Trappier on February 23. A reveal of police records revealed Trappier to be a convicted murderer.

*

Alice McGillion, the deputy police commissioner assigned to public communications, began leaking information to the press: Benjamin was a suspect. Trappier was probably in on it. Both men, it was reasoned, were working for a drug dealer named Mustafa. The drug dealer was in jail on a charge of threatening to kill Arjune. Benjamin was given a lie detector test, the results of which were inconclusive. The police commissioner, Benjamin Ward, was walked out and propped up before the television cameras. He all but indicted Benjamin in time for "Live at Five."

Unfortunately for Benjamin and the public, neither McGillion nor Ward had any idea what they were talking about. The chief of detectives, Robert Colangelo, was equally ill-suited to be discussing a murder investigation. Unknown to the public, Colangelo had never, ever, solved a murder case. His work in the Byrne case consisted of telling detectives to put the murdered officer's clothes in paper, rather than plastic bags. This allowed the evidence to breathe. The advice was right out of the Detective 101 textbook. Still the threesome had looked smart and keen on television.

There was, however, absolutely no basis in fact for identifying Benjamin as Public Enemy No. 1. It was later determined that Benjamin had returned home at 3:30 A.M. after a night of drinking at his bar, Willie's Fishing Club, at 106-38 South Road. Benjamin had just one set of keys for the car, and they had never left his possession. At first the detectives assigned to interrogating Benjamin thought him clever. Later they realized he knew absolutely nothing about the crime.

In his drunken stupor, Benjamin had probably even driven through the intersection of Inwood and South Road, a block away from where Byrne sat dead. In his desperation to help the police, to see anything of importance, Arjune may have mistaken Benjamin's crapped-out Oldsmobile for a getaway car. Most of the detectives believed Arjune to be mistaken from the start, or even worse, lying to protect his wife. They believed Arjune had gone to the window upon hearing the shots and then retreated to his bedroom phone. His wife reported seeing a black man in a three-quarter-length ski coat leaning into Byrne's car. That would have been the Shooter. Arjune saw a brown coat. No one was wearing a brown coat. Mrs. Arjune also told police she had seen the man run north on Inwood. Mrs. Arjune never reported seeing any car.

Arjune himself, interestingly enough, never made any mention of seeing a getaway car during his three-minute 911 call. Arjune later told police he did not want his wife involved with the case. Many felt Arjune was talking about what his wife had witnessed.

Still Arjune was a brave and honorable man.

Richie and Pete Pistone left the 103rd Precinct at 6 P.M. on February 26. The men drove home together, trauma-weary and anxious. This was, quite obviously, the case of a lifetime. Joanne made Richie a small chicken dinner, which he only picked at. He laid down for two hours, but never really slept. He returned to the precinct at midnight.

By then, the detectives had lost interest in Benjamin as a murder suspect. Everyone from One Police Plaza was now of the opinion that Mustafa had ordered the hit from jail. The crack dealers Webster and Johnson were still in jail. A frantic search had begun for Yusef Qaadir, alias Joe Sharp. Police discovered the crack dealer a changed man, working for a security firm, studying to take the policeman's exam. The police commissioner's flacks were now telling reporters that Benjamin had probably loaned his car to someone in Mustafa's crew. They spent all of Saturday spreading more misinformation. Reporters, cut off from the assigned detectives by McGillion, could only pass along the deputy commissioner's mistakes.

The newspapers were wild for the story. The *Daily News* and the *Post* identified Mustafa as the man behind the slaying. The *News* also ran a front-page headline on February 27th reading: REWARD $30,000. The accompanying front-page editorial read,

"The *Daily News* calls on the people of New York to help find Edward Byrne's killer and send the drug scum a message—We will not be frightened into silence." It was the first front-page editorial of its kind since the paper had come out against the Axis powers.

There was no shortage of suspects. Informants, many of them hoping to claim a bounty that ultimately exceeded $130,000, rushed to the phones, dialing a special hot-line number. There were about 150 calls in the first 48 hours. All the tips and confessions had to be checked out. At the height of the investigation, there were more than two hundred detectives working the case. They filed a total of seven hundred detective reports, called DD5s.

An army of narcotics cops, meanwhile, descended on South Jamaica, arresting two hundred suspected crack dealers in the first forty-eight hours. Ordinarily, cops averaged ten to fifteen arrests in a similar period. Every person taken into the system was interrogated as to what, if anything, they knew about the assassination of Police Officer Edward Byrne. And here was a bitter irony. In death, it seemed, Edward Byrne, a cop who had never made a drug arrest, had killed off crack trade in Queens.

Everyone, Richie Sica soon found, had talked with Byrne's killers. An informant named Eddie walked into the precinct at 6 A.M. and stated that he had just overheard Claude Skinner telling a girl on the street, "My boys bumped the police officer to scare the witness." At the time, Skinner was sitting in a room speaking with Eddie Granshaw. The detective was making a deal with the drug dealer, or so Skinner thought. In December 1985, Skinner's brothers had been named as suspects in a murder. There was no evidence, however, linking them to the crime. Granshaw told Skinner, "Listen, if you help us get the guys that killed the cop, we'll forget about your brothers' case. Don't help us, and your brothers go down for the homicide." Skinner promised to help, not knowing that he had been tricked.

As it turned out, Skinner had no information on the killing. Not that Skinner didn't try to help. By nightfall the drug dealer was offering his own reward, a $50,000 contract on the life of the person who killed Byrne. Skinner wasn't about to rat anybody out. But he had no problem ordering an execution.

The most ridiculous leads came from those facing arrest on narcotics charges. One prisoner said Supreme McGriff had done the killing. Unfortunately, Supreme was in jail. Another informant said the killing had been ordered by Jazzy and Lefty Jennings. The Jennings boys were in direct competition with Mustafa. The feeling was that Jazzy and Lefty had killed the cop to bring down the heat on Mustafa, thereby putting him out of business. Sica and Pistone spent a day chasing this lead.

Lefty Jennings, it turned out, had a lot of enemies. Still awaiting trial for an April 1987 murder, Lefty was reputed to have shot no less than half a dozen people. No less than ten people called the police hot line, stating, "Lefty killed the cop." Another six reported, "Lefty's brother Jazzy did the killing." One caller said, "Jazzy shot the cop. Now he's framing Lefty."

Actually, a curious thing had happened. Frustrated citizens were for the first time seeing an almost immediate police response to their complaints about drug dealers. Cops swept in and arrested the dealers. The dealers had nothing to do with Byrne's murder, but at least the blocks were clean.

The cops were getting frustrated, too. Lieutenant Dunbar came out of his office and spotted a detective sleeping. The detective was on loan to the investigation from an elite Manhattan-based detail. "Get the hell out of here," Dunbar screamed. "We got a dead cop here. I don't want anybody sleeping. Sign out and go back to your command." The lieutenant than slammed his door, the remaining detectives turning to stare at each other.

The cops had to warn people not to give money to people walking the neighborhood seeking contributions in the name of Edward Byrne. There was no such fund. Only in New York would someone turn a tragedy into a racket.

Some of the information being gained in the interviews was fantastic. An informant walked into the precinct at around 8 P.M.

on Saturday, February 27, and laid out an entire racketeering case.

The information, found in DD5 No. 120, read:

"Informant stated that he knows the persons that are involved in drug trafficking in South Jamaica.

"He stated that the Nichols family is at the top of the drug trade. He believes Fat Cat's mother and his sister are running the drug operation while Fat Cat is in jail. Mort (sister of Fat Cat) definitely supplies drugs and is always accompanied by an unknown male Oriental. The following families are supplied by the Nichols family: Earlie Tripp, Abaduba, Mustafa, Pappy (currently in jail), and the Supreme Team.

"He further states that a person named Skinner is on a level just under Fat Cat's level and operates independent of Fat Cat's family through an agreement. He further states that Earlie Tripp operates in the area of 150th St. and 107 Ave. Earl's mother, Nettie Stanley, operates a store on the east side of 107 Ave., between 150 St. and 154 St. Earl uses the second floor of the store to package drugs. The following persons work for Earl: Kandu, Stanley, and Boom.

"Abaduba, unk m/b, unk. first and last name, sells from the game room located at 106-56 150 St. The following persons work for Abaduba: Red, Fats, and Ben.

"Informant states that the Mustafa family is currently being run by Bugout, aka Emory Matthews. The following persons work for Bugout: Saleem, Cee, Homes, and Unique. Mustafa's territory was Inwood St., from Lakewood Ave. to Liberty Ave. Bugout's people are currently located at a Spanish bodega on Sutphin Blvd. and 109 Ave. They keep drugs behind a steel door in the back of the store. The owners are not involved because they are intimidated.

"Pappy Mason's organization is being run by Marshal. The following persons work for Pappy: Marshal, Divine, and Scott. Call themselves the Bebos."

The information in this one police report was as good as anything the FBI had, and the Federal agents had been working on the crack dealers in southeastern Queens since Billy had joined them in early 1987.

The informing was not left to men alone. Another C.I. (Confidential Informant) named Missy was walking through the Queens Woman's House of Detention on Saturday when she spotted Fat Cat's niece, Pumpkin. "They took one of ours, so we took one of theirs," Pumpkin reported. "Abbie did it. Blew the guy's head right off his shoulders." Cops spent two days running down the mysterious Abbie. Still another set of cops rushed off to Greenhaven prison, interviewing an inmate named Anthony Lloyd. The reason for the interest? Lloyd had gotten into a prison knife fight with Fat Cat back in 1979. Some of the information was downright spooky. One detective called the DEA offices in New York to check on a suspect named Phil Rodney. The agent answering the call was named Everett Hatcher. In January of 1989, Hatcher would be sitting alone in a car on a desolate patch of Staten Island when a drug dealer would walk up to his window and shoot him dead.

But there were no secrets in the streets. Still another informant had said, "Tommy Mickens did it. He's mad because the FBI is after him now. They got this big case going against him." The FBI investigation of Mickens, incidently, didn't become public knowledge until three months later. Still another informant had stated that he had heard someone named Kandu discussing the hit at about 9 P.M. on February 25. "Kandu was saying that he had to stay low and get his shit off the street because Prince and his boys were talking about hitting a cop. The word in the Forties Houses is that Prince (Gerald Miller) and his boys did the hit." Still another informant said that Eddie Lyons, aka Freedom, did the killing.

There were those, of course, who confessed to the killing. One was a Francis Pierre. Mr. Pierre told a set of Brooklyn detectives he was coming back from Kennedy Airport with two men when they pulled over and shot the cop. The detectives were more than a little skeptical. Mr. Pierre could not describe his accomplices and was extremely short on motive.

"Are you sure you killed the cop?" Mr. Pierre was asked.

"Of course," he said. "I was there. I did it." Mr. Pierre would never back off his confession. Later, Mr. Pierre admitted to a second murder. "I killed President Kennedy, too," he admitted.

There were other wackos, too. Another prisoner said he had overheard his cellmate admit to arranging the killing. The cellmate had been moved to another prison. The informant volunteered to wear a wire and move in with his old cellmate. But it turned out that the two men were lovers and only interested in sharing the same cell again. A former detective in Brooklyn had information on a man who said the killing was part of an overall plan to kill Ed Koch. "First the cop, then the mayor," the suspect had said. The ex-detective's friend was ultimately arrested for threatening the mayor.

Still another man called to say he had seen Fuji Brown running from the scene. Police then sought out Fuji Brown, locating him in prison. Mr. Fuji said that he used to work for Fat Cat as an enforcer back in 1978 when three Rastafarians were killed. "I was there, but I didn't do the Rasta killings," he said. "Silvester McCord, who is known as Sneaky, shot them Rastas. Ice and Magnet were also there. The case went on for fourteen months. The case against the other three was dropped when I took the blame. I got five years, but I didn't do it." Mr. Fuji stated that he had seen two men on the street at the time of the Byrne killing, but that he wasn't really sure because he had been cracked up since getting out of jail. Mr. Fuji also said Pappy Mason had offered him $100,000 to kill a cop. Then he proceeded to identify a photograph of Todd as Pappy and Marshal as Fat Cat.

"But I really wants to help," Fuji said, as he was led back to prison.

The detailed stories were fascinating and yet maddening. One inmate telephoned police, saying he shared a dayroom in prison with Supreme, Prince, and Mustafa. The following report was then filed:

"Subject stated that once Fat Cat got sentenced, Mustafa felt he had to get back onto the street to widen his area. Mustafa told this subject that 'the time is right for me now to make money.' Mustafa was anxious to get out of jail.

"Subject stated that he was in the TV room with Mustafa, Prince, and Supreme. All four are playing cards. During the game, conversation about Fat Cat and Pappy takes place. They also talked about Fat Cat's sentence. Mustafa states, 'I'm not going out like that.' Mustafa states he's going to knock off that witness. Mustafa could not believe the witness had the heart to testify. Supreme and Prince ask how are you going to do that when you can't find the witness. Mustafa states, 'We know where he lives.' Subject stated he overheard Mustafa on the phone the next day, saying, 'Do what I tell you. Use the .380. You know where it is.' This subject then again plays cards with Mustafa, Prince, and Supreme. At this time Mustafa tells the others, 'My homeboy went to the house last night but the cop car was there. And they didn't do nothing.' Mustafa says, 'The plan is to take the cop out of the car and walk him to the door. The witness will see the cop and open the door. Then do whoever's there, you can leave the cop.' At that point Prince says, 'Do all of them.' Supreme says, 'It don't make no difference.' During a break in the game, Mustafa calls his homeboy and says, 'Do what I told you to do. Get the .380 and blast the family.'

"The morning the cop got shot, Mustafa tells this subject, 'These stupid motherfuckers, they kill the cop and leave the family.' Subject states that Mustafa was really pissed off. Later that day Mustafa gets transferred. Supreme and Prince were laughing how fucked up the papers got the story, stating that Fat Cat had nothing to do with it. Prince tells the subject that now is the time for him to make his move since Fat Cat and Mustafa are both jammed up."

The lead was considered a hot one. Mustafa had, police learned, been in the prison dayroom playing cards on the days the informant described. Prince Miller, however, was in the Brooklyn House of Detention. Supreme McGriff was in an upstate prison. Still, the informant would never back off his statement.

"I heard what I heard, man," he said. "You don't want to solve this shit, that's fine with me."

Some of the other information was more interesting. One crackhead reported, "The Bebos done it. They shoot all their enemies in the head." Another stated, "A female named Jackie told me that Fat Cat could only call on three people to do the job. One is named Bugout, the other is named Mike Bones, and the third is named Todd." Still another man arrested on a drug charge said, "This is the kind of thing the Bebos would do."

There were also missed opportunities. In the first hours after the killing, detectives had grabbed James McCaskill, the Shooter's friend "Homes," as he walked along Sutphin Boulevard with two crack vials in his pocket. It took another day before cops got around to questioning McCaskill.

"Homes stated that he knows Mustafa from the neighborhood and his brother Saleem," a detective wrote. "McCaskill further states that he does not know anything regarding the police officer that was killed and did not hear any word on the street."

At the time of his capture, Homes had just walked out of the Carmichael Diner, leaving Marshal, Todd, the Shooter, and the Driver still sitting in the back booth.

The first break.

"We were all pretty frustrated. The old guy, Benjamin, was pretty exciting for a while. Everybody worked on him. And we were thinking, 'Man, for an old man, he's all right.' Nobody could break him. We figured he was an old guy and that somebody had used his car. That was done all the time. They had nothing to say about it if one of the dealers wanted to use their car. They were either going to get their ass kicked if they said no, or they'd just give up the car. Todd was living on the second floor below where they found Benjamin's car. It fit. But then we get the old guy in and he's saying, 'I don't know nothing about it.' We all worked on him. The guy lost two days of his life.

"We hung up photographs of all the suspects on a wall in the robbery office. Fat Cat, Skinner, the Corleys, Mustafa's people. I had Pappy's picture up there, Marshal's picture, and Todd's picture. I had been reaching out for Billy the whole time. Couldn't find him anywhere. Finally, on Saturday morning he comes in around 8 A.M. I remember he even cried for a while. Billy always liked a cop. And I remember sitting him down and talking to him. He was wearing a big snorkel parka. He looks at me and says, 'What are you fucking around for?' And then Billy turned around and pointed to the pictures on the wall. 'You know this man here had to call the shot,' pointing to Pappy. 'And you know he called Marshal and Marshal took care of it. You know Marshal took Todd with him, because that's his main man.' And we all sat there listening to him. And I said, 'Billy, how did you hear it?' He says, 'No, I didn't hear it from nobody, but that's the way it works, and that's the way it's gotta be.' So we grabbed Dunbar. The lieutenant liked Billy. And Dunbar's the kind of boss, if you have an idea, he'll always listen to you. He'd sit down and listen to what you've got to say. And that's why I liked him there, why all the guys liked him. Some bosses will tell you, 'Listen, this is what I'd like you to do.' Dunbar has his opinions, but if you have something you really believe in, he'll let you run with it. But in this case we had so many people to focus on, it was hard, just with one small team trying to do all the work. We had all the manpower at our disposal. I mean we had 100 detectives in that squad room at a time.

"So we called Dunbar in the back room. Billy ran over it again with the lieutenant. And Dunbar liked the idea. So the lieutenant made the decision that our team would focus on Mustafa and Bugout, the group from down there. And the task force was going to focus on Todd and Marshal. It was apparent, if you just looked at it on the surface, that Mustafa had the cop done because of Arjune. He had the most to lose. I had some C.I. in the street who pointed us toward Lefty and Jazzy Jennings. It was feasible, possible, that they had hit the cop to put pressure on Mustafa. That's when Pete and me went out into the street. We were out about three hours. When I came back, Dunbar ripped me apart. Screamed at me in front of everybody. Because as the stuff was going on, Colangelo and the bosses wanted the case detective.

Dunbar knew I was out on the street. That's how I handled all my cases. But I understood Dunbar's point. This case was different. I put my tail between my legs and went back into the room. I was pissed and hurt at the same time. That's when me and Eddie Granshaw started coordinating the thing. Eddie says, 'I'll go out in the street. You and Pete stay here.'

"The 27th, the 28th, and the 29th were like the bad days. I was putting too much pressure on myself and the other guys. I wanted a collar before they buried the kid."

The city was in mourning. Matt Byrne and his wife were on the front page of every newspaper in the city. The attack on Edward Byrne, or more precisely what he stood for, had become national news. Matt had appeared on his front doorstep with the rest of the family on Sunday morning. He was wearing a blue suit, a blustery wind in his gray hair. He looked puffy in the eyes. He spoke and everyone was surprised by the man's voice. It came out robust and gallant.

The ex-cop's wife, Ann, wore sunglasses and held his left arm. The kid, Kenny, was wearing one of his brother's NYPD tie clasps. Steven stood at attention in full Marine dress.

"If our son Eddie, sitting in a police car representing and protecting us, can be wasted by scum, then none of us is safe," Matt Byrne said. The lawyer was reading from a yellow legal pad. The dead cop's girlfriend, Lisa D'Ambrosio, stood behind the family slightly, whimpering.

"A little of all of us died because Eddie represented the decent people of the world," Byrne continued. "Time has come, I say . . . to put your money and your resources where your mouth is. The family wants the public to know that they are hurting. They want a sign of public outrage for what has happened to Eddie."

Everyone had been struck numb by the murder. John Cardinal O'Connor had talked about the killing after Sunday Mass at St. Patrick's Cathedral, saying, "The city is at a sorry pass." Daniel

Moynihan, the United States Senator from New York, had rushed to the cop's wake, saying, "This is a fundamental assault on our law."

Koch, still afraid that someone would lay the blame for the city's demise on his shoulders, took the offensive. He bought a full-page advertisement in the *New York Times,* writing, "Officer Edward Byrne was murdered in cold blood. Let's make sure he didn't die for nothing." Then Koch went on to do what he did best, blaming New York's problems on Ronald Reagan. Not that the President wasn't watching. Reagan called Matt Byrne at home, saying, "Eddie's death will not be in vain." The President did not say, however, what he would do.

The funeral, the largest in police history, was held at St. James Catholic Church in Seaford, Long Island, on Monday morning, February 29. Ten thousand cops stood in lines six deep, the formation covering eight blocks along Hicksville Road. Some of the cops came from as far away as Texas, forcing traffic on the Southern State Parkway to a standstill. At least a million people watched the funeral on television.

With the exception of Homicide Team C, the entire 103rd Precinct was in attendance. As the day grew colder, the mood grew more somber. An associate pastor, Thomas Devita, delivered the eulogy.

"We commit him back to our God and our Father who gave him life twenty-two years ago. If only it had been a little bit longer." The family priest went on to compare Rookie to an all-American boy, calling him a man worth imitating. The department chaplain, John McCullough, quoted the words of Christ in describing the treachery of Judas Iscariot: It would be better for this man if he wasn't born.

The coffin was draped in a green, white, and blue department flag. One cop played taps on a bugle. Another cop, this one in the plaid kilt of the department's Emerald Society bagpipers, played

111

"Irish Soldier Boy." Five police helicopters appeared over the church and then thundered off. An injured city cop, Steven Mc-Donald, had sat in the back of the church in his motorized wheelchair. McDonald had been shot by a fifteen-year-old in Central Park in 1986. He sat paralyzed, a tear in his eyes. At one point, the only sound to be heard in the church was the reverberation of McDonald's respirator.

Koch, never at a loss for words, said Byrne's death was as symbolic as those of FDR, JFK, and Martin Luther King. Given the chance, he screeched again about the need for a state death penalty. Federal prosecutor Rudolph Giuliani, an unannounced candidate for mayor, stood in front of the cameras with Larry Byrne, an assistant in his office. "When a police officer is killed, the death penalty should be available," Rudy said. "I think that would get the message across to the drug dealers. Maybe the people that oppose the death penalty don't understand that you're dealing with uncontrollable behavior." Death seemed to be the only answer anyone had for a savage taking of young life.

In Washington, President Reagan was saying, "With all the headlines about how we're losing the drug war, let's keep in mind the progress we've made." The First Lady had chimed in, "If you're a casual drug user, you're an accomplice to murder." Nancy did not think to add that the same could be said for casual presidents.

The gray hearse was escorted from the church by eight white-gloved officers. Edward Byrne was ultimately led to Farmingdale Cemetery and buried under a stand of sugar maples. His coffin was shiny and black with silver fittings. It was lowered into the ground across the road from Republic Airport. The grave-side service lasted fifteen minutes, with Robert Noonan, commanding officer of the 103rd Precinct, handing Ann Byrne a folded American flag. Three young women laid single roses on the coffin, accenting a spray of gladiolus, daisies, and carnations.

And then the survivors were led off, Edward Byrne left dead in the ground. Across the road from his grave, small planes soared into an ashen sky.

*

"The television stations were cutting to the funeral all morning. The weight of the drama was overwhelming. But there was also the burden of the case, this pressure to solve it. We felt like the whole country was watching.

"I was also crazy for Todd. I didn't know if he had anything to do with it, but I knew we could work him for information. We had the Connecticut homicide hanging over his head. Bernie Porter, one of the guys from anti-crime, had found Todd's uncle, this guy Roger Phillips. Bernie comes to me and says, 'I can get Todd's uncle in here, do you want him?' This is the twenty-ninth. I said, 'Shit, yeah. Get him in here.' Bernie and Maurice Mingos go out, they get Roger from the apartment. They bring the guy in and he's totally distraught. He was crying and totally unable to talk. I says, 'Listen, Roger, this is all I want from you. I want to know where your nephew is. We're going to grab him one way or another. It's no secret that he killed that girl in Connecticut. But if he don't come to us . . .' I was trying to bullshit him. Nothing. He's not even responding. I thought he was going to have a nervous breakdown. I thought he was going to have a heart attack right there in the precinct. We spent about twenty minutes with him. I said, 'We're going to let you go home with Bernie. I want to talk to you, but I'll let you compose yourself. I'll let you relax. But I want you back in here.' Then we let him go, not realizing what he knew."

The phone call came into the 103rd Precinct just after 3 o'clock the following day, Tuesday, March 1. A man known to New York City detectives as Mr. Law, registered Confidential Informant No. 2797, said he had information. Mr. Law requested an immediate conference with police at the offices of his attorney, who was also known to police.

Two detectives were dispatched to the offices of the unknown lawyer, arriving at 3:30 P.M. A police officer assigned to the 109th

Squad, C. Jackson, took notes of an interview conducted by Sergeant Kevin Reilly of the Queens Homicide Task Force.

And here is what Officer Jackson wrote in DD5 No. 354.

"Mr. Law states the following facts referring to the morning of February 26th, 1988, between the hours of 0330 and 0400.

"I was driving my 1977 light blue Caddy (TWK-348) west on Rockaway Blvd. at 134th Street, when two girls I know as Debbie and Muka flagged me down. They got into my car and both were very nervous and visibly upset. I tried to find out why they were upset. Debbie said, 'Muka's boyfriend just did it.' Later in the conversation I asked what the boyfriend did, and Debbie said, 'Scott had just shot a cop.' Debbie also stated that Scott told them he was going to ask the cop for a match, but instead shot the cop through the window. The girls told me they had walked a long way from where Scott and Todd dropped them off. Mr. Law states he took the girls to his house (address known to this department) and they left that location at 0800 hours. At no time did the girls identify the car they were in."

Someone called Richie at home. He wasn't scheduled to come in until midnight.

"This guy says he has two girls who were with the shooters."

"Did he give you any names?"

"Yeah, two. Scott and Todd."

Richie hung up the phone. He knew his face was white and bloodless. Richie called Granshaw at home and then Billy.

"Does our guy Todd hang out with a guy named Scott?"

"Sure," Billy said. "Todd Scott and that other Scott. They're always driving this beat-up yellow car through the Forties. I saw them out there the day before the shooting tightening the wheels and racing up and down the block."

The voice of Todd Scott.

"Marshal wanted to go to his mother's house. Then we went to the city to see some sex shows on 42nd Street. I called my girl

Tonise, she said the police officers had come around looking for me, but her brother said it wasn't a homicide. I went to Brenda's house where I live on Friday night. The next day I went to the parking lot in the Forties. I called Brenda because I had a beige snow parka and it was getting cold. She told me a lot of police came up into the house with guns out. They was telling her mother that I was wanted for murder, but they didn't say who. So then when I went back upstairs where my uncle live at 109-10 168th St., Shareema came up there. She told me they had asked her whether she knew Todd. This was at 10 P.M. on Saturday, the 27th. She told them I hadn't been around there. They said there was a reward for my arrest. At 11 P.M. I called Tonise and she said they wanted her to come down to the precinct. I went back outside and stayed at my father's house for the next two days, Sunday and Monday, 103-08 Remington. The penthouse. Tuesday I stayed at a hotel, Kennedy Inn on North Conduit Ave. Registered under the name of Kevin Brown. Got there by cab, stayed there with Tonise. Everything was cool. I wasn't worried about no cops."

No one knew the Shooter's name yet. He was still new to the game, much closer to Fat Cat than Pappy. He had spent an awful lot of time with Fat Cat's sister, Viola. She was a fat, hideous woman with a terrible temper and a foul mouth. The Shooter was lean and dark, his body strong and hard. He wore glasses. People told him that he looked like a young Malcolm X. The Shooter liked that. He would tell them, "By any means necessary."

The Shooter would sit up nights with Viola in her bedroom, the girl's head spinning with crack. He would talk Viola off to sleep. Once the fat girl had reached for him, pulling him to the bed. He had not protested, but he had not enjoyed the love-making either. But it was bad business to be rude.

Viola had got him started running packages of crack. The Shooter was loyal and trustworthy. But he could also see that Fat Cat's power was waning. He had befriended Marshal and then

Todd. Business was friendships. Knowing Todd and Marshal was good business. They were always making fun of the way he looked. The Shooter wanted money for gold and clothes. He wanted to look like something, to be somebody people would notice.

A veteran cop in the 75th Precinct named Richard Brew had his own murder to solve. Hell, Edward Byrne had only been one of a dozen to die in New York that week. Brew's precinct alone had about a hundred open murders dating back to the advent of crack. Brew couldn't even keep track of the East New York homicide count anymore. Crack had come and the precinct had gone haywire, the murder rate doubling from 55 in 1986 to 110 in 1988. The blond-haired detective had been assigned to the ghetto precinct since July of 1982. He had worked on the Palm Sunday Massacre, the biggest one-day killing in the city's history. Some lunatic had killed seven people in one morning, leaving women and children scattered through an apartment. Brew had twenty years on the job. He was long past the point where dying still upsets a man.

A murder indictment had been returned this day against a dealer in Brew's precinct named Brian Gibbs. Nicknamed Glaze, Gibbs worked as a Fat Cat lieutenant. Glaze was as big as it got in East New York. The drug dealer had probably killed a dozen people, certainly no less than ten. The most recent indictment, obtained that afternoon, said Glaze had killed another dealer named Clifton Rise.

At around 1 P.M. on Monday, March 1, Brew and his partner Hank Mathas had spotted Glaze sitting in a red Jeep Cherokee. They knew Glaze well enough to know there wasn't going to be anything approaching violence. Glaze's Jeep was parked outside a grocery store on Lincoln Avenue between Sutter and Blake. Glaze was sitting next to a lean, dark fellow wearing glasses. As Brew approached the car, a third man with dreadlocks walked out of the supermarket.

Glaze offered no fight and was placed under arrest for the homicide. The Jeep was impounded. As a courtesy, Brew invited Glaze's friends back to the precinct house.

During the course of the ride over to the precinct, the man in the dreadlocks was asked his name.

"Philip Copeland," he had replied.

Brew had then turned to the lean passenger, sitting between Marshal and Glaze in the back seat.

"And you?"

"McClary," the Shooter replied, truthfully. "David McClary."

The names meant nothing to Brew, nor could they. Gibbs was questioned and booked. Marshal and McClary stood around the station house, talking with the cops. By then, Brew had called the 103rd Precinct, inviting cops over to interview Glaze. McClary, Hank Mathas noticed, looked very nervous. The Shooter agreed to pose for a Polaroid snap shot. Glaze gave McClary his car keys and jewelry.

"Am I free to go?" McClary asked.

"Yes."

The Shooter was scared. He walked out of the precinct, only to return a few minutes later.

"I want to return this jewelry," McClary said.

The Shooter was led back to Gibbs in the holding cell. Glaze didn't want to voucher his valuables with the police department.

"You hold them," Glaze said. "I will see you later."

The Shooter walked out of the precinct a second time, only to return again. He summoned Mathas to the corner.

"I need to be put in protective custody," McClary whispered.

"Why?"

The Shooter shook his head.

"I can't put you in protective custody if you won't tell me why you need to be protected."

"You got to drive me home and put me in protective custody."

"Why?"

McClary shook his head.

117

Brew had wandered over. "You got to give us a reason," Brew said.

"I can't."

McClary then took a seat in an interview room, pondering his situation. All around him, cops were talking about the dead cop, saying things like, "If I see these guys I'd just shoot them down. No questions asked." Marshal had very little to say. He sat on a detective's desk for a while and then laid down. He slept for a while in the middle of the squad room.

The Queens detectives arrived at the precinct at 3:15 P.M. They were interested mostly in Glaze. The dealer refused to speak to them. As an afterthought, the detectives conducted interviews with Marshal and McClary.

David McClary, a former star basketball player in the Police Athletic League, told the cops: "I've known Brian Gibbs for three months. I call him the man. I used to go with him to the Red Parrot, a disco in Manhattan. I met Phil at the Parrot. I don't know Phil, I just met him. He came to my house this morning at 11 A.M. because I promised him a kitten. Phil came with his uncle Bernard Ingram. We were waiting for a call from Brian. When he called, we went in Unc's van. He dropped us off and Brian picked us up. I know the drug dealers 'cause I live in the area. I like Fat Cat 'cause he gives me money at times to buy sneakers to play basketball. I know Pappy sells drugs on 150th Street and Sutphin. Skinner sells drugs, but he is a nice guy. I don't like Mustafa. If anyone killed the officer, it should be him, Mustafa."

Another detective from the Queens Homicide Task Force, David Dallenegra, conducted a brief interview with Copeland. He later prepared a DD5, writing:

"Subject is 22, 5'6", 150 pounds, small dreadlocks, short beard and mustache. He states he knows Fat Cat, Pappy, and Ruff. He runs errands for Pappy's mother while Pappy is in jail. He states that on Fri. 2/26/88, he went to the Red Parrot with David McClary. They met Glaze there. Arrived at 1 P.M., left at 4 A.M. on Saturday. Subject states that on Thursday, Feb. 25, 1988, at about 2 or 2:30 A.M., he went to the Kennedy Inn Hotel on North Conduit. He was with a female, a black woman named Audette Wills. They used room No. 504. She signed in using her real name. He used a Suzuki Jeep, green, that he borrowed from a friend, Paris Williams. He further states that he did not leave the hotel until noon on Friday."

The two men, having posed for photographs, were just getting prepared to leave when they got a call from the 113th Precinct in Queens. Copeland was wanted on a bail-jumping charge. On March 13, 1986, he had assaulted a man in the Bronx. A bench warrant for his arrest had been issued six months later. Then he had been arrested on drug charges on October 7, 1987. He had posted bail and skipped again.

Copeland was an interesting yield. His father, a merchant seaman, had been washed overboard in 1980. With her husband lost at sea, Marshal's mother, Carolyn Barbee, had lost her son to the streets. "I raised him as a God-fearing child and took him to church every Sunday until he was in his teens," Mrs. Barbee would later report. "After that, it's up to him."

The detectives would find it incredible, later, to think that one of the city's most wanted criminals had spent the better part of an afternoon sleeping on a detective's desk in the middle of a squad room. But Copeland was always cool around cops. As a teenager back in 1980, he had worked as a summer file clerk at One Police Plaza. Marshal knew the paperwork game. He was looking at an overnight stay in jail, nothing more. The cops led him outside to their car. The Shooter was still free to go.

"Can I have a ride back to Queens?" McClary asked Detective John Califano. The two detectives looked at each other for a moment.

"I don't think that would be possible," Califano decided. And with that the detective drove off, leaving the Shooter alone and free on a Brooklyn street.

*

An anonymous male placed a telephone call to the hot line at 6:30 P.M. Michael Falciano, a veteran cop nicknamed the Falcon, caught the call. The anonymous man was calling from a phone booth. He claimed to have a friend that "knows who shot the cop, because his friend works for the drug dealers who were responsible for the murder." The caller was nervous. The Falcon had smoothed him with talk of a reward. The detective convinced the anonymous caller to meet him at the corner at 95th Street and 57th Avenue in Maspeth.

The Falcon and John Williams reached the intersection just before 7 P.M. A black teenager walked up to their car and announced himself as the anonymous caller. A second teenager, Martin Howell, also got in the car. On the way to the station house, Howell had started talking.

"I'm involved with the drug dealers that killed the police officer," Howell said. "Todd Scott killed the police officer on the orders of Pappy Mason."

Howell had refused to say anything more until he reached the precinct. He was led into the robbery office, the same room where the photographs hung on the wall. Howell had walked immediately over to a picture of Todd Scott.

"He killed the cop," Howell said. "He is the Shooter." Howell then pointed to a picture of Philip Copeland. "We call him Marshal. He was involved, too. There's another guy named Scott. You don't have his picture up here, but he was involved, too. They drive a 1979 beige Chrysler two-door with tinted windows."

Falcon went to find his supervisor, who in turn called Sica at home.

"You better get in here," Richie was told.

By the time Richie arrived at the station house, Howell was giving his statement. Howell seemed particularly at ease with a detective from the Homicide Bureau named Steve Weiner.

"You hungry?" Weiner had asked.

"Yeah."

"Me too. Let's order out for some Chicken Delight." This was

Steve Weiner at his best. The detective was fast-talking and something of a blowhard, but a fine investigator. Weiner and the Falcon worked on two sheets of paper, writing the subject's version of events on one and their case notes on the other.

Subject's version:

"The night before the shooting. In The Clubhouse with me—Marshal Copeland, Todd, Todd's Uncle Roger, Darry, and Stevie O. Todd announced that the boss 'Pappy' wanted a cop hit, that there was $8,000 a head for the job. I thought they were kidding. They started sniffing coke and drinking beer. They had drew straws. Marshal and the two Scotts drew straws. Todd picked the short one, so he had to do it. After that I went home. Friday morning I woke up. Turned on the TV and saw the news about the shooting. I went outside and saw Scott all flashy, new clothes, big gold chains, showing big knots of money. When we got to The Clubhouse, there was Roger and Kevin. Scott started saying how it happened. How Scott came up to the car asking for directions and pulled out a sawed-off shotgun and shot the cop five times. Marshal then came to the club and said the same thing, primarily. Then he said, 'Business as usual' and not to say anything more about it."

Case information:

"Subject belongs to the Bebos (drug dealing group). They hang out at a location in the Forties project. There is one member whose first name is Scott. Scott's uncle is legal tenant of the apartment in the project where they hang out. Thursday before shooting met 2100 hrs. in apt. Present were Todd Scott (not same as Scott whose uncle rents apartment), Philip Copeland, Stevie O, Darry (Copeland's cousin), Kevin Curry, and Scott (owner's nephew). All in room when Todd Scott makes offer of $8,000 to kill cop.

"The order to hit a P.O. was given by a big dealer who is presently in jail and goes by the name of Pappy (kingpin drug dealer in area). It is common knowledge among the group that there is a police car with a P.O. guarding Arjune's house around the clock.

121

"When offer to kill P.O. made by Todd, there was a discussion of consequences for killing P.O. Four of the group went into next room and got high on coke and beer. They came out and drew straws to see who would do the shooting. Todd Scott drew the short straw. At about 11 P.M. they all left."

"The next day, Friday morning, Feb. 26, subject awakens and sees on the news about cop shooting. He returns to club but no one present. Shortly after, Scott arrives and tells subject, 'We all did it.' Subject asks Scott, 'You all did it?' And Scott answers, 'Yes.' All now come to apartment in new clothing. They bragged about it. Sometime during conversation, Copeland, who was the driver, relates about how Todd Scott blew the cop's head off. That he shot the cop's head off and was laughing. That he went to the cop's window and asked for directions and that he drew the shotgun from the sleeve and shot the cop 5 times."

Richie arrived at the precinct, studied Howell's statements, and saw immediately that there were some major problems. For one thing, Howell had his Scotts confused. Either that or the interviewing detectives had confused the names for him. There was also the matter of the shotgun. Byrne had been shot five times with a pistol, not a shotgun. Eventually, Richie realized that Howell was mixing hearsay with what he had eyewitnessed. Howell had been present for the drawing of straws and planning. He knew nothing first-hand beyond that. Still, the kid had been a godsend. Granshaw was absolutely ecstatic with the witness, but more than a little distressed with mention of the shotgun. All detective notes and DD5s in the case, called discovery, would be turned over to defense counsel if and when the case came to court.

Weiner's own DD5, based on his own interview with Howell, cleared up a lot of the problems. Or so the detectives thought.

"Subject stated that last Thursday night he was in a room at Todd Scott's uncle's house, located in the 40's Houses, 109th Ave. and 160th St. The subject stated that he was there with Todd Scott and Scott Cobb. At approx. 9 P.M. subject stated that Todd Scott and Scott Cobb entered the room and said, 'The boss put out orders to hit a cop, and it's easy, he sleeps on the job.' They told us you can get $8,000 a head. The subject stated the following individuals were also in the room at the time the above was said: Todd Scott's uncle, Kevin Curry, Stevie O, Darry (Copeland's cousin). This subject thought they were kidding about icing a cop. This subject informed the undersigned that no one in the room accepted the request to ice a cop. Subject stated that at that point Todd Scott and Scott Cobb went into another room.

"Subject continues stating that Todd Scott along with Scott Cobb and Copeland (aka Marshal) cut up straws, and that Todd Scott got the short straw. 'So he had to do it.' The undersigned asked, 'Do what?' And Martin replied, 'Ice the cop.' This drawing of straws took place at 2300 hours. Subject stated that all those present snorted coke and drank beer. Subject left at that time and went home.

"Subject stated he heard the news the next morning and thinks to himself, 'Holy shit. They did it.' This subject then has a conversation with Scott Cobb (1100 hours) and states, 'You did it.' Scott replied, 'Yeah, man.' Todd was really bugged out. He was laughing. Todd is crazy. Scott Cobb also stated that they shot the cop five times.

"Subject was asked if anyone described the scene of the shooting. Subject replied by stating that Scott Cobb told him after they shot the cop that the cop's brains were splattered all over the front seat of the car."

Richie Sica: "I came in with Eddie Granshaw at around midnight. The place was buzzing. At first the guy with Marty was doing all the talking. He was like the mouthpiece. He was just some shithead who knew nothing about the case. He saw all the dollar signs and he had talked Marty into coming in. So, eventually we figure out, Marty knows all the information, this guy got it from Marty. So we throw him the fuck out after about twelve hours.

"Now Dunbar tells me and the guys in our team, 'Let's work Howell, I think we got a break. It looks like Todd is the guy.' So now everything is clicking. Now I know why Roger Phillips is so upset. So Dunbar sits down and he goes through this whole thing. They met at Roger's apartment on 160th Street in the Forties. Marshal was there. This guy Scott Cobb was there and another guy. The order came from Pappy. Everything was clicking.

"Eddie and I went out to the 113 to see Marshal. We go into the room, they have their interview room in the 113, and Marshal is sitting there. We walk in and he says, 'I suppose you guys are going to beat the shit out of me, too.' I said, 'No, you know I don't work that way.' So me and Eddie sit down with him. And I ask him about Todd. And he says, 'I ain't seen Todd.' So we told him, 'Listen, we're interested in Todd because of the case in Connecticut.' And that's the line we were using. And then we started to talk about Pappy. And he says, 'I ain't got nothing to say about Pappy.' And I told him, 'I understand that Cat's losing all of his juice on the street. Pappy's got the upper hand.' And he just looked at me and smiled. And then he started talking about the round table ring. He was dressed in a tan leather suit. He had this big ring on his finger with a map of Africa on it. Big diamond, too. We asked Marshal where he got it and he told us Pappy. But we got nothing. He had an open case so we couldn't take a statement from him anyway. It was just idle conversation. He wouldn't talk about Pappy anymore. He said, 'I ain't no Perry Bellamy.'

"We went back to the precinct. The Falcon and John Williams had brought Howell into New York for a polygraph. We were still waiting for him to return. At around 3 A.M. Dunbar comes into the squad and I'll never forget this. He looked like all the blood was drained out of him. He says, 'I got something to tell you guys. Marty failed the polygraph.' So I looked at Eddie, and I says, 'So what the fuck, he failed a polygraph? What does that mean?' So Dunbar says, 'I don't know if we can use him, I don't know.' So now me and Eddie were at wit's end. Marty had done very poorly on the test. On a conversion table of minus 24 to plus 24 Marty had scored a minus 10. Anything below minus ten is deceptive. Specifically the machine said Marty had lied on questions about not being in the car himself and about being offered money by Todd to join in on the hit.

"He was too good not to be true. Too much fit now. I had had Roger in the day before. Now I know why he's so distraught, not because his nephew's wanted on a homicide in Connecticut. He killed a cop. It was planned in Roger's apartment. Marshal was there. The order came from Pappy. This is what Billy told us. So me and Eddie tell Dunbar, 'Let's go over and we'll drag Roger in.' He says, 'No, no, no, you lay off Roger.' And Dunbar has never said anything like this to us before. It's always been, 'You guys do what you want to do. I don't care what you get him on or how you get him in, just go.' Eddie and I just sat around talking, saying we got to get this guy. Eddie decided to start with the car."

Eddie Granshaw's investigation.

"Richie and I were sitting there, talking about the car. All of a sudden, Pete Pistone reaches into a drawer and pulls out a piece of paper. He says, 'I got the plate number.' I was taken aback. It turns out that Pete had been given a description of Todd's car and a plate number from an informant a few weeks before. This is when they were looking for Todd in the Connecticut case. The car was supposed to be a tan Dodge with tinted windows, North Carolina tag number IB something 6648. I couldn't believe it. Pete had the plate sitting in his drawer the whole time. That wasn't kosher. We should have found Todd and the car weeks ago. Maybe even before any of this happened.

"I left the office with another detective, Al German. We started driving through the Forties Houses' parking lot. All of a sudden I see a dirty yellow car with tinted windows parked near the corner of 109th Ave. and 160th Street. Al and I look closer and see an Alabama plate on the car, IBC 6448. Pete had the wrong state, but he was only a number or two off. This is it. Fuck the polygraph, Marty Howell is telling the truth. I radioed back to the squad. This is at about 3:30 in the morning. 'Don't let that kid go.

He's right on the money.' We waited until somebody showed up to sit on the car and then rushed back to the precinct. Richie and I were flying now. I went in and talked to Marty Howell. The shotgun thing still bothered me. I ask him, 'Tell me about the shotgun. Did they tell you that or did you hear it on the radio?' And the kid said, 'No. I heard that shotgun on the radio.' I could have kissed the kid. We sat around waiting for dawn, ready to give Roger Phillips the wake-up call of his life."

6

"WE GOT TO DO THIS FOR THE BIG MAN."

Darius Newby was stretched out on a beige, crushed velour couch, deep in the sleep of innocence. A round-faced kid, who did not yet shave, Newby spoke in a low, rumbling voice. Not that Newby was given much to sentences, even in the waking hours. He probably said more in his sleep.

By the morning of March 2, 1988, Darry had been selling crack out of Roger Philips's apartment in the Forties Houses for six months. He was never more than a good shout away from apartment No. 7E at 109-10 160th Street. In the vernacular of the street, Darry was a drone, a pissant worker. He roamed the Forties project, circulating through the brick shoeboxes with a plastic bag of crack vials in his coat pocket.

He worked twelve hours a day, seven days a week, hawking crack. He retreated to apt. 7E—called The Clubhouse—each night and turned over the day's take to his boss, Todd Scott. Darry knew enough not to steal or skim. Another worker, Omar Little, seventeen, had tried to short Todd $20 once. Darry had watched

Todd plug a curling iron into a wall socket. Then he had seen Todd hold the iron against Omar's skin, severely burning his friend on the neck, both hands, and wrists. As Omar screamed, Todd had yelled, "I should shoot you like I did Princess, but I ain't gonna shoot you."

Still sixteen, Darry held no legal job and dated no woman. Although he wore a watch on his right wrist, Darry knew just two periods of time, dark and light. Most of his $800-a-week salary went right back to his employer, Todd Scott. He was living in the vial.

Darry had quit school in the fall of 1985, the same day he scored his first crack vial. He had spent every subsequent day in a crack stupor, smoking as many as thirty crack vials a day. When he couldn't get crack, Darry smoked pot and drank himself dizzy. It did not matter to Darry that crack had robbed him of all those attributes that constitute a healthy young man. With his thought process stunted and his speech muddled, Darry knew only the emotions of a dealer. He thought scoring drugs exciting and a crack rock pretty. He began each day pining for the taste and smell of the drug. Darry Newby was, above all else, a first-generation crackhead.

So Darry did not hear the first knock at the door to apt. 7E. He mistook the second, sharper knock at 7:30 A.M. for the throbbing in his ruined head. But then the knocking grew so loud as to startle Newby to semi-consciousness. He had gotten up and opened the unlocked door, coming face to face with the members of Homicide Team C.

"Is Roger Phillips here?" Eddie Granshaw asked.

"He be sleepin'."

"Get him."

Newby trudged off toward a back bedroom and then returned to the couch, drifting off to sleep in a room full of homicide detectives. Phillips appeared a moment later.

"Is your nephew here?" Richie asked. He was looking past Roger down the apartment hallway.

"Nopes. But I know you gots to see for yourself."

The detectives had rushed in at the invitation and searched the rest of the apartment. Granshaw had seen a body under a sheet in the back bedroom. The detective had pulled back the sheet, revealing a teenaged face. Granshaw turned to Sica and shook his head.

"I know this guy from the street. This is Kevin Curry." Eddie covered the sleeping crackhead with the sheet.

The cops were here on their own. Dunbar had not yet given them permission to question Roger Phillips again. The cops believed in Howell enough to risk trouble. Roger was their only shot at corroboration, so they were being delicate.

"Would you come back to the station with us?"

"Okay."

Richie and Eddie led Roger into the squad room through a back door, secreting him in the anti-crime office. Richie started out gentle, maybe too gentle. Eddie stood back, listening. It was not Granshaw's custom to play bad cop, but Richie was being too tame. Roger had gone right back into his shell, sobbing. He would only admit that his nineteen-year-old nephew, Todd Scott, beat him up on occasion. Granshaw slapped a locker with an open hand.

"This fucking guy, he's your nephew. He's supposed to respect you. And you're letting him slap the shit out of you? He hits you in front of people and disrespects you. He throws you out of your own apartment. What are you, some kind of asshole?"

It hadn't taken much more than that. Talk might free him of Todd Scott, Roger reasoned. Some years ago he had testified against his cousin in an assault case. The cousin had gone to jail. That had been easy. No one in the projects had minded. Roger rubbed his red hair and pulled at his short beard. He was twenty-four and an alcoholic. He had been fired from his last job. All he had in life was the apartment. Shooting a cop had been wrong. Kicking a man out of his own apartment was wrong, too.

"Can you protect me from him?" Roger wanted to know.

"Of course," Richie said. He wasn't lying.

Roger started talking. He went through the story one time telling it in a haphazard, disjointed manner. Then he took a pen to a white legal pad and started to write. The twenty-four-year-old man wrote in the small, looping hand of a frightened child.

"On February 25, 1988, about 8:30 P.M., I was in my apartment with my friends Kevin and Darries. My nephew Todd came in the house with his friend Phil. We had some beers and about an hour later two of my nephew friends come in and me and my friends went into the living room. My nephew Todd stay in the kitchen with his friends. They were talking about some business they had to take care of. I heard them say they were going to hurt a cop that was watching somebody. Then heard them say to my nephew, you have to do it. I saw Todd flick his eyebrows. I heard Todd say, Let's go, I have no time to waste. Then Todd and his friend left banging on the elevator as they went down.

"At about 3:30 to 4:00 A.M. Todd came back by hisself and say I motherfuckin' bad and know one can stop me. I say to him you a got damn fool. He said mine your fucking business an push me and then I went to my room. The next morning I went to the kitchen. I found straiws (2) on the kitchen table. One was half the size of the other. Roger Phillips."

Eddie Granshaw's notes.

"Richie stayed with Roger in the precinct. He went in and broke the news to Dunbar—Roger was giving it up. I went back to Roger's apartment with Al German and two sergeants to get the other two idiots. We got there at about 8:45 A.M. Darry was up by now. He opens the door and says, 'How you doing?' Like we're old friends. We go in and wake up Curry. We get them both back to the precinct at about 9:30. Richie puts Newby in a room in the Community Relations office with Al German. The sergeant and I go in a room with Curry. The sergeant, Phil Panzarella, has arrested Curry before on a robbery charge. After about five minutes of nothing, Phillie wants to stomp the kid. But Phillie gets like that. He's a warrior. I think he's shot maybe ten guys on the job, definitely killed five. All good shootings. German comes out of the room with Darry and says, 'He ain't saying nothing.'

"Now I know Curry. He's a wise-ass. He's thinks he's tough. So I tell him, 'You're in the soup, kid. This fucking Todd is taking you down. Roger, that pussy, he let the guy run his life. You're afraid of Todd, too. I think you're both chickenshit. You make me sick.' All of a sudden, Curry jumps out of the chair and says, 'I'll kick Todd's ass. I ain't afraid of nobody.' So then he gives it up. He says, 'Scott, Todd, and Marshal were talking about knocking off a cop down on Liverpool somewhere. They are talking about getting big money, in the thousands, eight or eighty it was. Todd mentions something about shooting him five or six times. Marshal is saying we are going to get him, and at one point, Todd is elected to do it because he is the maniac of the bunch. They stayed for a while and then they left. About two hours later, Todd comes back and he says, 'It's done, there won't be no testifying done now.' Roger starts calling Todd a fool and Todd slaps him. So there's one. Kevin is good.

"The other guy, Darry, is like brain-dead, a lump. We go in and tell him Kevin has given the thing up. Then finally, he starts to talk. Actually the kid could write. That surprised us all."

"I Darry, Todd, Marshal, Scott, Roger, Kevin, we was sitting in Roger's apartment. Me, Kevin, Roger was sitting in the living room. And Scott, Todd, and Marshal was sitting at the kitchen table and Todd was talking about killing the cop and Marshal and Scott agreed and then Dave came about 2:30 and told Todd, Marshal, and Scott to come on and they all walked out together. Then me, Kevin, and Roger was talking and saying that they crazy, they going to jail. And then we went to sleep. And I woke up about 10 A.M. and I went to use the phone on 109-160 St. I called my brother and we was talking and then Scott walked up to me and said, 'We killed the cop, I'm leaving,' and then I finish the conversation with my brother. I went up to Roger's house and I told him I saw Scott and I said what Scott said. Then Scott came back on Monday and collected the cracks money and Roger asked Scott how they did it. He said they pulled behind the car and they shot the cop. And then he said he was going to Marshal house. He came back yesterday and we went upstairs and was just talking and getting high. Darry Newby."

Sica and Granshaw still had a couple of major problems. No one had, as of yet, put the informant Marty Howell in the apartment. Howell had an awful lot of good information for a guy that hadn't been put in the room. Granshaw went back at Curry with a photograph of Howell.

"Do you know this guy?"

"Yeah," Curry said. "That's Mortimer. He was there, too. I forgot him. We calls him 'Shah.' "

Darry Newby was questioned again. By now, the crackhead's life was coming back to him. He made a second statement, which was typed by someone else and then signed by Newby.

"In November I had a conversation with my cousin Philip Copeland. I asked my cousin what had happened to Princess. My cousin told me that Todd Scott and him shot her and dumped the body on the side of the highway in Connecticut.

"In an earlier statement, I told the police about portions of a conversation I heard between Philip Copeland, Todd Scott, and Scott Cobb that I heard on Thursday night in Roger's apartment. A few days before this, Kevin Curry, Scott Cobb, Shah, and me and maybe some other people were by a pay phone on 109th Avenue and 160th Street. Todd walked up to us and said, 'Do you want to go with me to kill a cop?' We told him 'no' and then he began to curse us. Scott Cobb than asked Todd Scott, 'Where is the cop at?' Todd then said, 'I'll show you,' and the two drove away in Scott Cobb's yellow car."

The other difficulty centered on the mysterious "Dave." Only
Darry had reported seeing "Dave" in Roger's apartment. Richie
Sica had been given a picture of David McClary by the cops from
the 75th Precinct. None of the narcotics guys seemed to know any
Dave. Richie walked into the room with Roger and showed him
the photograph. He was fishing.

"That's Dave," Roger said. "He the new guy. He was at the
door, but he wasn't in the meeting."

By high noon, the detectives had their most wanted list. Marshal Copeland was already in jail on a bench warrant. Todd Scott
and Scott Cobb were loose in the neighborhood, probably not too
far from the Forties Houses. No one had any idea as to the
whereabouts of David McClary.

Richie and Eddie, having worked twenty-four hours straight,
were sent home, ordered to return at 10 P.M. the same night.

The remaining detectives, now hot to the scent, spent the rest
of the day interviewing relatives and girlfriends of the suspects.

With the suspects identified, Sica and Granshaw had drawn
closer, centering their own investigation on Todd Scott. They
began their evening tour raiding the homes of Scott's girlfriends.
Todd managed to keep one hour ahead of them. The detectives
assigned to the Queens Homicide Task Force concentrated on
Scott Cobb and McClary.

The getaway car had been impounded and crime-scene detectives had dusted it for fingerprints. The owner of the car was a
twenty-two-year-old race track groom named Clifford Manning.
Almost immediately after moving to New York in the summer of
1987, Manning quit fast horses for an even faster high. The crackhead met Marshal in December, trading him rides for crack. At
one point, Manning had been introduced to one of Marshal's
associates, a man known only to him as Todd. The two men had
borrowed Manning's car in January, never returning it. When
Manning asked for the car back, Todd beat him with his fists.

Knowing that he was up against dangerous guys, Manning went back to his job as a Brooklyn and Queens handyman. He happened across Marshal and Todd two days after Byrne's murder outside a crack house on the corner of 155th Street and 107th Avenue. When Manning asked for his car back, Todd told him, "I told you I wasn't giving you your motherfucking car back. Now get the fuck out of my face before I kill you like I killed that blue-eyed cop." At this point, Marshal grabbed Scott by the arm and said, "Forget about him, let's go."

The voice of Todd Scott.

"I stayed out all day Wednesday. I had seen Phil the day before. He asked me why the police were looking for me. I said, 'I don't know.' Then we laughed. Phil called me on Thursday at the safehouse. Phil had been arrested. He was calling from the precinct. He said the cops were looking for me. Phil says, 'If they catch you, just tell the truth.' That was a good one."

Lillian Cobb had been expecting the police. She was a large, decent woman who had spent most of her life toiling as a domestic. Poverty had not stolen her perception of right and wrong. On March 6, 1979, at the age of fifteen, her son Scott had beaten and robbed an eighty-two-year-old Hungarian immigrant, Joe Kardy. Kardy had come out of his house to buy a newspaper. Scott, working with a girlfriend, Leslie McCullough, had cut the man with a knife, making off with fifty cents. Kardy, who had come to New York from Hungary in 1905, would later remember, "It made me fearful about going out." Lillian Cobb had been deeply hurt, thinking herself a failure. But then a rage had come to her. Upon his release from family court, she had beaten the boy unmercifully. She had been embarrassed by the crime, screaming over and over again, "Fifty cents? You throw your life away for fifty cents?" Sentenced to one to three years in prison, Cobb had been arrested a second time on November 19, 1982, for possession of a knife. He pled to disorderly conduct. He had two other arrests for drug possession in 1983 and 1984.

At about the time of his last arrest, Scott had met a girl, Maria Hutcherson. For a time, Maria had been able to cool Scott's fury. She'd even borne Scott a son, Anthony, in 1986. Scott's younger sister was found murdered the same year. By then crack had come, and Scott had abandoned his issue to sell crack on the corner of 160th Street. Maria saw him out there every day in front of the grocery, using a corner pay phone as his business office.

At one point Scott had offered to give his mother money. Lillian Cobb turned down the cash and felt better of herself for doing it. She wanted no part of the child's failure. Lillian Cobb still loved her son. But she hated her broad-shouldered offspring for his weakness of character.

So when the police came to her apartment, 3B at 106-05 159th Street in the Forties Houses, Mrs. Cobb invited them in. When the cops asked for a photograph of her son, Lillian produced the family photo album, giving them the clearest photo she could find. Having watched the police funeral on television, Lillian would later recall, cooperation came easy.

Lillian Cobb's oral statement to police was brief and damaging.

"Scott came home early Friday morning and said that he wanted to talk to me. I went in the room and he was sitting by the window drinking a beer. He wasn't acting like himself. He said, 'Someone did something to someone.' He then said someone shot someone in the head and it was a cop. He was in the car by himself. Scott said he did not shoot, but he was there . . . Does it really matter?"

The detectives discovered Maria Hutcherson to be equally agreeable. Scott had visited her shortly after the shooting and announced, "I was in the wrong time at the wrong place. Todd shot a cop." Hutcherson had seen Scott several times since then, as recently as that morning. She reported that he kept money in a safe in his mother's apartment and loved his son dearly.

"I ask Scott for money to buy new baby shoes this morning," Hutcherson, twenty-four said. "He had money in his hand. But Scott say he got to give Todd the money 'cause it's not his. It's that there, you know, cracks money. I don't know what good the cracks money is if it can't buy a baby no shoes."

Later Maria allowed detectives to record her conversation with Scott's mother. When Maria asked Lillian what Scott had told her, Lillian told the same story she had told police. By then the police even liked Lillian Cobb. She did not know how to lie.

Kenneth Haynes, a patrolman assigned to the Queens Public Morals Division, was driving along South Road at about 10:30 P.M. when a streetwalker approached his unmarked car. The girl was filthy, her clothes and hair wretched and ruined.

"Let me in," said the prostitute. She was twenty-two, with natty hair and disheveled clothes. To call the girl a hooker, Hayes later thought, would be to say something kind. Mostly the girl tackled her dates. The girl was a crack whore. Haynes had thought at first that the woman had mistaken him for a john. He had not been in the mood to make a soliciting arrest with a cop dead and his killers still on the loose.

"Do you know who I am?" he asked.

"You a cop. Now let me in."

The woman was shaking. She had begun talking even as Hayes drove off the block. "I saw who shot the cop," she said. "I was standing on 107 Ave. and I saw this grayish car come by me with three guys inside. I seen them do it."

The girl's name was Rachel Moore. On the streets people called her Black Rachel. The mother of two children, Moore worked the streets each night turning tricks. Prices varied, but Moore never got more than $20 for any one date. Mostly she had sex with men in their cars. She smoked crack between dates.

Moore had lived with her mother in South Jamaica for the last sixteen years. She was driven back to the 103rd Precinct and shown an array of photographs. As the stunned detectives looked on, Moore stopped at picture #8186 in photo album No. 10.

"That's him," Moore said. "That's Todd Scott. I saw him shoot the cop and then get into the car at the corner of Inwood."

"How can you be sure?"

"Man, I went to school with him."

"And the car?"

"I been in the car before."

The streetwalker went on to tell Detective Peter Fiorillo that she had jumped under a car at the first sound of gunfire.

Having said this much, Moore started to shake and cry uncontrollably. Most of the emotion had to do with the woman's fear. But her body also ached for crack. She was smoking up to twenty vials a day at this point, turning ten tricks a night. The interview had to be terminated. Rachel Moore, the only known witness to the murder of Police Officer Edward Byrne, than left the station house, escaping back into the night, and the vial.

By now, Mr. Law's scared friend Debbie had turned up. Detectives found her walking aimlessly through the street and brought her back to the precinct. The girl, Debra Scott, twenty-five, rendered an oral statement, being too nervous to set anything to paper herself.

"I went to my girlfriend Pooh's house between 9 and 10 P.M. on the night of February 25. I stayed in front with Pooh. Her sister Muka came down. We hung around outside. Kevin Curry came by, we were just standing around, and some kids were playing.

"Later we went up to Muka's apartment. About 11 P.M. Scott Cobb came around and we went back down. Roger, Kevin, and Scott started fighting. They stopped, Kevin and Roger left. Todd Scott was there then and he wanted Pooh to stand in the box.

"Scott Cobb said he was going to get something to eat. I asked him to get me something. He said, 'Let's get in the car and go to

White Castle (3 of us).' We came back and parked by the seven-story building on 160th St.

"Scott Cobb said, 'I'm going to kill this cop.' He also threatened me that he would splatter my brains if I told. He also said, 'There a cop on 107. He's going to die tonight.' He also said he was ordered to do this. But he did not say by who. At about two in the morning we drove by, Friday, February 26, 1988, the three of us drove past the cop on 107. He was sitting in the K-9 car reading a newspaper and the light in it was on. Cobb said as we drove past the cop, 'I have orders to kill this cop.' Scott Cobb stated that Tawana—that's Pooh's real name—should go in her house and get the grenade that was there so that he could blow up the car with the police officer. At that time Tawana said that she could not get in her house to get it. I told Tawana she was crazy and ask, 'What are you doing with a grenade?' I also said that if Tawana was getting the grenade I was getting out of the car because I wasn't going to get blown up. We then returned to the 40's project.

"Me and Tawana went to the seven-story building and up to apartment 7E. Tawana was looking for Todd Scott. Darry was with us at this time. I was standing at the elevator holding the door open. All of a sudden at 3:45 A.M. Todd Scott came running up the stairs and said, 'Boop. Boop. Boop. Boop. Four to the head.' I gasped, stepped back into the elevator with Tawana. Then we heard a lot of sirens. We went to the street. We walked over to 107 and saw all the police cars. I wanted to get closer but Tawana didn't. We walked until we got to Foch Blvd. We walked along Foch and crossed the Van Wyck Expressway. When we got to 134th Street, we turned down toward Rockaway Blvd. We stayed at a friend of Tawana's house with a guy named Sam. This was about 4:30 or 5 in the morning when we arrived. In the morning, Sam said, 'You girls got a problem, you know about the cop shooting.' He heard the radio and stood in the room and said, 'That's what's wrong with you girls. You knew about the cop shooting.' We left Sam's house. I returned on Monday, February

29, and told Sam what happened. I then left and walked the streets until you guys picked me up."

By Thursday morning, March 3, the trappers had their snare in place. Detective Henry Hassell, an eighteen-year veteran of the department, had led a team to Lillian Cobb's door at 6:30 A.M. Mrs. Cobb had let Hassell and Ronnie Waddell into her apartment. The cops had a search warrant allowing them to remove Cobb's safe. Once the empty safe was removed, Hassell asked Lillian for permission to place a trapping device on her phone. The trap, sometimes called a Pen register, would be used to isolate and identify the origin of incoming calls. Lillian agreed to this, signing a consent form.

Detectives from the department's Tactical Assistance Response Unit arrived thirty minutes later. One cop hooked a self-starting tape machine to the bedroom phone. The machine was activated each time the phone was lifted and shut off each time the receiver replaced. With the trap and tape recorder in place by 8 A.M., and guarded by police officer William Synenko, the cops sat back, waiting. With a member of their own family murdered, the cops were confident that Scott Cobb's affection for his own mother would lead to his apprehension.

The voice of Todd Scott.

"That day, Thursday, I called the 103 about two in the morning. I asked to speak to Lt. Dunbar. He wasn't in, though. I talked to this guy John Williams. I said, 'Why you cops looking for me? I didn't kill no cop. That shit was stupid.' The guy wanted me to come in. I said, 'I'm afraid you guys would hurt me.' I said I ain't coming in without my grandmother, Rita Phillips. I told him meet me over her house. Then I hung up. But I stayed put.

"Scott came over at nine in the morning. He said the police had come to his house and he was scared. They wanted to question him. So I called the project pay phone on 107th Street and 160th Avenue and asked for Shareema. We talked for a while. All my girls was wondering about me. On Sunday I had sent my uncle over to see my girl Pooh, Tawana Blakney. She 17 and nice. I had him tell her, 'I has to go away for a while but I still love her. If I send for you, you got to be blindfolded. I had called my girl Tonise, too. She 18 and pregnant with my baby. Tonise ain't so pretty no more.

"Anyway, my girl Shareema says she wants to come over. The cops had come to see her the day before and ask her did she know I shot a cop. The housing was doing work in her apartment and she wanted to come over. She took a cab and come over with her sister Kisha about 10:30. These the Robinson girls here. Shareema talk about being shown a photo, but I didn't say nothing. She cooked spaghetti with meat sauce around noon and started doing some cleaning. We was watching soaps and a Run-D.M.C. movie. Kisha went out and come back with some herb. I was laying with Shareema. Kisha went back out to get some rolling papers. Scott came over and then he go out to buy some sneakers. He come back and say he spoke to his mother and they looking for us. I laid down with Shareema again. I really likes this Shareema."

The telephone in the bedroom of the Cobb residence rang at 2:30 P.M. Lillian Cobb was standing in the kitchen with Police Officer Synenko and his partner from the 109th Squad, Detective John Kiselewsky. The ringing had startled them. Lillian pointed to the phone and indicated she wanted to pick it up. The cops nodded.

"It's him," Lillian said, covering the mouthpiece with her hand. And then she went back to the phone. In the bedroom, a tape machine was spinning. Kiselewsky picked up his portable radio and walked into the living room, calling for Sergeant Philip Panzarella back at the 103rd Squad.

"We got him on the line now," Kiselewsky reported.

Panzarella went back into an office where the TARU detectives were working. He told a detective that Scott Cobb was on the phone. A moment later the technician came back. "He's calling from 93-08 209th Street over in Bellrose. The phone is in the basement apartment. It's registered to a Paris Williams."

Paris Williams, Panzarella thought, the registered owner of the green Suzuki jeep. Also Pappy's girlfriend. Panzarella strode over to Richie and Eddie Granshaw, grabbing them by the shoulders. Panzarella was not the type of guy to wait around for the arrival of the department's glory boys, the Emergency Service Unit.

"Grab your vests, let's go," Panzarella said. "I think we got something good."

They had just turned out of the precinct when a second call was placed to the Cobb residence. Again Lillian Cobb picked up the phone, turning to the cops and mouthing the words, "It's him again." The tape machine in the bedroom was rolling again.

Scott was calling to give her the number where Todd could get hold of him—"At the corner of 165th Street and Jamaica. Ma, get a pen real quick"—but his mother had a surprise for him.

LILLIAN COBB: Do you know I got detectives sitting in my house?

SCOTT COBB: Yeah?

LC: Yes.

SC: Saying what?

LC: Saying that they want to talk to you, Scott. This is very serious.

SC: Oh—I'm waiting, waiting for a lawyer first before I go in.

LC: Yeah, but you should go before it makes it hard on you and hard on me, because they sittin' here. Anthony is here and Marie's here. They were around there, scared the hell out of Marie yesterday.

SC: Anthony too? Marie too?

LC: Yeah.

SC: Tell 'em I go over to a lawyer. I don't need no reason.

LC: What?

SC: I, (stuttering), I'm waiting for the good lawyer to come.

LC: Not the point—it, it—just like the detective just told me just now, he said them cops is out there in the street and they got your picture and some of them is goin' to shoot the minute they see you, Scott. That don't make no kinda sense.

They talked for a few more minutes, Lillian and then Marie, pleading with Cobb to come home. Cobb kept going on about the lawyer—"Pappy send me a lawyer"—asked again for Todd to call him, and hung up.

Panzarella had received a message on his portable radio redirecting him to the corner pay phone outside the Coliseum Mall on Jamaica Avenue. By now, every news organization in the city was monitoring the police frequency. By the time the sergeant and his detectives rolled up to the mall five minutes later, the place was covered with cops. Granshaw saw a reporter from WNBC News, John Miller, standing near the pay phone Cobb had used to call home. Scott Cobb had left, missing his chance to make "Live at Five."

After a ten-minute search, the detectives left the mall and resumed their journey to Paris Williams's apartment on 209th Street. The cops were on the block by 4:00 P.M., passing the house twice. The block was filled with detached one- and two-family homes. The suspect's house was a white, two-story wooden frame dwelling containing three apartments. The building included floor-through apartments on the first and second floors and a basement apartment. Cobb had used a phone registered to the basement apartment.

There was a small driveway on the side of the house and a backyard. There were too many windows and doors for three cops. Panzarella radioed back to the squad, requesting a backup team. As the cops watched the house from a half-block away, two detectives from the Queens Robbery Squad, Nick Rodelli and Joe Cicalone, pulled up. One of them said, "The last call just came in from this house."

They climbed into the sergeant's car, four cops listening to Panzarella's instructions on how to best surveil the block. The five cops sat in the car for about fifteen minutes, their nerves raw, their senses keen. Panzarella was not very good at waiting.

"Fuck it," the sergeant decided. "Let's just hit the fucking house."

In that same instant, Eddie Granshaw had looked toward the white house. Scott Cobb was standing in the driveway, wearing a blue snorkel jacket, pulling up the hood.

"There he is," Granshaw screamed. "It's fucking him."

Panzarella started to yell into his portable radio, calling for the troops, "Panzarella, 1085. Forthwith."

Steve Weiner, riding with three other detectives, demanded, "Philly, what's the address? What's the correct address?"

"Ninety-three, oh-eight, Two hundred and ninth."

All across Queens, homicide detectives were slapping red lights onto their car roofs and flicking on sirens.

The case detective makes an arrest.

"We all jumped out. By the time me and Eddie got around to the other side of the car, they already had him on the ground. Then Panzarella and Rodelli had him on top of the car. And then I turned and saw Todd peeking out the side door. I yelled, 'There he is.' Panzarella turned and saw him, too. He yells, 'Get the motherfucker.' We ran to the door. Me, Granshaw, and Rodelli. I hit it first and bounced right off. The ground was slippery. I know it sounds funny, but we were all kind of laughing. So now Rodelli hits the door and drops. Granshaw hits it again and the door ain't going. So now Rodelli and Granshaw lock arms and they're kicking at the door. Eddie hurts his ankle. And I remember saying to Eddie, 'Did you try the doorknob?' And he just looked at me like he was upset. So I figured this is no time to fuck around. Rodelli smashed his hand through the window and tried to open the lock. But it was a dead bolt, the kind you need a key for. I went and checked the back windows just to make sure the guy didn't jump out. I went back out front and then the door came crashing down, all the glass all over. And then we went down into the basement. We had one fucking flashlight, a little baby thing. So we get down there, and our eyes are still adjusting. We all have our guns out. Can't see a fucking thing. I take the front with Eddie and the others go in the back. There are two other guys there now, too, Al Sabo and Steve Weiner. And then I hear a dog barking. Eddie opens a bathroom door and yells, 'Pit bull! We got a pit bull.' And then he slams the door. And I'm saying 'Oh, fuck.' I got my gun out and everything, but you can't see shit, because my eyes are still going from brightness to darkness. I did the front closet and I did the bedroom. I turned the light on in the bedroom. Eddie had the next room over. Eddie comes into the bedroom and says, 'Did you do the bedroom closet?' I said, 'No.' We go to open the closet door and there's a dresser there in the way. Eddie pushed the dresser aside. He's holding the door open and I look in. I see what I think is a pile of clothes on the right. And I look again and I says, 'Holy fuck.' Todd is right there staring at me. As I back out with a flinch, I yell, 'It's him. It's him.' And then I'm screaming, I mean the guy could have just taken my head off, 'Come on out of there, motherfucker.' He wouldn't come out. I leaned in to get him and looked to my left. I see two sets of eyes. Now I'm fucking spooked. I jumped back and yelled, 'There's two more in there.' And Eddie and I were screaming, 'Get the fuck out of there. We'll fucking kill you. Get the fuck out.' Todd isn't moving. He could have a gun. I don't know. I'm listening for any metal sound now. I reached into the closet and dragged him out, throwing him on the floor with Eddie. Now Rodelli is there, Weiner has cuffs and we get a cuff on him. The other guys grabbed the two girls, the Robinson sisters. And now everyone is fucking going bullshit.

"Everybody was screaming, 'You cocksucker. Why'd you do it? Why'd you kill a cop?' We put one cuff on him, and all I saw was fucking guns all over the place. And I said, 'Put those guns away.'

So he's cuffed now. Guys are screaming, 'Where's the gun? Where's the gun? Why did you do it? Why did you do it?' Now we pick him up. And everybody was, like, furious. I had never known rage like this. I was just standing there, screaming."

Eddie Granshaw's last arrest.

"Richie and I took the guy out of the closet. We bring him up the stairs and one guy's choking him, one guy's got him by the balls, and one guy's ripping his arms off. We start bringing him up the stairs and Richie yells, 'No, bring him back down.' We brought him down and I started yelling, 'Let's kill him. Let's kill him.' I picked him up by the neck and lifted him right through one of those false ceilings. I didn't know I was that strong. I was yelling, 'Where's the gun, motherfucker?' and he's saying, 'I don't know. You can kill me, but I don't know where no gun is.' And then I got scared. I was afraid someone would actually try and kill the guy. I wasn't scared for him so much. I was just afraid somebody was going to let a round go and hit me. But we didn't let up. I had never acted like this before in my career. I kept screaming, 'You cop-killing son of a bitch, you're going to tell us where the gun is.' That was the adrenaline talking. And he's saying, 'I don't know nothing about the gun. I didn't kill no cop.'

"He was wearing a pair of dungarees and a Chicago Bears football jersey. William Perry's number, 72. He was barefoot, too. We led him out and he walked right over the glass. Son of a bitch, didn't even cut himself. We led him out and put him in Panzarella's car. Phillie had never come into the house, which was a good thing. I'm sure Phillie would have shot somebody. We drove away. I sat in the back between Todd and Cobb. Richie was in the front passenger seat. Phillie was driving. We were supposed to go to the 113. But we got a call directing us to the 105. Our precinct was too hot with reporters. No one said a word in the car. It was eerie. When Richie and I got back to the station, we put the guys in separate rooms. Then we went into the squad dorm room. It

was a little room, we were just by ourselves. We were taking our
vests off and it was pretty emotional. I guess we both just couldn't
believe that we got these guys. I grabbed Richie and we were
hugging and crying and I kept saying, 'We got these fucking guys.
We fucking got them.' We were standing there hugging, and this
was funny, someone opened the door, saw us, and said, 'Sorry, I'm
sorry,' and backed right out. I guess we stayed in there for twenty
minutes, hugging and crying."

The voice of Todd Scott.

"I was getting dressed to go back out. Scott said he was going
to the store for some socks to go with his new sneakers. After that
I heard a lot of yelling. I heard a loud bang upstairs. We were all
in the basement. A lot of detectives came in and starting beating
on me. They had me on the ground and handcuffed me. They were
all kicking me and one of them was hitting me in the knee with
a hammer. The other ones were pulling my testicles. They kept
asking me where the gun is and why did you do it. 'Did what? Did
what?' They kept hitting me. One guy, Richie, was holding me and
hitting me in my face and stomach. So as we were going to the car
the man hit me in the right eye with a walkie-talkie. I was bleeding, but no stitches."

They went right for Cobb. Richie and Eddie entered the room, and
a detective who had been baby-sitting the suspect left, closing the
door. Cobb was about five-foot-eight, Richie saw, with a thick
neck and yellowish black skin. He had a weak beard and short-
cropped hair. Mostly, Richie decided, Cobb looked soft and
scared.

"Listen, the bullshit is over. We know what happened, you
know what happened. I want you to tell me."

"Nah, I don't know nothin'. I don't know about no cop. I know
Todd was running scared cause of that Connecticut shit."

"Nah, you ain't telling me what I want to hear."

"You know, I got a baby."

Eddie stepped forward into the unfamiliar role of bad cop.

"Listen, asshole, you ain't gonna see your kid."

They left the room. Cobb was just sitting there, thinking. A lieutenant, Stanley Carpenter, sent two veteran detectives into the room, Jerry Shevlin and James Curran.

"If I were there," Cobb asked Shevlin, "and I didn't do the shooting, would I be just as guilty?

"I don't know."

"Ah, fuck it, I'm going to tell what happened."

And then Scott Cobb started talking to Curran and Shevlin. At one point, Shevlin poked his head out, seeing Richie and Eddie.

"He's giving it up," Shevlin said.

A captain who looked after Pete Pistone sent him into the room to sit in on the interview. Granshaw, who was never particularly fond of Shevlin was heard to say, "I could kiss Jerry Shevlin."

Eddie and Richie walked into the room with Todd Scott. The barefoot prisoner was handcuffed, sitting in a chair. It was the prisoner who spoke first.

"I ain't no Perry Bellamy," Todd Scott told the detectives.

An anonymous police witness.

"There were about 100 detectives in the squad room. I looked in and Todd was sitting on the edge of his chair. He was saying, 'I don't know nothing. I don't know shit.' The guy was barefoot. And everybody is jumping on his feet. Two detectives were in there with a lieutenant. They were choking him. The lieutenant had him on top of the couch. They were bouncing Todd off the walls. One of the bosses was afraid that the television and radio people outside could overhear what was happening. So one of the guys turned the radio way up and shut the blinds. Then Todd says,

'I want a lawyer.' One of our guys tells him, 'Let me tell you something. There ain't no lawyers in this one. You ain't talking to no lawyer, you ain't talking to nobody. And if you think this was bad, every motherfucker out there is going to come in here and take a piece of your fucking ass. You got 30 minutes.' Those detectives left. Another guy goes in, Al Sabo. I hear Sabo saying he's the guy that kept the cops from hitting Todd with the hammer back at the house. Todd tells him, 'I'll tell you what you want to know. Just don't let those other guys back in here'."

As Sabo sat talking to Todd Scott, Richie reentered the room, reading the suspect his rights. In turn, in an admission that he had indeed been read his rights, Todd signed a Miranda card D203172. Still, Todd kept insisting that he had nothing to do with the killing. Sabo attempted to soothe Todd, telling him, "If you have something to say, or if you know anything about this, now would be the time to say it." Todd asked to have his cuffs removed and Sabo complied. Richie left the two of them alone.

"Have you ever been in trouble before?" Sabo asked.

"Yes," Todd said. "But it was a long time ago and it has all been taken care of."

Scott was lying. He still had three open cases. Had he told the detectives this, they would have been precluded from interrogating him any further without the presence of an attorney. It was his biggest mistake this side of getting into the battered yellow Dodge.

As Sabo softened Todd Scott to the task of confession, Scott Cobb sat with Curran and Pistone, stuttering through an oral confession. The detectives asked Cobb to scratch out a written confession and he complied.

The three-page written confession, which was started at 7:30 P.M., took ninety minutes to write. The confession made Cobb's position clear. He would maintain throughout the rest of the case that he had no prior knowledge of the killing and was merely the driver.

*

By this time, Al Sabo was there, taking an oral confession from Todd. Sabo took shorthand notes in a reporter's notebook as Todd talked. Todd had only agreed to talk after being told that the detectives had impounded the battered yellow Dodge and that they knew about the meeting in Roger's apartment. Todd went through the story once with Sabo. Then he turned to Sabo and said, "Listen, I know I have to go to jail. But can we do something to see if I could pick the jail I go to?"

"It isn't up to me to make any deals," Sabo said. "Would you be willing to talk to the case detective now?"

Richie reentered the room, reading Todd his rights again. Todd repeated the story a second time, insisting that he had not killed the cop.

"David did it," Todd had said. "This guy Dave."

At that point Richie reached into his pocket and produced his photograph of David McClary. Todd looked at the photo and said, "That's him. That's Dave. That's the dude that shot the cop."

Scott refused to write out a confession but dictated a statement to Sabo. He, too, renounced responsibility for the killing, claiming that David McClary had been the triggerman. He signed the statement at 11:45 P.M.

Meanwhile, Steven Weiner had drawn the assignment of going to David McClary's home. He had arrived at the home at 8 P.M. and been met at the door by the suspect's mother, Luis McClary. Weiner had pulled a picture from his pocket as he entered the home. It was the same picture taken by Richard Brew in the 75th Precinct, the only photograph of David McClary in police possession.

"Do you know who this is?" Weiner had asked.

"Yes. That's my son, David."

As the other detectives searched the apartment, Weiner talked in a small, gentle way with the mother. In November, Mrs. McClary's oldest son, Roger McClary, had been arrested for murder. He had shot a crack dealer dead and then rushed home. Luis McClary was a church-going woman; the murder suspect had found no sanctuary in her home.

"Listen," Weiner told her, "I would like to speak to you one-on-one. Is it all right if we go in another room?"

McClary led the detective into a back bedroom. Weiner spoke to the woman for twenty minutes, explaining that her son's name had come up in the investigation of a cop killing and that he was wanted for questioning. He told her the picture in his hand was going to be duplicated by the thousands and put in the hand of every uniformed member of the NYPD.

"What's your impression of the uniformed force?" Weiner had then asked.

"Well, now, they are like, they are all my son's age."

"That's right. Generally, the majority of the uniformed force has under five years' experience. And this photo is going out to them. Because of that inexperience, there is a problem, a good chance that something might happen."

McClary knew exactly what the cop was talking about. She already believed that there was a very good chance her son could be killed in a shootout with police.

"I have been doing this for twenty years," Weiner said. "If your son comes home, you contact me. I will guarantee you that nothing is going to happen to your son."

The move was cheap, and the talk cliché, but Weiner was right. There could be a shootout. And besides, the detective could always use the collar. This had only become the city's biggest police investigation since Son of Sam.

"I'm a deacon in a church," Luis McClary said. "I handed my son Roger over. I did it with one son, I will do it with this son."

Richie Sica was sapped, his face drained, his shirt sweaty. He left Todd Scott and walked out into the squad room. Someone gave him a cigarette. He hadn't really noticed the confusion in the room until now. A lot of the cops were standing around near a desk reading the confession. The detail was a little more than a few of them could bear. At least one cop was sobbing in the bathroom. Others were slamming desks in anger and screaming. A lot of cops, particularly the patrolmen, came up to sneak a peek at the suspects. Most of them said the same thing. "These guys are nothing." A few bragged, "I seen that one, Todd, on the street. I told him to get his ass off my block once." There were those, too, who in the presence of black detectives, had screamed, "Fucking niggers."

The detective's lament.

"Todd had kept saying that it was David that killed the cop. But I kept thinking that it was him and not David. He was using himself as the third party. 'David did this. David did that.' When he got to one point where he said that he saw the hair fly up when David was shooting into the car, all I could think to myself was, 'Why don't I just do him right here?' But then the case was so important. To lose the case because I wanted to beat the cock off this fucking guy. You gotta weigh it at that point. And I was thinking, 'I can't believe I'm sitting here listening to this guy.' Usually I would be looking to fucking break his face. And now I gotta sit here and listen to what he did to a brother officer. Some things ain't right. I went and got him dinner instead, a hamburger, french fries and a Sprite. Everybody wanted to spit in his food. But I wouldn't let them.

"I kept thinking back to when I had him in the closet. I could have shot him then. A lot of guys have told me I should have shot him then. It could have happened that way. He goes for the gun and I shoot him. I'm scared. It's dark. He goes. I know Eddie had the same feelings. And then you know why you can't do it. You do something like that and you're nothing, you're like them. You don't decide not to do it because killing someone will fuck up a case or get you arrested. You don't do it because you're incapable of doing it. They're the bad guys. I'm the good guy. We all have dark sides, but character is varying degrees of darkness. There is no gray area when it comes to murder. You can either pull the trigger or you can't. Pull the trigger and you've lost. But honestly, I still think about when I had my chance to shoot him in the closet. I think about it at some point every day. The thought used to make me feel weak. Now it gives me strength. I know I had the chance to take a life and I'm not one of THEM."

Scott Tulman, the Assistant District Attorney assigned to the case, had arrived at the precinct at approximately 9:00 P.M. An assistant followed him in, carrying a large black case. One of the city's most grizzled crime reporters, Jim Peters of the *Daily News,* had recognized Tulman on the way into the precinct. He knew the meaning both of Tulman's appearance at the precinct and of what was in the black case. A week before, Pappy Mason had stood in a Queens courtroom, and upon his conviction, pointed an imaginary gun at Tulman. Then Pappy had pulled the trigger. The man with the black case had to be a technician.

"Look," Peters had said, pointing. "The mutts are going to make videotaped confessions."

7

"IF WE LOSE ONE,
THEY LOSE ONE."

Scott Tulman was getting out of the confession business. A chunky man of average height, with thick fingers and a full, brown mustache, the Assistant District Attorney had worked in the Queens Homicide Bureau for four years. He had seen more murders during that time than some major American cities and a European country or two. With the advent of videotaped confession, Tulman was, on an average, sitting down with a half-dozen killers a month.

He was a genteel man, a Queens kid, who did not look or sound comfortable on camera. His rapport with suspects, although it sounded clumsy and forced, had a way of disarming people. Sinners talked to the priestly prosecutor. Tulman was known around the office as Father Confessor. There was no slight intended by the nickname. For his part, Tulman even enjoyed his first hundred or so homicide investigations. But, as so often happens with sharp prosecutors, Tulman woke up one day and discovered himself a poorly paid lawyer. Even before arriving at the 105th Precinct on the evening of March 3, 1988, he had made the decision to join the Manhattan firm of Jack Litman and Associates. A tenacious sort, Litman had just won a partial victory for the unspeakable Preppie Killer, Robert Chambers. Like Eddie Granshaw, Edward Byrne was to become Scott Tulman's last hurrah.

After arriving at the precinct, Tulman had read and reread the statements of Todd Scott and Scott Cobb. As the street cops like to say, he knew all the South Jamaica players. The suspects in the Byrne assassination, Tulman could see, were trying to minimize their role in the killing. That was normal. Very few killers would admit, flat out, that they had stabbed or shot someone. There were always mitigating factors.

It fell to the prosecutor to show that Scott Cobb had driven to the scene with full knowledge of what was to transpire. Todd already admitted to being on the scene. Most of the detectives believed Scott to be the trigger man. He certainly needed more on Philip Copeland. And what about David McClary? Did a guy with no police record simply walk up to a cop and shoot him?

During the course of his interrogation, Tulman hoped to get the suspects to admit talking to Marty Howell, planning the murder in Roger's apartment, and speaking to Debra Scott. There was also the matter of Pappy Mason's involvement. Tulman had not yet, nor would he ever, forget the brazen image of Pappy standing in an American court of law, shooting him down with an imaginary gun.

As it would happen, it was also within Tulman's domain as a special investigator to explore allegations of police brutality. Neither Todd nor Cobb, he noted immediately, had any cuts or bruises. Neither man would make a brutality complaint in his presence. They would appear on tape for a jury to see in perfect physical health. And for this, Tulman was grateful. While Tulman was not a police buff, he did not want a scandal, either. Forget beatings. Scott Tulman had every intention of slaying Edward Byrne's killers with the state's sharpest statute, murder in the first degree.

The technician, Enrique Williams, had set up a video camera and tape machine in an interrogation room. Scott Cobb, wearing a navy blue shirt and new blue dungarees, was led to a seat against a green cinder-block wall. James Curran and Pete Pistone, the detectives who had taken Cobb's written confession, were asked to sit in on the taping. Tulman took a seat facing the suspect, his back to the camera. The detectives, both coatless and worn-looking, sat to his immediate left. Tulman, the embodiment of criminal justice, was wearing the traditional blue suit with a paisley tie knotted tight at the collar. He had entered the room at 10:04 P.M. He turned to the camera and announced himself, a red light coming on, a blank one hundred twenty minute video tape rolling.

"Okay," Tulman began, "Now, Mr. Cobb, may I call you Scott?"

"Yes, you could," Scott replied, rubbing his face. He was holding a chain with a golden crucifix in his right hand.

Tulman then read Cobb his rights and asked if he had been mistreated by police. Cobb said he had been treated well and added that the cops had given him food and drink. At that point, Tulman held up the three-page written statement.

"Whose handwriting is it?"

"Mines."

Already, a problem with language. Tulman did not want a jury thinking a detective named Mines had written it for Cobb.

"It's your handwriting?"

"Yes."

"You wrote that out yourself."

"Yes."

Cobb than added that he had initialed every page and denied being forced to write the confession. Cobb spoke in a raspy voice, stuttering from one thought to the next. An asthmatic, he had to be reminded to stop and catch his breath. With the preliminaries out of the way, Tulman asked Cobb to relate his story.

"I ain't known about this till after it happened."

"Okay."

"Then I, I gets information about what happened. I was being a driver that didn't know what part of the crime I was being involved in."

"All right . . ."

"And that's what happened to me before, driving them someplace, people that's involved in a crime."

"Yeah."

"That's what I was given the car for."

Cobb was shrugging his shoulders and spinning the crucifix in his right hand. He sat back and sighed.

"Well," Tulman continued, his voice light. "When did you first get involved with driving them?"

"I had the car, I just started dealing with them for, like, three weeks. I'm a newcomer to them. I was given the car 'cause the Todd, the Todd, was wanted. Todd Scott was, like, wanted for other charges, and Philip Copeland was, too, so they had to stay, like, underground, like, stay hidden out for a while. So I had to be the man to pick up their money. I was, like, like their lieutenant. I was taking care of their drug business for them, while they sat in their houses."

Cobb slapped his thigh and blew out a soiled breath. He rubbed his meaty face with both hands and shuddered. He wanted desperately to make a friend in the prosecutor.

"You have to calm down," Tulman said. "You seem, like, excited. You want to get this . . ."

"Scared, man."

"I understand that."

"Scared."

"Well, you know, it's a serious thing that has happened."

"My life is on the line."

"I understand that. This is an opportunity to tell your story. What happened?"

"We was, like, before this happened, we were hanging out on 109th and 160, me, Roger, Kevin, Todd, and all of us, we were hanging out downstairs drinking beer with the girls. I had this girl,

I was going with her. Todd's girlfriend, Tawana, she got this cousin named Debra. I was talkin' to her a little bit. I was drinking beer a little bit."

Tulman checked a name on a sheet of paper in front of him. Cobb had just put the witness Debra Scott in the middle of the story. Debra had heard Cobb say, "This cop is going to die tonight." Prior knowledge. Judges call this type of thing corroboration. Tulman wanted to know about the meeting.

"Did you go upstairs?" Tulman wondered. "Like to Roger's house?"

"Yeah, yeah, we go up there. Standing outside, we go up there to hang out. We sitting around up there for a while. It was me, Darius, Kevin Curry, and Roger, Todd's uncle. So we were sitting there for a while. We got back outside, so I went and picked up Todd."

Tulman checked off three more names. Cobb was moving people in and out of rooms better than most movie directors. The cop's witnesses, Darry, Kevin Curry, and Roger had all been placed in the right spot at the right time.

"Which car?" Tulman asked, laying another trap. "Now which car is this?"

"In the Chrysler, the car that they say was on the scene of the cop being shot."

"Well, was the car on the scene?"

"The car was not on the scene."

"Okay."

"The car, for all I know, had nothing to do with that, but I find that it does."

"That was the car you were driving?"

"Right, right. That's the car, that is the car that we was driving that shot the cop."

So now Tulman had a getaway car and a driver. He was never sure when this would end, how far Cobb would go. He needed detail on the meeting.

"You were drinking up there?"

"Forty-Five, we were drinking Forty-Five."

"By the way, where were you in the apartment? Where were you sitting?"

"In the kitchen, at the round table. There's a round table in the kitchen. I was sitting by the window. We were sitting around the table drinking."

"Who were you?" Tulman asked. This was a move aimed at getting a head count.

"Me, Kevin, Roger, and Darius. Todd came in out the bedroom, took some beer, and went in the bedroom, and sooner or later his girlfriend knocks, Shareema, the one that was arrested with us today. He goes in the back room with her, so I leads them outside. Meanwhile we're outside. Todd yells out the window, 'Scott, don't forget to come back and get me at 3:00.' "

"Where did you go?"

"We came downstairs and they went with me to the store to get more beer, then I left them. I left them because Roger started arguing with Todd's girlfriend, Tawana, and Todd's girlfriend's sister. And Roger smacked Todd's girlfriend's sister. Roger was drunk from drinking all the beer, so I told him to go back upstairs."

"Okay."

"So I had the two girls with me. I said, 'Let's go to White Castles. We goes to White Castles, me and the two girls. It was me and the two girls, Tawana, Todd's girl, and the girl Debra that I used to deal with, the one I was talkin' to at the time. I, I, I even told them about the cop."

Tulman pounced. Cobb had made a mistake. Any admission of knowledge by Scott before the killing would mean an easy conviction.

"You told them, what, where, at White Castle?"

Cobb retreated beautifully.

"I told them about the cop after we came back from the scene."

"Oh, I see."

"See, I confessed that I was, I didn't even tell this in my state-

ment, 'cause, like, I'm trying to get all this out now where I can
. . . I might, like, hesitate and, like, put something somewhere else
ahead of time. That's why I take my time and slow down and get
it together."

"Okay."

"So they knew that Todd had shot the cop." Cobb had slipped
again, no longer making McClary the Shooter. "I mean that Todd
was there, they knew."

Cobb then gave Tulman the address of the White Castle he had
visited and resumed his narrative.

"I took them back and said, 'Yo, see you all later.' Then I went
and bomped the horn for Todd. It was, like, 3:00, a little after."

"Yeah."

"And he come down, and he tells me, go drive, go get David.
I'm like, I'm like where . . ."

"What's David's last name?"

"David McClary. McClary, McClary. David McClary."

"Is he also involved in the . . ."

"Cop shooting."

"Oh, he is, right?"

"He is involved in it, too."

Tulman gave Scott a surprised look, almost as if to say, "Not
my old friend David McClary." Actually the prosecutor knew
nothing about the man.

"But is he also involved in drug dealing?"

"He works for Fat Cat."

"And who do you work for?"

"I was working for Pappy."

"For Pappy?" The hair on Tulman's neck was standing on end.

"I just started."

"Who is Pappy?"

"Pappy is Cat's second man."

"Okay," Tulman continued. "So you work for Pappy and
Pappy works for Fat Cat?"

"Pappy is the boss. While Cat is gone, Pappy's in charge. Pappy is the boss man now and Marshal is lieutenant. Pappy relays a message to him through phones and prison visits."

Tulman could see now that Cobb was his. He was not going to quit the session. The prosecutor moved Cobb back to the murder itself. He could resume a line of questioning on the murder conspiracy later. Marshal, Pappy, and Fat Cat were in jail. David McClary was still out there.

Tulman had continued: "Where did you pick Dave up?"

"The first time we went and got him, Dave wasn't there."

"Okay."

"Dave was not there. I don't know, Todd went to the house. He told me park back. He didn't let me see the house that he went to. He didn't let me see 'cause I'm, like, a newcomer. I ain't supposed to know too much."

Cobb leaned forward. He was being intimate.

"See, like, they, you know. You got to show that they can trust you. I'm not supposed to know where certain houses is until I'm, like, really into the family."

"Right."

"Dave came out and got in the car."

"Okay, what time was this, about?"

"About, about, about 3, 3:15, 3:20 somewhere around there—'cause right after that, we left and went to the scene."

Cobb then volunteered to show Tulman where he had picked David up, where he had parked his car, and where he had hidden out. With this done, Cobb resumed his drive to the Inwood Post.

"He runs in, Dave gets in the car, and they said drive. We were riding up Sutphin Boulevard, we was riding, they said go to 107, just like that. We is driving and then they say, 'He's sleeping, he's sleeping,' like that. I said, 'Where to next?' He said makes a right, so I makes a right."

Cobb had his right hand in the air, moving the hand from block to block. Tulman spoke and Cobb parked his hand on his thigh.

"What did they mean by that, 'He's sleeping, he's sleeping'?"

"I didn't know what was going down at the time."

"Prior . . ." Tulman was looking for knowledge.

"I guess he meant the cop," Cobb said with a shrug.

"Had you passed the cop car?"

"I didn't never pass the cop car. See, I followed. I didn't know what was going on. They just told me to drive. I was just, just, just guided. Sometime they blindfold us sometime when we go places. They blindfold females so they don't know people where they be."

"Okay, do you remember passing the police car?"

"A cop car passed us, but I didn't see no police car squatting."

"Okay, where did you go then?" For a guy that would only admit to following orders, Cobb was having a hard time following Tulman's direction.

"So I makes a left on to South Road," Scott said, continuing to negotiate turns with his hand. "So they told me, I turned the corner. I said, 'Where to now?' and I parked on Remington. I was parked on the dirt, like a dirt sidewalk. I parked. The guys said they be right back. I rolled my windows down. I listening to music. I just sitting there."

"Right."

"So I'm just sitting there, and they, they walked off. They went behind the car 'cause they, they . . . I would know they weren't in front of me, 'cause I'm right there in front of Liberty Avenue, right there by Austin's Lounge."

"Did both of them have weapons at this point?"

"Not that I know of. All I know is that David had the weapon."

"Okay, now you saw that gun prior to them leaving the car?"

"No, I seen it when they came back."

"Oh, I see."

"See, I ain't know what's going on—they was telling me they was coming right back. So they walks off, so then all I hear is POW, POW, POW, POW. I heard four shots. Then here they come jettin' around the corner."

"Okay, could you see the cop car from where your car was parked?"

"No, I'm on Inwood. . . . They said I'm on Inwood. I'm on the last block."

"Now after that you heard shots . . ."

"I hear POW, POW, POW, POW. I jumps. I gets nervous. I jumps and get nervous. I see them come running hard around the corner, breathing hard. David opened the door first and pulled the front seat down, because it's a two-seater, and lets Todd in the back seat, and then David gets in and close the door. I said, 'Yo, what's up? What's up?' They said, 'Yo, ride slow, just ride, play it cool.' So I said, 'Yo, where to?' and they said make a left on Remington Street toward the Van Wyck. We went down the ramp to the highway and we got off on Jewel Avenue. I kept asking, 'What's up? What's up?' in the car while we were riding. And it, it finally came out. I got scared ever since then."

"What was the conversation?"

"Dave was tellin' Todd, 'Yo, man, you fucked up, man, you fucked up.' "

"Who said that?"

"Dave was telling Todd, 'cause Todd, I think—Dave said after he fired, Todd was standing there, laughing at the car. Todd was leaning on the car."

Cobb brought a hand to his mouth, mimicking Todd's laugh.

"He go, 'Heee. Heee. Heee. You blew his brains out! One of the bullets came through the door.' "

Cobb was talking fast, rushing from the scene again.

"This is what Todd was saying. Todd said, like a joke, he said that he shot the cop, 'Brains, I seen the cop's brains come out, I seen the brains.' Dave said he tried to get, pull Todd from the car, and tell Todd to come on."

"Okay." The prosecutor did not look so well. Detectives Pistone and Curran slumped in their chairs.

"They was, Todd was laughing."

"Right."

Cobb took a deep breath and leaned back into the cement, his hands folded in his lap.

"After Dave shot the cop, Todd was the one that distracted the cop."

Tulman slid his chair forward.

"Okay, how did it work?"

"They was planning, Todd was saying 'Yo man, look at that shit split, look at that shit split.' I'm like, 'What happened, explain what happened.' He said, 'We better split up, we better split.' Todd said he walked up on one side, took his hood off, he said he took his hood off. He walked up to the car, the cop had his window up and he say . . .'"

Cobb suddenly shook his body, demonstrating how Todd had acted like a monster.

"He go, 'Arrgghh, arrgghh, arrgghh.' He's telling the cop 'Arrgghh.' "

"Just like making that noise."

"Yeah, the cop had his window rolled up. Todd said he approached from the passenger's side. He wanted to distract him. I guess, he wanted to distract the cop when David come on the driver's side. This is how David came."

Cobb hooked his left hand in and around an imaginary police car.

"Dave just, Dave came along the passenger's," Cobb said, catching himself. "He came on the driver's side and fired the shots while Todd was distracting the cop."

"And where did he shoot him?"

Cobb twisted a heavy gold watch on his right wrist. There was a cup of water in a white plastic cup at his left hand. He started for the water and then stopped.

"I don't know. Todd said he seen the cop, the first shot, he seen the cop's brain come out."

Cobb brought his right hand to the right side of his head and then let it fall. The cops squirmed upon seeing the spilling motion. The suspect went back to spinning his crucifix.

"He says that was what he was laughing at. He said one of the bullets had come through the door, almost hit him. He be tellin' David, 'You almost fucked me up and hit me.' This is the argument in the car. 'That shit was swift.' "

"You've got to slow down."

163

"Sorry."

Cobb took a deep breath and smirked.

"Todd was telling Dave, 'Yeah, man. You almost hit me, man. Man, what's wrong with you?' He said, it's a big hole, a big hole in the door. He's, like, tellin' Dave, 'Man, what the fuck you shoot him with?' "

"And what kind of gun did he shoot him with?"

"He said it was a .357 with .38 bullets in it."

Cobb made a face, as if to say, "Can you believe that shit?" He was looking for a supporter.

"I seen the gun. It was a silver gun. Todd was telling Dave, 'Throw it. Throw it in the water,' when we was going to Flushing. And Dave's like, 'No, I'm gonna take it home with me and take it apart. I'm gonna bury a piece here, a piece there.' "

"I see. How many shots, did they say how many shots were fired?"

The suspect leaned into the question, counting bullets on his fingers.

"Dave said he had six shots in the gun. He said he wanted to save two in case he had to kill a witness, if he seen a witness. He said anybody who had been walking by. The gun was a six-shooter. He said he wanted to save two in case he run into a passerby that might have seen something while he was running."

"Now you drive on the Van Wyck and where do you go from there?"

"Get to Jewel Avenue and I get lost."

The Driver laughed.

"We started just discussing what happened. Dave said he had to pull Todd from the other side of the car, 'cause Todd's at the cop car, 'Heeee! Heeee!' laughing."

"That was after the cop was shot?"

"Yeah. But, but Todd, he didn't have no feelings toward it. Dave said Todd was leaning like this on the window."

Cobb put his elbows on the edge of the prosecutor's table and pretended to look into a police car.

"I asked Todd did he leave any fingerprints on the car. I ask him, 'You leave any fingerprints on the car, if you did, you finish.' "

"He said that his hands were not on the car?"

"He said he's like on the window, leaning in. The cop told him to come around and Dave had fired already."

"So the last words from the cop were . . ."

" 'Come around.' "

"This is before?"

"Todd said his gun was in his lap, too. He had his gun in his lap."

"Todd saw the gun in his lap."

"Yeah."

With this revelation, Todd Scott was no longer just an interested bystander standing a car length behind the killer. If Todd had been close enough to see the gun in the cop's lap, he had either killed the cop or distracted him.

"Okay, so the gun was in the lap and then he's making funny noises and the cop . . ."

"The cop don't hear him. Todd said that. He's like, 'Booooooo! Boooooo!' " Cobb said, waving his hands like a ghost. "He said the cop told him, 'Come around.' "

"I see . . . and then the cop, you know, come around here if you want to talk."

"Yeah. By that time it was too late. Dave was bustin' on the cop. He was bustin' and shootin'."

"Busting and shooting?"

Cobb laughed lightly. He had been back in the projects for a moment, talking the crack language.

"I'm saying bustin' because that's a street word that we use. Bust mean shootin'. If they say they gonna bust somebody, they going to shoot somebody."

Tulman pushed on, seeking a motive.

"Well, why was the cop shot?"

"It was an order. Todd was saying it was an order given."

165

"Okay."

Cobb stopped spinning his crucifix. He sat back, his manner reluctant. He was wondering how much he should tell. But he had already come this far. He knew, almost certainly, that he was going to jail. Trapped, he sought to save himself.

"From Pappy," he said of the order. "To Marshal."

"Pappy gave an order to Marshal?"

"To Marshal, Philip Copeland. And it was supposed to have been seven people to do it."

Tulman thought immediately of Brian Rooney. Pappy had taken a half-dozen gunmen with him to assassinate Fat Cat's parole officer.

"It was supposed to be seven people open up on the whole car. We surround the car, open up on the car."

"Why that car?"

"Dave, like, said that they had the car timed when Pappy was out here. They said the car was marked."

"When Pappy was out, when?"

Mason had only spent about ten days on the street since being arrested for the Rooney homicide. A judge had released him pending a bail hearing. That was back in late January, early February.

"He was out before they remanded him the last time. He was organizing at that time. It was already planned. Not saying it would be that cop, but a cop. Whoever cop that was going to be in that area. That's how they had it, that's how it was."

"Who went to scout out the area?"

"David said he did. David was, like, the man who planned it. But Pappy was the man who delivered and gave the order to Marshal, Philip Copeland."

"Okay, and that is the chain of command?"

"Pappy's the chain of command. Then Marshal. He tell him, 'Blah, blah, blah, blah, I want this person knocked,' whatever, boom."

Cobb was now holding an imaginary gun to his own head. And

that was the perfect image, Tulman knew, for the murder suspect was killing himself. Quite suddenly, Cobb's manner took on a righteous tone.

"They got a thing where they call 'One Love,' and when Pappy say you do, you do."

"What does 'One Love' mean?"

"One Love mean, hey, we do or die. This is, this is how they think. One Love, One Love mean, 'Hey, we all tight. We all, we all family.' "

Cobb's hands were clenched, the fists held tightly against his chest.

"I give you an order, you do. When Pappy give you an order, you do. On the phone when Pappy calls, his name is Bebo. We don't call him Pap on the phone 'cause the phones be tapped. Just say, 'Bebo.' That's what we call him on the phones. They'll all talk Jamaican. They slur and they, like, you couldn't understand what they saying."

Cobb started to speak in a tongue that sounded to Tulman and the detectives like rapid-fire pig Latin.

"Like you wouldn't understand what they were saying. But I would understand what they was saying on the phone."

"Okay, so why was the decision made to kill a police officer. I mean, why?"

"Todd said 'cause Pappy felt he went back to jail, so they have to pay for that. There was a thing behind Fat Cat, too. They said that, 'We lose one, they lose one.' This is what they were saying and they said that there be more."

"This is who talking?"

"This is what Marshal been saying. 'If we lose one, they lose one.' They saying, 'Cat got twenty-five years to life—Boom.' He had nothing to lose. So Pappy knows he's facing time, it's 'Hey, let's send them a message. Send a message out.' "

"What's the message being sent out?"

"That's the message. That even though they behind bars, they still give orders, and the orders be tooken, and it be done. They was proving, 'Hey, 'cause all of them be in, that don't mean the show stops.' "

"I see." Tulman really thought he was going to be sick.

Cobb added: "So they still got strength from jail."

With Pappy in jail, Tulman knew, it would be tough to prove murder conspiracy. No one had, as of yet, said a whole lot about Marshal's direct involvement.

"When did you see, well, Marshal?"

"When we was going to Brooklyn, this is the next day, in the morning. Marshal was not there on this, on the scene. Marshal wasn't involved, he wasn't on the crime scene, he wasn't involved in, like, being there. But he is the one who got the message from Pappy. He gave the order, 'cause this is what I was told. I was there. Marshal was, like, after it happened. They started to trust me a little bit. But they still kinda, still even after the cop got shot, they will still go to the side on certain things they don't want me to hear."

"What kind of things can you hear about?"

"If they got somebody pickin' up money, they don't mind me hearing. If they're gonna beat somebody down or they're gonna kidnap somebody, something like that, I can hear. 'Cause they do a lot of torturing people. Like when you mess up on packages and drug money, you get tortured. You get sanctioned. They cut your arm off, something like that. Or they stick a hot comb in your ass and they burn you up. I seen them beat people, beat people down, and stomp 'em out and cut them up, shit like that."

Tulman deftly moved the conversation back to the cop killing, steering Cobb home again from the Inwood Post. Cobb related dropping off McClary at his home and described the clothing Todd and David had been wearing. In another slip, Cobb put Todd in black clothing and David in the hooded sweatshirt, switching their roles in the process. Mostly, Cobb remembered his friend's sneakers. David had stalked Edward Byrne in black Adidas. Todd, he said, had worn a pair of Nike Air Jordans.

"Where did you go after dropping David off with the gun?"

"Todd said take me back to his uncle's house. So we goes back to Roger's house and we go upstairs and Todd was telling them, 'Boom, boom, boom, boom,' saying this is what he did to the cop, how David did this, how David did it to the cop and all this now."

Cobb then folded his arms across his chest to show how Todd had stood talking in a pose of defiance made famous by street-corner rap singers.

"Todd say, 'Yeah, that shit was fun, man, Boom, you should have seen what happened. Dave made that shit split. Boom, boom, boom, boom.' That's all he was saying."

"Who was up in the house at that time?"

"Todd, Roger, his uncle, Kevin Curry, a kid named Darius, and me."

"Shah?"

"Shah, yeah."

"You know Shah, right?"

Cobb nodded. "Shah, yeah, Big Lips."

"He was there, too?"

"Matter of fact, he was, 'cause he heard about it, too. He was up there, 'cause Todd told everybody. Todd even went and told his girl Tawana after that."

"Todd what?"

"He went and told his girl Tawana after that. Told all of them. He came in the house and say, 'Yeah, we did it, right. Yeah. Boop, boop, boop. Yeah, we did it, we killed a cop. Yeah: boop, boop, boop.' "

Cobb was mimicking Todd's rap pose again.

"The word 'boop,' he was using Jamaican style. Instead of 'pow, pow, pow,' the Jamaican style is 'Boop, boop, boop.' Bebos trying to be Rastas. That's how they talk. Todd talk, like, 'Boop, boop, boop.' That's how the Jamaicans talk. So Todd can pronounce how the shots was."

Having finished the linguistics lesson, Cobb then denied that there had been any meeting in Roger's apartment prior to the shooting. Tulman had expected as much. Cobb was too smart to

169

admit being anything but dumb. He did, however, put all of the police witnesses in the right place at the right time, including the lynch pin—Marty 'Shah' Howell. Cobb's confession, Tulman felt, also corroborated the statements of Howell, Roger, Darius, Kevin Curry, and Debra Scott.

"When I get back to the apartment, I'm, like, scared," Cobb had continued, holding the crucifix in his right hand. "I'm, like, I'm like out of here. Man, I have to go home. I was scared. I was petro."

The petrified suspect then recalled speaking with his mother, Lillian.

"I told her. I confessed to my mother. I said, I said, 'Ma you know Todd just killed a cop.' I said, 'Ma, I didn't know what was going on.' I 'splained to her, I let her know. She's, like, 'Be careful. Scott, what happened?' I just told her what I had to tell her, 'cause I thought it was my confession to her."

"Who else did you tell?"

"I told my girl (stuttering) Ma, Ma, Maria Hutcherson. I said, 'Maria, they got me in some shit that I don't even know what I'm into.' She said, 'See that shit. Start hanging with them and look what happened.' She saying she didn't want me hanging with them in the first place. She knew something was gonna happen. She kept saying it."

"What do you have to do to become a member of this family?" wondered Tulman. The prosecutor sounded like he wanted to join up.

"Nothing," Cobb replied, leaning toward his recruit. "You just have to be a strong person. See, they wanted to use me for a strong arm. I supposed to have been one of the strong arms they was trying out. They say, 'Go beat this man up, go beat that person up.' Like that. Make a position."

"Was there money involved?"

"It had to be money involved. I didn't hear no prices, but there had to be money involved, 'cause after it happened, when we was going to Brooklyn to Pappy's uncle's house, Marshal then went and got some money. We was in a Suzuki Samurai, green Suzuki Samurai. After what happened, Pappy gave the Jeep to Todd. He gave Marshal a van."

"Whose Jeep was it?"

"Pappy's Jeep. His girl was driving it. Mimi, Paris Williams. Everything that they ride in is Pappy's, but the cars are circulated out. They're not in Pappy's name."

"How do they do it? How do they work it?"

"They got people in the family they just sign cars to. These people is willin' to take the fall. So they sign the car in their name. But everything is Pappy's. He got two Mercedes, BMW, customized van, Jeep . . ."

"Right. What about cash? Where do the monies go that you get from drugs? Where does that go?"

"The money goes to certain houses. I would give the money to Marshal or Todd. See, they would never let me know where the money houses was. I just was the pick-up man. Just pick up money and give people packages of crack."

"What about the people in Roger's house? Were they dealing crack, too?"

"Everybody was in the house worked. Marshal told everybody when Pappy gets snatched, we got to know where everybody is from now on. Everybody have to stick together. So we all stuck together. We drink Forty-Five and sit and get drunk. We didn't bother nobody."

The prosecutor was fatigued. He had never before met a suspect so ingrained in the crack subculture. Cobb had his own language. It took all of his energy just to decipher Cobb's speech.

"So we're going in a lot of different areas," he said finally. "We'll take it step by step."

"You're making me feel relaxed right now," the suspect said with a smile. "So that's why I can get this out."

"Okay. How many members are there of this . . ." Tulman stopped, almost choking on the word "family."

"It's a army."

"It's a army?"

"It's an army," Cobb repeated. "About 300 people, no bullshit.
They had a war one time in the projects, Pappy and the Cat. For
every one of the people they was shooting it out with, for every
one that the other crew had, they had ten."

"In the shootout. You had 300 people?"

"It's Fat Cat's crew, too. They're all family and associates. You
got Supreme Team, you have Fat Cat's crew, you got Marshal's
crew, you got Mustafa, and you got Pappy's crew. That's all the
same. All that's Fat Cat's. All that come from the same person."

"We have a lot to talk about here. Would you be willing to talk
to the detectives about all this?"

"I'm willin' to tell them everything. If I can wish something, I
would just say I wanna live. I don't want to turn my back and look
every minute. I don't want to be in jail wondering if I'm gonna
get knocked. They can get messages through jail to get you
knocked."

"I gotcha."

"I'm willin' to go on the stand. I came this far now. Why stop.
I wanna prove myself right. I wanna get back what, what, what
I can do to help, to help convict them."

Tulman wasn't making any deals. Certainly not yet, anyway.
But if Scott Cobb wanted to help get his friends convicted, the
prosecutor wasn't going to stop him.

"All right," the prosecutor proceeded. "How much monies
were coming? Not just generally either. When you go back into
Brooklyn now, you're getting money?"

"Exactly eleven hundred dollars, 'cause Marshal came out and
he gave me, like, five to hold. He gave Todd two, gave Dave two,
and he kept two. He told me to hold the five, 'cause he didn't want
to drive around with the five hundred on him. It was all five-dollar
bills in a rubber band. He didn't want to drive with all that and
get pulled over. As I figured it out it had to be eleven hundred
dollars."

"Okay, where's the five hundred now?"

"The five hundred we spent in the city on going to sex shows, movies, and eatin'."

"Okay."

"Pappy say he couldn't give out that much money right now, 'cause he didn't want nobody get busted with too much money on them. The cops would say this is part of the hit money. So he tells us, 'Here's a little money and go chill, go have a little fun.' This is what Marshal tells us. Pappy called Marshal and Pappy told Marshal where he can get the money from, that's Unc, Pappy's uncle. The money that they would get, that's their payoff. Everybody was also supposed to get an eighth of a key theirself. Whatever you sell it for is yours. He gave away cars to them and all, so that's their pay. They do anything for Pappy. If he ordered it, they do it again."

"I see. I see."

"Whatever Pappy say go."

"Now, did Dave say anything about the money?"

"Dave wasn't really expecting no money. He said he did it for Pappy, 'cause he loved Pappy and that's his man, he owe it to him."

"Oh, so he would have killed the cop for nothing?"

"Yeah. He said he owed that to him."

Tulman wanted more on the money. He could not believe that four men had entered into an agreement to kill a police officer for what amounted to Edward Byrne's bi-monthly paycheck.

"Todd told me, like, boom, that they supposed to get hit with a package where the money be worked off, a package."

"When were you supposed to get paid for this?"

"I don't know. When the shit cool down."

"And you haven't yet gotten any money in connection with the shooting?"

"Nope. And I don't wants none."

Cobb then proceeded to list each and every individual with knowledge of the shooting. He included everyone with the exception of one he knew about—Sphinx—and another he would only learn about months later, the scared streetwalker nicknamed Black Rachel.

With one exception, there wasn't a whole lot left to talk about.

"Oh, yeah, by the way, where is Dave?"

"The last time I saw Dave was when we went to the city. We went to celebrate. That was it, that was it."

"Okay, are you willing to speak further, 'cause I'm not going to speak to you anymore at this time? The detectives might have some additional questions, you have any problem with that?"

"I'm willin' to do anything."

"Would you want to go back to the scene and just reenact the whole thing."

"I volunteer. I volunteer."

Tulman felt Cobb had already volunteered to go to the Inwood Post once too often. The prosecutor turned toward the camera, the confession completed. The prosecutors face was ashen, his suit still perfect.

"We conclude this interview," Tulman had said in a dead, colorless voice. "The time now is approximately 11:12 P.M." In the background, Scott Cobb, having just hung himself, was hanging a tiny gold crucifix around his neck.

Richie Sica had given Todd Scott a pair of sneakers. The suspect had been allowed to place a phone call to his grandmother, Rita Phillips, and Tonise, the mother of his child. The old lady had cried on the phone. Richie had met the woman a couple of times. He even liked her. By now, Richie had been working for something like twenty-four straight hours. He had called Joanne at some point and talked about his murdered friend, the cop Larry Stefane. The detective and his wife cried together.

After all his searching for Todd Scott, being in the same room with Todd had left Richie with an empty feeling. The kid was so, well, ordinary. He had no personality to speak of. He was a handsome kid, Richie would give him that. He had soft brown eyes and a quiet way. He was not a screamer or a wiseass. He was just another slender drug dealer from the streets of South Jamaica, sitting there, dangerous as all hell. The narcotics part in the Kew Gardens courthouse was filled with Todd Scotts. Richie could even understand a poor kid pushing a schoolbook aside for the vial. The vial meant Nike sneakers, heavy gold jewelry, and a BMW. The vial was fulfillment. Some of the kids would even become murderers. But to kill a cop, like that? He looked at Todd and tried to imagine how it had been for Michelle Garland and Crystal Bynum, the girls seeing a gun in his hands, frozen with fear. And then the flash. The detective could not fathom the violence.

The voice of Todd Scott.

"You want to know who I am? I'm Todd Keenan Scott and I was born in Jamaica Hospital on Nov. 23, 1968. I was raised in Bayshore until I was eight by my great-grandmother, Jessie Kelly. My grandfather, John Phillips, took custody of me when I was about ten or eleven. It was him and my grandmother, Rita Phillips. That's Roger's mother. I rarely see my mother, Brenda. She lives in Manhattan, and has this problem. I don't like to talk about it. My father, Leroy, still lives in South Jamaica on Remington, not far from where this here happened. I sees him regular.

"I went to elementary school at Samuel Huntington, P.S. 40. I graduated okay. I went to intermediate school at Richard Grosley over on 108th and 167th Street. That was three years intermediate school. Graduated. I went to Andrew Jackson High until my 11th year. Then I quit. Looked for a job, couldn't find one. I'm 6 foot-1 and 175 pounds. I guess, there's not too much to me, is there?"

His grandmother's version.

"Todd was raised between my mother, Jessie, and me, Rita Phillips. We were out on the Island then. My mother died and we moved to Hollis, Queens. Todd's own mother, my daughter Brenda, is caught up in drugs. She's still alive, but of no help. She been a prostitute, too. I know that. She was in jail, too. I never had no control of that boy from when my daughter went to jail.

"Todd graduated from Public School 40. He was an average student. At I.S. 8 they said he had above-average intelligence. I don't know. I'm just telling you what they told me. Todd went south to live with a relative when he was 13 years old. He stayed there two years, came back lonesome. He got a fellowship from the church. He was baptized and he could lead a prayer. He hates cigarettes. He's an asthmatic.

"Todd went to Andrew Jackson until he was 16 years old. They caught him with a gun in school. The case was dismissed, which did him no kind of good. Todd quit school. He was shot in the thigh by some other kid right about then, too. It had to do with drugs. Todd wouldn't say nothing to the cops. He said he was playing with the gun and it went off.

"He got arrested in some drug sweeps after that. This was out in front of the Forties in July 1986. This was dropped because he was 16, still a youthful offender. He was arrested again in October, they say, with 51 packets of cocaine. There was a group of them standing around, I heard. Todd went to Rikers Prison four months on that. They gave him five years' probation. He came back and worked some odd jobs. I think a snack bar. Todd reported to his probation officer on time for seven months. The officer quit and Todd quit going. They assigned a new officer three months later, but he was unable to find Todd. In 1987, I guess it was October, they stopped his jeep and found some stolen credit cards. Todd didn't go back to court on that one. He was arrested again for having some crack on December 18 and they let him out on $250 bail. He slipped through the cracks there. Somebody made a mistake. He's on probation until 1991.

"My son, Roger, Todd's uncle, they call him Red. He did this testifying against his other nephew, William Phillips. William cut someone across the neck with a knife to protect Roger. Roger testified against him, and William went to jail. This was seven years ago.

"Todd's father, Leroy, is still alive. I think he lives on Liberty Avenue now. Todd's middle name is Keenan. He's five-foot-11. Oh, and one more thing, Todd worked at Mary Immaculate Hospital one year as a volunteer. Isn't that where they took the dead police officer?"

Todd Scott was led to the interview room at midnight. There was a great clamor in the streets below, television lights hot on the precinct. The television stations were already reporting that the murder of Edward Byrne had been solved. Many of the reporters were jumping to conclusions, the *New York Post* among them. Murray Weiss, a *Post* reporter, would come up with the most inaccurate report, writing that there were two women in on the hit and that the killers "would have pretended to be two couples out on a date" if pulled over by the cops. WNBC reported, correctly, that the killers had drawn straws. Someone in McGillion's office had, as is sometimes their policy, denied the truth.

There was also word filtering through the crowd of a surprising visit to the corner of Inwood and 107. Edward Byrne's brothers, Steven and Larry, had visited with Arjune, telling him, 'Hang in there. Don't give up.' Arjune had said he had wanted to go with flowers to the funeral. The police said it was too dangerous. The Byrnes said they understood completely.

During his days as a fugitive, Todd Scott had followed the story in the news. The cops had found a copy of the *Daily News* with a story headlined, "Bounty Goes Up," on the dresser in his safehouse. The fingerprints of both Todd and Cobb were later found on the paper. So Todd knew of his infamy even before he sat down with Richie Sica, Al Sabo, and Scott Tulman to make his videotaped confession. By the time Todd finished with his statement, the *Daily News* was already getting ready to run his picture on the front page under the headline, "Dance of Death."

*

The prosecutor had washed his face and straightened his tie. He was still wearing his prosecution clothes, the blue suit. Scott Tulman began: "Now, can I call you Todd?"

"Uh huh."

It took several minutes before Todd warmed to the camera. He said he had been treated fairly by the detectives and been read his rights. A closeup of his face revealed no marks, no bruises. Todd asked for no lawyer, no quarter. He sat in the Bear's uniform shirt, leaning forward, hands on his knees.

"Well, it's like this," he said. "We was all at my house, you know, it's not my house, it's my grandmother's house, but my uncle was in charge of it and he be lettin' people sell drugs, come up there and rest or count money. So, we was all up there one day; me, Kevin, Dave, myself, you know, everybody I had written in the statement. We was up there and Dave was talkin' about somethin', somebody . . ."

"Was Philip there?"

"No, I had seen Philip by hisself earlier."

"Okay, then what happened?"

"Dave said somebody wanted him to do something to this cop who be sleep by hisself, who be stationed by hisself, be dozing off in the early morning hours. So he had, you know, left. He was supposed to come back and met us, right. But we really didn't believe him. We didn't believe him. We thought he was going to get somebody else, you know, like a fight over turf. So then I was with my girlfriend Shareema, right, and Scott came and told me he was going to get Dave. So he went and got Dave and came back a couple of hours later. It was almost three and we went over to my father's house, right, which is where the incident, like, happened, right. Dave and Scott went over to the bar, Austin's Lounge. I was talking to the girl, Rocky. I was trying to get her to come to my father's house, right, so I could stay with her, right. She wouldn't come. So then we went back, I met Scott at the car, the yellow car, we went to Inwood Street where the officer was parked with his back facin' us. Scott parked around the corner. So what happened was Dave got out, because he was in the front, I was in the back and Scott was driving. Scott was parked on the corner, so he couldn't see what happened, but me and Dave went. Dave was on the right-hand side. He started out on the passenger side. And I was on the driver's side. I was, like, two or three cars away. I could see the whole thing, right. I was on an angle where I could see everything that happened. But before I walked up there I was on the corner and that's when a squad car came by and said something to the officer. Then they rode by and they stopped at the corner where I be standin' and flashed the light on me. I went like this (lifting up shirt) to show I ain't had nothing. They kept going and, like, eight or nine minutes later we proceeded. He had come out the yard where he stepped into because he had on dark clothes. So he snuck up behind the car. Like, the officer, I think he was readin' somethin', or doing somethin'. He had his head down. He didn't never see Dave comin'. He had a canine car and the cage was blocking the view. So at that Dave stood with the gun this far away (showing hands about ten inches apart). So I seen the first bullet that hit him, killed him. I seen that part, the first bullet, then the rest rang out. I ran back to the car and got in the backseat. I didn't believe he was gonna do it, you know, I just wanted to see what was gonna happen. Later on, I went back to my house.

"So the next morning Philip came to my house. He said, 'You know a cop been killed, you know everybody who got a name in this neighborhood, they gonna come after. They gonna come after you, too.' So he was tellin' me to lay low and be cool. So then we went to Brooklyn to Philip's house. But we stopped at a store to get some clothes, right, and it was another guy from Queens that we know, he was talkin to the guy who owned the store and the guy said, 'You guys from Queens are getting real crazy shooting cops.' Dave started braggin' about it, you know, feeling all big about it and everything. He was all souped up."

Todd Scott was under control. He would tell the story in a way that would put him in the best light. He was not going to give up the names of potential witnesses or say much of anything that could be corroborated independently. The confession became like a game. Whenever Tulman showed interest in a particular subject or person, Todd would feign memory loss. Having put a gun in David McClary's hands, he was reluctant to implicate anyone else, even Cobb. He knew, for instance, that Martin Howell had been picked up by police two days earlier. He would not, then, put himself in a room with Howell.

"Was Shah around that night?"

"He was outside working."

"Did you ever see Shah in The Clubhouse?"

"Not that night."

Scott was also fiercely protective of Marshal. Family order, Cobb had already told Tulman, depended on this.

"Okay, did Marshal ever show up there?"

"No."

"When did you first hear the conversation about the cop—hurting a cop?"

"Earlier, right after Marshal told me Dave was looking for me."

"Now did Dave ask if anybody wanted, if he needed anybody to help him with this or something like that?"

"No. He said he was gonna do it by hisself."

"By himself?"

"He said he didn't need anybody. He just said him and his gun."

What kind of gun?"

".357. Yeah, and Dave told me to come get him at three."

"And how was it that you came to go along?"

"'Cause we didn't believe him. We didn't believe him. We thought he was going after somebody else. We thought, you know, like fighting over turf. You know, like, 'It's my ground.' We went and parked around the corner."

"Which cop did you say you were gonna . . ."

"It wasn't no, he didn't know his name. It wasn't like he was picked out. It was just that he was the one that always fall asleep. That's how he knew him as."

"I see, the one who's—"

"It was planned. The one who falls asleep all the time in the morning."

Richie was sitting in the corner, squirming. He had not yet met the dead cop's parents, but he knew this was going to hurt them. It was bad enough to have lost the kid, but to have his reputation defiled, Richie felt, was like urinating on his grave. In truth, Richie hoped the kid had been sleeping. He hoped death had come fast, blind, and painless.

"I thought he wasn't gonna do this. He was going after somebody else. He was just saying that just to be sayin' that, 'cause I ain't known him for doing nothing, really. Dave was really like a sneaky type, quiet."

"What's his last name?"

"I don't know his last name. I know him from his brother Roger. I know Roger, we used to play basketball in Baisley Park tournaments. He was our coach one year. Sponsored our team."

Even the most harmless story had a sinister twist. Roger "Nacy" McClary was a convicted murderer and drug dealer. The team he coached had been playing in SNIFF tournament games sponsored by Fat Cat and Supreme.

"We came down South Road, right, before we got there, went through 107, didn't say nothing but, 'Yeah, that's the one.' "

"Dave said, 'Yeah, that's the one.' "

"Uh huh."

"Now at the time that the car pulled up and you parked the car, did Scott Cobb know what's going to be going down pretty much?"

"Yeah. He been knew."

"He knew from when, Wednesday morning?"

"Yeah."

Tulman looked down at his notes to keep from smiling. So

much for Scott Cobb. He wouldn't be getting any deal now. Not with prior knowledge.

"When did you see Dave with the gun?"

"When he went to get it."

"Where did he go?"

"He went to Tawana and them house to get it."

For a time, Tawana had been Todd Scott's girlfriend. Now Scott was not only trying to put the shooting on David McClary, but dumping off his girlfriend on him. Ultimately, Scott said, McClary had gotten the gun from Tawana's sister, Muka. The sisters lived together on 160th Street in the Forties. The cops had hit their apartment with a search warrant at 1:30 in the morning on March 3. They'd found nothing. Tawana, seventeen, was tough beyond her age. She had looked Richie Sica squarely in the face before he left and said, "Go fuck yourself."

"I tried to talk to Tawana one time," Todd continued. "But then I left her alone. You know, she held guns for everybody. But, you know, it was a brand-new gun and Dave had no bullets for it."

"How do you know he got the gun from Tawana's sister, Muka?"

" 'Cause that's who he was talking to. Dave liked her, too. Me and Scott stayed in the car. He went up and got the gun and came down, so he had on gloves. The gun was brand-new, nickel-plated. He had no bullets, but he knew where to get some. He said the guy who be selling guns on 115, some Jamaican guy, at the weed spot. He only had .38 bullets. And Dave said, 'That ain't gonna fit in there. You can't shoot .38 bullets in a .357.' The guy was telling him you can, but you can't shoot .357's in a .38. Dave was surprised. We were walking to the car, right, and that's when he was loading the gun. But he also had more bullets. He gave him a handful."

"At the point you stopped and were getting the gun, why was he getting the gun?"

"For the cop."

It would be almost impossible now for Todd to say he hadn't

known prior to reaching the Inwood Post what was going to transpire.

"Let me ask you a question: Why kill a cop?"

"I don't know, he got a call from somebody. I don't know, somebody told him to do it."

Tulman and Sica had almost certainly heard enough. But Todd was taken through the actual shooting one last time. It was at this point, Richie would say later, that he again wondered why he had not killed Todd Scott when he had the chance.

"He didn't never see Dave when Dave shot him. Dave was right up close to the window. When I heard the first shot, and I saw it, I saw his head, you know, I just seen fragments, like his head moved. I seen his chin in his chest and that's when I turned and heard the rest of the shots."

"How far away were you down the block at this point?"

"I was like two cars away. But I'm on the sidewalk."

"On the driver's side."

"Yeah. But I could see everything, though. Just seen the bullet hit him 'cause he was up close to the window with the gun and I heard the first bullet hit and his head went down and his hair was flying, you know, like a blow dryer and I seen stuff, you know, blood and stuff and I ran."

"How many shots were fired?"

"Four. I heard four."

Richie Sica spilled his coffee cup, startling Todd.

"When Dave got back in the car, he said about when he was shooting him, he seen his head jerkin', you know, every time the bullet hit him. His head go up and down. He said he didn't know if the last one hit him. He said he didn't think it hit him, because he didn't see him move. After that, he was talking about the way his head was movin'."

"You didn't almost get shot yourself at one point."

"I wasn't even on that side of the street. I was behind him."

"Did you ever tell anybody the story of what happened, which is a little different than what you're telling me now?"

"No, I ain't even mentioned it to nobody."

"You didn't tell anybody about this, did you?"

"I didn't tell nobody."

"Okay. You didn't, for example, Scott, tell Marshal?"

"I just think that shit is sick."

"Sick? You think it was sick to do that?"

"Boy, it had to be, man. I still been around here."

It was Richie Sica that felt sick now. He pushed his chair back and covered his eyes. It was all so sad, so damn unnecessary, he thought.

Scott had not implicated his friend Marshal in any real way and he had been a good Bebo, keeping Pappy's name out of the videotape altogether. Tulman tried one last time.

"Okay, now, let me ask you this: Was there any money that you got in connection with this case?"

"I didn't get nothin'."

"Marshal ever give you any money?"

"No, nobody. Nobody gave me any money. I wasn't there for money. I wasn't there for killing. I was there to see what Dave was really about, you know. To see if he was really gonna do anythin' or nothin'. He was really talking about doing a cop in."

The interview was concluded at 12:40 P.M., the tape sealed and vouched. Todd Scott was led to a holding cell. By 2 A.M., when Richie Sica looked in on him, he was dead asleep. Richie had stood there a good while, remembering his friend Larry Stefane, and a night many years before in Bellevue Hospital when he watched a cop killer named Singleton shake through a nightmare.

Many months later, Todd Scott would take a blue ballpoint pen to paper and begin writing. The suspect's rantings, written on a yellow legal pad, would wind up in a lawyer's safe.

"I don't know David that well. Not well enough to call him a friend. Phil was nowhere around when this happened. There was no meeting. There was no plan, there was nobody in that house but me, Shareema, Roger, and Bea. I received no money, I had no part, I just went for the ride. I had other intentions like looking for girls. Neither me nor Philip had anything to do with it. I was there but wasn't a part of it. Philip was nowhere around all day. Im not protecting nobody, and thats the—truth. Most of the confession the police madeup. Sica, Sabo, Dunbar, and Panzarella. The wanted me to lie on Philip and Pappy. And that's the truth. They said if I cooperate I would go in a protection thing for a witness. But I didn't accept 'cause they didn't have nothing to do with it. It might all sound strange but that's the whole story. It was just us three and no one ELSE. I didn't have no gun. I didn't shoot no one. And I was no where near the car. I was never in no real trouble, so I didn't know just BEING THERE WOULD END UP LIKE THIS. THIS WAS A MISTAKE OF A LIFE-TIME. I THOUGHT WE WERE GOING TO PICK UP GIRLS. I had nothing to do with it. At all. They just wanted me to lie on Philip. My Uncle lied. Kevin lied, Shah lied, and Darry also lied. Whoever said Phil was there lied, too. I WAS JUST BEING CURIOUS. I DIDN'T KNOW IT WOULD LEAD TO THIS. I DIDN'T KNOW BETTER. I didn't know what he was going to do. I didn't have a gun. I had on party clothes, you know, BRIGHT COLORS. You don't go out and shoot somebody in the middle of the night with bright colored CLOTHES ON. WHEN I GOT THERE IT WAS A NO CHOICE SITUATION. I had to go with him. There was no girl out so I stuck with him. Rosalyn didn't want to go with me as I planned so I left with them. Philip wasn't around so I couldn't have been with. This wasn't no jail or hit. That is a bunch of SHIT!!! The one who did it did it on his own. I guess he had something to prove. All I know is that I didn't do nothing. I just was there. And that is the whole story. The real story. JUST NOBODY TRYING TO BE SOMEBODY. Or try-ing to impress somebody."

8

"JUST THINK OF IT AS TURNING A TRICK."

The detectives left the 105th Precinct at 4:00 AM. Along with the reporters, they had been instructed to return for something called The Walk. In New York City, where television is almighty, there had, over the years, developed a strange and curious ritual. Whenever the police cracked a big case, they would put on an elaborate dog-and-pony show—walking the prisoner past a gauntlet of television cameras and still photographers. The Walk made for great television and was a particularly New York phenomenon.

The custom dated back to the advent of the television minicamera and served as a way of drawing public attention to good police work. But there was also a practical matter. Showing a suspect's face on television sometimes jarred victims into fits of recognition. "That's him, Harry. Son of Sam. He's the one that took the radio out of our car." Occasionally, suspects yelled something of importance to a reporter. There was, for example, a case in which a murder suspect had refused to make a statement to police. He was arrested anyway, but the case was weak. On his way past the cameras to the police wagon, the suspect had screamed, "Damn right I killed him. He had it coming." The ad hoc confession was subpoenaed and played before a jury, resulting in a conviction.

By the winter of 1988, most young criminals had learned to cover up their faces with jackets or sweatshirts. It was not uncommon to see a fifteen-year-old hiding his face with his hands. It was just one of those things criminals learned at a young age. Reporters had come to regard The Walk as light theater, a chance to yell outlandish things. Mike Pearl, the dean of the city's court reporters, prided himself on his ability to get into every available camera shot. Chris Oliver, a street-wise reporter for the *Post* had, some months earlier, stood outside a Fort Greene precinct waiting for an overweight murder suspect named Anthony to be walked. Anthony had followed a pretty woman home from a grocery store. He had then returned with a gun and, after being spurned, shot the woman dead in her vestibule. The rotund suspect, Oliver saw immediately, bore a resemblance to the star of the sitcom, "What's Happening."

"Hey, Rerun," Oliver yelled, "Why'd you shoot that poor girl?"

Anthony had thrown Oliver a murderous look. But it was too late. From that day forward he was to be forever known in the city's tabloids as "Rerun, the plump killer."

The police department's flack patrol regarded The Walk as serious business indeed. McGillion and her assistants in the department's media office played D. W. Griffith, over-directing the events to the point of absurdity. Most walks tended to be saved for prime time, television reporters being able to go live with the suspects on the six and eleven o'clock news.

There was no way suspects Todd Scott and Scott Cobb were going to be walked in the middle of the night. The lighting was all wrong for that kind of thing. So Richie Sica, Eddie Granshaw, and Pete Pistone were told to wait till morning to lead their suspects off to jail. They were told to return at 8 A.M., which would give their police commissioner, Ben Ward, and his police chief, Robert Johnston, time to finish their breakfast.

"We went back to the precinct and laid down for a while in the dorm. It was me, Eddie, and Pete. We were tired but not tired enough to sleep. We laid down for a while, maybe an hour or so. We went downstairs early, got washed up, and went back over to the 105. Panzarella set up The Walk. It was a real hype sort of thing. I looked out the window once and the place was mobbed, hundreds of people, just waiting to get a look at these guys. Me and Eddie were assigned to Todd. As soon as we appeared with him at the front door, people started to shout Byrne's name. 'Ed-die. Ed-die.' It was unbelievable. You might expect that from cops. But these were ordinary people, neighborhood people. They had come down to chant, 'Ed-die. Ed-die.' Todd heard that and he kind of bucked, you know, like a horse that sees something in his stall. He was spooked. Then Todd recovered, throwing a look of disgust at the people. He wasn't shaved. And he was still wearing that Bears football jersey, No. 72, William "The Refrigerator" Perry. People were hissing and chanting. 'Ed-die. Ed-die.' Todd kept his head up and walked to the car, didn't even try to cover his face. God, those chants were great. I can still hear them. 'Ed-die. Ed-die.'

"Then we got in the car, and me and Granshaw were in the backseat with Todd. Panzarella was in our car, too. No one said a word, just letting the chants rain over us. It was really touching. And then the other guys came out, Cobb went into the car behind us. We had the Emergency Service guys there with machine guns all over the block. And we took off from the 105, headed for the 103 Precinct. It was lights and sirens the whole way. And it was like a fucking motorcade. It was unbelievable. Nobody said anything. Me and Eddie are, like, misty-eyed. We never got to go to the kid's wake. We missed the funeral. This was our time. I hadn't really thought about the kid much until that moment. It was always a uniform rather than a person that this had happened to.

"We went up to Jamaica Avenue, up to 122nd Street and

Jamaica. We made a right on Jamaica, and went all the way down to the 103. And we passed the precinct, but, it's funny, they didn't telephone ahead to let the cops in Eddie Byrne's precinct know we were coming. We wanted to do this out of respect. Just to pass by the kid's precinct with these mutts in the car. Have all the cops out there. But nobody was out there. They forgot to call ahead. A couple of guys came out because of the sirens. But they didn't realize who we had in the cars until later on. It was like these guys had been able to sneak up on an entire precinct this time.

"We went to Central Booking in Kew Gardens. Everybody in Central Booking knew we were coming. There were remarks being passed back and forth, people applauding. It was really quite electric. There were a lot of cops around, extra forces. Nobody wanted an incident. The upper echelon didn't want anything to happen to these two guys. Not that I didn't want to kill the guy myself, but this was my case. How the fuck was I gonna explain Todd Scott with a bullet in him?

"We lodged them. Then went back to the precinct and Chief Johnston was there. Earlier, before we left, Eddie and the chief had gotten into a playful argument about where the best cheese-cake in the city was made. While we were gone, the chief had sent one of his guys out to a place in Whitestone for cheesecake. And he says, 'You guys did such a fine job, I want to present you with this. It is, despite what Det. Granshaw here says, the best cheese-cake in the city. And I left something in this paper bag here. Not that I know what it is, now. But I'll leave it on the desk here and let you guys figure it out.' There was a bottle of Scotch in the bag. And Eddie has a piece of cheesecake and says, 'Sorry, chief, but this isn't the best.' We were just sitting there, drinking Scotch and eating cheesecake. It wasn't even high noon yet."

Steve Weiner had been up for two days. The detective was sitting in the 103rd Precinct coffee room watching television. Weiner was, without question, one of the department's real success stories.

He had come on the job in 1969. Most cops never earn a gold shield. Weiner got one in two years. He had toiled for fourteen years in the 110th Precinct before joining the elite Queens Homicide Task Force. Weiner had been awakened from bed in the first hour after the Byrne assassination. Above all else, Weiner prided himself on his ability to interview. The detective was large and yet quick, brash and yet charming. He was everything you wanted in an interrogator.

"I am an aggressive person," Weiner would later say. "I'm good at what I do."

He had already done fine work in the case, gaining the confidence of Marty Howell, Lillian Cobb, and Luis McClary. Todd Scott had put on Weiner's handcuffs. At around 10:30 A.M., Weiner looked up from the television and saw a gang of people enter the third-floor squad room. Weiner looked closer and recognized Mrs. McClary and her suspect son, David. The mother had been true to her word and was surrendering her second son in as many years to the police. Weiner rushed to greet them, his manner that of a maître d'.

"Take a seat," Weiner said, politely. "I'll be right with you."

He then walked over to his boss, Lieutenant Daniel Kelly, and said, "Mrs. McClary is here with her son, David. I think I have a rapport with her. I want to do the interview."

Kelly thought this a fine idea. He instructed a second detective, John Glover, to sit in on the interview. Weiner approached a third detective, Ronnie Waddell, telling him, "Do me a favor, sit in on this with me. I know the mother. I asked her to surrender the kid last night. She did."

Weiner searched for an open room and decided upon a makeshift office in the middle of the floor. The room was separated from a second office with a tin wall. He led the suspect's mother to a row of seats outside the wall and said, "Listen, if you want, you could sit right here and I will be in that room with your son. I will have the door closed, but it won't be shut and you can hear what is going on in that room."

Then Weiner banged on the wall, a tinny sound reverberating

through the office. Mrs. McClary looked worried, fearing a police beating was still a possibility.

"Anytime you want to come in that room," Weiner told her, "you can come in. Anytime that your son wants you to come in that room, I will let you come in."

Mrs. McClary then led her son into the interrogation room, introducing David to his confessor. "This is Det. Weiner," Luis McClary said. "This is the one I spoke to last night."

The suspect took a seat. Weiner's technique was first to gain a subject's confidence and then move in for the kill. The men talked about basketball, girls, and religion for twenty minutes. Weiner read David his rights. On one of four visits to the room, Mrs. McClary told the detective, "I'm a religious woman. He has to tell the truth because he's going to meet his Maker." Then she left.

"Do you believe in God?" Weiner asked.

"Well, my mother is a deacon in a church."

"Okay, well, I know she does that. But do you believe in God?"

"Yes," David McClary replied.

Weiner reached into his pocket and pulled out a picture of Todd Scott.

"Do you know him?"

"Yeah, that's Todd Scott."

"How long have you known Todd Scott?"

"About three to four months."

"Where do you know him from?"

"The area," McClary said, meaning the neighborhood.

Weiner then produced a picture of Scott Cobb. McClary denied knowing Scott Cobb.

"Have you ever seen Todd Scott with a gun?" Weiner then asked.

"I never seen him with a gun, but everyone knows that he carries a gun."

"Does your girlfriend, Shaunte Traynham, know Todd Scott?"

Weiner had been given the name by McClary during the preliminary bullshit session.

"We had friction over that. Todd tried to hit on her."

"Do you know Todd's uncle?"

"No."

"Have you ever been in Todd's uncle's house?"

"No."

Weiner paused for a moment, giving the suspect time to think. Nothing worked more wonders on a suspect than a well-placed dead moment.

"Todd has said many times that he don't like police officers. I heard him say he would like to ice one."

"Do you know what kind of car Todd Scott has?"

"He drives a beat-up old yellow car. It used to be Marshal's car."

"Is Marshal Philip Copeland?"

"Yes."

With this much said, McClary said he had first learned about the cop killing when he turned on the television at 3 P.M. on Friday, February 26. He claimed to have seen Todd at Fiesta's restaurant two hours before the killing and then again on Sunday afternoon, February 29. Both meetings, McClary claimed, had occurred at his hangout, Fiesta's, a restaurant on the corner of 116th Street and Sutphin Boulevard.

"Do me a favor. Describe the conversation."

"Todd asked me if I heard about the incident. I said, 'Yeah.' Todd said, 'It was good for the cop. It was good for him,' meaning the cop. Todd don't like cops. Then Todd says, 'If I tell you something, don't tell anybody.' Then Todd began to tell me he was down for the icing of the cop. Todd said Scott had drove the car, the yellow car. He said they drove westbound on 107th Avenue and passed the cop car. Todd said they saw the cop was nodding. They parked the car around the corner on Pinegrove and 107th Avenue. Todd said he approached the cop car on the driver's side, while Scott was standing on Pinegrove, which is behind the cop car. I think they only used one gun. Todd did something to divert the cop, and got the cop's attention. I don't know if he got the cop's attention, but he fired four shots, fast into the car."

"Where did the shots hit the cop?"

"They hit the cop in the rear, in the left rear."

McClary was pointing with his left hand to the rear of his own head.

"You know, the cop had blue eyes," McClary said suddenly.

Weiner was sitting two feet away from the suspect.

"How do you know?"

"I seen them."

"How could you see them?"

Weiner stood up and walked over to the light switch. It was the early afternoon, the sky gray. He returned to his seat, moving even closer. Now the detective was sitting right on top of the suspect in a darkened room.

"Hey, look into my eyes," Weiner then said. "What color are they?"

"I don't know. I can't see."

The blue-eyed detective pushed his seat back.

"Well, how the fuck do you know the cop had blue eyes?"

McClary flinched, as if ducking a punch.

"Oh, I remember, the inside lights were on, you know the inside of the car."

The suspect, paused, realizing his mistake.

"Yeah, Todd . . . Todd told me the inside lights were on."

McClary went back to his narrative, describing how Todd had told him that the cop's gun was in his lap and that he had a newspaper folded on the seat beside him. He also repeated Todd's claim that Edward Byrne had been sleeping.

"I don't know if the cop looked at him, but Todd fired four shots. He said there was no one on the street when this happened. Todd said after he fired, he seen the cop's brains on the front seat. Todd then ran back to Pinegrove, got back in the car, and they left."

Weiner sat back again. He remained silent for what might have seemed to McClary an eternity, two or three minutes. Then the detective leaned forward.

"Listen, Dave. You gave me chapter and verse here. You also had to be there. You know too much about it. You know the cop had blue eyes. You know the gun was in his lap and you know about the newspaper. You had to be there."

There was another long silence. David McClary had, up until this point, looked the cop in the eyes. Now the suspect sat slumped in his chair. He held himself and leaned back, defeated and deflated.

"I was the driver," the suspect whispered.

At this juncture, Mrs. McClary entered the room again. McClary asked for twenty minutes alone with his mother. "If you give me twenty minutes alone with her, I'll tell you everything." The cop left the room.

Weiner reentered the room about fifteen minutes later. The mother walked out and McClary resumed telling his version of the story. He could not remember what Todd was wearing or where anyone was sitting. He did recall, though, that he had been wearing green sweatpants and that Scott Cobb had been wearing green Army fatigues. He then reported hearing the shots, waiting for the killers to return, and driving onto the Van Wyck and then home.

"When did you see Todd again?"

"Like I told you earlier, I seen him that next Sunday at Fiesta's."

There was a knock at the door, this one much bolder than Mrs. McClary's. Lieutenant Kelly entered the room at 3:35 P.M. and announced, "His lawyer just called. All questioning of the suspect is to be halted." Weiner was furious, but he knew the rules. He walked out into the squad room and started typing up his notes.

David McClary's girlfriend, Shaunte Traynham, twenty-four, had called Fat Cat's lawyer, David Louis Cohen. The attorney had called the squad room and asked for David McClary. Informed that the suspect was being questioned, Cohen had said, "Stop it. Stop it right now."

Cohen, married with children, had found Fat Cat to be good business. The drug dealers were always getting arrested, making Cohen rich in the process.

By 4 P.M., svelte, bearded, and handsome, wearing a blue suit and carrying a briefcase, he arrived at the station house. Despite the general conception, there is very little ill will between detectives and criminal defense lawyers. Ultimately, they are all part of the same club. Lieutenant Dan Kelly, however, had no use for David Cohen. It was the lieutenant's opinion that, in the case of Cohen, criminal and criminal lawyer were close to being one and the same.

Still, there was no arguing. The lawyer had the Constitution on his side. Cohen was led into a room with McClary, and the two sat alone together for the better part of an hour. Finally Cohen exited the room, telling cops, "I don't represent him. You can do anything you want with him."

In all his thirty years of police work, Kelly had never seen anything like this. Could they now go in and question McClary again? Cohen left as the cops debated whether they had the right to resume questioning the suspect. Kelly decided to send McClary off to jail. McClary would later say that Cohen had asked him for a $30,000 retainer, he had balked at the price, and Cohen had left. Most cops theorized that Cohen had only appeared at the station to deliver McClary a message from his client, Fat Cat. Cohen would deny this publicly and invoke the Fifth Amendment when called to testify about his actions.

David McClary was placed under arrest at 5 P.M. and charged with first-degree murder—killing a police officer or a corrections official—and criminal possession of a weapon in the second degree. He was transported to Queens Central Booking in the basement of the Kew Gardens Criminal Courthouse on Queens Boulevard and lodged in a holding cell to await arraignment.

At about 10 P.M., Detective Jerry Shevlin called his supervisor, Sergeant Kevin Reilly. Shevlin had transported McClary to his cell.

"Look, I'm here with McClary at Central Booking," Shevlin reported. "We're having a conversation. McClary is talking. Does he have a lawyer or not?"

"Ask him," Reilly decided. "Then see if he wants to make a videotape."

Shevlin, like Weiner, had spent most of his police career with the detective bureau. Having held the gold shield for nineteen years, Shevlin was currently assigned to the Queens Homicide Task Force. It had been Shevlin, along with Detective James Curran, who had broken Scott Cobb some thirty hours previously. Like Weiner, Shevlin was a skilled interviewer, a big man who would sit at a table twisting a huge gold detective ring on his right hand. Cobb would later say that Shevlin had induced his confession with a slap of the ring hand to the defendant's left ear. Shevlin would deny this at a hearing, twisting the ring as he spoke.

Shevlin arrived back at McClary's cell at approximately 10:30 P.M. The detective escorted McClary into a room in the intake bureau and removed the suspect's handcuffs. He then inquired as to whether McClary had a lawyer.

"No," McClary said. "This guy Cohen same to see me. But he wanted $30,000. I told him forget it."

Shevlin saw a huge opening.

"You know you're taking the weight for this whole thing," he said.

McClary looked genuinely amazed. None of the suspects, to this point, knew what any of the other suspects had said.

"What are you talkin' about? I was driving the car."

"Bullshit. Todd Scott and Cobb said that you're the Shooter, that you shot him."

"Nah, I didn't shoot him. They shot him. Todd shot him."

Shevlin shrugged his shoulders.

"All right, Dave, but we got it on videotape."

"That's a lie."

"Well, that's what they said. You're taking the weight."

McClary was seething. Todd Scott had broken the cardinal rule. Why, McClary realized, Todd Scott was no more of a stand-up guy than that rat Perry Bellamy.

"Would you like to see their videotapes?" Shevlin offered.

"Can I?"

"Certainly."

Shevlin led McClary back to his cell. The detective then tele-phoned back to the precinct, requesting that the taped confessions and a tape machine be rushed over. By midnight, McClary, Shev-lin, and his partner, Stanley Strull, were sitting in a small room, watching Todd Scott tell the whole world about this cop killer named Dave.

"I think he was readin' something, he was doing something, he had his head down, 'cause he didn't never seen Dave coming . . ."

"That's a lie," McClary gasped, as Scott identified him as the Shooter. As the tape progressed, McClary exclaimed, "He's fuck-ing crazy," and "What is he talking about?" When Todd called him "the sneaky type," McClary laughed. Once Todd Scott's confession had been played, Shevlin put Scott Cobb's into the machine. McClary watched about fifteen minutes of Cobb and then announced, "I've seen enough."

David McClary wanted revenge.

"Fuck them," he decided. "I wanna do one of those things, too."

Shevlin called for an Assistant District Attorney immediately, getting David Dikman from the Homicide Bureau. McClary was camera shy, however, afraid that he would wind up on television. He asked to be able to call his sister, Bunny. Shevlin handed him a phone. McClary spoke with his sister for ten minutes, Shevlin only able to hear David's end of the conversation.

"But I want to do one, too. I want to tell them my side of the story. They putting it all on me."

McClary hung up the phone and announced, "I'm ready." Dikman, awakened from bed, had arrived at the intake bureau at 1 A.M. He commenced the interview at 1:43. About seven minutes into the discussion, McClary announced, "This is where I screw up." Shevlin ordered the camera be shut off.

"You don't want to make a statement?" Shevlin asked.

"No, it's just the camera I'm scared of."

David Dikman and his technician left the room. McClary was under the mistaken impression that he was being seen live on every television in the city. Shevlin opened the camera and handed him a tape.

"It's not going on television," Shevlin explained. "It's just us in here. No one out there is watching."

McClary then agreed to try it again. He made a complete taped statement, insisting Todd Scott had done the killing and then laughed about it later. McClary did not tell the camera anything he had not already told Detective Weiner, except that he, too, had left the car. McClary claimed he had agreed to accompany Todd only because he had thought the intended target a drug dealer. Each of the suspects, interestingly enough, had thought it wrong to shoot a cop, but perfectly all right to off a rival dealer.

Still, McClary had made a tape. He had even admitted to a prior knowledge of the killing. He had also insisted that Scott Cobb had knowledge of the killing prior to the actual shooting. Having seen Todd Scott's detailing of the grisly killing, McClary stayed away from the gore.

Shevlin was tremendously pleased, of course. A jury was going to get to see David McClary up close and personal. He also chuckled at another thought: Once the hearings started, every television reporter in the city would be handed a copy of the tape to put on the six o'clock news. David McClary would be seen on television, after all. Payback was a bitch.

No one knew about Black Rachel. She was still out on the streets, working men and smoking crack. The cops had offered to put her on ice, but the streetwalker had protested.

"I'm safest in the streets," she had told them.

Even as David McClary was being arrested on the afternoon of March 4, Rachel was sitting with a man. The man was being very nice to Rachel Moore, much nicer than any john. Only the man wasn't interested in the streetwalker's body. Detective Nick

Rodelli was interested in her eyesight. Rodelli, on loan from the Queens Robbery Squad, had placed a photo display before the hooker. Having already selected Todd Scott as Byrne's killer, Rachel now pointed to picture #2 in the six-man photo spread, positively identifying David McClary as the driver of the battered yellow Dodge.

But Rachel was full of secrets. On the morning of March 3, the morning of Scott Cobb's arrest, Rachel had been sneaked into a room with Detective Steven Weiner. Only a few detectives in the 103 squad room knew her name, even fewer knew that she claimed to have eyewitnessed the murder.

The interview had commenced at 9 A.M., even as detectives were hooking a tape machine to Lillian Cobb's phone. Weiner listened and then typed up a report. The forms in that sequence all relate to police action in the early morning hours of 3/3/88. Weiner, typing on a script typewriter, dated DD5 No. 538—a number also altered in such a way that it could be read either 3/1/88, 3/3/88, or 3/13/88. It is impossible to know, then, just when Rachel Moore was saying what she was saying.

Here is what Weiner filed:

"On this date the undersigned and Det. (Michael) Connor did interview the above-named subject at 0900 Hrs. at the 103 Sd. Subject states that she has lived in South Jamaica for over 11 years and that she is a crack user and prostitutes herself to pay for her habit. Subj. has been using crack for the last three yrs. and 'copes in the neighborhood.'

"Subject states that on the early morning hrs. on 2-26-88 she was on her stroll at 107 between Pinegrove and Inwood. Subj. stated that approx. 0300–0400 hrs. she noticed a grey auto pull up alongside the radio car, but she paid no attention to it. Subject stated that she had seen this car earlier at about 0200 hrs. on Sutphin/108 Ave. At that time she saw Todd Scott in auto on passenger's side. Stated she knows Todd since 6th grade up to H. S. Todd was seated in front passenger's seat. He was wearing a dark coat with a hood. Subj. saw 3 m/b's in car (including Scott).

Subj. saw a m/b with 'dregs' [dreadlocks] sitting in the rear. Subj. states the next time she saw the auto was when it pulled up alongside the radio car. At first she did not pay any attention to the car. Then she noticed that Todd was standing on the passenger's side of the car with a handgun and his arm fully extended. Subj. also noticed a m/b (same one as previously described with 'dregs') standing alongside the driver's side of the RMP holding a handgun with his arm extended. Subj. states this m/b had dregs and was wearing a blue coat. Subj. has seen this m/b on numerous occasions in the area. Subj. heard multiple gunshots. Subj. said the shooters said something to the driver of the car. Car made a turn, does not remember if it was right or left, and as the car was turning, both shooters got into car.

"This subject viewed two photo spreads and positively identified Todd Scott (#5) and Copeland (#3) as the shooters."

Rachel Moore had not only put Marshal on the scene, she had put him at Byrne's car door with a gun in his hands. This account made Marshal the Shooter. It also got him arrested. The only known witness to the scene had not even put Scott Cobb, a man who readily agreed to being there, in the picture. She also put the car on the same block with the getaway car. In three separate confessions, with not one of the others knowing what the others had said, Scott Cobb, Todd Scott, and David McClary had put the getaway car on another block. That was pretty curious. Just as curious was the fact that none of the assassins had seen Rachel Moore, either.

"I brought her to the D.A.'s office on the 4th. I think it was the 4th. I was embarrassed to walk in with her. She looked like shit. Her hair was standing up. She was a mess. She sat down with the assistant district attorney, Gene Kelly. Gene came out and he says, 'She's fuckin' good.' And I was looking at her, she looked like she was going to die any minute. I had talked to her. I don't remember the whole thing. See, what she told me isn't what she said on the stand. She told me Todd shot the guy. Never mentioned Marshal. She mentioned David. But she just said that Todd shot the cop. And then I left her with Gene Kelly for a couple of hours. First Gene came out and said, 'She don't even put Marshal there.' And then he comes out a while later, and Marshal was there, the car was on the block. She didn't mention the car to me. Not that it passed and picked them up and went north on Liberty. I mean, basically, I backed right off. I wasn't going to do anything that hurt the case. At that point there's no argument. However well it fits, that's the way you go.

"She went back on the streets. At that point the arrests are over. Rachel was on the street until April or May 1988. That was amazing. A witness that valuable out on the streets. Anything could have happened to her. A john cuts her throat and we're dead. She has a crack attack and drops dead, I mean, where does that leave us?"

Philip Copeland, who had been held without bail on a bench warrant since his March 1 arrest, was charged with second degree murder at 7 P.M. on March 5. He made no statements and made no phone calls. None of the other defendants had placed him at the scene, so Copeland even allowed himself a smirk at his arraignment, turning to blow a kiss at his alibi witness, Audette Wills. Marshal was a stand-up guy. But not as much of a stand-up guy, apparently, as Rachel Moore.

Odds and ends.

Derrick Smith, Scott Cobb's sparring partner, was located on March 3. "Sphinx" was interviewed in his mother's apartment in the Forties at 6:30 P.M. by Detective John Conaboy of the Major Case Squad.

"Derrick, do you know Scott Cobb and Todd Scott?"

"Yes, they are crack dealers for Pappy Mason. I know them since 1980."

Smith then related the story of his street fight with Cobb an hour after the Byrne killing. The scuffle had ended with Scott sticking a gun in Sphinx's ear.

"He put the gun in his waistband and said, 'Listen, you are gonna hear about a cop being killed on 107 and Merrick. Listen to the news.' I heard the news bulletin that the cop had been shot on 107 and Inwood. I knew Scott had done it, or was there."

"Do you think Scott Cobb killed the cop?"

"Cobb was there. Todd Scott would pull the trigger. He thinks he's macho. The word on the street is that."

Shaunte Traynham, twenty-four, was grabbed within minutes of David McClary mentioning her name. The woman stated that she was the mother of David's four-year-old son and that although she knew Todd Scott, she had never seen him with McClary. She knew both Todd Scott and Marshal by sight, and stated that Scott worked for Todd and Todd worked for Marshal, and that Todd used to tease David, saying he was a "bum" because he didn't have money or clothes.

And then Shaunte Traynham opened up some. In his report on the interview, Ronnie Waddell quoted her as saying:

"Scott (Cobb) used to work on 150th Street selling drugs. Scott used to come to my girlfriend Linda's house on 145th Avenue. My mother was a guidance counselor at Scott's school when his sister was murdered in 1986. My mother used to walk him home. He used to come see a girl named Tawana who lived across the street. One day, my girlfriend Linda went to the Forties projects looking for Scott. Linda wanted some money, and we all thought Scott was a drug dealer working for himself. Debra (David's sister) overheard Todd say to Linda, 'Scott works for me, not himself.' Todd is a bad guy. He have hurt several people. I know Pappy and he is in jail. The order did not come from Fat Cat.

"You can get killed talking about these people. I want to leave. This interview is over."

The following items were recovered from Todd Scott's closet and vouchered by Jerry Shevlin's partner, Stanley Strull, on March 3:

One leather jacket "Polo" with the word "Bebo" on back. Newspaper photo of Howard "Pappy" Mason found in pocket. Possible blood thereon.

One pair of leather pants.

One red/white "Saxony" jacket. Possible blood thereon.

One "Puma" jacket.

One pair of "Polo" boots.

Six Guinness beer bottles with Todd Scott's fingerprints.

One Moet champagne bottle with Todd Scott's fingerprints.

A grand jury was impaneled on March 7 and heard testimony for two days before returning murder indictments against Scott, Cobb, McClary, and Copeland. Gene Kelly and Scott Tulman presented most of the evidence. They were assisted by their homicide chief, Robert Alexander, a prosecutor known not so affectionately in precinct houses throughout the borough as "that fucking used-tire salesman."

Some months earlier, Alexander had attempted to console a police inspector who had given the order to shoot and kill a deranged man threatening cops with a loaded shotgun.

"I know what you were thinking," Alexander had said in front of no less than a dozen people. "You were thinking, 'Go ahead, make my day.' " Alexander, witnesses said, had been very lucky that the infuriated inspector's gun was empty.

Upon being asked for a search warrant to inspect Todd Scott's safehouse on March 3, Alexander had scribbled out a note on a crumpled piece of paper. "Just go in with this," he had said. The cops should have known better, but they were anxious. After all, Alexander was supposed to know the law. The cops went in and found Todd Scott's leather Bebo jacket. There was a blood spray on the right sleeve. There was also blood on the chest of his hooded sweatshirt. The blood type matched Edward Byrne's. Ultimately, all evidence gained in the illegal search was ordered suppressed. The police were still looking to complete a DNA test on the blood when the court ruled. And that is too bad, because the jacket might have been used to show that Todd Scott, and not David McClary, had shot the sitting policeman.

Two dozen witnesses were paraded before the grand jury. They included Sica, Pistone, Granshaw, Curran, and the officers who had identified Byrne's body at the morgue. Martin Howell and Roger Phillips also testified. Arjune, having set the investigation back two days with his positive identification of William Benjamin's Oldsmobile as the getaway car, was not called. The most interesting witness, the only witness to elaborate on her earlier statement, was Rachel Moore. The streetwalker had been reluctant to testify until Eddie Granshaw took her aside.

"You can get through it," Granshaw was heard to say. "It won't be so bad. Just think of it as turning a trick. You can understand that, right? Just close your mind to what's actually happening and do it."

The streetwalker had smiled and then entered the room.

Rachel Moore, residing at 107–31 Sutphin Boulevard, county of Queens, was called as a witness and having been duly sworn, testified as follows.

"Rachel, I want you to relax and speak slowly and loudly so all these people can hear you, okay?"

"Okay."

"I direct your attention to the date of February 26, 1988, the Friday before last, specifically, at approximately 3:30 in the morning. Where were you?"

"I was on 107th and Pinegrove."

"And when you were there, where were you at that time?"

"On the corner of Pinegrove."

"And where were you facing at that time?"

"Facing the police car."

"And was the police car parked near the next block?"

"Yes."

"And, in effect, what block were you facing?"

"Inwood."

"And what direction was the police car facing?"

"107th, straight up."

"Was it going toward Inwood, looking in the direction of Inwood?"

"Toward it."

"Were you on the same side of the block as the police car?"

"Yes."

"And did there come a time now that you saw a person by the name of Todd Scott?"

"He was on the right-hand side, on the passenger side."

"Was that on the sidewalk?"

"Yes."

"And did he have anything with him at that time?"

"Yes, a gun."

"Had you known Todd Scott before February 26, 1988?"

"Yes."

"Did you go to school with Todd Scott?"

"Yes."

"Did there come a time when you saw a person by the name of Marshal?"

"Yes."

"How long have you known Marshal?"

"Years."

"Do you know his real name to be Philip Copeland?"

"Yes."

"Now, do you see a person by the name of David?"

"Yes."

"And where do you see David?"

"On the side of Marshal by the police car."

"In effect, there were three people there at that time, David, Marshal, and Todd Scott, is that correct?"

"Yes."

"Did any of these people have guns?"

"Yes. Marshal, David, and Todd."

"Now do you see a person by the name of Scott Cobb?"

"Yes."

"Where do you see Scott Cobb?"

"In the car."

"Where was that car in relationship to you?"

"On the side right behind the cop car."

"Toward the end of the block?"

"The end of Pinegrove."

"Was it near where you were standing?"

"A half a block, like in the middle."

"That would be 107th Avenue in the middle of the block?"

"Yes."

"If the car drove off, would it be headed toward Inwood Street?"

"Yes."

"Now, the person that was in that car, did you know his name?"

"Yes."

"What's his name?"

"Scott."

"Is that Scott Cobb?"

"Yes."

"How long have you known him?"

"Several years, too."

"Now I am going to show you a series of photographs, which for the purposes of this hearing I will mark Grand Jury Exhibit 4 A, B, C, D, and E. I would like you to take a look at all five of those pictures. Look at all of them. Have you had an opportunity to view all those pictures?"

"Yes."

"Do those pictures show a car?"

"Yes."

"Is that the car that Scott Cobb was in?"

"Yes."

"Now have you ever seen that car before that night?"

"Yes."

"Have you ever seen anybody else drive that car?"

"Yes."

"Did you see any of these individuals drive that car?"

"Yes."

"Who did you see?"

"Dave."

"Is that David McClary?"

"Yes."

"Had you known David from before?"

"Yes."

"Did you later learn his true name to be David McClary?"

"Yes."

"Did you ever see any of those other people on the block drive that car before?"

"Yes."

"Who?"

"Marshal."

"Marshal?"

"Yes."

"What about Todd. Did you see him drive that car?"

"I have seen him in it."

"You stated before that Marshal had a gun?"

"Yes."

"Had you ever seen him with a gun before?"

"Yes."

"When did you see him?"

"Several times. I've seen him at night."

"Did you ever see him with a gun before?"

"Yes."

"How many times?"

"Several times."

"Now, after, did you hear shots fired that night?"

"Yes."

"After the shots were fired, what did you do?"

"I jumped on the car."

"Did you see how anybody left the area?"

"No."

MR. KELLY: I have no further questions. Do any Members of the panel have any questions?"

"A member of the jury would like to ask you a question. When you say you jumped on the car, that was not the yellow, that was another car on the block?"

"I dropped under the car."

"But it was not the yellow car?"

"No."

MR. KELLY: Do any members of the grand jury have any questions?"

"You stated before that you saw—that you heard a number of shots, is that correct?"

"Yes."

"Did you see who fired the shots?"

"When they first started shooting, I seen Todd Scott shooting."

"You were on the same sidewalk as Todd, is that correct?"

"Yes."

"You saw Todd doing the shooting?"

"Yes."

MR. KELLY: Anybody else?

"Thank you. I have no further questions. Thank you very much, Rachel. You can step down."

To Kelly's astonishment, Rachel Moore had reduced the art of testimony to two-word answers, using the King's English like there was a meter attached. She used a total of 140 words to

answer roughly 70 questions. In addition to this, the state's princi-
pal witness had done another flip-flop. Three men had become
four men. Scott Cobb drove the car now instead of Dave McClary.
She had a new killer, too, with Todd Scott firing a gun from the
sidewalk. If this were the case, and it certainly was not, Todd Scott
would have stood a better chance of killing Philip Copeland and
Dave McClary than Edward Byrne.

Rachel Moore, everyone could see, was going to be a big problem.

The voice of Todd Scott.

"The bitch wasn't there."

9

"HELLO, KILLER."

Sal Alosco was not the city's best criminal defense lawyer or even the brightest. At age forty-five he was chubby-faced and dapper, an avowed Manhattan bachelor who spent his evenings bouncing from one Upper East Side club to the next. He was a favorite of Elaine, the East Side bar owner who ran a restaurant of the same name. The restaurant was a favorite of the famous and nearly famous, a gathering place for movie stars and moviegoers. Elaine had become celebrated after the city's last major newspaper strike. Out-of-work newspaper columnists and reporters had gathered to commiserate in the saloon each night, most of them leaving open tabs. Elaine had let some writers keep their bar checks open for months. When the strike had ended, the writers paid off their tabs with cash and kindness. A table at Elaine's came to mean notoriety. And while Elaine always made room for the city's stars, she never forgot her friends. Sal Alosco, a marginal legal talent with a warm heart and quick wit, remained one of Elaine's favorite people. It was not uncommon to find Alosco at one of Elaine's best tables, surrounded by the likes of Woody Allen, Jackie O., and Mike Tyson.

Alosco had a winning way with blue-eyed models and blue-chip stocks. Neither of these talents helped Alosco much in a courtroom, but he was rich enough to wear sleek Armani suits and slick Bally shoes. A Bronx kid, Alosco had attended Fordham Law School and enlisted in the Army ROTC. He had risen to the rank of captain and spent a tour in Korea before returning home to join the Bronx District Attorney's Office. The lawyer had worked as a prosecutor for a couple of years before setting out on his own.

Fame was always a step away. Alosco helped to publish a rock and roll magazine and managed a rock band for a time before turning back to criminal law. For a time, he shared an office with Bruce Cutler, the lawyer representing mob boss John Gotti. He made the newspapers once or twice, defending a white teenager in the Bronx who had stabbed a black child to death. The defendant had made a confession, which Alosco managed to get thrown out. An acquittal followed, Alosco feeling a bittersweet victory.

"I'm not saying the guy didn't do it," Alosco would tell his friends at Elaine's. "I'm just saying he wasn't guilty in an American court of law."

This was the familiar requiem of the criminal defense attorney. Each time you kill someone with the law, Alosco was fond of saying, you die a little bit yourself. About a year after Alosco won the acquittal for the accused child killer, his client was arrested a second time, for shooting a police officer, while in the process of robbing a Bronx hamburger stand. This time the defendant was convicted. Alosco turned back to his two great loves, corpulent women and stocks. Sal Alosco, Esquire, seemed doomed to anonymity. He gave up his downtown office and started working out of his modest East Side apartment.

Sal Alosco had followed accounts of the Byrne shooting in the newspaper. Like every New Yorker, Alosco had been repulsed by the crime. He saw the shooting for what it was, a declaration of war on the city by crack dealers. He also read of the emergence of a new city hero, Arjune. On March 8, 1988, following the announcement of the Byrne indictments, Arjune had held a press conference at his house.

Edward I. Koch, desperate to look tough on law and order with an election on the horizon, announced the formation of a Tactical Narcotics Team. The 118-member TNT Unit set up operations in Arjune's house. The unit looked great on paper, and arrested dealers by the bus load, but everyone in law enforcement recognized the unit for what it was, a political salve. Hitting the South Jamaica dealers with TNT was not unlike hitting a water droplet with a hammer. Once smashed, the problem splashed into new neighborhoods.

Still, Alosco saw, Arjune had become someone to cheer for. The immigrant's bravery had become part of the national dialogue.

"If the police stay here and they keep the dealers out of the neighborhood, this will be a beautiful place to live," Arjune said. "I don't want to go back to Guyana. I want to stay in America. If something belongs to you, you should have it and stand up and fight for it."

Alosco also watched the political emergence of Matt Byrne. The murdered cop's father, the lawyer saw, was now lining up with those conservative one-issue politicians who favored the restoration of the death penalty. On the day after Arjune spoke of American values, Matt Byrne and his family visited the Inwood Post. Arjune and Byrne met on the spot where his son died, their heads bowed in prayer. Ann Byrne was there, too, her misty eyes covered with sunglasses. Kenneth Byrne presented Arjune with a gift basket wrapped in yellow plastic. The moment was so private, Alosco read, that no photographers had dared snap a picture. Matt Byrne, his face flushed with anger, later read nine pages of handwritten notes on a yellow legal pad. The grieving lawyer promised to push for the death penalty, and attacked the state's governor, Mario Cuomo, for his veto of a death bill.

"I think people are finally coming to realize that we are losing the drug war," Matt Byrne said.

The police commissioner, Benjamin Ward, dropped a bombshell during a speech at a religious breakfast on March 13. Arjune was going to be given a new identity, presumably a first and last name, and enrolled in the Federal witness protection program. The city had agreed to pay him $126,000 for his house and troubles. Arjune thus became one of 5,153 federally protected witnesses. Only three percent of those people, Alosco read, were law-abiding citizens.

"It's the right thing to do," Arjune said. "I can't live here anymore. I am stepping into a world of darkness."

Alosco's world was also changing. On March 14, a lawyer-friend of his, Frank Hancock, had telephoned, asking him to take a defendant in the Byrne case. Hancock, a lanky man with gray hair and a hang-dog face, had once worked as an assistant prosecutor in the Queens District Attorney's Office. As criminal lawyers go, Hancock was unremarkable, but the South Jamaica drug dealers trusted him, so he had plenty of work and money. Alosco and Hancock had worked together on a Manhattan drug case with mixed results. They'd lost, but got paid. Hancock had come to regard Alosco as something of a mentor.

Hancock explained that he had been retained by someone named "Unc"—Bernard Ingram—to handle Philip Copeland's defense. A fee of $100,000 had been promised. Unc was described to Alosco as a dealer on a par with Pappy Mason.

"Do we get paid in advance?" Alosco wanted to know.

"No."

"I don't like that," Alosco said. "That's bad business."

"Don't worry," Hancock assured his friend. "They're good for it. You handle the law and I'll handle the money."

The arrangement sounded shaky, and it went against Alosco's better judgment to handle a case on a promise of money. Still, it was a chance for celebrity. The murder trial, he reasoned, would be a huge media event. Hell, the President of the United States was already talking about the case.

"Which guy do I have?"

"Todd Scott," Hancock answered.

Alosco buckled. To take the case would be to become the most unpopular man in the city. But he was a criminal lawyer, sworn to defend bad guys. Big crimes meant big money down the line. No one hated F. Lee Bailey for the Boston Strangler. Charlie Manson's attorney was still doing pretty well. In New York, Jack Litman had defended the Preppie Killer to rave reviews. Joel Steinberg's attorney was the talk of the town. Bruce Cutler was as big as Gotti. Every gun owner in the city was calling Bernie Goetz's lawyer, Barry Slotnick, a hero. Alosco figured this was his big shot at celebrity.

"Is my guy the Shooter?" Sal asked.

"Could be."

Alosco arranged to meet Scott at the Queens House of Detention the same day. He called his friends and his mother on his way out the door. Alosco's friends managed to hide their disappointment. Mrs. Alosco made no such attempt.

"I'll never talk to you again," the lawyer's mother said.

The lawyer had made his decision. He could not have known what was to come. In due course, Alosco would become the city's pariah. Cops would spit on him. People would call his home day and night, threatening to kill him. His car tires would be slashed and his mailbox filled with threatening letters. East Side bartenders would refuse to serve him. Diners would scream at him and challenge him to fights. Only Elaine, the Upper East Side saloon keeper, would remain his friend.

"Hell," Elaine would tell Alosco after her customers had all left, "it ain't like you killed nobody. If I refused to talk to every actor in this place who took a shit part, I'd be out of business."

Sal Alosco's big case.

"I went to see the kid's grandmother first, Rita Phillips. She was a beautiful, God-fearing woman who loved her grandson. We talked about his parents and I could see that she had no use for them. Todd had been recruited into the gang by Philip Copeland. As best as I can tell, Copeland had gotten into some kind of bike accident. He wound up at Mary Immaculate Hospital and befriended Todd, who was working there as a volunteer. Todd saw the gold and he went for it. He couldn't see working at McDonald's when there was so much cash to be made. He had no patience for society. Todd saw a Mercedes and he wanted one. Drugs meant cash and money meant success. The kid was probably making $1,500 a week when the contract came down to hit a cop. Todd wasn't the first kid to go for the money and he won't be the last. There are a whole generation of Todd Scotts out there now.

"The whole case intrigued me. How does a kid go this far? That's what I wanted to know. And where does it end? There was also this, too: I knew it was a career case. Byrne's death was going to make a prosecutor famous, no question. I knew that. But it was also a chance to test my skills. A criminal lawyer spends his whole life waiting for a case like this one. If you turn it down because you're afraid of publicity, you have no right being in this business. Everyone deserves a defense. And Todd Scott was going to get the best one I could afford him.

"I went to Queens to see the guy on March 15. The names had me confused—Scott Cobb and Todd Scott. Hell, the names had everyone confused. Todd came in and I put my hand out to him. My mind went blank. I couldn't think of his name. So that's when I said it. 'Hello, Killer.' Todd looked at me like I was crazy. I've called him a killer right out of the box, scared the crap out of him. Todd took a step back and we just started staring at each other. I'm sure he's wondering what team I'm on. It was a very stupid thing to say. I don't know what I was thinking. I mean, I call everybody 'killer.' If I like you, I call you 'killer.' If I hate you, I call you 'pal.' And then I just laughed. I told him, 'Listen, Todd, I'm sorry. But that's just the way I am. I'm very loose. I'm a regular guy. But I'm going to defend you. I'll never lie to you and I'll work my butt off for you. But sometimes, hey, I may say the wrong thing.' We got along fine after that. He scratched out a handwritten note on a white piece of paper saying he retained me to represent him in respect to indictment #1662–88 and agreed to pay me at the rate of $100 an hour. But it took another couple of weeks before I asked him the big question, 'Todd, did you kill the cop?' "

The city's Irish cops, a number that had once included Edward Byrne, had great cause for celebration on St. Patrick's Day, 1988. Even as the Emerald Society bagpipers were making their first public appearance since the Byrne funeral, marching down Fifth Avenue, a roar was being heard a borough away in the Kew Gardens courthouse on Queens Boulevard. Pappy Mason, wearing dreadlocks and a white sweater that looked to be an Irish knit, stood beside his attorney, C. Vernon Mason, in the well of Judge Leon Beerman's court, ready to be sentenced on a conviction of gun possession.

"You gotta do what you gotta do," Pappy told the judge. "I look crazy, so people are going to judge me on that."

Although Mason had not yet been convicted in the Rooney slaying or even named publicly as a suspect in the Byrne assassination, he felt compelled to discuss the killings.

"This is two cops I supposedly, allegedly, killed," the defendant said. "Cops come to me at the precinct and say I'm the leader of a drug ring. I've never been arrested for drugs in my life. I don't know what they're talking about."

The attorney, Mason, no relation to Pappy, had earned a reputation as one of the most hated men in the city. C. Vernon Mason and his friends, Alton Maddox and Al Sharpton, were perpetuating a great hoax on the nation. Claiming to be a great black activist, C. Vernon Mason had rushed to and fro, demanding justice for a black teenager named Tawana Brawley. The girl claimed to have been raped by white cops in an upstate New York town named Wappinger's Falls. The racially explosive story had divided the city. Only later was it determined that Brawley had fabricated the attack. In his defense of Pappy Mason, C. Vernon said his client had been framed by police and called the conviction "racist."

Beerman was not impressed. He sentenced Pappy Mason to three and a half to seven years on the gun conviction. As Mason was led away, the prisoner turned to the prosecutor, Scott Tulman.

"Jive ass," Pappy muttered.

Even as Pappy Mason was being sent to an upstate prison, another cop from Edward Byrne's precinct, Bobby Kisch, was telling his friends a remarkable story. Kisch, a burly white cop who lived in a Queens housing project, was considered one of the 103rd Precinct's most active cops. At age twenty-five, he was a throwback to a different era. Kisch, nicknamed "The Iceman," had a reputation for street toughness. He took it personally when dealers congregated on his beat, and used force to move them along.

Three weeks before the Byrne killing, Kisch had happened upon Pappy Mason in the street. Mason had just been freed on bail, and he was standing on a South Jamaica street corner drinking a can of beer. Kisch approached him, demanding respect.

"Do me a favor," Kisch told Pappy. "Don't drink beer in front of me. Put the can in a paper bag."

Pappy Mason was stunned. No cop had ever dared tell him what to do. His friends were all around. Mason was nothing on the street without respect.

"Do you know who I am?" Mason asked.

"Yeah," Kisch said. "You're the guy who is going to put his beer in a paper bag."

Mason's friends began to walk off. This was, in the parlance of the street, a situation.

"Fuck you," Pappy told the cop, bringing the beer to his lips.

Kisch pounced, pushing Pappy against a metal window guard. "You either put that beer in a bag or I'm going to arrest you for disorderly conduct. Who do you think you are, talking to a cop like this?"

Mason threw the beer in a garbage can and walked off the block. His friends were taunting the cop, insisting Kisch had made a grave mistake. Mason said nothing until he was off the block. Then he turned to a friend and said, "That cop has to die. He dis'ed me," using the street shorthand for "disrespect." Within a week, Kisch had been called in off the streets. A supervisor had explained to Kisch that it was just too "hot" in the streets to have him out there.

"We're getting too many death threats against you," Kisch was told. "The word is that Pappy is going to kill you."

Kisch had been kept in the precinct even after the Byrne assassination. Bobby Kisch had a secret. He knew, even before any police officer, that the bullets that had killed Edward Byrne had been meant for him.

On May 20, 1988, even as Alosco was complaining to Hancock that the drug dealers were reneging on their promise to pay, the Fat Cat cartel was struck a killing blow. A car full of gunmen from a rival gang screeched to a stop in front of Fat Cat's mother's home. Louise Nichols, seventy-one, was sitting on a couch in the living room. She turned in time to see a firebomb crashing through her window. A gunman in a multi-colored jacket then sprayed the burning wood home and family cars with automatic gunfire. Then the assailants sped off. Fat Cat's mother survived the attack. The dealer's wheelchair-bound sister, Mary, however, expired in the fire.

Fat Cat Nichols was aghast. The attack on his family, coupled with the kidnapping of his wife a year earlier, had destroyed him in the street. At age twenty-nine, he was a vanquished emperor. Police theorized that the bombing had been done as a way of sending a message to Nichols's wife, Joanne, warning her not to testify against her kidnappers. Other detectives believed the bombing had been ordered by Brian Gibbs, the dealer nicknamed Glaze. Gibbs, cops said, was attempting to take over the Nichols/Mason empire. Three of Nichols's children were in the house at the time of the attack.

Fat Cat Nichols, incarcerated upstate at Shawangunk prison, was not allowed to attend the funeral. He sent a weepy message from jail, which was read at the service.

"If in any way I'm the cause of this, I'm sorry, because you know I would most definitely trade places with her," Fat Cat wrote. "I never took the opportunity to tell baby sister I loved her. Now it's too late."

The letter, which was read by the Reverend Charles Norris during a sparsely attended thirty-five-minute service in a St. Albans funeral home, began "Dear Momma." Fat Cat was furious with police who said it was too dangerous for him to attend the funeral.

"This is just another way of them trying to torture me by not letting me say goodbye to my sister," Cat wrote. "Times like these is when a family really needs to stick together. As I'm sitting here, writing this, I keep thinking about baby sister. If there is a heaven, she's there."

As Norris read the letter, he stood a few feet from a three-foot-tall floral exhibit of red roses in the shape of an "S"—a tribute from Kenneth (Supreme) McGriff, another deposed crack deity.

Nearly six months after the Byrne killing, on August 11, 1988, the police got the Nichols family together. A team of FBI agents and Queens narcotics cops moved in to smash the drug ring of Fat Cat Nichols. The campaign, code-named Operation Horse Collar, was the culmination of information supplied to the government by Richie Sica's informant, Billy. Fat Cat, Pappy, and thirty other suspects were arrested on Federal racketeering charges. The arrested included the mothers of Fat Cat and Pappy, as well as their girlfriends and sisters. The United States Attorney for the Eastern

District of New York, Andrew Maloney, was thrilled with himself.

"The death of Officer Byrne has led to the demise of the Nichols organization," he said.

In announcing the arrests, Maloney revealed that the Feds had placed wiretaps on the phones of Viola Nichols and her mother, Louise. Agents had listened in as the dealers complained about police pressure on their business following the Byrne killing.

In one such conversation, Viola Nichols wondered whether Pappy Mason had gone over the edge.

"He's my man and everything," Viola said. "But why did he do that stupid shit?"

"He mad," replied Brian Gibbs, the Brooklyn crack dealer nicknamed Glaze.

"Yeah," Viola continued. "He mad. Do you think he did it for the weight to fall back home . . . or do you think he was a goddamn fool?"

Still later, in a conversation recorded on March 31, 1988, Viola's daughter, Pumpkin Connally, discussed crack dreams with her boyfriend, Gucci Brown.

"I want a piece of land in Jamaica," Gucci Brown sighed. "I know your Uncle Cat's action is all around here. I wish I could get me a spot that bubble up about 10Gs a day."

"That sounds like on the right track," Pumpkin said. "But ever since they killed that cop, you knows it's going to be slow."

Most of the Queens detectives felt cheated by the Federal case. They also suspected that the indictments could have been announced in January 1988, a full month before Byrne's murder. With Nichols in jail for life, and Mason facing life in the Rooney case, the Federal case was anticlimactic. An Assistant United States Attorney named Charles Rose, perhaps one of the most egotistical and unpopular prosecutors in the city's history, handled the indictments. Rose, having never handled a murder case in his life, bragged of taunting Pappy and Fat Cat in an underground parking lot as they waited to be led upstairs and arraigned on Federal charges.

"Look," Rose reported having told Fat Cat and Mason. "There's some other people upstairs that you know."

"Who?" Mason asked.

"Your mother," Rose said. And then turning to Fat Cat. "Yours, too."

The prosecutor's move was pure grandstand, right out of a James Cagney movie. But in the world of Federal drug enforcement, where a prosecutor is nothing unless he has had his life threatened, Rose's move had the desired effect. It wasn't long after this that Rose was heard bragging, "Pappy Mason wants to have me killed for arresting his mother."

One of those arrested with Fat Cat was his sister, Viola Nichols. Viola had been very brave at the time of her arrest, kicking and spitting at a television newshound named Mary Murphy who had stuck a microphone in her face. Within hours after her capture, Viola had mellowed and cut a deal with the Feds. A team of Queens detectives, including Richie Sica and Ronnie Waddell, arrived at the Brooklyn office of the U.S. attorney, determined to know what, if anything, Viola Nichols knew about the murder of Edward Byrne.

"When the Feds made the arrest, we went back to 26 Federal Plaza, and they bring Viola in. The Feds wouldn't let us talk to her. This guy comes in and he's dressed to the nines. We're sitting there with no ties on. This guy, who is an assistant U.S. Attorney, comes in and says, 'I'll go in there and talk to her. And if she says anything worthwhile, I'll come out and let you guys know.' So we were on their turf, you know. But we've had it up to here with their government bullshit and FBI secrets. So the U.S. Attorney comes out about a half hour later and says, 'She's not really saying anything. She's just talking about this guy Pappy in jail.' So Panzarella is standing next to me. And he says, 'Are you fucking kidding me?' Now Lt. Dunbar doesn't say anything. He just looks at the government guy. Dunbar finally says, 'We've been waiting to hear this for five months now. Do you know who Pappy is?' The guy says, 'Yeah. I heard of him.' So now Panzarella jumps right in the guy's face. He says, 'You know, you fucking guys don't know shit.' He went through his whole routine on him. You could see the cops and the Feds squaring off up there. There was a lot of tension up there that day, a lot of tension. They had a lot of our guys working on a Federal case, but the Feds were running the investigation. There were our guys against one wall and the Feds against another. I thought there was going to be a fight. No New York City cop respects a Fed. The FBI doesn't trust us or share with us. But they can't get the job done without us. The FBI's idea of an undercover is sending some white agent in tennis shorts up to Harlem to hit a tennis ball against a wall. They are professional white guys.

"Anyway, Dunbar is very diplomatic. He tells Panzarella, 'Back off.' So we do. Viola finally agrees to talk to Ronnie Waddell. They have some history. Viola certainly doesn't like cops, especially white cops. She thinks it was cops who burned down her house and killed her invalid sister in the fire. But she'll talk to Waddell. And it turns out she's got plenty to say."

August 15, 1988.

"Understanding all my rights, I make the following statement concerning what I know about the murder of Police Officer Edward Byrne.

"I returned home on January 11, 1988, after being in jail for approximately two years. At that time Howard Mason, who I have known for approximately six years, was in jail at the Brooklyn House of Detention. (I know Howard Mason by his 'street' names, which are 'Bebo,' 'Pappy,' or 'Star.')

" 'Pappy' was released from jail approximately one week before Police Officer Edward Byrne was killed in Jamiaca, Queens. 'Pappy' returned to jail on Thursday, February 25, 1988, the day before the officer was killed. I know it was a Thursday because it was the day after my regularly scheduled visit to my parole office.

"During the week that 'Pappy' was out of jail, he came to my house every day so that he could receive telephone calls from my brother, Lorenzo Nichols, whose 'street' name is 'Busy' or 'Fat Cat,' who was in jail. Usually with 'Pappy' was two men I knew as Philip, also known as 'Marshal,' and Todd. On one or two occasions, 'Pappy' came with 'Scott.' On several occasions, 'Pappy' met David McClary at my house.

"I have known Philip for approximately three years. I have known David McClary for many years. I was introduced to Todd and Scott by 'Pappy' during the week that he was out of jail. After 'Pappy' went to jail and until the four of them were arrested, I continued to see the four men every day. They usually drove a green 'Jeep.'

"On August 11, 1988, I was shown photographs by Detective James Ronald Waddell of the New York City Police Department. I identified those photographs as the four men I know as Philip, also known as Marshal, who I now know to be Philip Copeland (Government Exhibit No. 1); David McClary (Government Exhibit No. 2); Todd, who I now know to be Todd Scott (Government Exhibit No. 3); and Scott, who I now know to be Scott Cobb (Government Exhibit No. 4). I signed and dated those photographs on August 15, 1988.

"Every day until they were arrested, the four men came to my house, usually between 6:00 and 6:30 P.M., so that they could receive telephone calls from 'Pappy.' The night that 'Pappy' was returned to jail, February 25, 1988, Philip Copeland and Todd Scott came to my house to wait for such a telephone call. 'Pappy' called at the scheduled time, and spoke with Philip Copeland. Most of the conversation was in what I call 'Bebo talk,' and I couldn't understand it. However, I did overhear Philip asking whether he should contact 'Bobo,' who I know to be Mike Bones. I learned that 'Bobo' was not to be contacted.

"Police Officer Edward Byrne was killed on Friday, February 26, 1988. Within the next two days, I received telephone calls from my mother, Louise Coleman, and my sister-in-law, Joanne Nichols, in which they told me that 'Busy,' my brother Lorenzo Nichols, was mad about what 'that stupid motherfucking "Pappy'' did.' At first, I didn't understand what they were talking about. When I asked, my mother and Joanne told me that it was about what 'that stupid shit "Pappy" had done.' My mother told me that it was about the killing of the police officer and that 'Busy' was very mad at 'Pappy.'

"A day or two after I spoke to my mother and Joanne, I got a telephone call from 'Busy.' During the call, 'Busy' asked me whether I had spoken to 'Bebo' yet. I told 'Busy' that I hadn't and 'Busy' then said to me, 'Man, I don't know why "Bebo" did that fucked-up shit. What "Bebo" did was fucked-up. He messed up everything for everybody. Now nobody will make no money! Now he won't make no money, either.' I understood from the conversation that 'Busy' was talking about the killing of Police Officer Byrne.

"One or two days after I spoke to 'Busy' about the police officer, 'Pappy' called me. I asked 'Pappy,' referring to the murder of Officer Byrne, 'Why did you do that?' 'Pappy' told me, 'You don't understand. The man dis'ed (disrespected) me!' I told 'Pappy' over and over, 'I still don't understand why you did it.' 'Pappy' kept telling me that it was because the police officer 'dis'ed' (disrespected) him by ordering 'Pappy' to put a can of beer that 'Pappy' was holding in a brown paper bag.

"Within the next day or two I again spoke with 'Busy.' At the time, 'Busy' told me that ' "Pappy" had the wrong fuckin' cop killed.'

"On what I believe to be the second Sunday after the murder, and after the arrest of the four men, 'Pappy' called me from the Brooklyn House of Detention. 'Pappy' told me to tell 'Homes,' who I know to be David McClary's friend 'James,' to get the 'thing,' clean the prints off, and to 'break it up and get rid of it.' I understood 'the thing' to mean the gun used to murder Officer Byrne. Because I didn't want to be involved, I told 'Pappy' that he should tell 'Homes' himself. 'Pappy' told me to find 'James' and that he would call back.

"I beeped 'Shawnee,' who is David McClary's girlfriend, and told her to tell 'James' that 'Pappy' wanted to speak to him. A little while later, 'James' came up to my house and the two of us waited for 'Pappy's' call. I answered and gave the phone to 'James.' Then, 'Pappy' had a conversation, which I didn't over-hear.

"After the conversation, I asked 'James' what he was going to do. 'James' told me that he was going to do 'what "Bebo" told me to do.' 'James' then left.

"A few days later after the telephone call between 'Pappy' and 'James,' I saw 'James' on the block. I asked 'James,' 'Did you get rid of it?,' referring to the gun. 'James' told me, 'Yes.'

"Prior to the telephone call between 'James' and 'Pappy,' I asked 'Shawnee,' 'Did David do that?,' referring to the murder of Officer Byrne. 'Shawnee' told me that David had done 'it.' 'Shaw-nee' also told me that the police had come to her basement win-dow, and she had fled. She told me that the gun was at her house, and after the police had left, she hid it somewhere in the neighbor-hood.

"There are additional details which I could provide concerning my conversations with the people named in this statement. This statement is only a summary of those conversations.

"Signed, Viola Nichols."

Another one of those scheduled for arrest was Philip Copeland's benefactor, Bernard Ingram. "Unc" blew town before the cops hit his house, however, only stopping to phone Frank Hancock.

"Marshal is on his own now," Unc told the lawyer. "There isn't going to be any more money."

Hancock relayed the message to Alosco, who promptly announced both lawyers fools. Hancock had been paid $3,000 to handle the biggest murder defense of the year. Sal Alosco got $1,500—which wouldn't even cover his expenses at Elaine's for a month. Todd Scott, now penniless, offered to cash in a $2,500 life insurance policy he had taken out as an eighteen-year-old.

"You have a life insurance policy?" Alosco said.

"Sure," Scott said. "It's very dangerous out on the streets. I was always prepared to die."

Alosco shook his head. That same day, he had been given a copy of Viola Nichols's deposition. The state of Connecticut, Alosco also heard, was about to indict Todd Scott in the execution murder of Michelle Garland. Connecticut was a death-penalty state.

"You keep the policy, Killer," the lawyer decided. "You may collect on it yet."

10

"THEY WERE FIVE SHOTS THAT WERE FELT ACROSS ALL OF AMERICA."

State Supreme Court Justice John A. Leahy was, by reputation, the most uncompromising jurist in all of Queens County. It was Leahy who'd stunned a young detective named Richard Sica when he'd dragged a jury to a Queens hospital room to pronounce a guilty verdict on the young man who had killed a soldier for his girlfriend's boombox. Although judges are picked at random to handle cases in New York City, no one was going to trust the Byrne case to chance. The leathery judge was the logical choice. He had already told many of his friends that he was looking forward to handling the case. One of those he reportedly told was the murdered cop's father, Matthew Byrne.

Leahy, a cantankerous sort and something of a cop buff, was, like Matt Byrne, a member of The Club. Actually, the men had been friends for years, and on the day that Edward Byrne died, Leahy mailed Matt Byrne a handwritten Mass card, expressing his condolences. He followed up the card with a phone call. Unfortunately for the Byrne family, word of the Mass card leaked out, and the card was subsequently destroyed.

Still, Leahy's actions made the newspapers. Sal Alosco demanded, with all due respect, that Judge Leahy recuse himself from the case. The judge refused. Alosco was not that upset, however. He believed the judge's friendship with Matt Byrne would provide a marvelous basis for an appeal.

Pretrial hearings in the case opened on October 12, 1988. When Sal Alosco reported to the Kew Gardens courthouse on Queens Boulevard, he was directed to the borough's grandest courtroom, Part K-2, on the first floor of the building. Alice Crimmins, the infamous child killer, had been convicted in the same courtroom. More recently, the room had been the stage for the Howard Beach racial trial. In Part K-2, however, Alosco had an unpleasant surprise waiting for him. Judge Leahy was not there. Instead, Judge Thomas A. Demakos, white-haired and firm, was sitting on the bench. Demakos, having just finished with Howard Beach, was regarded throughout legal circles as the borough's *second* toughest jurist. He was also the one hearing the fire-bombing and witness-tampering cases involving Arjune.

"How did Your Honor get this case?" Alosco asked.

"I don't know."

"Could we have a hearing to determine how it was Your Honor was selected to preside over this proceeding?"

"That application is denied."

Alosco then asked for an adjournment so that he could go to the state's Appellate Division for a ruling. Judge Demakos's response to this set the tone for the trial.

"Going to the Appellate Division is not going to be worth anything, because what I decide is not appealable," Judge Demakos replied.

"Shall I read the law?" Alosco said.

"No, don't read the law. I don't need the law," Demakos snapped. And with that, the judge banged his gavel.

There was more legal parrying on the issue, but as Alosco said himself at a sidebar, the die had been cast. The defense did not have a friend in Judge Thomas A. Demakos. Matt Byrne, having studied the judge from a seat in the fourth row, turned to his police guard as he left the room.

"I like that judge," Matt Byrne said.

Matt Byrne also liked the two prosecutors handling the case. Gene Kelly, the star of the District Attorney's Homicide Bureau, was a ruddy-faced, sharp-nosed Irishman from Rockaway. Although Kelly had a smooth dancer's name, the prosecutor was chubby, disheveled-looking, and awkward of step. He was very sharp on the law, however, rarely losing a case. Kelly's assistant was A. Kirke Bartley, a newcomer to the Homicide Bureau. Bartley was Kelly's physical and intellectual opposite—lanky and neat, silent and Waspy. Bartley had grown up in Douglaston on the Nassau County border, one of the borough's most posh neighborhoods. He shared a backyard with the tennis star John McEnroe. The closest Bartley had come to Rockaway was when he sailed past it on a friend's yacht. Having never tried a murder case before, Bartley was an unknown commodity.

As the lead prosecutor in the case, Gene Kelly became, like Richie Sica, something of a surrogate son to Matt Byrne. The men spent many hours together, discussing strategy. The assassination of Byrne had cut to the soul of Kelly's being. He could not imagine a more brazen crime. He spent many evenings with his friends at a Rockaway saloon, an anger tearing at him. Byrne was the case of a lifetime, and Kelly knew it. And while Kelly could, over the succeeding months, be accused of pandering to Matt Byrne to the point of obsequiousness, he never lost sight of his mission. A cop had been killed, a message delivered. Gene Kelly had every intention of sending a return message to Pappy Mason's minions: We lose one. You lose four.

On the first day of the hearings, Todd Scott's videotaped confession was played. Ann Byrne, the cop's mother, sat holding a Mass card, crying. Matt Byrne remained stoic. At one point, David McClary turned to the grieving parents and grinned. The videotapes of Scott Cobb and David McClary were played the next day. Richie Sica took the stand on the third day. The detective was

talking about the assassination, having just put Todd Scott and
David McClary behind Byrne's car again, when words failed him
completely.

"May the record reflect that the witness appears to be in tears,"
Alosco said. A recess was called, the weeping detective excused.
Todd Scott had sat at the defense table writing notes on a yellow
legal pad. The defendant, taking a cue from courtroom artists,
drew a sketch of Sica, complete with tears.

"YOU SHOOK HIM UP," Scott wrote. "SICA. He went back
on some of his words."

As the hearings continued, the city was struck by a second shock
wave. On the night of October 18, 1988, two city police officers,
Christopher Hoban and Michael Buczek, were gunned down
within hours of each other. Hoban, an undercover assigned to a
crack detail, was shot while making a drug buy. Buczek was killed
after he and his partner stumbled upon two Dominicans robbing
a crack dealer in Washington Heights.

With the mortified city reeling and the political hard-liners
demanding the return of the death penalty, the Republican presidential nominee, George Bush, flew into New York for a campaign rally on October 20. The Vice President was welcomed to
the stage of a Catholic Queens high school by Matt Byrne and five
hundred uniformed police officers. Bush then received the en-
dorsement of the police unions at a school where, it was noted,
management had broken the teacher's union. The most compel-
ling moment in Bush's visit came when Matt Byrne presented the
vice president with his son's badge. As the cops and high school
kids chanted, "Death, death, death," Matt Byrne stood off to the
side, his hands clenched in fists of rage.

Bush and Byrne became fairly good friends in the succeeding
months. In an interview on "NBC Nightly News" just prior to his
election, Bush said the most moving moment of the campaign had
been when Matt Byrne "handed me the badge of his fallen son."

By then, Matt Byrne belonged to the Republican Party. On November 18, 1988, outgoing President Ronald Reagan signed a drug bill, dedicating it to his wife, Nancy, and a murdered policeman named Edward Byrne. Matt and Ann attended the signing, listening as Reagan said, "We salute Eddie Byrne. We salute his family for their determination that his death will not be in vain." In a quieter moment, Nancy told Ann Byrne, "It's regrettable that it took a tragedy like this to propel this bill to national prominence." Edward Byrne was one of only 2,000 New York City murder victims in 1988; police say that more than half the killings were drug-related.

So taken was George Bush with the martyred cop's survivors that upon being elected President, he invited Matt and Ann Byrne to the White House for a private dinner.

"I can't believe I'm here," Byrne reportedly told the President.

"I can't believe I'm here, either," quipped the President.

Matt Byrne did not think to tell reporters for several months, however, that the badge he had given the Vice President of the United States was only a replica of his son's badge, one of a dozen or so he had ordered up to pass out to politicians who favored death as a solution to murder.

The pretrial hearings resulted in a split decision. The prosecution was allowed to use the videotaped confessions of Todd Scott and Scott Cobb at trial, but precluded from entering David McClary's videos into evidence. Demakos also decided that the police had conducted an illegal search of the house where Scott and Cobb had been arrested. He threw out all the evidence taken from the house including the two bloodstained jackets belonging to Todd Scott. The blood on both jackets had the same type as Edward Byrne's.

Kelly had been prepared to argue that Scott had actually done the shooting, accounting for the blood spray on the jacket arm of his gun hand and chest. With the evidence lost, Kelly had no choice but to go with the stories of Todd Scott and Scott Cobb, making David McClary the Shooter. A DNA test on the blood was never completed.

Because each of the defendants had made statements incriminating the other, Demakos decided to break the case up into three separate trials. Todd Scott and Philip Copeland would stand trial together. Scott Cobb would get his own jury, as would David McClary. The Scott–Copeland and Cobb juries would be seated at the same time, however, one jury box situated in front of the other. This was only the second time in the history of the state that two juries had been placed in the same room. The first was Howard Beach.

With jury selection under way, the witness Arjune suddenly appeared at an evidentiary hearing on January 31, 1989. While getting ready to testify against Mustafa on March 24, 1988, Arjune had shocked prosecutors by telling them he had recognized Byrne's killers on television. Although the prosecution did not think enough of Arjune's memory to call him as a grand jury witness in the case, the witness was adamant. Arjune's memory improved with time. By April 15, 1988, Arjune was saying that he had seen Todd Scott and Scott Cobb together outside his house on ten different occasions prior to the shooting. With his credibility attacked, Arjune turned the hearing into a circus, challenging Demakos himself.

"I saw Scott Cobb driving the car," Arjune snapped. "I saw him driving the car. You weren't there, but I was there and he was there and I saw him. I was there and I saw what happened. It wasn't right."

Michael Fishman, the attorney representing Scott Cobb and a petulant match for Arjune, failed to break the new witness.

"Were you with anybody when this happened?" Fishman asked.

"Yes. Jesus was with me."

Although it was clear to everyone in the court that recognition of the defendants had come to Arjune quite late in the story, Demakos ruled the witness credible. The ruling dealt a stunning blow to an already weak defense. Moments after hearing the ruling, Alosco visited his client.

"Do you know what's happening here?" Alosco asked.

"Yeah," Scott replied. "They're dropping a gun on me."

Alosco was sick. He believed two things about the case. First, he believed, or wanted to believe, that Todd Scott had gone to the Inwood Post not knowing what David McClary would do. Second, he believed, with some justification, that his client's confession had been coerced. Later that night, he sat at a table at Elaine's saying once more, "I'm not saying the guy is innocent. I'm just saying he isn't guilty in an American court of law." When the check came, he reached into his pocket and discovered a handwritten missive. The note had been written in the small round hand of a child.

"Thank you for everything you're doing, Mr. Alosco," Todd Scott wrote. "I appreciate it." Sal Alosco drank very hard that night, unable to understand the dichotomy of a teenager who kills brutally and then writes a thank-you note.

The trial opened on February 21, 1989. No one thought Edward Byrne's parents would survive the day. For twenty-two years the date February 21 had meant something joyful to the Byrne family. There had been many cakes and cards in the beginning and then two years prior, when Edward Byrne came of age, some champagne. But now the birthday had been lost to something twisted and evil. On February 21, 1989, Police Officer Edward Byrne would have been twenty-three. Instead, with the kid lying dead in a Long Island field of stones, his mother and father came to Part K-2.

Matt Byrne, his hands huge and his eyes bagged, sat in the fourth row, gripping the back of an oak pew. His wife, Ann, wearing a cop-blue dress, sat at his shoulder. They did not cry, there being no tears left. They just sat and watched, hoping the kid's death would matter for something in the end.

The reporters, about thirty of them, were crowded into the first three rows of the courtroom. Special high-intensity lights had been installed in the ceiling to facilitate television cameras. The reporters' necks went stiff trying to keep an eye on the Byrne family.

"Nothing from them today," said a cop guarding the Byrne family. "Today was the kid's birthday."

No one came to see the defendants, that being a large part of the story. To the man, they were regarded by court watchers as a loathsome lot who had tried to find family in a gang empire. Todd Scott, the youngest of the defendants, dressed entirely in black, sat at an oak defense table next to Alosco. He didn't come from a place where kids got birthday cards and cakes, so he showed no emotion. Once, he turned to face Matt Byrne, their eyes locking. It was Todd Scott who looked away first.

Both juries were led into the room and read a preliminary charge by Demakos. The judge then excused the Todd Scott–Philip Copeland jury to allow opening statements in the Scott Cobb case. Bartley had been chosen to give the opening in the Cobb case. No one was sure what to expect from the willowy prosecutor. He looked nervous, his hands shaking as he brought a glass of water to his thin lips. Bartley wore a dark blue suit and a red tie with yachts on it. But then the prosecutor started to speak, the tenor of his voice both strong and startling. A. Kirke Bartley, everyone agreed, was a find.

He first read through the indictment, his manner kind, and then shifted gears, going right for the throat.

"Edward Byrne, a young police officer, was following in the steps of his father, a police officer. Ladies and gentleman, ironically, on this very day last year, Edward Byrne celebrated his twenty-second birthday."

Several jurors lunged, as if rear-ended by a car. Michael Fishman jumped to his feet.

"Objection," he screamed.

"Overruled."

"Ladies and gentleman, we are going to focus now on the twenty-fifth of February 1988, a little less than a year ago. And the evidence will show that on that date, Edward Byrne reported to duty sometime before midnight for his late tour in the 103rd Precinct. And as he is reporting to duty, at the 103rd Precinct, a little less than a mile away in an apartment on 160th Street, Scott Cobb, together with Todd Scott and Philip Copeland, are planning to kill a cop. Not just any cop, ladies and gentleman, a cop in uniform. A cop who sits alone at night guarding a witness. Not to kill Eddie Byrne. To kill a cop.

"But, ladies and gentlemen, at this point that late evening of the twenty-fifth of February, as Eddie Byrne put on his blue uniform, the cruel hand of fate reached out for Eddie Byrne because he was given an assignment. A special assignment. He was to guard a witness by the name of Arjune. And the manner of which he was to guard this witness was to sit alone in a police car in front of this witness's house.

"At this point, ladies and gentleman, Eddie Byrne's fate was sealed. It was sealed because an order was given. An order from an individual by the name of Pappy Mason. An individual who had gone to jail just the day before, a boss, ladies and gentlemen. A boss who was not going to let his going to jail pass unanswered.

"Ladies and gentlemen, a message was delivered, an order was given, an order was given from jail. And that order was given to Pappy Mason's lieutenant, his trusted alter ego on the outside, Philip Copeland. And Philip Copeland, following the chain of command, enlisted and recruited Todd Scott, Scott Cobb, and David McClary. Enlisted them for one purpose. Pappy Mason wanted a cop dead."

The jurors were his now, Bartley could feel it. One elderly white woman in the back row was twisting a gold crucifix in her hand. A black man in the front row with a diamond earring was holding his head, his eyes misty. Bartley turned and pointed at the defendant, Scott Cobb. It was important, he had been taught, to point at the accused.

"He will attempt to place the bulk of the blame on his accomplices. But, ladies and gentleman, you will also hear the witnesses testify from this stand that prior to the murder of Edward Byrne, that Scott Cobb drove past the place where Edward Byrne was parked guarding that witness's house an hour or more earlier, and pointed to Edward Byrne and said, 'THAT COP IS GOING TO DIE TONIGHT.' You will hear that testimony."

After telegraphing the testimony of Black Rachel and Arjune, depositions that would ultimately put Scott Cobb on the same block with Byrne, Bartley described the shooting.

"Ladies and gentlemen, the order given from jail was carried out. The message was delivered, a young police officer was found minutes later slumped over in his patrol car, five bullet wounds shattering his head, ending his life. Ladies and gentleman, the evidence, the associates of Scott Cobb, the eyewitnesses that you are going to hear, Scott Cobb's own statement, the physical evidence will reveal to you Scott Cobb the planner, Scott Cobb the driver and, moreover, Scott Cobb the messenger. The message, ladies and gentlemen, was a message of death to Eddie Byrne. It was, as you will hear from the testimony on videotape, as Scott Cobb says, 'You take one of us and we'll take one of you.'

"Thank you."

Scott Cobb, wearing a yellow shirt, dungarees, and red shoes, tapped a ballpoint pen on the defense table. It was the only sound in the courtroom. Fishman shuffled a sheaf of yellow papers. Matt Byrne took off his glasses and then rubbed his eyes.

"Mr. Fishman?" Demakos said, inviting a follow.

Fishman, a small man with a ratlike snout and thick mustache, moved to the well, pulling a lectern close to the jury box. The scratching of the wood on tile filled the room with annoyance.

"I've felt you've had enough of having your heartstrings pulled," Fishman began. "Mr. Bartley was very competent in evoking emotion. We'll find out how competent they are in bringing forth facts."

Fishman then went into a dissertation on the law, insisting Cobb had been an unwitting dupe. He referred to the cases of Joel

Steinberg and Howard Beach, noting that jurors had acquitted defendants in both cases on the most serious murder charges. He talked about coercion, saying, "The death of a police officer under any circumstances is a terrible, terrible thing. The death of a police officer under the circumstances here mobilizes the police force . . . The police totally mobilized to do everything they could, including, when they thought they had the proper suspect, threatening physical coercion until young Scott Cobb gave in and was willing to tell them anything that they wanted to know and did so." After a few words about credibility of witnesses, Fishman sat down.

The Cobb jury was then excused for the day, Demakos explaining at a sidebar that one of them had tickets to see some fake drama, *Phantom of the Opera.* After the jury left, Matt Byrne walked over to Kirke Bartley and slapped him on the back.

"Thank you," he said.

Now it was Gene Kelly's turn to address the Todd Scott–Copeland jury. Kelly stood in the well of the court, an experienced man, shaking. He tugged at his tie and picked at his brown suit jacket. The crime still had him scared. He wanted the jury to see him trembling in the presence of Todd Scott and to imagine the terror Edward Byrne might have felt upon being this close to the killer. He rolled his shoulders and began talking, stopping briefly to wipe a lock of brown hair off his forehead. As the big man talked, the facts chased away his nervousness. Kelly talked about a murder known to the detectives as Case No. 435 of 1988, a body ticketed No. 1339 of 1988 by the medical examiner, a killing known to the grand jury as Case No. 1662 of 1988. And then, with great intensity, Kelly gave the numbers a policeman's face.

"To us, ladies and gentlemen, this is the case of a young man, a member of your police department, who was the recipient of a symbolic message by the agents of death to the people of this city that they are above the law, and if you interfere with them or interfere with their leaders, they will shoot you even under the cover of darkness and even if you happen to be dressed in blue."

Alosco and Hancock lurched up, demanding a mistrial. Kelly pushed on through their objections, identifying Pappy Mason as the architect of the hit, explaining the Bebos and their contract. He described the testimony of Martin Howell and Darry Newby as to conspiracy, and hinted to the existence of Rachel Moore as an eyewitness to the killing. Eventually he wound up discussing the testimony of the medical examiner who had examined Byrne. His voice boomed through the court and, because of the cameras, the city itself.

"She will testify that upon her examination, she found evidence of five gunshot wounds. Now that is five gunshot wounds, ladies and gentleman, that snuffed out the life of a young man who was a member of your police department. And those were five shots that were heard on the streets of Jamaica, and, ladies and gentlemen, they were five shots that were felt across all of America."

Kelly sat down. Todd Scott was trying to be invisible, his chin dropped deep on his chest. Philip Copeland had turned to face a friend in the audience. The nervous defendant smirked and waved, like a fighter trying to shake off a blow to the head. Alosco rubbed a line of sweat from his forehead. Hancock bit his bottom lip.

"Mr. Alosco?" Demakos inquired.

"Your Honor, on behalf of defendant Todd Scott, I waive my opening."

"Mr. Hancock?"

"I waive opening statement."

A television with a forty-inch screen was then rolled into the room and Todd Scott's videotape inserted. All eyes remained riveted to the television set as Scott's voice and murderous plan filled the room.

"Somebody wanted to do something to this cop who be sleeping by hisself in the early morning hours," the jurors heard Scott say. "He didn't never see Dave coming."

Matthew Byrne brought a hand to his face, time not doing

much to make the loss any easier. Later Alosco stood in the hallway, pitching his defense to a jury of reporters.

"Todd went to see what the other fellow would do," Alosco said. "It was like being on a runaway train. He didn't know when to exit. Is he guilty? Yeah, he's guilty of being stupid."

The trial continued on Wednesday and Thursday, Kelly parading a steady line of prosecutors and detectives to the stand. Scott Tulman, now in private practice, was called as the state's first witness and used to introduce the devastating videotapes into evidence. "This is an honor," Tulman told his friends. "Being called here is like being called to serve your country. How can you refuse?" At one point, Tulman caught Todd Scott's eye and stared him down. Sergeant William Norfleet, a huge man with twenty years on the job, recalled signing Edward Byrne's memo book moments before his death and then returning to find the young cop's head shattered.

Richard Sica, the case detective, followed in the afternoon of the second day. He wore a dark blue suit, his gold shield hanging over his top pocket. Worried about breaking down on the stand again, Sica avoided eye contact with the Byrne family. He was shown a series of color crime scene photos, the dead cop's blood still fresh-looking. As Sica talked, the photographs were circulated at the defense table. Cobb and Scott strained to see the pictures. Todd Scott snickered and brought a hand to his mouth. It was like he was peering into the car again. Alosco requested a sidebar, objecting to the photos being placed into evidence.

"I didn't object before," Alosco said. "But I have re-examined the photographs and what I didn't notice before is that pieces of the officer's brains are on the seat in the photograph . . . I mean, there's actually chunks of his brain on the seat."

Demakos agreed to re-examine the photos before showing them to the jury. Sica continued with his narrative, his manner confident and perfect. Although Alosco and Hancock tried to get Sica to admit to having beaten their clients into confessions, Sica survived the questioning unmarked. After being excused from the stand, Sica met Matt Byrne in the hallway. The men hugged, tears in their eyes.

Sica's partner, Pete Pistone, followed him to the stand, describing his trip to the hospital with Byrne's body. Bullet fragments were produced and circulated at the defense table. As Alosco spoke with Hancock, Todd Scott picked up the bullets. It was a damaging image. Alosco heard a gasp from the jury box and turned to see his client with the bullets. Again. He grabbed Scott under the table.

"Put those down," he muttered.

Bartley was about to introduce photographs of Byrne's bloody uniform into evidence when Alosco called for another sidebar. It was a bloody uniform that the defendants had wanted to see, Bartley had decided. Let's show the jury the uniform.

"What are you offering for evidence?" Alosco asked.

"The photographs of the clothing of the officer," Bartley said. "It is not gruesome."

"It is irrelevant," Fishman countered. "The shooting took place in the head. The gloves, the T-shirt, the underwear. There's just too much blood."

"It is relevant that he is a uniformed police officer that was guarding a house," Bartley said. "Blood is unavoidable."

Demakos ruled against the uniform. He did not mind the jury hearing what had happened to Edward Byrne, but allowing them to see, well, that was more than any jury could be asked to bear. Although the trial was scheduled to resume on Friday, Michael Fishman advised the court his client had joined a Muslim sect in prison. Friday, Fishman explained, is the Muslim high holy day. Demakos was furious, but unable to do anything. He canceled all Friday court dates.

In the hallway, Richie Sica called a friend aside.

"It's too bad Cobb found religion so late in life," he said. "If Cobb is a Muslim back on February 26, 1988, Eddie Byrne is still alive."

"How's that?"

"Eddie Byrne was killed on a Friday."

Richie Sica on the ghost of Edward Byrne.

"I went to dinner at a friend's house out on Long Island. It was the first time, really, that I had taken a break from the case. This was on the night of February 25, 1989. We were having a good time, but then I started to get moody as it approached midnight. It was a very eerie feeling. I didn't say anything to the hosts at first, but finally my friend sees something is wrong. He says, 'You're thinking about Byrne, aren't you?' And I was. An idea had suddenly struck me. It was the anniversary of his killing and all I could see was the way he had looked in the car. I started to think about driving out to the Inwood Post. I just felt I should be there at 3:30 A.M. on February 26, you know, the one-year anniversary. I wanted to go, to see what it felt like to be there again at the precise moment in time. My friend talked me out of it. I remember, the guy knew a lot about the case. He said, 'You know who you'll meet out there if you go? Matt Byrne. The two of you will be standing out there in the middle of nowhere, feeling sorry for yourself.' He said, 'This case isn't your life. You have to move on.' And I felt the guy was right, so I stayed away. In the morning, I went to the precinct. The guys were there, talking. They looked kind of spooked. I asked, 'What's up?' And one of the guys said, 'Matt Byrne was out there at the Inwood Post last night. He was just standing there praying. It was like the two of them, Eddie and the old man, were together again.' I guess, on the whole, cops are pretty weird guys."

Part K-2 had become a kind of Mecca for good and evil. Crack dealers and cops waiting to make appearances in a narcotics court killed time at the Byrne trial. The dealers stood in line waiting for a chance to walk through a metal detector. They wore long trench

241

coats and new black army boots, the latest in South Jamaica street fashion. One kid after another stepped up to the court officers.

"Is this the trial for the Bebos?" they asked. The court officers replied, "No. This is the murder trial of Edward Byrne." The kids shrugged and laughed. "Same thing," they said.

The court officers handed each of the dealers small gray trays, requesting that all telephone beepers be checked at the door. Members of crack society found seats on the left side of the courtroom behind the defendants. The cops, dozens of them, sat on the right side of the court behind the prosecution table, in pews marked "Reserved M.O.S."—cop shorthand for Members of the Service. In Queens, the distance between noble and diabolic was an eight-foot-wide aisle.

The kids were listening one day as Scott Cobb's written statement was being read.

Todd said, "We rocked that nigger."

One of the beeper kids started to laugh. Amazingly, no one in the M.O.S. section came across the aisle. A white-shirted court officer rushed over instead, ordering the spectators quiet. The officer was still walking away when the kid with the beeper used his index finger and thumb to form an imaginary gun.

"Pow, pow," the dealer whispered, pulling the trigger. A few minutes later, the kids left, laughing, heading off to their own arraignments. The lesson of Todd Scott, apparently, was that he was no lesson at all.

The first eyewitness to the murder plan appeared on Wednesday, March 1. Darry Newby, first-generation crackhead, took the stand, looking chubby and clean, having gained forty pounds since leaving the Forties Houses. He had been living in a hotel for a time, and then moved to a secret location where he worked odd jobs.

Darry Newby spoke in a barely audible voice and played with a gold watch on his right wrist. It was the first public look, really, at the life of a crack dealer. The sixteen-year-old witness described his life as a crack seller and reported having been at the meeting in Roger Phillips's apartment where the killing had been planned. He was very bad on details, misspelling the name of his own gang—the Bebos—and being unable to remember if he was drunk or sober when the meeting took place. His testimony could be reduced to a single sentence.

"Todd Scott was talking to Philip Copeland and Scott Cobb. He said that, 'We have to kill a police officer regarding a witness.' "

Alosco and Hancock hammered at Newby's credibility, getting him to admit he had been given immunity in two drug cases in exchange for his testimony. Fishman was particularly reckless, the judge calling him insolent. Still, Newby survived, making a single cultural mistake.

"You never got high?" Hancock asked.

"No."

"Never smoked marijuana."

"Oh yeah, reefer. But that's it." There was some chuckling in the jury boxes—Queens residents living in a city where marijuana was no longer even considered a drug. During a recess, Philip Copeland's mother stood in the hallway, holding a Bible. She would not pass judgment on her brother's son, Darry Newby, or even her own son.

"Only God knows if Philip done it," she said. "If he did it, God knows. If he didn't do it, God knows. If he done it, God be taking care of him. He gets what coming then. You can't raise a boy but so much."

A mob of reporters had also surrounded Alosco.

"I was hoodwinked into this case," he said publicly. "My family is pissed off at me. My friends are pissed off at me. But I'm still doing the job. I'll go tonight for dinner and have a clear conscience. I'll be eating alone, but I'll have a clear conscience."

11

"WE GOT TROUBLE."

Martin Howell moved to the witness stand in the late afternoon, searching the defense table as he sat in the box. He found defendant Philip Copeland and smiled the smile of a boxer at a prefight weigh-in. As a seventeen-year-old in South Jamaica, Howell had called him Marshal; he had been all the law a crack gang respected, a policeman of sorts. Howell had not sold crack since the day after Edward Byrne had died. Like Newby, he had gained forty pounds, and his mind and eye were powerful. He was not terrorized anymore.

"Marshal ain't nothing no more," Howell had told Sica before taking the stand. "I'm the shit now. If they get out, they got to worry about me."

Howell was sporting a Mike Tyson haircut and wearing a tan suit jacket, gray tie, and olive pants. He had a gold bracelet on his right wrist and a gold watch on his left. His knees twitched as he spoke.

"What was your association with the Bebos?" Gene Kelly began.

"I was a narcotics trafficker."

Howell then began his narrative, putting the conspirators in Roger Phillips's apartment on the night of the cop killing. Although Kelly did not need to prove conspiracy to convict on murder charges, he felt he needed a meeting. In truth, Kelly now knew, the killing had been set up in Viola Nichols's apartment. But he had already decided not to call Viola as a prosecution witness. He did not want the jury hearing about any rough-and-tumble cops, or hearing that Pappy Mason had wanted Officer Bobby Kisch murdered instead of Edward Byrne. So he went with the story he had.

"What, if anything, did Todd Scott say?"

"Mr. Todd, he said that the boss had put out an order to hit a cop," Howell replied. "And whichever one of us was to participate, will receive $8,000 dollars."

"Where was Scott Cobb at this time?"

"He was right next to him."

"What did you say?"

"I asked Todd what if we got caught, and he said that we wouldn't get caught because the guy sleeps on the job and it would be easy."

"What did you say?"

"I said, 'I ain't with it.' "

"Was Philip Copeland there?"

"Yes. Philip Copeland asked Scott Cobb, did he have the 'Jammies'?"

"What do you mean by the word 'Jammies'? "

"It's street terminology for guns. Scott said he was going to get the artillery from Ninja."

"Who is Ninja, by the way?"

"He's another member of the gang."

The direct testimony was devastating. Howell was excused for the night and celebrated his first anniversary as a guest of the New York City Police Department with a room-service steak and beer.

*

Howell returned to court the next morning, March 2, 1989. The oak-paneled room was angry and uneasy. Overnight, an undercover DEA agent named Everett Hatcher had been gunned down while sitting in his car on a desolate Staten Island lot. People were already comparing the assassination to that of Byrne. Some of the jurors later admitted to having read about the case. Agent Hatcher, ironically enough, had been the only DEA agent to work on the Byrne murder.

Alosco directed his cross-examination of the witness to the question of Howell's credibility. The lawyer knew Howell had flunked a polygraph, but failed to get the results of the test into the record. He then hit Howell for being an opportunist, trying to portray him as man who would say anything to get reward money. Howell was not, by any stretch of the imagination, your classic hero. But he had done the right thing in the wrong age.

"I was feeling guilty," Howell said of his decision to come forth. "It was on my conscience."

Conscience. No one had mentioned the word in the case before. Alosco heard it and moved on, quickly. Howell explained that he was making $1,500 a week as a crack distributor, and the jury gasped at the figure. With so much money to be made in crack, it seemed unreasonable to believe Howell would turn in a friend for a reward.

"Well, reward money is good," Howell admitted, finally. "But that ain't the full reason that I'm up here."

"You are not here to finger someone so the street is clear for you, are you?" Alosco said.

"I'm here so the street is clear for everybody."

Fishman didn't fare much better.

"Did you pay income tax?" Fishman demanded. Howell smiled. The jurors laughed. The judge said, "Mr. Fishman. Please."

Finally, in closing, Howell spoke to motive.

"Pappy said that he wanted to see on television that a cop got iced."

He also reported on a conversation he had with Philip Copeland when some crack money turned up missing two days after the assassination.

"Marshal said, 'If you don't want to wind up like that motherfucking cop, then the money better turn up.' "

On his way out of the court, Howell stopped to throw Copeland another look. All told, Howell had testified to six incriminating conversations that he had never reported to police originally.

"Damn," said Copeland, squirming.

"Hummph," said the witness.

Roger Phillips refused to testify. He was staying with his grandmother in North Carolina when the telephone rang. Roger picked it up and heard Todd Scott. "If you testify, I'll kill you," Roger reported Todd Scott telling him. Roger hit the bottle immediately and remained in a drunken stupor for days. Kelly was too scared to put him on the stand. Kevin Curry, another witness, also refused to testify.

"Lately I been forgetting things," Curry told Sica.

"Like what?"

"Like anything Gene Kelly tries to ask me."

With Phillips gone and Curry playing games, Gene Kelly went to his secret witness. At 12:30 P.M. on Wednesday, March 8, he produced Rachel Moore. With the exception of what was to follow with the witness Arjune, Moore's testimony was the high point of the trial, a riveting display of courage, and yes, perhaps, storytelling.

Rachel Moore stepped to the stand, wearing a black dress with a scarf around her neck. The cops had dressed her, picking out clothes that made the streetwalker look like a cop widow. The scarf covered up a nasty scar. Rachel had stayed on the street for two months before being located in the South. She'd gotten into a fight with a neighbor who'd slashed her throat with a knife. It took twenty stitches to keep the Byrne prosecution from bleeding to death.

Rachel's hair had grown back and she had gained twenty

pounds. She was reluctant to look at the defense table, appearing shy and coy. She spoke in a raspy, naughty voice. A. Kirke Bartley conducted the direct examination, Rachel testifying that she had known Todd Scott since grammar school and Marshal and Scott Cobb for a period of three years. Eventually, they worked around to her employment.

"How were you making money at that time?" Bartley asked.

"I was a working girl."

"Now, Rachel, did you have any customers that evening?"

"Yes."

"Now what, if anything, did you do with the money you received from these individuals?"

"I bought crack with it."

Moore gained confidence as she talked, describing how she had been waiting for a customer at the corner of 107th Avenue and Pinegrove, a block behind Edward Byrne's police car.

"Well, I was standing in between Inwood and Pinegrove. I was like in the middle of the block, about three houses down from the cop car. I was on the sidewalk at the time fixing my shoes, tying them up. Then I stood up, halfway in the street. I looked up the block and saw Scott Cobb stuck his head out the car, looked down toward my way, then he looked in front of him."

"What happened at that time? Would you tell the jury?"

"All right. Todd, he walked on the sidewalk, on the passenger side of the cop car. I seen Marshal and Dave McClary. Dave was standing in front of Marshal on the driver's side. Todd bent down looking inside the cop car. And then all of them came out with guns and they started shooting. I hit the ground, ending up under a car. I crawled up under a car. Scared. I was like in between two cars."

"For how long a time did you remain underneath this car?"

"About five minutes. I went to the back streets. I ran around behind Pinegrove and all the way home, running scared and crying."

"Where did you run, Rachel?"

"Home. I heard sirens. Took my coat off and threw it in the garbage. Didn't want anyone to see . . ."

"For how long did you stay home?"

"For the night and next day."

At this point, a fire alarm started to clang. Demakos jumped at the sound, as did the jurors. The timing of the alarm, although accidental, was perfect. The bell was tolling for Todd Scott, Philip Copeland, and Scott Cobb. Rachel Moore had put herself three doors down from Byrne and situated the yellow Dodge directly behind herself and the target. She had also spotted three of the four men on the block with guns in their hands. As the bell rang wildly, Alosco and Fishman reviewed their sets of Rachel's prior statements and grand jury minutes. The eyewitness had never, ever, told the story in this way before.

"I am told it is not an emergency," Demakos said of the alarm.

"I beg to differ, Your Honor," muttered Alosco.

After a recess, Rachel Moore resumed the stand under direct examination. Moore was standing at a model of the block, placing the killers around the police car again, when the fire alarm went off a second time. Moore continued testifying through the ringing bell. She placed herself in the middle of the block and Bartley ended his direct examination, turning the witness over to Alosco.

The task of attacking the witness's credibility had fallen to Alosco. He was ready to allow that Moore had been on the block, but was certain that she had been too high on crack to remember what, if anything, she had witnessed.

"Okay," he began. "How many dates was it that you had on February 25, if you recall?"

"A number of them, I wasn't counting. Probably ten dates."

"Well, were you getting paid for these dates?"

"Yes. Twenty dollars, ten."

"How long did each date last?"

"Oh, about twenty minutes."

The witness was being both naughty and coquettish. She

brought a hand to her face and giggled. The jury laughed with the mischievous witness.

"Yeah, but some wasn't twenty minutes," Rachel said. "You know . . ."

Alosco was beet-red.

"I understand," he continued. "Now—I won't say a word. In either event, you had ten dates or more and each of them lasted twenty minutes . . ."

"No," said Demakos, interrupting. "She said some . . ." Then he, too, gave the jury an embarrassed look. Rachel Moore saw the judge in trouble and rescued him.

"Some last a little longer than others," she said with a wink. A few of the jurors actually clapped. Alosco waded on.

"Were all the dates in cars?"

"Some wasn't. Some was in hotels."

"Well, how long did you stay at the hotel?"

Alosco had stepped into a clean right hand.

"I stayed there thirty minutes. Hotels is usually, you know, longer."

"Did you register at the hotel?"

Rachel brought a hand to her face and peeked through her fingers at the lawyer.

"No. You don't register."

Now, even Matt Byrne was smiling. Demakos hid his face from the television camera.

Alosco quit the subject of prostitution and pressed on to crack smoking. Rachel Moore, a young mother, admitted smoking twenty to thirty crack vials a day, including ten vials on the night of Byrne's murder. She insisted she was not high, however, when she witnessed the attack on Byrne. The witness was completely unable to pinpoint the time of the shooting or explain her previous versions of the assassination. She was also soft on the shooting itself.

"They started shooting. All I heard was the shots and I jumped on the ground."

"Did you see Todd shooting?"

"I saw a gun in his hands. When I heard the shot, I hit the ground."

Moore was, quite obviously, mistaken. Todd Scott may well have fired a gun into Byrne's car, but he could not have been on the passenger side door, firing. The forensic evidence showed that all the shots had been fired through Byrne's window.

Pressed on the issue, Moore stammered, "They had guns in their hands. I don't know who shot."

"So you don't know who shot?"

"No."

There were other problems too, now, Moore's testimony beginning to unravel. She had originally said she saw Todd Scott get back into the getaway car. Now she was saying she had never seen anything after the first report of a gun.

"I said I thought he got in the car. I don't know. Probably did. I don't know."

"Did you tell them that Todd Scott was the shooter of Police Officer Byrne?"

"I said they all pulled guns out. I don't know who shot. Hey—I seen them with their guns."

"And you didn't see any flashes of guns."

"No."

"No further questions."

Alosco felt triumphant. Rachel Moore was all over the map. She was, he felt, an eyewitness who had not seen the shooting. After a ten-minute recess, Frank Hancock started his cross-examination. Moore was the only witness to place Philip Copeland at the murder scene. Hancock had discovered a court document that showed Rachel had reported to court on the morning of February 26, 1988—six hours after the shooting—to answer a prostitution charge. That meant Rachel had not been home crying for two days. The witness had been caught in a contradiction.

"I don't remember going to court the next day," she said, when confronted. "What for?"

"Indeed, what for?" Hancock countered. The lawyer then produced the document, forcing Gene Kelly to eat Rachel Moore's

memory lapse. Hancock then got Moore to admit she had continued to smoke crack for a month after the shooting, an admission that meant she had been high when she testified before the
grand jury. He then revealed that Rachel had continued to prostitute herself for four months after the shooting, getting arrested for
the last time on June 8, 1988. Hancock also produced a photograph of Moore taken on March 2, 1988, that showed her to be
a sallow-faced skeleton of her present self. The made-over Rachel
Moore looked at the picture and went wild-eyed. Kelly squirmed.
The case against Copeland was falling apart. Hancock proceeded
to expose a fatal flaw in the witness's made-over account of the
shooting.

"We have Mr. Copeland and Mr. McClary directly on the other
side of the car on the passenger side, right?"

"Yes."

"Mr. Scott shooting into the car?"

"Yes."

"Did you see Mr. Copeland fall?"

Kelly bounced to his feet, Demakos sustaining his objection.

"Well, did you see anybody injured as a result of that shooting?"

"I didn't see nobody. I was under the car when they were
shooting."

Hancock was sneering. Moore was wiping her face with a hand-
kerchief.

"No further questions."

With Moore now reeling, Fishman moved in for what he hoped
would be a kill. Moore had made many mistakes. She had flip-
flopped on her identifications of the getaway car, the number of
people on the block, the position of killers on the block, even her
own position on 107th Avenue. Moore could not even remember
going to court on the day of the shooting. Fishman needed to show
that crack had boiled her brain free of memory.

"When did you start using cocaine?"

"Approximately 1986."

"Did you ever use cocaine in a form other than crack?"

"Well, I cooked it. I used to cook cocaine. I cooked it up. It's crack."

"When did you start smoking marijuana?"

"When I was sixteen years old."

"Did you share crack with your johns?"

"Yes."

It was approaching 6 P.M. Demakos called an end to the questioning and ordered Moore back to the stand in the morning. Moore walked off the stand, her legs shaky. Gene Kelly rubbed his face and cursed.

"We got trouble," Kelly decided.

A. Kirke Bartley worked with the witness for many hours that night. He wanted to keep her story simple. All the prosecution needed was for Rachel to say she'd seen all of the killers on the block—including Philip Copeland. She was coached to say she saw guns and heard guns. It was not important to know who had shot, only that the four had been there when the shooting was done. In a pinch, Rachel could always blame the cops for misstating what she had told them in her reports.

Rachel Moore retook the stand at 10:50 A.M. She was wearing a gray business suit. The former professional woman looked, well, professional.

"Did you see who fired the shots?" Fishman asked, resuming his cross.

"When they first started shooting, I'd seen Todd Scott shooting."

Kelly objected immediately, sending a message to his witness. Fishman asked the question a second time. Moore, having seen Kelly's reaction, modified her answer.

"I saw him with a gun in his hand."

Fishman showed Moore her grand jury minutes, in which she had testified that Scott had shot Byrne.

"And did, in fact," Fishman asked now, "Todd Scott do the shooting on that night?"

"He had the gun in his hand. I don't know whether he shot or not."

"On February 26th, 1988, isn't it a fact that you heard more than one gun being fired?"

The witness did not hesitate. "Yes," she said.

Kelly stood up, waving a ballpoint pen.

"Objection, Your Honor. And I ask that be stricken."

"No," Demakos said. "Overruled."

Now everyone in the courtroom was confused. Matt Byrne looked as if he would be ill. Fishman spent the next two hours getting Moore to admit she had "misspoken" about quitting crack within a month after her arrest and misstated the length of her continued employment as a streetwalker. Moore admitted she had once performed sex in the yellow Dodge with a man other than the defendants and blamed the police for misstating her eyewitness accounts of the shooting. Finally, Fishman tried to prove that Moore had not come forth voluntarily as previously stated.

"Isn't it a fact that you were picked up for having committed another crime of loitering when you got into the police car on March 2, 1988?"

Kelly objected, but Demakos overruled him, repeating the question himself. "Were you picked up for loitering?"

"Well, I was on the corner, I got in the car. I wasn't . . ."

Demakos saw, quite suddenly, the question's importance.

"Please," he insisted of the witness. "Were you picked up for loitering at the time?"

"They didn't arrest me, no."

"They didn't arrest you, but you were picked up for loitering?" Fishman said.

"Objection."

"Sustained."

"You were working that night?" he continued.

"Yes."

Fishman smiled. He had no further questions. Kelly was shaking. It had been bad, but not bad enough to ruin the case completely. Kelly had a decision to make. He could patch up the holes in Moore's testimony with a series of questions on redirect examination. But that would mean allowing the defense another shot at his floundering witness on re-cross.

"Any redirect?" Demakos wondered.

"No, Your Honor, we have no redirect."

Rachel Moore walked out of the courtroom and the city. She was relocated in the South along with her mother. The pity of the streetwalker was that while she had put her life on the line for the police department, she had never been able to tell the story as she knew it. Rachel Moore had, no doubt, been at the murder scene, high on crack. She knew too much about the killing. As she first reported, she might have even seen Todd Scott fire into the car, blood spraying his jacket, David McClary at his side. But she probably never saw the car parked behind the patrol car and she certainly never saw Philip Copeland at the murder scene. She saw enough to get Todd Scott and David McClary convicted of murder and enough to create a whole lot of trouble for Scott Cobb. Rachel Moore was an eyewitness to murder. But she testified to another man's vision of the crime.

A month after testifying, Rachel Moore's mother was arrested on a shop-lifting charge in Alabama. A woman that had been relocated after her daughter had decided to help the police, she died in police custody under mysterious circumstances. An investigation into the murder was scuttled.

He used to be the man with one name. But by the time Arjune arrived at Judge Demakos's courtroom on March 15, he was completely anonymous, a witness in a Federal witness-protection program. There has never been an American success story quite like him, Guyanese mechanic turned professional witness.

Arjune walked to the orange witness chair in Part K-2, the first hint of a swagger in his step. He wore an ordinary brown suit and black shoes with a plastic sheen. Richie Sica, unsure of what to call the Federally protected witness, settled on a nickname—Mr. America. A brave and yet insolent man, Arjune carried himself into court like a man who has seen it all. At the hearing, Arjune said he had recognized the men who killed Byrne at a distance of sixty-five feet. The defense was intent upon putting the distance at one month, saying Arjune needed until March 24 to get his story straight.

Philip Copeland was actually singing at the defense table before Arjune took the stand. He was talking to himself by the end of the afternoon. Arjune's testimony had an even worse effect on the defendant Scott Cobb. During a lunch break, Cobb punched out another inmate who asked him to share a bench.

Arjune had taken the stand against drug dealers twice before, both cases resulting in conviction. In each case, he had testified the way Roberto Duran punches—with contempt. The last time Arjune had said he saw something happen on the street, the guy got fifty-to-life.

Arjune arrived at court in a splendid motorcade, sirens screeching against the morning. A helicopter covered him from the sky as Arjune walked into court, a coat covering his face. He was not, Demakos had warned the defense attorneys, someone to be trifled with.

"Arjune," said the court officer swearing him in. "A-r-j-u-n."

The witness pointed a bony finger at the clerk and said, "E. You missed the E."

And then he was off, placing Todd Scott at the shattered window of Edward Byrne's patrol car.

"Now after Todd Scott left the cop's car, he took two steps facing the car that was waiting for him. The car driven by Scott Cobb. Then Todd Scott turned around and looked to my house, like as if he wanted to come for me now. He looked to my house, but he made the decision not to come there, because I was waiting, too."

The screaming started right there, and never really stopped. The jurors, having already spent most of a month hearing from witnesses weak of voice and even weaker of character, were ecstatic. Arjune, the runaway witness, was their revenge.

Arjune calmed down for a bit, testifying that he had rushed to his window after hearing "five heavy shots," in time to see Todd Scott at the cop's window. He then saw Scott and another "colored guy" get into a yellowish car driven by Scott Cobb. Arjune failed to mention, however, how it was possible to see Cobb at a distance of sixty-five feet through a tinted window. Arjune made no attempt to place Copeland at the scene, but then he was never asked to.

Alosco began his cross-examination and immediately found himself in trouble.

"Were you in the bedroom with your wife?"

"Obviously. I always sleep with my beloved wife."

"Now when you got out of bed, did you get out of bed at the same time or did your wife get out of bed, or did you go first?"

"I went first. She ran to jump out of the window and go away, but I said, 'Take it easy. We are alive.' "

"What did you see, the first thing you saw?"

"The first thing I saw was Todd Scott."

"And you saw my client near the driver's side, is that right?"

"Listen. I told you this before. I'm telling you the truth, that is what I'm here for."

"What was it that you saw him doing at the time?"

"He was looking at the poor kid that got killed."

"Did you see what he looked like that night, how he was dressed?"

"Well, he looked exactly like that guy (indicating Todd Scott). That's him. He wore a brown jacket."

"You were able to see the mustache?"

"Oh, sure. I am not blind."

"How much did he weigh?"

"I didn't have a scale."

The audience was clapping and laughing. A half-dozen of the twenty-four jurors in the room were holding their stomachs. Alosco demanded that Demakos admonish the witness. Fishman demanded that the judge admonish the entire audience. Demakos buried his face in his hands.

"Okay," Alosco continued. "Who else did you see that evening?"

"I saw the driver of the car," Arjune said, pointing his finger. "That gentleman right there."

"Scott Cobb?"

"Your buddy, yes."

"My friend?"

"Yes."

Alosco didn't like that answer much. It was one thing to defend a cur. It was quite another to have someone call you a dog's best friend. He stepped back and shuffled his papers. It was going to be a very long night at Elaine's.

Alosco moved on to Arjune's 911 call, but the witness remembered little about the call. He only recalled that he had talked to a female officer after hearing five heavy shots. He did not remember having told a police operator he saw a man running from Byrne's car or giving a description of the suspect. Arjune could not explain, either, why he had waited until after seeing photographs of Scott Cobb and Todd Scott on television before volunteering his testimony. For his part, Alosco made a major mistake in not asking Arjune how he could have positively identified William Benjamin's car as the getaway vehicle. Still, Arjune was masterful at slipping punches.

"I am lucky I am still alive," he volunteered, apropos of nothing.

"I am happy you are alive," said a startled Alosco.

"You are sure you are happy?"

Alosco took off his glasses, wiping them clean.

"Do you wear glasses, by the way?"

"Yes, I wear glasses to read. Not like you, sir."

"Your vision is not impaired in any way, you're not nearsighted or farsighted?"

"I'm not blind yet, sir."

Alosco handed the witness some photographs of his home taken at night.

"This is the way it looked back then," Arjune said. "But it's dark. I don't think you could see without your glasses. But I could."

Alosco sat down a minute later. He was exhausted. Fishman followed, faring little better.

"I remember you," Arjune said. "You're Mr. Fisherman, right?"

"Close enough," Fishman muttered. Arjune got the occupation right, if not the name. Fishman spent much of his time on the 911 tape, noting that Arjune, like Rachel Moore, had changed his story too many times to remain a credible witness. Frank Hancock, noting that Arjune had never even mentioned Philip Copeland's name, passed on cross-examination altogether.

The jurors were excused and filed past the witness. Arjune made eye contact with them all, winking and nodding. The jurors, to the man and woman, smiled back. Gene Kelly rested the prosecution's case the next day. Much later, long after rendering their verdicts in the case, nearly all of the jurors would say the same thing: Arjune was the prosecution's best witness. Only he was embellishing.

12

"OPPOSE US AND YOU DIE."

Philip Copeland had an alibi. Audette Wills, a petite and well-mannered South Jamaica housewife, took the stand and pronounced Copeland her secret lover. It was all the murder trial had been missing—the sex angle.

Wills, twenty-seven, testified that she had spent just one evening with the suspect, Copeland picking her up at 7 P.M. on the night of February 25, 1988. The couple had spent time with two other people over drinks at the Flagship Diner. Two other women, Dietra Holloway and Linda Barnes, were also produced, testifying that they had seen the happy couple together at various times in the evening when other witnesses had Copeland in Roger Phillips's apartment. Eventually, Wills said, she retired with Copeland to Room 504 at the Kennedy Inn on Baisley Boulevard. The two had fallen off to sleep at 2 A.M., she testified, after a night of take-out shrimp and amorous love-making. Copeland slept between his date and the wall, Wills recalled, making it impossible for him to get out of bed without her noticing. She awakened between 3:30 and 4:00 A.M., saying there was a chill in the room. Philip Copeland, she said, was sleeping in his clothes.

A crack user with a failing marriage, Wills had left her children at home with her husband. She had awakened at around 7 A.M. to find Copeland still in the bed beside her. Wills sounded believable and produced a receipt for a hotel room for the night in question.

In rebuttal, Kelly provided a detective who said that, despite a thorough investigation, he had been unable to verify Copeland's alibi. A night manager the detective spoke with could not remember seeing Copeland or Wills, but identified the hotel receipt as being valid. A maid said a man and woman had spent the night in the room, but she could not recognize them.

Ultimately, the question of Copeland's direct involvement in the murder remained open. He had certainly planned the killing. But only Rachel Moore had placed him at the scene at a time when another woman placed him in bed. Then again, the witness had not put Copeland on the block until after meeting secretly with Gene Kelly. Copeland also had time to leave the hotel, kill Byrne, and return before Wills awakened. The question of Copeland's guilt or innocence was going to be the jury's toughest call.

Philip Copeland had one last play to make. He figured he was the only defendant with a decent chance of winning an acquittal, so on March 21 he moved to protect his flank. He spoke to Todd Scott as the two waited in a holding cell, warning his co-defendant not to take the stand in his own defense.

"You've said enough already," Copeland warned Scott. "I don't want to see you on the stand. You know I still got juice."

Copeland then asked Hancock to excuse him from the rest of the proceedings, hoping the jury, upon seeing Copeland absent from court, would further sever him from Todd Scott.

"He doesn't want to be here," Hancock told Demakos at a sidebar. "He certainly has the right not to be present."

Demakos saw through the stunt.

"He is on trial before this jury. And he is on trial, whether Mr.

Alosco calls the witnesses or you call the witnesses or the District
Attorney calls the witnesses."

Sal Alosco rushed into Part K-2 on the morning of March 22,
looking ashen and scared. His client, Todd Scott, having been
threatened by Philip Copeland, was now refusing to take the
stand. Alosco approached Demakos, along with Hancock and
Fishman, for a private conversation.

"I have been preparing my client to take the stand for at least
two to three weeks. We have had many, many discussions. About
five minutes before he was set to testify yesterday, I was called in
and told that he did not want to testify. I asked the court for some
time to be able to speak to him. I did speak to him last night, and
reaffirmed that position. I told him overnight, you know, to recon-
sider his position.

"I went in this morning. He was hesitant, and then he said he
was going to take the stand; however, he didn't wish to answer any
questions posed to him by the District Attorney. And I said, you
can't do that, you know, you have to do what you have to do. I
am not saying he was threatened, nor am I saying what went on
or why he is here, but I can tell from his demeanor that he is
definitely afraid. It's a sudden change in his character, his demeanor. I definitely think he has been threatened—he is afraid of
something. Give me some time."

Demakos called a recess. Sixty minutes later, at high noon in
Queens, Todd Scott walked to the witness chair. He nodded to
Philip Copeland once and then began talking. Talk was all that
Todd Scott had left.

"Do you live with your parents, Todd?" Alosco began.

"No." The voice was low and hollow-sounding.

"Have you ever been employed, Todd?"

"No."

"Have you ever applied for jobs?"

"Plenty."

"Did you ever get a job?"

"No."

Alosco then directed Scott to the day of his arrest. The defense attorney knew that the most incriminating evidence against Scott had been his own words. In a final, desperate effort, he needed to show that the statements had been beaten out of his client.

"Who was the first police officer that you saw?"

"Richard Sica."

"Tell us what, if anything, occurred between you and Det. Sica."

"Well, when they came in, they grabbed me. I wrestled with them. They tried to throw me on the floor. They started to kick me."

"And after Det. Sica grabbed you, what, if anything, did he do to you at that time?"

"Well, after he grabbed me, he asked me, 'Where is the gun?' And he said, 'Why did you do it?' "

"And did you know what he was talking about?"

"Yes."

"What were they doing?"

"They was hitting me in my ribs and kicking me in the balls and stomping me, and putting the gun to my mouth."

"Now who was it who put the gun to your mouth?"

"Det. Nick Rodelli."

"And after he did this, did he say anything to you?"

"He said to Det. Sica, 'Let's do him now, Richie.' "

"What did you understand that to mean?"

"He wanted to take my life."

Scott went on to describe a series of beatings, claiming he had been whacked in the face with a walkie-talkie by Sergeant Panzarella and stomped in the office by Lieutenant Eugene Dunbar and Eddie Granshaw. He then claimed that the entire videotaped statement had been fabricated and rehearsed.

"They wanted me to lie on people," Todd Scott said. "They

wanted me to tell untrue stories about certain individuals. I thought I had to do whatever I had to do for my own safety."

Todd then retold the murder story in a new, less incriminating fashion. He claimed that they had parked the car around the corner from Byrne on Pinegrove, facing Liberty Avenue.

"Did you see Rachel Moore that night?"

"She was not there . . . If Rachel Moore was there we would have run into her."

"Who was in the car, other than you and Dave?"

"Scott Cobb."

"Anybody else?"

"Nobody else."

"You got out of the car. Did Dave say something at that time?"

"I would rather not say."

"Why were you there, Todd?"

"I guess I was stupid."

"And did you see him approach the police vehicle?"

"I'd rather not say."

Kirke Bartley was scheduled to cross-examine Scott after the lunch recess. He sat in a room reviewing Scott's police file. He passed up a chance at a sandwich, deciding to cross-examine the witness on an empty stomach. Edward Byrne, he remembered, had died hungry.

"Now, Scott Cobb," Bartley said, after leading Scott through his drug history and various assaults and beatings, "he's just a driver for you. He knew nothing about what was going on the evening of the murder?"

"No, I assume he didn't."

"And Mr. Copeland didn't know anything about it, right?"

"No."

"So the only one person that knew anything about it was Mr. McClary, right? The person who is not here?"

"I decline not to answer that."

"Isn't it a fact, sir, that you had conversations with Marshal and David McClary and Pappy Mason about killing a cop before Pappy Mason went back to jail?"

"Incorrect."

"And isn't it a fact that on the morning of the shooting, at about 10 o'clock, you, together with Marshal and David McClary and Scott Cobb, went to Viola Nichols's house and received a phone call from Pappy Mason?"

"I don't know Viola Nichols. I wouldn't have been in her house if I didn't know her."

Scott was flustered, his eyes bewildered. He looked to Alosco for help, just as Rachel Moore had once looked to Gene Kelly.

"Now with regard to the video statement," Bartley continued. "Was that statement true or was that statement false?"

"It's particularly true, some of it is, some of it ain't."

Bartley then produced three photographs taken of Todd Scott by prison officials on the day of his arrest. The photographs showed Scott stripped to his underwear. The prisoner was scowling, but unmarked.

"Mr. Scott," Bartley said in closing. "Did you fire the first shot into Police Officer Byrne or would you rather not say?"

"I never fired the first shot," Todd Scott said.

Scott stepped down and retook his place at the defense table. He looked to Copeland for support. Marshal was staring straight ahead, shaking his head. Alosco rested his case. The lawyer was standing in the hallway a few minutes later, talking to a friend.

"My client is a liar," Alosco said. "Sure, he committed perjury. But whose perjury does the jury want to believe—Todd Scott's or Rachel Moore's? Todd Scott's or Arjune's? Everyone is lying and I'm tired of being spit at. My mother told me last night, 'I see you on television and I think you are a defendant.' "

*

Scott Cobb walked to the orange chair an hour later. He was sweating and scared, never having spoken to a group of more than six or seven people in his life. On direct examination, Cobb repeated the same story he'd told the District Attorney's video camera on the night of his arrest. Scott Cobb continued to deny that he had any advance warning of the assassination.

"They didn't trust me not to tell the police," Scott Cobb said.

The morning of Monday, March 27, 1989, broke wet and gray. Michael Fishman got dressed at his Long Island home, wearing a starched blue shirt, tan tie, and gray shirt. Scott Cobb, scared and alone in his prison cell, put on a gray sweater and a pair of gray slacks. The gray couple sat at the defense table, their manner calm and unthreatening. Cobb mouthed a prayer as Fishman studied his summation. The room was packed with police officers from the 103rd Precinct, most of whom only knew Edward Byrne by name. Richie Sica and Eddie Granshaw sat in a row with Matt Byrne. The detectives were nervous, still not daring to believe the case had worked out right.

Fishman played with a bump on the right side of his forehead and pulled his hair over a bald spot on the top of his head. Cobb waited, holding his head with his left fist. Demakos entered the room, spoke to the jury briefly, and then recognized Fishman.

"The loss of a life," Fishman began, "anyone's life, is felt by all mankind. The death of a police officer is a crime that cuts into the very fabric of our society. Yet, as horrendous as that crime is, you must put aside all sympathy for Edward Byrne's family. All fear for the destruction of society, all desire to avenge what has occurred. To succumb to the obvious pressure, to convict Scott Cobb of this crime without affording him a fair and impartial trial, would be an even greater crime against our society and civilization as a whole. Our system of justice has been devised to ensure a fair and impartial trial, to insure that no defendant is railroaded into a conviction due to public outcry or moral rage or through prosecutorial misconduct. If you cannot do so, then, I submit, you must step down now as a member of this jury and let someone replace you who can."

No one stirred in the jury box. Fishman continued in a soft, pleading voice.

"You all swore that you could. You all promised the court, gave your word. If you can look solely at the facts of what this case is about, if instead of Officer Edward Byrne, if it was not him in the car but if it was a person of a different profession and it was just a murder—and that's tough to say, and it's even tougher for you to accept, for anytime that we can say 'just a murder,' it means we have lost something—but if this was just another murder, then I submit, your job would be much easier."

Fishman probably lost his jury right there. Nearly all of the jurors had either been a crime victim or known a crime victim. No one had ever paid attention to their anonymous crimes. Byrne was their shot at reprisal. And now Fishman was asking them to think of Byrne's death "as just another murder." The lawyer continued attacking the credibility of Martin Howell, Rachel Moore, and Arjune—noting that they had all been paid money and were in line for a reward. Of Moore, he said, "She has no brains left. She is cooked, in the vernacular of the street. Boy, did they do a job on her. Rachel Moore said she turned her life around. God, all she didn't do is say she got God." Fishman was also correct in his assessment of the witness Arjune, saying, "He kept us all in stitches but, again, he is a person who has been prepped. Arjune has made himself into more than a public figure. He has made himself into a public savior. I submit to you that, if he could, he would testify on every case that would come down the line concerning drug deals in South Jamaica."

But for all his words about fabricated testimony and paid witnesses, Fishman could not change the videotaped statement of his client—a man named Scott Cobb who admitted to having been paid a reward to have a cop shot. Whatever emotion Fishman had been able to take out of the case by suggesting that the jurors think of Edward Byrne as a murdered drug dealer rather than a cop was quickly replaced by A. Kirke Bartley.

"Scott Cobb contends that he was sitting alone in a car somewhere, unaware of what was about to take place, unaware that a police officer was about to be murdered," Bartley said at the start of his summation. "Ladies and gentleman, I suggest to you that the only person seated alone in a car on the early morning hours of February 26, 1988, unaware of what was going to happen was Police Officer Edward Byrne. The killing of Police Officer Edward Byrne was more than just another brutal murder. It was a declaration of war against our society. Ladies and gentlemen, it was an act calculated to deliver a message, and that message is "oppose us and you die."

Fishman was standing with one foot on his chair, screaming. Scott Cobb, seeing the weight of Bartley's words on the jury, banged both his fists on the defense table.

"Objection," Fishman shrieked. "Inflammatory, not necessary." Bartley would not stop.

"Ladies and gentlemen, those bullets that tore away the life of that young police officer also tore away the fabric of our very society. Eddie Byrne was more than a young man on the threshold of his life. Edward Byrne was a police officer. He was a symbol."

Demakos stood up now, demanding that Bartley deal with the evidence and the evidence alone. But it was too late. The jury had already heard, and Bartley pushed on further still.

"Ladies and gentlemen, the evidence revealed that Edward Byrne was in fact assigned a post and that post was to protect a witness. Scott Cobb, in his video, indicates that Pappy Mason had chosen the Arjune guard post to send his message, his message of death. Consider this, if you will: The enormity of that message was not lost on those people who were ordered to carry that message out. The awesome consequences of that act, and the response that the act would be reasonable to evoke, would not be, and was not, lost on those people who were going to carry out the murder.

"Now, what I'm suggesting to you is this: that a person or

persons going out to commit such an act would not take with them someone that they could not trust. Reason compels us to believe that if you're going to go out and assassinate a police officer, you're not going to take with you somebody that you cannot trust. I ask that you think about that for a moment, because that is what Scott Cobb is suggesting to you. That he was just someone in the mailroom. Well, ladies and gentlemen, he's told you he was much more than that within the organization. I would ask you to reflect on that for a moment. And I would suggest to you that Scott Cobb was a trusted insider.

"Let us conceive of the scenario that may have happened if Scott Cobb was just a driver, devoid of any knowledge of what was going on that evening. Triggermen get out of the car, five powerful shots ring out in the middle of the morning in Jamaica, waking up the community. The gunmen run back to the car and Scott Cobb is gone, he's gone to the bathroom, he's gone out for a beer. Those are the possibilities if Scott Cobb had no idea of what was going on.

"Consider again what type of message this was. Consider the manner it was delivered, five shots to the head. Consider that type of message and ask yourself, is that the type of plan that someone would leave the getaway just purely to chance: Well, I hope he's still there when we get back? What does logic and reason tell you about that? If you're going to have a plan to go and assassinate a uniformed police officer, perhaps the most heinous crime in this past decade, are you going to leave the getaway purely to chance? Purely in the hopes that the guy that you have as the driver is going to stay there and not go off someplace? Consider it, ladies and gentlemen. I suggest, when you do consider it, that it flies in the face of common sense, it flies in the face of reason."

There was more, but nothing as dramatic. Bartley had the jurors' full attention. Two, a man in the back row and a woman in the front, were already crying. The prosecutor ended his summation most poignantly, with a discussion of Arjune.

"Ladies and gentlemen, we talk about Arjune. Arjune was a

character, I concede that. It's suggested by Mr. Fishman that Arjune was well prepped. I defy anyone to prepare Arjune. I defy them. God knows, I tried."

Just after the jury was dismissed, the room broke into applause. Police officers in the audience rushed Bartley, slapping his back. Someone barked a command and they separated, making room for Ann Byrne, in a cop-blue dress. She stepped forward and kissed the prosecutor.

Frank Hancock didn't have much to say in summation, in part because the witnesses hadn't had much to say about his client. Despite all their confessions and testimony, neither Todd Scott nor Scott Cobb had ever placed him at the scene. Scott Cobb, especially, had no reason not to name Copeland. He was, in the old street vernacular, a scaredy-cat. Cobb never accused the police of beating a confession out him. Indeed, on the stand, his own lawyer had elicited the same description of the killing as the Assistant District Attorney with the video camera, Scott Tulman. In the absence of a credible rebuttal witness, the story told by Copeland's alibi witness, Audette Wills, remained quite reasonable. It seemed completely unreasonable, Hancock argued privately, that Philip Copeland would contract out a hit and then carry out the killing himself.

"Ladies and gentlemen," Hancock said in closing. "Philip Copeland is a drug dealer. Philip Copeland is not a cop killer."

Sal Alosco had the least to work with. Even in the best possible scenario, Todd Scott had problems. He got out of the car knowing a cop would be killed. Then he stood back and watched a cop being killed. All Alosco had was a legal technicality. Had the Queens District Attorney added a murder conspiracy count to the indictment, Scott would have been dead. But Scott had been charged with straight, cold murder. And legally, Alosco knew, there was a difference between being at a murder scene and being a murderer.

"He says in the video statement, because I don't call it a confession, he says, 'I was across the street during the whole thing. I didn't know.' He could have been stupid. He could have been there because he is dumb. Because he's a jerk. Because he's a tough guy. Because he's trying to challenge this individual to see who he is. But that doesn't make him a killer. That does not make him a killer. There is a difference between someone who pulls the trigger and someone who witnesses the crime. And I suggest to you that he was there—he shouldn't have been there, he had no right to be there: But that doesn't mean he participated.

"Had he, and if you believe the other testimony, been at the car, and he pulled the trigger, or he tried to do something affirmative, then you can consider it. But even after he's beaten and he testifies, and this is his first statement, he never says he did anything to kill this officer."

With his defense finished, Alosco felt the need to reconcile his own performance. He had taken this case, in part, because there was some fame in it. But fame quickly turned to infamy. He was a criminal defense lawyer, a trial lawyer. Just as policemen police neighborhoods, firemen put out fires, and bouncers at nightclubs bounce people out of clubs, Alosco was a criminal lawyer who defended criminals. He did not, ultimately, like Todd Scott very much. He found the kid to be a liar and a danger. But he also understood Todd Scott. And he had seen nothing in the prosecution of Edward Byrne's killers to dissuade another teenager from approaching a patrolman's door.

"You know," Alosco said, no longer talking about his client or case, "trials are sometimes like ends to a healing process. After there is a deliberation, you know, we try and harmonize what happened with what's going to happen. We live today in a very, very troubled society. We have drug dealers all over the place. It's like the morality is gone. There are no ethics today. And that disturbs all of us. And the Todd Scotts, it's not only Todd Scott, there are millions of Todd Scotts. He might have failed, ladies and gentlemen, but there's a lot of failures out there. And maybe you and I could do something about it. Maybe, you know, we could be a little more caring about these people. And I don't want you to feel any sympathy for the Todd Scotts of this world. But I ask you to consider where they're coming from.

"And I ask you not to close the door on the Todd Scotts of this world, because the Todd Scotts are going to be out there. They're our generation. They're our youth, our children."

The summation had to be as scary as anything the jury had heard on a videotape. Even Gene Kelly had been impressed. He nodded to Alosco in fairness, and then waited, allowing some space to creep in. As in most dramas, this was a star's place, the final scene. Kelly reached for a glass of water and rubbed an abscess on the back of his neck. Like the inflammation's owner, the sore looked ready to burst.

Kelly, speaking without notes, started off by apologizing for the world he had brought the jurors—a humanity of deceit, ignorance, violence, and evil, the sphere of Martin Howell, Darius Newby, and Rachel Moore—the crack world of South Jamaica, Queens. It was only through these witnesses' eyes, with their voices, Kelly argued, that the world of Todd Scott and Philip Copeland could be revealed. He made no apologies for Marty Howell's drug use or Rachel Moore's prostitution. Quite to the contrary, he maintained, it was their personal wreckage that gave them credibility. This was not, Kelly reminded the jury, a Wall Street case. This was instead a tour of America's domestic Vietnam. To make it understandable, Kelly had needed to produce the crack soldiers.

"If I had brought in a doctor or a priest, a rabbi or a minister, and told you that he was standing there at 3:30 in the morning on a Thursday night, Friday morning, you legitimately would have had every reason to be somewhat skeptical. But if you take the testimony of Rachel Moore and the testimony of all the other witnesses, why isn't it plausible that she would be there at 3:30 in the morning on February 26, 1988? She was a survivor, another person who lived in the world of the Bebos."

Kelly spoke for more than an hour. He spent much of his time on the case's weakest link, Philip Copeland.

"Audette Wills goes out to a hotel she has never been in before, stays with an individual she had never stood over with before, goes to the Kennedy Inn, and she is up all night. She is nervous, can't sleep. Miraculously, Philip Copeland is the only one that seems to be able to sleep. He falls asleep with his clothes on at 3:30, 4:00 in the morning. Philip Copeland, amazingly, on the biggest night in the history of the Bebos, the preconceived murder of a New York City police officer, Philip Copeland is not involved. Philip Copeland is sleeping in a hotel room.

"What, are you kidding?"

Kelly discussed the credibility of witnesses again, but the jurors were losing interest. They had heard enough of Rachel and Arjune, Marty Howell and Darry Newby. In truth, they had probably heard enough of Gene Kelly. Not everyone was attentive. Some of the jurors looked on with drugged faces. One yawned wide and turned absently to the left, meeting the hard gaze of a dozen armor-plated policemen. The jury snapped to attention, though, as Kelly worked to his big, foot-stomping close.

His big Irish voice boomed off the oak walls, "These people had great, great power. They had the power to hire workers, the power to sell drugs, power to distribute drugs. This is awesome power. Ladies and gentlemen of the jury, on the morning of February 26, 1988, these two individuals, Philip Copeland and Todd Scott, decided to reach an even greater power, a power almost godlike. It was a power, ladies and gentlemen, over the life and death of another human being. And on the morning of February 26, 1988, these two individuals, Todd Scott and Philip Copeland, exercised that power. The results are what we are here for today."

Kelly stopped, pausing a full measure. He ran his eyes over the jury box from left to right, his jaw hard.

"Ladies and gentlemen of the jury," he said, the prosecutor's voice low and respectful again. "On the morning of February 26, 1988, Edward Byrne reported for duty. Edward Byrne, on the morning of February 26, 1988, he did his job. And now, ladies and gentlemen of the jury, I am asking you to do yours."

13

"I DON'T WANT THEM CUTTING MY HAIR."

The jurors got the case the following day, on the windy, angry, gray morning of March 28, 1989—thirty-four days after first taking their seats in Part K-2. The once-anonymous jurors arrived at the courthouse by bus, taxi, and private car. It was easy to spot them. They were the ones carrying luggage—makeup bags, garment bags, and curling irons—into an American court of law, most of them smiling like excited school kids on an overnight camping trip. They would be sequestered until reaching a verdict, spending time, if need be, in a Queens hotel.

For once, Richie Sica and Sal Alosco arrived in Part K-2 with something in common—monumental hangovers. Sica had spent the night with prosecutors, drinking through their false fears. Alosco had treated a group of reporters to cocktails and dinner at Elaine's. The lawyer stood outside the courtroom, shuffling through a series of blue American Express receipts. The evening totaled out at $450.

"How can so much fun feel so bad?" Alosco said, his eyes bleary.

Sica stood about fifteen feet away, around the corner from Alosco, dragging hard on a cigarette. He started down the hallway toward the courtroom, accidentally bumping a short, red-eyed lawyer. Sica steadied the man and then caught himself, recognizing the face.

"No hard feelings, detective," Sal Alosco told Sica.

The detective was embarrassed. Still, the protagonist shook the lawyer's hand.

"I won't say good luck," Sica said. "But you're a decent man, Sal."

The detective was thinking back to when he had cried on the stand. Alosco, seeing the tears, had stepped back, agreeing to a recess.

"Just business," Alosco said.

"That's all," Sica agreed. The men entered the courtroom together, taking their places on opposites sides of the aisle as Demakos ordered the doors locked. The judge then charged the jury.

"We are judges, you and I," Demakos told first the Cobb jury and then the Copeland–Scott jury. "You are a judge of the facts. I am a judge of the law. Don't try and be detectives."

Demakos then explained the three elements needed to find a defendant guilty of second-degree murder. Basically, the state's law was pretty simple. A defendant, acting in concert with others, had to: 1) have shot Edward Byrne 2) have intended to cause Edward Byrne's death, and 3) in fact, killed Edward Byrne. The law, as charged by Demakos, held that a person playing a minor role in the murder is just as guilty as one who plays a major role. Ultimately, then, it did not matter so much who shot Byrne, as long as everyone in the group knew that it was their intent to shoot and kill a cop.

The Cobb jurors deliberated for two hours and then requested to see Scott Cobb's videotape a second time. Cobb's trial testimony was also reread. A jury request to visit the scene and look out Arjune's window was denied. The jury also wondered, while pondering a charge of weapons possession, whether an individual had to physically possess the gun. Demakos explained that so long as a person knew there was a gun, he did not need to hold it in his own hands. Unable to reach a verdict by 6:30 P.M., the Cobb jury was taken out to dinner and then sequestered for the evening.

Demakos then received a note from the jury deliberating the fates of Todd Scott and Philip Copeland. This jury had five requests. They wanted to: 1) see pictures of Todd Scott after his arrest 2) get a read-back of the testimony of Marty Howell and Darry Newby relating to Copeland's involvement 3) see Todd Scott's videotape again 4) have Todd Scott's direct testimony read back, and 5) see a model of the area, along with pictures of Arjune's house. Demakos ordered the jury to cease their deliberations at 7:30 P.M., retiring them to a hotel for the night.

The Cobb jury had not been heard from since mid-afternoon. The second day of jury deliberations, March 29, had broken bright and sharp, the temperature unseasonably warm. Matt Byrne had taken off his tweed, sky-blue jacket, rolled up the sleeves on his striped shirt, and loosened his blue tie. He stood in front of the Kew Gardens courthouse, waiting, the calm spring evening his friend. After all the months and all the hours, he seemed comfortable at last. He stood amongst an integrated group of new and old friends. Kirke Bartley stood with Ann Byrne, his own suit jacket draped over his shoulder. Sica and Granshaw did the cop thing, pointing out drug dealers they knew to Matt Byrne.

The court officers, two of them, pushed through the doors at approximately 5:35 P.M. There was an urgent look to them, their jaws firm.

"The Cobb jury has returned a note," the court officer told Bartley.

"A verdict?" Bartley asked.

The court officer nodded. Bartley put on his coat and turned to Matt Byrne.

"You have a few minutes," Bartley said.

Byrne pulled on his jacket and reached for his wife. He put his arm around the woman and walked across a concrete mall, their backs to the courthouse. It was a nice picture, the two of them walking alone. For all their hope in the legal system, for all their confidence in Detectives Richie Sica, Eddie Granshaw, and Pete Pistone; witnesses Marty Howell, Rachel Moore, and Arjune; prosecutors Bartley and Kelly—the murdered cop's parents were still anxious. They chatted for a moment about strength and then stepped back toward the courthouse.

"Let's go," Matt Byrne told his friends.

They entered the building and pushed past the cameras, entering Part K-2, reluctant to take their seats. Sal Alosco stood in the hallway, stealing his last drags off a cigarette.

"Got to be guilty," a friend told him.

"Oh, yeah," Alosco said. The idea didn't bother him much.

Michael Fishman was already seated at the defense table, his face ashen. The jury had not liked him very much. The verdict, Fishman realized, was for him, too.

Cobb entered the courtroom wearing a faded dungaree jacket and jeans. He was led straight to the defense table. The defendant no longer wore his designer glasses. He sat down and started drumming his fingers on the table as the Byrne family took their seats. Cobb rubbed his face and rolled his eyes. He turned around once, spotting Sica and Granshaw in the fourth row beside the Byrne family. Byrne put his left arm around his wife and pulled her closer, waiting. Ann Byrne held Edward Byrne's Mass card in her left hand.

Judge Demakos came onto the bench at 6:10 P.M. He was holding a piece of paper.

"All right, I have a communication from the jury," he announced. And then he read the note: "Dear Judge. We have reached our verdict."

The jury filed in, their work done. All told, they had spent less than twelve hours deliberating Cobb's fate. Most of the men were coatless, the women faded-looking and grim. Not a single juror afforded Cobb even so much as a passing glance.

The clerk stood in the middle of the well. He then asked, "Madame Forelady, has the jury reached a verdict?"

"Yes, we have," replied the forelady, Claudia Tyler. Cobb flinched, surprised by the strength in the woman's voice.

The jurors and then the defendant were ordered to stand. Cobb came right up, his pose defiant.

"Madame Forelady, under the first count of the indictment, murder in the second degree, how do you find the defendant?"

"We find the defendant guilty."

Uniformed cops in the back of the room began to hoot. Byrne hugged his wife. Ann Byrne turned to her right and embraced her youngest son, Kenny. The kid was still wearing his brother's NYPD tie clasp.

The jury returned a guilty verdict on the gun charge, too, but it was murder that counted. Cobb knew that. The defendant fell to his seat, his legs gone, and listened as each of the jurors was polled.

"Is that your verdict?" the clerk asked twelve times.

"Yes, it is," came the reply, twelve times.

Scott Cobb shook his head and cursed.

"You jive motherfuckers," he said.

And then Cobb was swept out of the room like so much garbage, the bounce in his step gone. Byrne sat in the row, an appointment book in his lap. He turned to the page with April twenty-fourth on it and wrote the words "Cobb sentencing." The Byrne family remained in the aisle for several minutes. The cops, many of them from the 103rd Precinct, formed a receiving line. The Byrnes shook each hand, patted each uniformed back. Some of the cops turned away, crying. Thirsty, Matt Byrne turned and drank from the prosecutor's water pitcher.

Larry Byrne, the couple's eldest son, rushed into the courtroom along with his wife. An Assistant United States Attorney, Larry Byrne prosecuted drug dealers for a living. He had seen many verdicts. He cried at this one.

"Thank God," Larry Byrne said.

After about fifteen minutes or so, the second jury was led into the courtroom to hear a read-back of Martin Howell's testimony relating to Todd Scott's offer of $8,000 to hit a cop. Moments later, Alosco stood in the hallway, looking very much alone. He had been sitting in the back of the courtroom with Frank Hancock when the Cobb jury came in with their verdict. A cop had turned to him and yelled, "Your guy's next."

"Todd was scared when I told him about Cobb," the lawyer said. "He knows if the driver goes, he goes. The kid is strange. He's worried about getting his clothes back. The cops took a black leather suit when they arrested him. He's going down for murder and that's what he's worried about. It's crazy."

The final note was sent in just after 7 P.M. A cop from the Patrolman's Benevolent Association rounded up the Byrne family, leading them to their seats at 7:28 P.M. The cops, about a hundred of them, followed them into K-2. They were all confident.

The seating arrangement in the fourth row had changed with the tension. Larry Byrne, a briefcase full of justice on his lap, sat next to his wife. Matt, Ann, and Kenny Byrne were seated in the middle of the row. Kenny wore a blue sweater, the sleeves rolled up. A small gold replica of his brother's badge hung on a chain around his neck.

Philip Copeland bopped into the room and smiled. Matt Byrne saw him and gripped the pew in front of him with his left hand. Todd Scott had not bothered to shave. Wearing a black sweater, he sat slumped over in his chair, fingering a long gold necklace. Ann Byrne gripped her husband's right arm with her left, and thumbed at his jacket as the jury was led into the oak box.

The jury began with Scott. Copeland sat to his friend's left, sneering. The response told spectators as much about Copeland as the crime.

"Mr. Foreman," said the clerk, addressing Fred Van Gassbeek. "Have you reached a verdict as to the defendant, Todd Scott?"

"Yes, we have," Van Gassbeek said evenly.

Scott was then ordered to rise before the already standing jurors. He looked scared and turned to his left, checking Copeland for support. Marshal nodded.

And then, in the next second, the mystery went away. Van Gassbeek said the word "Guilty," like it was nothing. He also pronounced Scott culpable on the gun charge.

Larry Byrne jumped to his feet, and punched his right fist into the air. Matt Byrne, scared of the jury system, acted as if his team had just scored a come-from-behind victory with no time left on the clock.

"Aw right!" he screamed.

Philip Copeland, the real test of the evidence, came next. But Van Gassbeek didn't hesitate on the murder charge here, either.

"Guilty," he said.

That was the verdict Matt Byrne had coveted. He knew, as a lawyer, that the evidence putting Copeland at the scene was suspect. Now, upon hearing the verdict, he clenched his fists and screamed.

"I'd like to send a message to that son of a bitch," he said.

The jurors were polled, each of them strong in their conviction. They watched from the box as the defendants were led out. Demakos banged his gavel, demanding order, but the cops could not be silenced.

"Death penalty," one screamed from the back of the room.

"Fry the bastards," screamed another.

Philip Copeland, a tiny man who had known great power on the streets of South Jamaica, bounded out of the room. He jerked to a stop at the door to a holding cell.

"I'll be back," he yelled.

The insult drove the cops to fury. They screamed and hooted. Matt Byrne cursed, "The son of a bitch, bastard." Copeland's mother sat across the aisle, clutching her Bible. She went weak with the chaos, sinking softly into the pew.

Scott was led out next. Richie Sica, watched, believing that Todd Scott would follow Marshal's lead. He always has before, the detective thought: That is why we have a dead cop in Queens.

"This only round one," Scott said.

Kenny Byrne turned to his mother and whispered, "We got 'em." Then the teenager began to cry. Matt Byrne removed his jacket and sat writing out a statement for the press on a yellow legal pad. No one was in any hurry to leave the courthouse, not wanting to let go of the moment. Byrne started to get up once, but was pushed back into the seat by his wife.

"You just sit there," she said, gently. Matt kissed his wife's hand.

Eventually, Matt Byrne wound up in front of the television cameras, a sheaf of yellow papers shaking in his hands.

"The jury verdict tonight was a message by society that it's going to take society back from the mutts," Byrne said. "It's also a message that you don't kill our cops. Hopefully, the verdicts rendered here will make this city safer.

"The verdict will never bring Eddie back. But hopefully, it will make this city safer for all of us, and particularly for our brave police officers."

This scene was perfect. The case had started thirteen months before with a drug dealer deciding he wanted to send a message to society: We lose one, you lose one. It ended on a cool evening with a dead cop's father at center stage, a message in his hands: "We lose one, you lose three." Never before, a jury had agreed, had subtraction been so important to their city.

With the family whisked from the courthouse by police, reporters turned to the remaining detectives who'd worked on the case. Richie Sica and Eddie Granshaw dodged the cameras, finding a quiet place in the corner. Sica had no words to match the verdicts. Granshaw kept grabbing him by the shoulders and yelling, "We did it. Those sons of bitches, we nailed them." Lieutenant Eugene Dunbar, near tears, stood with the press waiting for an elevator.

"I have a son named Tommy," the lieutenant said. "He knew Edward Byrne from school. Now my kid wants to become a cop."

"What did you tell him?" a reporter screamed.

The elevator had arrived. Dunbar stepped into it, pushed a button for the garage and turned.

"I told him 'No,'" Dunbar said, as the door closed.

*

On May 7, 1989, as the first batch of defendants awaited sentencing, David McClary went on trial for murder. Although his videotaped statement had been suppressed, there was more than enough
trouble for McClary in his written statement. Rachel Moore was
recalled, identifying McClary as one of those she'd seen at the
murder scene. The prosecution also produced Viola Nichols, the
witness swearing she had overheard McClary planning the murder. Gene Kelly did not, however, recall the witness Arjune.
Everyone was confident of a conviction.

On May 15, President Bush went on television before the nation
to announce a $1.5 billion crime bill. The money, Bush said, would
be used to take back the streets from the type of men who had
conspired to murder Edward Byrne.

"Last fall," the President said, "a retired New York police
lieutenant gave me badge number 14072 and I have it with me here
today, the badge his son wore the day he was gunned down by a
gang of cocaine cowards. Matt Byrne asked me to keep Eddie's
badge as a reminder of all the brave police officers who put their
lives on the line for us every single day.

"Matt, your son's badge, as I have told you, is kept in my desk
at the Oval Office.

"And during the debate on gun-related violence that has raged
in this country the past several months, neither it nor what it
represents has ever been far from my mind.

"At the trial of Edward Byrne's executioners, there was testimony that the hit was ordered from prison to send a message to
the people behind the badge, and one witness said they hoped to
see the attack on the television news at Rikers Island.

"Well, today, we have a message of our own.

"We're going to take back the streets by taking the criminals off
our streets. And it's an attack on all four fronts: new laws to
punish them, new agents to arrest them, new prosecutors to convict them, and new prisons to hold them.

"I am announcing today, and there is no more fitting place then right here, a comprehensive new offensive for combatting violent crime—for Eddie Byrne, for every police officer we honor here today, and for America."

Matt Byrne, flushed with pride and ruined by sorrow, had stood on the Capitol steps for some time, an American President having made his loss important. He had been particularly struck by another presidential acknowledgement.

"Not since Lincoln," Bush had said, "has a President stood in front of the Capitol and been just a few miles from the front lines of a war."

The defendant was worried about his hair. He sat in a holding cell on the morning after the President's speech, May 16, 1989, and pointed a finger at Frank Hancock. Philip Copeland was delivering a message, again.

"I don't want them cutting my hair," Copeland said on the day of his sentencing.

Copeland's lawyer, Frank Hancock, did not look well. He had been offered a deal by the U.S. Attorney, Charles Rose, some days before. A prosecutor looking for evidence against Pappy Mason in a Federal case had offered Copeland an amazing deal. Rose, scared of losing his own case, had offered Copeland a fifteen-year term in Federal prison and a promise to relocate his family. Copeland also faced a murder trial in Connecticut for the killing of Michelle "Princess" Garland. That indictment would be made to disappear. Word of the government's offer had infuriated both state prosecutors and city police. Matt Byrne had promised Rose political death—a phone call to the President. Ultimately, Copeland had turned down the chance to cooperate, telling Hancock, "I ain't no Perry Bellamy."

Copeland did not mind losing his head so much as he feared losing his hair. In jail, he hoped to hook up with a gang of Rastafarians. The dreadlocks were important. Copeland also worried about his sex life. He wanted a stay of sentencing in order to marry Audette Wills. A married prisoner, Copeland knew, was allowed wifely visits in prison. A bachelor sentenced to life remained eternally single.

Hancock had seen enough of the early morning scene in the Kew Gardens courthouse to know how these requests would play. The room was a great blue uniform, cops coming from as far away as Connecticut and Suffolk County to witness the sentencing. In a state without a death penalty, this was as close as New Yorkers got to revenge: listening to a judge whack a defendant with a twenty-five-years-to-life sentence.

"I'll mention the hair," Hancock promised. "Marriage is going to be, well, a problem."

Copeland paused. He had found family in a drug gang and more recently, when it suited him, religion. Some years before, after meeting Pappy Mason—would-be Jamaican from Brooklyn— Copeland had let his hair grow and pronounced himself a Rastafarian. Hancock had the sneaking suspicion that this was about all his client knew of the sect's teachings—the hairdo.

"No meat, either," Copeland reminded Hancock upon entering the courtroom. "They can't cut my hair and they can't make me eat meat."

Copeland did a half-strut to the defense table and sat down. The cops, about one hundred fifty of them, stirred. Copeland stole a peek at the cops over his right shoulder.

"Damn," he said.

Gene Kelly spoke first. He went right to the heart of the case, calling the assassination a message killing. Hancock followed, repeating his client's pitiful request.

"Mr. Copeland is a religious person," Hancock said. The cops snickered, knowing Copeland bent his knee to just one deity—the crack pipe.

Thomas Demakos made a face and went directly to his index cards, beginning to read his sentencing in a voice that cracked like a whip over the audience.

"Those of us who sat through this case and who heard the

evidence against Philip Copeland were left with but one conclusion. That this was an assassination—a deliberate, premeditated, intentional act to kill a cop. 'For every one of us you take, we'll take one of yours.' Can it not be said that this vile act was also a deadly declaration of war against the very foundations of our society and a defilement of the cornerstone on which our criminal justice system is based? A cop on duty, guarding a witness to a drug transaction, was executed. This arrogant act assaults our society and, in turn, affects each and every one of us, each and every neighborhood in our city.

"First we see how witnesses are stalked and killed in these drug-infected areas; then, a cop is brutally assassinated. Who will be next? Prosecutors and lawyers? Perhaps a judge? In this same city, a Supreme Court judge has had to have a twenty-four-hour police guard because he had the audacity to sentence a drug lord to prison.

"Philip Copeland was convicted of the homicide of Patrolman Byrne, along with Todd Scott and Scott Cobb. There is no doubt, that of the three, Copeland was the worst. He was the lieutenant in change while the drug lord was in prison. The order to 'ice a cop' was transmitted to him, not to those of lesser importance. And, Copeland, you carried your order to completion. In doing so, you have demonstrated that you are unfit to be a member of our society.

"I have received a multitude of letters asking that I impose a life sentence without parole. Under the law, I cannot do that. However, what I can do, and will do, is to promise you that I intend to make a recommendation to the Parole Board that you are never paroled. I know I will no longer be sitting on the bench in twenty-five years, but rest assured, my last judicial function before I retire from the judiciary will be to write the Parole Board to remind them of my strong feeling that I have expressed to you today. Sentence of this court shall be twenty-five-years-to-life with a recommendation to the Parole Board that you NEVER be paroled."

Copeland didn't even blink. The cops began to applaud, Matt Byrne clapping the loudest. Copeland turned and smiled as he was led away.

"Bye-bye," yelled one cop. "Have a nice life."

And then the door shut on the life of Philip Copeland.

Todd Scott was another story. He, too, had been offered the chance to cooperate by Charles Rose, the desperate Federal prosecutor. In making his racketeering case against Fat Cat Nichols and Mason, Rose had already given deals to Viola Nichols and Brian Gibbs, the dealer named Glaze who had left no more than twenty victims glassy-eyed and dead. By this time, Rose was being vilified in the press for his machinations. Having never tried a murder case himself, Rose remained deathly afraid of losing his Mason case. Ultimately, he would even give a deal to Fat Cat himself, taking Nichols into Federal custody while he testified about Mason.

Alosco could not believe his client's good fortune. He told reporters, "The government's offer is really quite wonderful. I wonder if they will give us medical benefits, too." Sica, Pistone, and Granshaw were furious with the Feds. They considered the FBI and Federal prosecutors lazy, too green to go out and make their own case.

Todd Scott's big decision.

"Todd used to tell me, 'Sal, I trust you, do whatever you think is right.' But I always told him, 'This is your case. I work for you.' After the convictions, the government called. They called and said, 'You know we're interested in talking to your guy.' Todd did not want to go. But I told him, 'Todd, before you make up your mind, you have to consider a few things. You're a young kid. You're facing the death penalty up in Connecticut. These guys here, you may not even remember their names in 15 years. I mean,

I know they are your family and everything, there's this One Love thing where you don't turn against your family, but there is something more important and that's called self-preservation. I just want you to go in there and listen.'

"And that's how I put the pressure on him. I felt I had to give him the opportunity to save his life. I said, 'Todd, you may think these people are important, but they are not.' I knew by then that there were a lot of rats in the Federal case. So I figure if everyone is going to rat everybody else out, I say the person that gets there first gets the bargains. So Todd listened. They put a lot of pressure on him. They wanted him very badly.

"Todd knew he faced the possibility of death, but it didn't really scare him. He faced the death penalty on the street, too. What did he do then? He bought a life insurance policy. It was very strange to look at him. Here's a guy, he's facing the death penalty, and I'm trying to impress upon him that in Connecticut, death is a real option. I kept wondering—does he realize, you know, that he may be seated down, an electric current running through him? I mean I was frightened. I was scared because this kid doesn't know or appreciate life. I was also scared, frankly, about losing a client to the chair. I couldn't live with that, and I knew it.

"So it looked like Todd was gonna turn. He even made a statement to the Feds—an offer of proof—that only I was able to make a record of. With that done, I asked the government for a cover story to present at his sentencing. The cover story would be that I was fired—get me out of the case and do what you want. They were supposed to call up Demakos and tell him the cover story. That morning, I made a statement to the press saying I was fired. Then I went into Demakos, and he looked at me like I had two heads. He said, 'The government didn't tell me and I wouldn't go along with it anyway.' So the Feds hung me out to dry. I felt vulnerable. I mean if the guys in the street think Todd Scott's lawyer is trying to get him to cooperate, they whack me out. It's one thing to be dedicated in this business. It's another to be foolish. The negotiations broke down right there. The deal was dead. I still had Todd Scott's last confession in the case, the one he gave to the Feds, thinking he had a deal. No one has ever seen a copy of it."

Todd Scott's secret confession, given to the U. S. Attorney on May 12, 1989.

"Pappy ordered the hit.

"Phil saw me in the project and said that Pappy wanted to talk to us. We went to Viola's house on Feb. 24, 1988. We got there at 6:30 P.M. Pappy was talking to Phil on the phone. Present were me, Dave, Phil, and Scott Cobb. Pappy talked to Phil only. How did I know who it was, calling? Viola said it was Pappy. He kept calling. Viola picked up the phone and said, 'Phil and Todd is here.' They talked for about an hour. I was watching TV, sitting on the bed. The phone has a long cord. Phil was sitting on the edge of the couch behind the TV. Scott Cobb was in the living room. Viola wouldn't let him in the room. The kid named Housecat was in the bedroom. Dave was at Fiesta's Diner by then. Viola was standing in the living room doorway.

"Phil said we had to see Pappy. He said it to me, but loud enough for all to hear. I was told to have Dave and Scott all around the next day. No other instructions. I had given Phil money for Pappy's lawyer. We left there together, me and Scott. Phil went his own way. We went back to the projects and my uncle's house. That night I left and went to the Kennedy Motor Inn. I registered under an assumed name. I don't recall the name anymore. I stayed there the whole night. In the morning I went to check on Pappy's workers. I met Scott at his house. We were just riding around. We were just driving around all day in my yellow Chrysler. We were riding around and I saw Dave at Fiesta's. I told him to meet me at 7 o'clock on Feb. 25th, 1988. Me and Scott went to Lucille's to get food and then to my uncle's house. Got there 6:30 P.M. Phil came and took me into my room. He had someone with him, a Jamaican guy. I was not introduced.

Scott Cobb was in the dining room. Phil showed me a ring he got from Pappy. It was a big ring with a flat surface. It had a round table on it. The ring had two P's on one side and a map of Africa on the other. Phil said Pappy had gave it to him and told about the police officer. Pappy said he wanted a police officer to get hit because he was mad over his conviction. He wanted to show the police officer he was still strong. He said, 'I want Todd to do it.' I said, 'No,' because I was closest to Pappy. I work for Pappy. Dave works for Fat Cat. I told him to get somebody else. Phil decided to let Dave do it because he was new.

"We left all down the elevator and I went to meet Dave and told him what had happened at my uncle's house. I was with Scott. At first, Dave wasn't around. We finally met him at a Kentucky Fried Chicken. I told him, 'They want you to hit a cop.' He goes 'Why me?' Then Phil and Dave was talking about it. Dave said, 'I'll do it.'

"We dropped Dave off on the evening of the 25th. Scott and I were driving around. We went to my uncle's house looking at movies. Scott came and got me about 2:30 A.M. on the morning of Feb. 26th in my car. It was planned for Scott to come and get me. We went to get Dave. We went to Fiesta's. Dave wasn't there. We went to get Dave at his house. We stopped off at my father's house, I saw my father. Then we went to Austin's bar across the street. They went in and I went to talk to my sister. We came back out and Dave said he had something to do. I didn't know whether he had a gun on him. Scott was driving. I was in the backseat laying down. Dave was in the front passenger seat. Phil was with a girl, no one spoke with Copeland that night.

"We were going to the city. We made U-turn on Remington, Dave said go back to 107th. We both got out, we're around the corner, we couldn't see the police car from where we was at. Another police officer's car pulled up, a marked car with two white guys in it. They talked to Byrne's car, gave him coffee or something. Dave was on the other side of the street. He was in the bushes on the side of Byrne's car about one block away. Scott could not see us. He didn't know what was going on. He didn't know because I didn't trust him too much. After the cop car come and shine a light on me, we started walking up the block parallel. I realized what was going to happen. I figured Dave had a gun. He came up from the back and I was, like, 12 feet away on the driver's side of the street. Dave ran up on him, he had both hands on the gun. He crosses the back of the car, the window is not down. I think the light was on. Byrne didn't see him coming. He had his head down like he was reading. He didn't never see what happened. I am 12 feet away, closest. I didn't see him pull the gun the first time. I didn't see him pull the gun. He fired five shots. I heard them. I know he shot a .357 revolver, a big chrome gun. No one said anything when we got back to the car. We never spoke. Scott had the music on, he couldn't hear no shots. Scott wanted to know why he wasn't going to the city, but no one answered.

"Dave took the gun with him. He told me about the .38 caliber ammo the next day. We got arrested, but we wasn't all in jail together. I spoke with Pappy on the phone. He asked me why I talk and I said 'cause I was scared. We had a corrections officer on the switchboard who worked for us. She would patch us all in together so we could talk. Me, Pappy, Dave, and Phil. We talked all during the trial.

"I didn't get piss for doing this. I wanted nothing to do with it."

By the close of D-Day, June 6, 1989, the case of Edward Byrne had drawn to a close. The morning was for sentencing. Todd Scott and Scott Cobb, having turned down the chance to cut a deal with the Feds, stood before Demakos. The judge hit the defendants with what amounted to an open hand. It was a fine sound, Richie Sica felt, the slap of a twenty-five-to-life sentence. Scott looked bored. Asked if he had anything to say before sentencing, Scott waved his hand. On the way out of the court, he turned to the police and grabbed his crotch.

The McClary jury had been deliberating since the previous day. After the sentencing, Matt Byrne walked outside, taking a seat on a stone bench with his wife. A wind came and blew their hair. Later Byrne would say, "We're going to disappear now. It's time for Eddie to rest in peace."

The final verdict came in—guilty on all counts—and this time the courtroom remained silent. David McClary, wearing a blood red shirt and a black tie, ran a hand over his chin. He then stood up and blew a kiss to his mother on the way back to his cell. He looked like a kid heading off to college.

It was quite anticlimactic. There were no curses from the gallery this time, no one-liners. By this point, everyone in the courtroom seemed limp to emotion. Matt and Ann Byrne heard the verdict and eased back into their seats. Ann put the kid's Mass card back in her wallet. The cops rushed from the court and out into the rain. It seemed to cool them further.

The last word from Richie Sica.

"After putting everything together now, I think there was just one big party at Roger Phillips's apartment. They were all going in and out of Roger's place. And nobody had any grasp on time frames. There was a meeting there, planning to kill a cop. They used Todd's car and Scott was driving. Scott always drove. I know David McClary said he drove, but that doesn't make any sense. It's not his car, so why would Todd let David drive his car? Todd said that David had the gun already, but he needed bullets for the gun. And that would be consistent. The Jamaican with the bullets was from 115th and Sutphin. That was David's turf. So David probably did have the gun. But they didn't go there with just one gun. I know that Todd had to have a gun with him that night. That's why he came up with the story that he lifted his shirt to the police car. He ditched the gun and now he's showing the cops that he's unarmed. But what I think happened that night was that David fired into the car. And then Todd came around, took the gun from David, and fired again. Why? 'Cause it shows on Todd's clothing. There was blood spattered on the outside of Todd's Bebo jacket. There was blood splattered on the inside of Todd's warmup jacket. But those jackets can never be used in evidence because they were thrown out. All the stuff taken out of the 209th Street safehouse was lost. Todd was not standing on the other side of the car when the shooting started. To do that would mean to stand facing the door with his chest area exposed. Do you think any-body, even Todd Scott, would be facing a gun? It's impossible then for the blood spray to have hit him on the passenger side. And the blood is on the jacket. I saw the blood and I've seen pictures of Todd in the jacket. It's his jacket.

"So here is what happened. Either Todd shot Eddie himself or he came around the car and took the gun from McClary. If Todd did fire a few more times, and he was the one who jumped up and down beside the car, and he's the person Arjune saw, that would be consistent. He comes around, and now there's no window there. He can get right up on Eddie, point-blank range, and fire. That's why Eddie had all the tattooing—powder burns and such on his face. Less than 18 inches, you get powder burns. But the powder burns Eddie had, the shooter had to be no more than a couple inches away from his face. Now the blood spatters all over the place. It would get up on his arm, his right sleeve, and across the front of his jacket. It's a spray now. There's nothing to stop it. There's no skull left. So the blood gets on him.

"But we'll never know conclusively. They never did a DNA test to determine if the blood was, in fact, Edward Byrne's. The blood was Eddie's type, we know that. But when you type blood, you destroy the blood that you typed. So the blood samples they did have were destroyed during the typing. We couldn't use the coats. But if we had, our biggest piece of evidence would have been destroyed.

"Was Philip Copeland there? Maybe. This never came out at trial, and Arjune is strange, but he did tell me the first night—I saw a girl in the back seat. A girl? Copeland has those dreadlocks.

Arjune could have mistaken him for a girl. If he was there, I doubt he was in Scott Cobb's car. Cobb was so scared at the time of his arrest. He gave up Pappy Mason. Why wouldn't he give up Copeland? It doesn't make any sense. I believe Copeland overslept. He may have been there later, in another car.

"I don't know what to think of Rachel Moore. She told me one thing and testified to another. I know she was there. She knew the names of the principals long before they became known. She also knew about the yellow car. The first time I talked to her, she told me flat out—Todd shot the cop. How she got the car on the block and Philip Copeland on the street, I can't speak to that. The terrible thing about Rachel is how all this wound up for her. She helps the cops solve a cop murder and then winds up down South, her mother dying in police custody. It's a terrible, terrible irony.

"Did Scott Cobb know what was happening? To a degree. He certainly knew he was hanging out with killers. The conversations about the killing are taking place all around him. Sure, Scott Cobb is dumb. But in order to not know what was happening, he'd have to be deaf and dumb. No matter what Scott Cobb says, he did drive by the Inwood Post with Debra Scott, point to Byrne and say, 'That cop is going to die tonight.' There was another girl in the car with them. Reason tells you the defense would have called the girl as a witness if she hadn't heard Cobb threaten to kill the cop."

Detective Richard Sica stood in the back of the courtroom. The juries had come and gone, the sentencing completed. Matt Byrne sat in the fourth row with a yellow legal pad, his hand and head working furiously. When Byrne was done, the words feeling right, he stood up and motioned to the detective.

"You coming, Richie?" Byrne asked. The television cameras were waiting.

"I'll catch up to you," Richie Sica replied.

The cameras made the detective nervous. He is not a public

man, the best investigative work being done in the shadows. Sica wore his best blue suit, the one he called the lucky one. He went into his pocket, looking for a cigarette, coming up empty. His hands shook.

"I don't know if I'll ever be the same," Sica said.

He was standing with Granshaw, thinking back to the moment he had arrived with Pistone at Byrne's shattered window. The city, after a time, got used to the crime. A half-dozen cops had been shot and killed in New York between the time of Byrne's murder and the completion of the cases against his murderers. A new cop was only a day in the ground. Sica, the memory of Byrne raw and sharp, was never really able to move away from the shattered window.

"This is the crime that changes us," Sica said.

"Yeah, well, I'm getting out," Granshaw said.

The two cops stood silent for a moment, unsure what to do or say.

"Did you say anything to Todd Scott?" Sica wondered.

"No," Granshaw replied.

"I wanted to say something."

"What is there to say?"

"I don't know," Sica said. "I just figured we would say something to the guy in the end."

Granshaw pondered this for a moment and then laughed. He was thinking a very private thought.

"Did you see him walking out, holding his crotch?" he asked.

"Uh huh," Sica said. "He was smiling."

"Well, he sure as hell wasn't smiling when I was trying to grab his balls," Granshaw said.

Sica blew out a stream of cigarette smoke to keep from choking. Then the detectives started laughing. They laughed for a very long time.

EPILOGUE

Arjune could not keep a secret. The federally protected witness was given a new name—Amos Hardeen—and a new job—mechanic in a Ford dealership—and a new home—Spokane, Washington. Arjune was very proud of himself. So prideful was the hero, in fact, that he felt compelled to reveal his true identity to his neighbors.

"Everybody knew who he was," a neighbor, Edeltraud Smith, later told reporters. "He was all the time bragging."

Arjune lived for a year in a wooden frame house on Maxine Street with his wife, Bina, and their three children. In a city of 185,000, where less than one percent of the populace is minority, Arjune was easily recognizable. His lawyer, Carl Maxey, who once laid claim to being the only black attorney between Spokane and Minneapolis, noted, "Black people stick out here like a sore thumb. And they get stopped by police for having a cup of coffee."

On September 1, 1989, Arjune was driving home when a Spokane police officer named Patricia Madsen pulled him over. Upon being stopped, the officer said, Arjune rendered a false name and, when asked for his driver's license, he stammered. The cop and the federally protected witness wound up pushing each other in the street, and Madsen claims Arjune struck her in the face. Making Arjune for a drunk, she administered a Breathalyzer. Arjune passed, and later claimed that Madsen had accused him of being a drug dealer.

"I don't do drugs," Arjune screamed at the cop. "See, I have been a drug fighter."

Spokane police charged Arjune with speeding, failing to stop at a stop sign, resisting arrest, third-degree assault, and failure to obey an officer. Immediately, a set of U.S. Marshals rushed to his aid, and Officer Madsen was given a lie detector test, which *she* passed.

Arjune was furious. He was so hurt at the idea of being called a criminal that he went to the *Spokane Chronicle* and broke his cover. Armed with a stack of newspaper clips on the Byrne case, Arjune announced himself a hero, and the resulting newspaper article was headlined: "Man who defied drug kingpins says he was attacked by officers." Four days later, the "For Sale" sign went up on Arjune's lawn, and he was relocated the same day, with his third identity in a year. The police stuck by their account of Arjune's actions. Ultimately, once again, no one was sure whether to believe Arjune or not.

The U.S. Marshal's Office, embarrassed by a lapse in security, would not comment on the Arjune fiasco. The protected witness was allowed to plead guilty to a reduced charge of resisting arrest in December 1989. The humbled defendant told the Spokane court, "It goes against everything I believe in to have harmed a police officer." The judge gave him six months probation.

One embarrassment was quickly followed by another. That same month, the informant named Billy Martin was jettisoned from the Federal Witness Protection Program.

In January 1989, Billy had been removed from the South Jamaica streets and placed in a New Jersey safehouse, then, six months later, relocated with his family to the West Coast. There, he made a mistake. Enrolled in a drug program, Martin revealed his past during a group-therapy session.

"Everybody else had a story," Billy said. "So I told mine. I wasn't thinking about security. I felt left out. I was thinking about getting better."

Besides the security lapse, it was also charged that Martin had brought drugs into the rehab center and had had sex with other patients. Those claims were never substantiated, but still, Martin was rushed to Detroit, where traces of Valium turned up in three of his urine samples. In mid-September 1989, Billy was "terminated" from the program and returned to the streets, with no identification and no money.

Billy's treatment infuriated city detectives and members of the Queens District Attorney's Office. As a secret informer, Martin had contributed as much as anyone—detective, FBI agent, DEA agent, prosecutor, judge, or American President—to creating the massive Federal racketeering and narcotics cases that had crushed the murderous crack gangs of South Jamaica. Billy had worn a radio transmitter in his Yankees baseball cap, carried miniature tape recorders, and starred in government surveillance videotapes of huge drug buys. Ultimately, and only with his help, the Feds had nailed drug kingpin Robert "Cornbread" Gray and such high-rolling gang leaders as Fat Cat Nichols, Pappy Mason, Supreme McGriff, Claude Skinner, and the Corley brothers. In exchange for his help, Billy was to have been given $65,000 and a new identity for himself, his wife, and children. The government reneged on both promises, even as George Bush was announcing an all-out drug war and holding up a vial of crack he had gotten in a staged bust.

Like Arjune, Martin went to the newspapers. His story, headlined "Out in the Cold," appeared on the front page of the New York *Daily News,* and the paper received hundreds of letters from outraged citizens, but the government never made a move to reinstate Billy Martin in the witness program. He remains on the street, a price on his head, wondering why anyone would ever agree to work with the Federal government in a drug case.

"George Bush is walking around with Edward Byrne's badge in his pocket," Martin says now. "What is he going to do for me? I was the first person to give the cops the names of Byrne's killers. Now I don't even have a valid driver's license in my name. I don't exist. I'm dead and I don't even know it."

Charles Rose, the controversial Assistant United States Attorney who had offered Byrne's killers a deal, continued to make unpopular moves. In quick succession, he gave deals to Brian Gibbs, Viola Nichols, and Fat Cat Nichols. On September 28, 1989, in an unusual secret court session, Fat Cat was allowed to plead guilty to two Federal racketeering murder charges, and in exchange for a chance at parole and reduced charges against his mother, Cat agreed to testify against his underling, Pappy Mason. In the parlance of Federal cooperation, this is called "testifying down." The agreement infuriated members of the state law-enforcement community, who claimed Rose had sold them out.

"Using Fat Cat to get Pappy," said one member of the Byrne prosecution team, "is like using syphilis to get gonorrhea."

One of those Fat Cat confessed to having had killed was his old girlfriend, Myrtle Horsham. Cat said he had ordered the December 1987 slaying because Horsham had stolen money from him and then "spent it on a dude." He made no mention of Horsham's threat to talk to investigators about the murder of Brian Rooney.

"Was one of the purposes of this to teach other people in the organization a lesson about not stealing from you?" asked Edward Korman, the Federal judge who accepted the surprising agreement.

"It wasn't just the stealing," Cat replied. "It was the fact that she was my girl and she took my money and spent it on someone else."

"Was there any other reason other than your desire—other than jealousy, shall I say?"

"Yeah. Because in other words, she made me look bad in front of the people who was within my organization."

The Cat turned canary also pled guilty to having had a rival dealer, Isaac Bolden, murdered in 1986. Cat told Judge Korman that Bolden and his friends had robbed people in his gang.

"I known him for years," Cat admitted. "And so I told him, 'Just don't worry about what you did. Just go ahead and point me toward the people that was with you.' And he did do that. He pointed me toward the people that was with him. And then he turned around and point the people toward me."

Nichols was not forced to say anything about having ordered the murder of Rooney, his parole officer. The plea agreement still allows for Fat Cat to be charged in a state court for that crime. It is unlikely, state officials say, that Cat will ever be freed by the Feds to face murder charges. Brian Rooney's wife, Susan, now living in California, cried upon learning of the plea agreement.

On October 1, 1989, Fat Cat's seventy-two-year-old mother, Louise Coleman, was allowed to plead guilty to reduced charges. Although Coleman had originally faced life in prison, she was given probation.

"I ain't did nothing," Coleman told the *New York Post,* moments before entering the courtroom. "I was always working. I ain't never had no drugs in my hand in my life."

This was the same woman who had been captured on a secret tape recording, warning an associate, "Don't come in the storefront no more . . . I don't care no more if I put two bullets in your head."

Pappy Mason went to trial alone in the Federal racketeering case. Harry Batchelder, Mason's lawyer, tried to enter an insanity defense at the November 1989 trial. He claimed that Mason had threatened to beat him up during a pretrial conference. A former hockey player with a Marine crew cut, Batchelder stood up to the intimidation. "There was the threat of violence on both sides of the table," Batchelder informed the court.

Mason boycotted most of his own trial, preferring to follow the proceedings on a specially installed speaker system in his cell. Richard Sica saw the Byrne case to fruition, sitting at a table in the court well with the Federal prosecutor. Scott Cobb was a surprise witness, saying he knew in advance of Mason's plan to kill a cop. Mike Bones, a Bebos enforcer, also testified, admitting to three murders. Viola Nichols spent three days on the stand, saying she would say anything to protect her brother. Fat Cat was never called to the stand.

The jury deliberated for three days before finding Mason guilty of ordering the Byrne murder. He is serving a life sentence in Federal prison. Mason still faces a state trial in the assassination of Brian Rooney.

In September 1989, Edward Koch was defeated in his bid to be re-elected to a fourth term as mayor of New York City. His police commissioner, Benjamin Ward, announced his retirement two weeks later, claiming illness. The department's Chief of Detectives, Robert Colangelo, also quit the force, and shortly thereafter, though she had never worked as a police officer, Alice McGillion was given the ceremonial post of First Deputy Commissioner. McGillion was the first woman ever named to the post, and, as a civilian, some argued, she was the most unqualified First Deputy in the department's history.

Detective Richard Sica was promoted to second-grade detective. He returned to the 103rd Precinct, where he continues to work on crack-related murders. Edward Granshaw, the department's second biggest overtime achiever in 1988, has retired to suburban Long Island. In October 1989, investigators who worked on the case got together for a retirement party in the Granshaw home.

"The only thing that really bothers me," Granshaw said, "is that I will never know, conclusively, who shot Edward Byrne."

Matt Byrne went back to lawyering. In a surprise move, he brought a $10-million suit against his old employers, the New York City Police Department. The Byrne family charged that the city had been negligent by not providing sufficient security, training, notice of danger, or equipment to Edward Byrne. The city, citing previous court rulings, argued that the police department could not be held liable for injuries suffered by officers in the line of duty.

The suit claimed that, rather than allowing Byrne to move as he was guarding the house, the police department ordered him to remain in a parked cruiser. This, Matt Byrne argued, made his son a sitting target. Matt Byrne also claimed that his son was inadequately trained and was not aware of the danger of guarding Arjune's home. There is mention in his brief of the dog cage which blocked his son's view of approaching doom, but no mention of the portable television found hanging from Edward Byrne's rearview mirror. On October 11, 1989, a Queens judge, Alfred Learner, ruled that the Byrnes had every right in the world to sue for wrongful death.

While waiting for his day in court, Matt Byrne campaigned heartily for a Republican mayoral candidate, Rudolph Giuliani. In the waning days of the race—a campaign Giuliani eventually lost—Byrne told friends that Giuliani had promised him a position in his new administration.

"He's going to name me police commissioner," Byrne reported.

The attorney Sal Alosco continued to find a table waiting for him at Elaine's. Gradually his friends came back to him. At first, his mother was reluctant to be seen with the convicted cop-killer's lawyer, and it was only after promising that he would not personally appeal Todd Scott's conviction that Alosco was able to coax his mother into a dinner date. On their first night out after the trial, Alosco looked up from their table only to see Matt Byrne and his family entering the restaurant. The lawyer looked at his mother and groaned.

"You aren't going to believe this," Sal Alosco said.

Mrs. Alosco turned and spotted the Byrne family. She let out a small gasp and pushed away from the table, leaving her son to dine alone.